THE MARK OF MAN

Mirador Publishing
Mirador
Wearne Lane
Langport
Somerset
TA10 9HB

The Mark of Man

Owen H Lewis

"That which is impenetrable to us really exists. Behind the secrets of nature remains something subtle, intangible, and inexplicable... Religion of the future will be a cosmic religion. It will transcend personal God and avoid dogma and theology...."

Albert Einstein

To Fran

Prologue

It happened first at 2:00 pm on 14th December 2014 in East Africa. Some said it was the water; some said that it was the vaccinations; some said that it was the beginning of the end. Whatever the cause, a natural born child arrived with the mark, placed clearly on the underside of her left wrist. It didn't look out of place, nor discoloured, but merely as an accentuation of skin tone, or perhaps as a birthmark. Each circle was encircled by another and then another. The mother counted 28 circles in all but thought nothing of it.

Moments later, in a small hospital in North East Japan, another child was born with a similar mark in the same place. This time it was noted by the resident doctor and the girl was given the usual metabolic screening tests which revealed nothing further. Appearing to be a perfect circle, filled in by a darker flesh colour, the doctor checked it under a microscope and made out 81 perfect circles, each one enveloping the one before it, and advised the proud parents that it was both strange and rare, but most probably a birthmark.

Meanwhile in Munich, a boy was born with a mark of 54 concentric circles, imprinted on his left wrist. The midwife was bemused and sought a second opinion. The baby was taken away for screening, leaving the parents anxious, but was returned 40 minutes later. The father remarked how the mark was similar to a burn, one that you would get from a car cigarette lighter, but again was reassured by the nurses, who referred to it as a birthmark.

10 days later and by 2:00 pm on the 24th December 2014, all the new born babies bore a similar mark, no exceptions, always in the same place, on the underside of the left wrist. The outer circle was always the same size, always exactly 14 millimetres in diameter. The only variant was the number of circles and the faintness of the outer line. By now it was an epidemic and by now no one thought that it was just a birthmark.

When the first child with a single faint outer line died, nobody thought anything of it. However when many more children, with similar marks died, the world's leading physicians were cautious over the causes of their death.

There were no signs of disease relating to the mark, nor was there any sign of manipulation prior to the births. A few children were born with one single faint circle; others had stronger, thicker outer circles; then there were those with two, three, four circles and those with many more. Some were born with other major defects, but rarely would it go undetected. No matter what type of mark the child bore, all tests that were run were inconclusive.

When local scientists and politicians tried to describe the causes to their people, there was no real explanation. There were no changes to the DNA; there were no changes to the causes of death. Those children born with a single faint outer line had died of natural causes; some were stillborn; some were cot deaths; some hearts had just given out.

In the New Year there was no change and no matter what explanation had been given, all the births had one thing in common; which the world's press were calling *The Mark of Man*.

It wasn't until June 2015 that a world council was formed to discuss the philosophical, theological and biological implications, imposed by this worldwide phenomenon. The underlying fact was that nothing had changed genetically, physically or mentally in any one of the 78 million children born, over the preceding 7 months. The planet's population was anxious for an explanation about this pandemic but, if it was a plague, there were no signs of disease.

Theories began to take shape in respect to the mark itself. Upon closer inspection, it resembled the growth rings that could be seen in a horizontal cross section cut through the trunk of a tree. Reasoning pointed towards the fact that each individual circle on the left wrist resembled one year of life, similar to these growth rings. A group of scientists alluded to carbon dating and their ability to determine the age of a preserved life form. Their theory extended to the living body and its ability to now reverse the process, thus determining its age from inception.

By the end of 2015 the world's human population was still increasing at an annual rate of close to 70 million a year, yet there were accidental deaths; murders, traffic accidents and untimely deaths, in which the fates would play their part. Nature's new death predictor could not foresee the future, but only the organic timeline of its host.

Unfortunately for the human race the mere knowledge, of one's timeline, would breed alternative philosophies, moralities, policies and even economies.

Chapter 1

The slow low thump thump on the ceiling gradually dulled, as the music from the apartment upstairs faded; something had taken its place; a ticking. As every second passed, it became louder, louder and far more intrusive; to the point where I could stand it no longer. I checked the bedroom, creeping over the crumpled damp towel on the floor as I passed by the unmade bed with its corpse like contents, until I reached the bedside table. I scratched around, not sure what I was looking for, but found nothing. I headed for the kitchen, where I opened all the cupboards but still found nothing. I ventured into the bathroom as the tick tick tick continued to drill deep inside my brain. I couldn't help but notice its similarity to the sound of the second hand on an old clock, in a ticking race against its own alarm mechanism, seeing which would be the first to - and then – peace - it stopped.

Silently, I stood in front of the mirror, adjusting my tie. Angling down, I ensured that my suit would make the right statement. Yet I was disarmed. The ticking couldn't have been a part of my imagination, but then again being a Forty, my time was precious. Perhaps it was my consciousness; reminding me of my own mortality. Whatever the noise, it had gone, and so, as I stood in front of my reflection, I was able to focus on the evening ahead; my opening night; which happened to be at the Saatchi Gallery in Sloane Square. The exhibition booklet would have had you believe that Hansel Laurence was a saint and a visionary but at 35 years old, I was neither a saint nor could I have staked a claim as a great harbinger of truth. I was known as Hal for a start, it had always been this way, for as long as I could remember.

I was in a hurry, as I had promised Laozi that I'd be on time for once, especially given the location and the intended clientele. However I noticed a stain on the lapel of my jacket. I brushed over it lightly with the tips of my fingers; leaving me to think that the suit was the wrong choice.

My father would have known what was right for the occasion; it was so frustrating that I couldn't ask him. He had passed away not long ago, succumbing to a rare form of cancer, which had hit him swiftly; thankfully the pain was short lived. With a particular interest in the stoics, he had been one of the most prominent historians of his time, blending his experiences with heroes of the past, creating an insightful understanding of the different

3

groups or factions; which had been borne out of what history called Mark's Day. He had often referred to 'the root of the problem being mankind's insistence on playing God'. Which given our mark being deeply connected to trees and to nature, I had always found not only quite apt but mildly humorous. I had let him know, on many an occasion.

With my time drawing to a close, I remain concerned; concerned with everything; not least with the barriers that have built up between the different factions, based on our expiration date rather than our culture or philosophies, economics or even capabilities. Pre-Mark's Day religion has been dead for some time and in its place has grown an ordered chaos. In my city, London, the Thirtys attack the Sixtys, the Fortys take on the Fiftys and the Twentys go for everyone. It's the same the world over; rarely does a Seventy or even a Centurian visit the city; preferring a life at a slower pace, without looking over their shoulder.

My mother, a Danish Eighty, albeit that we were all Eurafrican now, had promised to be at the exhibition. I knew she'd be nervous. I sure was. She was on her way from Cornwall with my brother Calvin, who as a Seventy, had ensured that we rarely saw eye to eye. The 42 rings on my wrist compared to the 76 on his, being the basis for our differing perspective. As with so many like him, he was unmarried, yet at 36 years old his own clock was ticking, before expiration.

In any case, the very use of the word marriage was a throw back to ancient institutions, as the union was no longer for the sake of the old gods, or their hackneyed religions and their disciples. I guessed that the term had just remained. Civil partnership had never really taken off; too staid, no doubt. My wife, Alicia, expired two years ago. I missed her but then again she was a Thirty and I was aware. We had gone into it with our eyes open, as did everyone else. We had no children, for their sake.

I have often thought of my future, with only seven years left before my own expiration. No matter how many tests I have, and believe me I have had many, the doctors haven't been able to give me a comprehensive answer as to the cause. My supposition has always been that it will be the same as my father, swift, unheralded and hopefully painless. In the past, and on more than one occasion, I thought of testing my mark by terminating early but I had always returned to the same thought, time and again, that this would have been a futile exercise, as nature's death predictor never accounted for accidents, fate or an unstable mind. That being said, since Alicia's expiration, I've been more than aware of the time left for me to make my own mark on this planet. My eternal wish being that the future of mankind extended beyond the knowledge of one's own mortality. Knowing was extremely frustrating and just so futile.

This discovery of a new planet in another solar system has given us all a little ray of hope, especially as rumour has it there could, quite possibly, be signs of life existing on the other side of our known universe. A broadcast *was imminent; one that I wouldn't miss for the world. It was obviously the Dane in me; morbid but never moribund.*

Yet standing there, in front of the bathroom mirror, my main focus should have been the evening ahead; especially as my choice of suit was so important. The only two left which weren't moth eaten, ripped or stained, were the royal blue and the light grey. The one I had on made me look like my father. Whilst that was not in itself a problem, I was a different animal, and I most certainly wasn't an historian or some great intellectual. By default I opted for the royal blue, with matching blue shoes and tie. The white shirt stayed. I retreated to my bedroom where I removed my original choice, placing the trousers neatly back on a hanger and the jacket in a dry-cleaning box. I returned to my reflection a different person; up to date and modernised. After all, my exhibition had been branded "The Faces of Our Future".

I straightened my tie, pushing the knot closer to the collar and up against the Adam's apple, taking a deep breath and then glancing quickly at my shoes, looking for scuff before heading for the door. The exhibition was a big deal and I wanted everyone to understand. We were all slaves; to the money, to the idea of notoriety, to the fame of existence. I was no different, I wanted to leave something behind; something indelible, philosophical or even whimsical but at least profound.

Chapter 2

Ama's heart pumped furiously, as the memories of her parents' brutal murder coursed through her veins. They reached her finger tips, turning them numb, yet the pain had neither departed nor was the sad reminiscence ready to be truly given up. Visions of embers that burned around her, as she escaped through the back door of her apartment, still fuelled her rage at life's gross injustice.

Her mind plumbed further the depths of her despair, as the tick tock of her internal clock caught her, hands gliding over the keys in front of her. She neither felt their weight, nor weighed down by her current circumstances. Voegel pointed in her direction, as if it were she who'd been keeping everybody from an important conference. She picked up the pace, letting her fingers do the work, skipping from note to note, building up to a peak, where at its most tantalising point, she dropped it again.

Voegel clapped his hands, signaling the end of the session. Finally she had the chance to look around, at the vast and now silent auditorium. She caught her breath at the moment's significance. She was at the Barbican Centre in London, England, which was extremely surreal, given that it had been only 18 months since she had run, in utter desolation, from Prospect Park to the 77th Precinct. Since that sad day, there had been an emptiness infusing her soul, catching her at times, listlessly drifting along, while the giddy world of music, with all its beauty and intrigue, had run along beside her.

Ama pressed down upon her stool, using the joint of her palm and her wrist, as she stood up, smiling at anybody who might be looking in her direction. She drifted on towards the door, trying not to give the game away, as she was running late. Voegel, her music director, gave her a look of spurious horror, as he tapped his watch. The rehearsal had run over; by nearly 90 minutes.

She still found it hard to fathom as to why she was even part of this orchestra. It wasn't as if she was a child genius. She had had to pinch herself on many an occasion. She just wished that her parents could have been alive, to see her now; Ama Pepper Clark, winner of a Gates Millennium Scholarship to NYU's Department of Music. She had become everything that her mother had wished for; a pianist with the New York Philharmonic. She'd made it out of Flatbush; propitious in the extreme.

She passed her colleagues, through the revolving doors, out into the chill dank air of the corridor. As she hurried along, free from unwarranted questions, a ticking sound surreptitiously crept upon her. At first she was not aware of it, but as she made it past the canteen, she had to stop; look to her left, to her right and above her. It reached inside her head. It was faster than the second hand on a clock, certainly louder. She detected another softer, slower, mellower sound; she knew that they were a tandem but they were gradually running out of synch.

She moved on and the sounds intensified, indicating that they were up ahead. She had wild thoughts of a group of Twentys breaking in. The earlier news had gone into painstaking detail of the latest twist in London power politics. The leader of each faction had met in a secret location in the Hackney area, in order to draw up plans for a truce. The meeting had gone disastrously wrong, as information of its whereabouts had been leaked to a separatist movement, comprising of Thirtys and Fortys, who'd decided to wipe out all of their enemies. Like the many headed hydra, this had created a thousand more problems and enemies for the new terrorist group. The Hackney area had been decreed a red flag zone, a no go area and off limits. The Barbican Centre was a little too close for comfort.

Ama's stomach turned over but she stopped herself, the sound was eerily familiar. The two beats were moving further and further apart but she willed them on to meet again. She wasn't a mathematician but knew that it was only a matter of time for the beats to join in unison for yet another fleeting moment. Each time forging new paths, until once again they'd meet, like a pair of oscillating spheres, for time immemorial.

She ventured on down another corridor, towards her intended exit and the revelation hit her; software metronomes. As she passed by another door, she knew that she was extremely close to the source and glanced inside. There standing on an empty desk, in the grey and dead light, compounded by the archaic fluorescent hallway glow, were two small 19th Century wooden metronomes, one running at 98 beats a minute and the other a fraction off; one light, one dark; one bold, one bright.

She was born on Caton Avenue and the area had been her home, for as long as she could remember. It just so happened that a group of Thirtys had decided that it was to be their home too. They'd taken over all of the buildings along Coney Island Avenue towards Prospect Park. Her parents had steadfastly maintained that they were not going to shift, just because of some crazed kids, who'd decided that all those more fortunate would have to pay for their hard luck.

Ama had become tired through sheer frustration. Society, the world over, had become so twisted. She understood the source of the violence; the projected life span of the individual but she had been close to giving up; it was the futility of it all. Yet she was now part of a team, with fresh purpose. It had given her a reason for being, no matter how insignificant.

7

She reached the restroom oblivious to Voegel who was chasing after her, waving a piece of paper in the air. As he neared, he coughed loudly, breaking her spell. She turned to face him. He was kind of strange looking, with scrawny features and thinning hair, but he was not only one of the most highly regarded conductors on the circuit but he'd also become Ama's protector and friend. She didn't have anywhere else to go. There was nowhere else that she preferred to be. The details of that evening's exhibition were on the sheet of paper.

Voegel had informed Ama on her first day that within the confines of the Philharmonic everything was done the old fashioned way. Everyone was to use a pen and paper; no cellhips or personal systems were allowed. They were all silently bound by those rules. They were there to play classical music and so they were to be classical in their methods. She studied the piece of paper and noted that it was already 7pm and that the doors would have already opened. She still had to change her clothes and cross town in a cab. Voegel left with an affectionate squeeze of her arm, as if to say good luck, be safe and have fun all at the same time.

Inside the restroom and within the safe confines of a cubicle, Ama unclasped her bag and pulled out a neatly folded red chiffon dress, deep in texture; deep in colour. She had saved it for her opening performance on the 2nd January but judging by Voegel's insistence on her going to the swanky exhibition; she'd thought the better of it and tried to look like she belonged in the company of all those famous people who were no doubt going to be there. She removed her sneakers, her sweatshirt, her pants and her underwear. She unfolded her dress and held the straps for her shoulders. She stood still for a moment before taking a deep breath, as if to give her the fortitude to don such a disguise and slipped in. She couldn't help but notice her mark; all 93 rings. The tattoo surrounding it had caught her attention. She had been 15 years old when she'd decided to set it within a dark blue sun and now that sun was beginning to fade. It had been a fad that she'd bought into at the time. It had somehow made the mark less foreboding.

Ama had always thought it quite macabre that not one of the maskers invented over the last 100 years had been able to change the mark. The flesh on and around it, up to 12 millimetres away from the perimeter circle, would not take any alternative marking, regardless of the method's design. She knew many who'd tried to cover their modesty with wrist bands, gloves, or even elaborate fleshbands with marks displaying alternative timelines. Unfortunately the fleshbands were easy to spot and they went out of fashion quickly. Likewise the gloves or wristbands highlighted a short or long timeline depending on who the bearer wanted to hide it from and whether they were in an urban area or the countryside. Yet most people Ama knew displayed their mark and wore it with honor and pride.

It was plain to see that the world had gone sour. The sharp taste of knowledge and foresight overshadowed what mankind once had, that which was now lost. Not long ago Ama had read a book that pointed to the dramatic change in both philosophy and theology since Mark's Day. At its core the author had laid out the basic principles of law and order in civilized society, those which were no more. The author Hector Laurence was an authority on the subject and had been on CNN a few times. She'd heard that he had died a few years back, just when people seemed to be becoming more receptive and attuned to listening. It suddenly hit her that he must have been related to the artist Hansel Laurence. They had similar names and they were both from England. Realising her oversight, she knew that she should have done more research. She'd been so wrapped up in her own cocoon that she was ill prepared.

Trying to remember the name of the book she put on her shoes, a contrasting deep blue, and she unlocked her cubicle door. She placed her crumpled rehearsal outfit into the bag and crossed over to a row of washbasins on the other side of the restroom. She gently applied her makeup, disentangled her hair and smoothed down the creases on her dress with the palms of her hands. As she did so, like a bulb of enlightenment, she remembered the book's title: 'A Cosmic Philosophy: Rules of Engagement'. It had explored the myth of 'ignorance is bliss' and the fall of man. With the message flooding back to her, she focused on its principle themes.

She put on her distinctive chic and cream Parisian overcoat and threw her deep blue cashmere scarf around her neck. Her cellhip pinged alive and she checked her messages. Her cab had arrived. She made her way to the building's exit. As she stepped onto the street outside a chill wind enveloped her, delving deep into her bones. It was winter after all; no different to New York; she fastened her overcoat, firmly drawing over each side, making sure that she was fully enclosed and headed over towards the waiting car. As she did so, she remembered Hector Laurence's vision; the natural universe within the realms of reality and how mankind could redeem himself, if only he could accept common guiding values and beliefs. She got into the cab and confirmed that she was headed for the Saatchi Gallery, Duke of York's. It sounded so intimidating.

The taxi turned left onto Aldersgate Street and headed south. Ama sat in the back contemplating the evening ahead, as the car stopped at the traffic lights. A dustbin lid caught up in the swirling wind, skipped along the pavement and hit the rear left hand side of the car.

"What was that?" The driver awoke sleepily from a trance and looked outside through the closed window.

"Just a trashcan cover." Ama responded serenely considering her noticeable discomfort with the scene outside. "I hope these lights change soon, as it's freaky round here. Have you had any trouble in this area before?"

"How about I put it this way, these windows are made of transalum, the strongest in the business. The entire fleet at Atlas Cars is fixed with transparent aluminum. I've got the whole car secured, so no one can get in without putting an explosive in the air chamber."

That makes me feel so much safer. Ama thought sarcastically as she sat back quietly, not wanting to continue with the conversation. She looked at her watch. 7:35pm.

I guess I'll make it in time for the presentation. The street was unusually empty, dark and hostile. Ama longed for some light, some life and vibrancy to usher her out of her sombre mood. It was as if the lights had read her mind, they flicked to green and the taxi pulled away. She had been to far worse places than Islington and reminded herself of how far she had come. She had only been with the New York Philharmonic for a short while but this was already her third tour. Shanghai had definitely been the most frightening place that she had been to. The number of duplicates walking the streets amongst the humans, pretending to be their parent was no doubt the most shocking part. She couldn't fathom the enormity of the problem facing not only Asiana but the entire planet.

It shouldn't have ever been started in the first place. How do you control something like that? You are damned if you do, damned if you don't. We're on a hiding to nothing playing with such unnatural things.

Chapter 3

December 31st 2144 - New Year's Eve – Fulham, London, England

Hal glanced at his tall frame in the hall mirror and gently smoothed over his tussled sandy blonde hair. His piercing green eyes stared back at him, engaged in a look of energised apprehension. With a sigh he walked over to the table, picked up his keys and checked his cellhip which had replaced all Gopple phones a few years before. He was going to be late and wondered whether that was still fashionable. He put on his overcoat, closed the door behind him and stepped out onto the quiet, tree lined street as a chill wind wrapped around him, digging deep at his bones. His body shuddered. It was at least minus nine degrees and the dead of winter. It was extremely cold. He fastened his overcoat, firmly tugging over each side, ensuring that he was fully covered. He walked briskly until he reached the corner and turned left, to the familiar environs of the bus stop, where the street lamp flickered; caught in its own indecision of colour and light. He pondered the evening ahead, as he shuffled lightly from toe to toe, keeping warm in the darkening night. A few minutes later the bus drew up and the side doors parted. A young girl with a pram, complete with a screaming baby, backed out. He stepped in, mindful of the gap between the pavement and its platform.

He glanced nonchalantly at the other passengers and conjured up a web of ideas as to who they were and their intended journeys. All he ever needed was a fleeting glimpse to work with. The girl with the red hat was an easy first; she was on her way to a New Year's Eve party, the bottle of wine was a dead giveaway. The young man, a Twenty, furtively looking between his cellhip and the others around, was no doubt heading for the West End and his faction leader. A Fifty, who was looking at the Twenty, with more than a degree of concern, stared out of the window averting her eyes for fear of inviting danger. He momentarily thought about her life, as he sat down close to her, quietly reassuring her that she was safe from any potential assault. She acknowledged his presence with a faint smile. He sat back in his seat and surveyed his surroundings once more, but grew tired of the exercise and reacquainted himself with the streets outside.

He subconsciously rubbed his left wrist in trepidation of the evening ahead. The mark had grown to its full adult size of 28 millimetres in diameter by his 21st birthday. To mark this occasion the celebrations had been long, amusing and intoxicating. They were tinged with a note of sadness as his older brother and Calvin's twin, Lars had passed away the year before. Yet this had not marred the occasion as there wasn't a mature soul left in the world who hadn't already resigned themselves to a loved one's passing. The moment that Hal treasured most of all was from later on in that evening when everyone else had left the restaurant, leaving him alone with his father.

They had talked of the old world, the religions of the past, the days when science was exploration into the unknown, a voyage of discovery rather than merely a pact with predetermination. His father had gone into great detail when concerned with man's shift in consciousness over the centuries. He had never made any grandiose or sweeping statement in his life and that moment was to be no different. He had presented a clear concise conviction of man's true place in the universe. By the time the third large cognac had been called for, Hal and his father were hugging and lamenting the days they had never truly known.

A siren snapped his attention away from his thoughts. He saw a flickering glow coming from the rear of the World's End Estate. He was hardly surprised, as this was now commonplace in all the housing estates, in all of the cities around the world. The factions had taken over and mankind's natural order had been reversed. The Thirtys, with little to live for but with enough experience, were the force in the inner cities. They controlled the violence; they dished out the pain.

The Fortys had more to protect, as did the Fiftys. The Sixtys had the promise of at least half a life worth living; leaving the powerbrokers of each faction to deal directly with the leader of the Thirtys; offering their greater experience and financial muscle in return for their own protection. The Teens and the Twentys would pick off anyone that they could find. Society had turned on its head, giving the youth control of the cities and the old guard the freedom of the countryside; or at least that which was left of it.

The buildings outside had changed dramatically from those of former glories. Storey upon storey of sheet glass, aluminium frame and retro coloured cladding had replaced what was left of the Kings Road. The Oil Wars of the late 21st Century had stretched so far into Eurafrica that London had been the scene of many a street battle, suffering decimation in most western parts. Kensington and Chelsea had been the epicentre, with many a beautifully ornate structure raised to the ground and replaced with what were proposed as radiant towers, which were merely glossing over the fact of their lost future.

The old buildings within the Cadogan Estate remained intact and seemed to have a musty quality about them; where memories of the past were now being seen through the eyes of lesser yeared Eurafricans.

He turned away once again, running his hand over his eyes, deep in concentration.

It could have been worse; I could have been a duplicate, slavishly worked to the bone from inception; without a single choice in my circumstances. At least, we humans, have the choice as to how we live our life, how we conduct ourselves, what we do to each other, as we march towards our definite end. The discovery of Kepler 3 certainly does throw up some interesting questions.

"Duke of York's."

The dulcet female tones of the electronic destination announcer broke the silence. He looked up to see that the girl with the red hat had gone and that the Fifty was making her way to the exit. He sidled past the young man who remained furtive and ill at ease. The Twenty wasn't a Twenty after all; he had more than 100 concentric rings which were just about visible from under the cuff of his black leather glove.

The bus drew to a halt. Hal let the Fifty off first, before stepping out into the cold. As the hiss of the passing bus faded into the distance, he felt a pang in his gut. He hated public speaking. Pulling out a pack of Marlboro No 5's and lighting up a cigarette, he crossed over the road. The gleaming white-washed walls of the Saatchi Gallery beckoned him on, he suddenly felt a sense of calm envelope him. He was only 35 minutes late. He climbed the steps and ambled in.

"Hal, Hal, where have you been? We've tried calling you a hundred times." Laozi's PA steamed over to him in a flustered combination of concern and anger. He removed the band from his right arm, detached his cellhip and showed her a screen no bigger than a square from a travel chess board.

"No missed calls - ah - hold that - I forgot to link up. You know that it would never have been deliberate." He winked at her as he manoeuvred himself away from the unintentionally frosty gaze that she had hoped was a smile and into the welcoming enclave of his benefactor, Laozi Veda.

"Hal, I'm so glad that you decided to grace us with your presence." Laozi boomed so that everyone could hear. He and Hal had become great friends over the years, ever since the day they'd met out in Singapore. Laozi recently referred to him as the son that he'd never had, most probably because his daughter had been turned against him by her mother, for reasons that only his ex-wife knew.

"I see that all the important people are here." Hal responded, with a little note of sarcasm, while scanning the room, taking in a lot of familiar faces and clocking his route round those that he would prefer to avoid later on.

"There are a number of people that I want you to meet, not to mention one specific group over there." Laozi pointed towards the corner on the other side of the gallery where a group dressed in modern suits, stood listening earnestly to one of Laozi's team briefing them on the artist. "They'd be interested in commissioning you for a private project over in Shanghai. We'll get to them later. In the meantime, you must meet Steven Le Mac; he's running for Mayor."

The whirlwind was now fully underway. He had been briefed by Laozi's team. It was well known by everyone, that he was neither good with large groups, nor was he likely to make a decent first impression. His propensity to say the wrong thing, to the wrong person, at the wrong time, had been well documented. He knew that he would have to make a serious effort not to damage Laozi's goodwill.

He stood still, mindful of the person talking to him and assumed an air of captivation, which he carried off well, until he felt a presence, one he had noticed before. It was momentarily exhilarating, chilling but not cold. He caught sight of her. She was somewhat taller than the people she was passing. She was graceful, serenely beautiful, but most of all, different to everyone else around. She meandered through the ever increasing crowd, slowly, picking her way through with an expression of mild trepidation but, most of all, reserve. Hal was mesmerised by her. He tried to concentrate on what the politician was saying. When he was expected to respond to a question, one which he had not heard, he politely excused himself and headed straight in her direction. He followed her trail through the crowd, desperately hoping that he could come up with something interesting to say in order to captivate her. However, out of a huddle next to him, a hand grabbed his arm and gave it an affectionate squeeze.

"Mother, how good to see you."

A startled Hal snapped himself back to reality, putting his latest potential conquest momentarily to one side, before continuing.

"When did you get here? How was the journey? Calvin, great to see you, it's been such a long time. Thank you both so much for coming along tonight. It really does mean a lot to me."

They hugged and kissed each other hello, as his mother looked him up and down, with a huge smile that emanated positive energy, so much so that anyone close by would have been swallowed up in the warm glow.

"Your father would be so proud Hal, really he would."

She let the statement linger, longer than usual, before gesticulating towards one of the paintings on the wall, a few feet away from them.

"It's not just the subject matter that has everyone buzzing; it's how you've captured every creature on canvas. It really is astonishing. The inscriptions within each outline are inspiring, as if they were your father's. You know that I keep saying it but you are so like him."

Hal had to interrupt his mother at that point, as he noticed his brother Calvin trying not to wince at the reference. Ever since his twin brother had died, Calvin had found it difficult to talk about anything emotional or familiar. Hal had always been at pains to understand the difficulty in growing up as a twin, where one was a Twenty and the other a Seventy.

Since Mark's Day all multiple births that were monozygotic produced the same mark on each identical offspring. However those that were polyzygotic would end up in a similar situation to Lars and Calvin, as they were dizygotic twins, fraternal but had developed from two separate eggs. They were divided from the start. For twins this must have been an exceptionally hard situation to deal with. The memories of their jealousies, and the fights, that ensued during their teenage years flashed through his already overcrowded mind.

"It's such a shame Alicia isn't here."

"I know."

Calvin jumped in, uncharacteristically.

"The Saatchi Gallery, I mean really? You're going to be world famous now. Your feet aren't going to touch the ground. From now on Laozi's going to cart you around, from city to city, spreading the good word. I know I'm coming across a little sarcastic but honestly Hal, well done, it really is spectacular."

His mood lightened, as even the thought of Alicia couldn't take away his growing sense of achievement. Calvin's words rang out, as a buzz of excitement and expectancy filled the show room. The sound of a tapping on a champagne glass filtered through the room and a hush descended upon the crowd.

A portly, sartorially elegant Indo-Chinese man sauntered through the milling throng and made his way towards the raised dais at the rear of the room, which was right in front of Hansel Laurence's pièce de résistance, 'The Legendary Weeping Tiger'. He stepped onto the platform, looked out across the sea of faces, paused for a moment and proceeded to talk into the cellhip controlled sound system.

"Ladies, gentlemen, distinguished guests, friends and even you art lovers, I am not an artist and so cannot speak for any one of them. However if I had to use a single axiom to describe the mind of an artist, I would have to refer to a speech by the multi-hyphenate Sir Stephen Fry, from the early 21st Century. He succinctly put it to his audience that one artist alone is a political party, two artists together are a rebellion and three artists in the same room are a civil war. Judging by Hansel Laurence's work on display tonight, if he were to meet another artist of such outstanding calibre, then no doubt we will have a rebellion on our hands.

"I first met Hal in Singapore when he was just 20 years old. He was visiting friends but had taken himself away for the afternoon, to get a bit of peace and quiet. I was standing on the street outside my apartment building, waiting for my driver to arrive. It was one of those days where I too needed some peace and quiet. Hal sidled up to me, unsighted and asked if I could take him to the National Gallery. Now I may not have been as well dressed or half as important as I would like to think that I am now, but back then I certainly didn't have the air or the grace of a chauffeur. However, I was intrigued by this young gentleman from London, and so offered him a lift, once my driver arrived.

"When my car did indeed pull up, I detected a look of faux surprise on my young friend's face, but dismissed this as possible embarrassment on his part.

15

We got into the car and set off for the gallery. It was during that journey that the seed of an idea was planted. Hal presented ideas on politics, art and culture that were way beyond his years and I didn't have a chance to ask a single question. It dawned on me that it was he who had known who I was all along, and had singled out the Vedas Corporation and its new CEO as his natural benefactor.

"It was only later, as I got to know him; his potential, his talent and his vision, that I took him under my wing and set him on a journey which, as you should all know by now, is entirely his own design. It is rare for the artist to introduce his work, but then again this is indeed a rare artist. Ladies and gentlemen, please welcome Hansel Laurence."

Hal paused a second before stepping out of the crowd and onto the dais. He cast a glance in the direction of his benefactor, whilst sucking up whatever air was left in the room, before exhaling. He spoke in a studied and deliberate manner.

"Good evening and thank you Laozi for the kind words. It has been a long road here. All the dreams and wild ideas of pure fantasy; the tetchy procrastination, the solemn procession, the flights of fancy have all led to this moment. In the past, as a younger man, as a Forty, living life on fast forward, I would have stood here and told you how I wasn't going to keep you long. It would have been my thought that the champagne and chatter was important to you but not the ideas; the substance. I would have let you know that I neither cared, nor that I would have even wanted to ingratiate myself to you all. However times have changed, not only for me but for everyone else in this room; in fact for everyone across the globe. Kepler 3 is a game changer, I can feel it. Don't ask me why; I just do.

"Ever since Mark's Day, we have been collectively heading into the void, where one crisis extrapolates another. We live in a violent world, built upon the rocky ground of our expiration dates, where duplicate development and the resultant subterfuge have only made matters worse. Our lack of wisdom and foresight has shown us how little that we have learnt from the past and it is all due to this damning mark.

"Today we find ourselves lurching towards a protracted but futile end. Our extraneous human conflicts based on our colour, our creeds and our nations' technological advancement are all immaterial in the eyes of the universe. These marks that we bear are a test of human endurance and it is my view that they are the manifestation of something subtle, of something intangible and of something inexplicable. It is through these thoughts –

She was there again in the crowd, slightly taller than those around her, with long dark sun kissed wavy hair, almond eyes and soft unblemished brown skin. Her eyes were fixed on him and his on hers.

"- that 'The Faces of Our Future' had its origins.

"It is for you to decide whether this is a true art form. It is also for you to decide whether this work is that of a true artist. But before any of you do decide, I would ask you to imagine what really is behind the eyes of 'The Legendary Weeping Tiger'.

"Look deep inside yourselves and reflect on how far mankind and the rest of the animal kingdom have come but also how much further we could go, if only we were to collectively believe that our mark was a necessary good and not this unnecessary evil that we have allowed it to become.

"You now know my message but unfortunately for me, you also now know where I am. With that being said, I thank you all for being here tonight. Please enjoy the rest of the evening and I will endeavour to speak to most of you before the night is through."

Contrary to his proclamation, he had no intention of speaking to anyone and immediately headed off in pursuit of the towering beauty. As he stepped off the dais, he was met by a rapturous throng of well wishers, press and members of Laozi's PR team. He was herded in the opposite direction from the girl, as cameras flashed and cellhips were turned on. Questions fired in his direction from every angle were met with a muted stare. One of his PR team stepped in, answered the questions and diverted attention away from Hal.

Within a matter of moments he managed to negotiate his exit, without causing too much of a stir. He backed away behind one of the pillars in the showroom, turned and walked briskly with his head down, careful not to make eye contact with anyone, as if he was deep in conversation on his cellhip.

Reaching the exit of the gallery, he turned and surveyed the room, pretending to talk into his responder. Remembering that she was close to his height, over 6 foot tall, *at least in heels*, he looked across the milling crowd, over the tops of heads to catch a glance; for a quick flash of recognition; for something he could work with. There was nothing. She was gone.

Dejected but not beaten, he put his thoughts of what might have been to one side and moved back into the crowd, this time accepting a glass of champagne and focusing on his real purpose; promotion and publicity.

The evening continued at a fast pace, as he was introduced to every politician, businessman, actress and international dignitary of the moment. He put on the performance of his life, which not only pleased the Vedas Corporation and all its employees, but also made his benefactor extremely proud. He managed to catch a quick conversation with his mother and brother before they left for home. He even made a mental note of how well his mother looked and that he would go visit them both, at least when his surprise tour of the three capitals was finished.

Laozi seemed to be unaware that he knew of what was in store. Whether this was true or not, he remained undaunted by the task ahead of him. He'd been to Singapore many times. Laozi's main residence was there. It was close to being his home from home. Likewise he'd been to Sao Luis, the capital of Panamerica and had his own contacts in the media and political world out there. These he'd accumulated over the years and would have no problem following up in the future. However it was the Eurafrican leg that he knew would be the most testing part. Being a Londoner, it never sat comfortably with him that the Oil Wars were engineered from within the walls of government buildings in Cairo. It riled him, especially given his views on international and local conflicts that had permeated most cultures on the planet.

Later on and as the crowd began to thin he, Laozi and a select group of suppressed sycophants, business associates and close acquaintances were ushered into a caravan of Range Rover Viitor's. Their destination was Laozi's apartment which overlooked Hyde Park in Mayfair. As the caravan of vehicles snaked up the spine of Park Lane, he looked out of his window. Towering 207 floors high and spanning to the north as far as Mount Street and east to Berkeley Square, the Vedas Corporation had taken over a quarter of Mayfair, providing shopping malls, restaurants, entertainment complexes, underground car parking, all surrounding the second tallest tower on the planet.

Later that evening as the clock ticked steadily towards midnight, Laozi stood in the corner of his principal entertaining room, with a few of his unnamed cohorts, speaking in hushed tones. Hal passed by, on his way to the bathroom, and couldn't help but overhear his benefactor confirming that, through all the support, faith and belief in him, his investment had at last, paid off. Not knowing that he should dwell on the underlying significance of that statement, Hal set about forgetting about the world's troubles for an evening, and for once basked in everyone's unbridled attention. His world now had a purpose; his was a momentary peace; found, just as his world was to be torn apart.

Chapter 4

December 31st 2144 - New Year's Eve – London, England

The taxi gathered pace as it crisscrossed the financial district, known as the City, heading towards the River Thames. 10 minutes later Ama felt a sense of calm wash over her as the lights of Blackfriars Tower loomed in the distance and the scene outside changed from gloom to revelry.

It is New Year's Eve after all. She exhaled with a sense of relief that the lackadaisical taxi driver failed to hear. However this sense of release emanated throughout the car, as they turned left briefly onto Farringdon Street, before crossing over onto Victoria Embankment. The car sped stealthily down the rampart onto the road running west along the river.

7:45pm. I'm going to make it. Ama noticed that the driver was listening to something through his cellhip earpiece.

"Could you put the infadio on back here please?" The driver slowed to momentarily concentrate on switching feeds and the car came alive with a news broadcast.

This Kepler 3 discovery is for real. I thought it was a hoax. Ama sat back in her seat and let the information wash over her. *I can't believe it. It's really happening.* Her mind drifted off, as she looked out of the window and up at the starry night. It was cold and clear. The reflection of the moon bounced along the Thames, shimmering in the dark, as if coaxed along by the ripples of the wind.

I wonder which one it is, up there, glistening in the dark day after day. The car buffeted against the kerb steering Ama's attention away. *He's been in a trance all journey; this news must be affecting him. I guess it affects us all.* On reaching the traffic lights at the bridge, they took a right onto Chelsea Bridge Road and headed for Sloane Square. Ama, sensing that she was close, quickly gathered her thoughts in order to focus on the evening ahead and not the sensational news that no doubt was currently sending shockwaves around the globe.

She felt a pang of nerves well up in her stomach, thinking of the evening ahead. She knew that she wouldn't know anyone personally; she might recognise one or two people but that didn't make it any less daunting. She knew nothing much about the artist, except for his famous father, uncle or even grandfather. She wasn't certain that they were related. She did know that he had been on the scene for a while and had been making waves over in the Brazilian state of Panamerica. She had however read an article about him on the plane to Shanghai, only recently, where she'd breezed over it as it all seemed a little superficial given the subject matter. One thing was for sure though, he was good looking.

Just the sort you'd let your Mama meet. She smiled ruefully.

The car followed Lower Sloane Street until it hit the lights, which were still on green, passed through, taking the left fork onto the King's Road, pulling up opposite Duke of York's.

"Here at last." The taxi driver almost sounded relieved. It seemed to Ama one of the longest cab journeys of her life but she put it down to nerves.

"How much do I owe you?"

"No bother, it's all been taken care of."

"Well, thanks, I guess. See ya." With that Ama slipped out of the car and crossed the pavement towards the gallery.

The wall of sound that greeted her, as she glided up the steps, was accompanied by a waft of heat that broke the cold snap encasing her. She had arrived. Ama picked her way through the main entrance towards the cloakroom. She deposited her overcoat and scarf; then was ushered, turning right, into one of the spaces that played host to Hansel Laurence's 'The Faces of our Future'. Although the gallery was famous for its high ceilings, white washed walls and Spartan design, this was not the scene that confronted Ama. Toe to toe, wall to wall; people mingled, talking animatedly at each other; glass in one hand, canapés in the other.

8:05pm, I'm sure I haven't missed the main presentation. Ama was offered a glass of champagne, accepted and ventured forth into the cohesive mass that was in front of her. She couldn't help but notice that she was one of the tallest women there. *Ok, in heels, but all the same.* Not many men stood taller than her. She scanned the top of the crowd, quickly assessing the situation, whilst trying to see if there was anyone that she recognised. She drew a blank.

Unperturbed but still apprehensive, she meandered through huddled groups of animation, wishing that someone would talk to her. She headed towards the rear of the room, weaving through another group of men in ultra modern suits and through a gap in the crowd, until she saw the canvas and stopped in her tracks.

It can't be. It's incredible. Oh no; the likeness. Ama tried to reason with herself until she got up close to the painting, hanging on the wall in front of her. She looked to side of the bottom right hand corner and read the brief description and title: 'The Ballad of a Crying Man'. *It has to be Papa. I know it's obscured by these inscriptions but where did he get this picture? When did he take it? I must find him I must talk to him. This is so weird.*

She noticed a group from Southern Asiana, most probably in their late twenties and all dressed as if they were Fiftys, staring at her, which made her distinctly uncomfortable, given the heart bursting reminiscence she'd just endured. As she backed away into the crowd she felt weak and nauseous. She steadied herself on the tall stone plant pot next to her, took a deep breath, and hurried through the crowd to get another drink. As she pressed through, she saw him, deep in conversation with an elegant and refined older woman and also someone who was his spitting image; only broader and less brooding.

It has to be his mother. She has the same nose; the same eyes. The guy's the same too; different but the same; must be a Seventy; must be his brother. Ama stopped, unable to move but also not wishing to. She knew that she couldn't just step in and interrupt this family discussion but she needed answers. The trio huddled together as people passed by; conversations ebbed and flowed, whilst Ama remained rooted to the spot. A small Panamerican gentleman sidled up to her and asked her a question in such a thick Colombian accent that she was unable to respond with anything showing that she had actually understood. He was dispatched quicker than he'd been expecting but her isolation was short lived, as she was awoken from her thoughts by the tap on a champagne glass.

A climatic level of silence fell over the assembled group, as an overweight, well dressed Asianaian man, who was most definitely of Indo-Chinese origin, strolled through the crowd and made his way towards the raised dais at the rear of the room, which was right in front of the piece called 'The Legendary Weeping Tiger'.

Damn that painting's good. Ama looked on and listened as the man spoke about the artist. She too felt like that she knew him already. She felt apprehensive, excited and breathless all at the same time. She had no one to hold onto. She couldn't steady herself. Her knees felt sure to buckle at any time. Laozi Veda finished his speech and there was an expectant hush as Hansel Laurence moved through the crowd towards the dais.

Ama was transfixed. Speechless; without a single thought, her entire focus was now on him. She looked on intently as he talked of man's extraneous conflicts. When he raised his left hand, just ever so slightly, he turned his gaze in her direction and their eyes met. They held each other's gaze momentarily while he drew breath and he carried on speaking, withdrawing his gaze and inadvertently giving her the necessary respite to gain her composure.

I've gotta get out of here. I can't stay, it's not right; there'll be so many people wanting to talk to him. I'll embarrass myself. I must go.

Ama immediately turned on the tips of her toes and retreated towards the exit. She made it through the doors whilst Hal was thanking everyone for coming along. Her impulse was to stay; to ride out the crowd and wait for her moment, but her head told her to keep walking. She knew that she wouldn't get a chance to speak to him.

For what? I'll never see him again. The picture of Papa? Pure chance.

On collecting her coat and scarf, Ama maintained her stride down the steps outside. She was resolute in her conviction to keep walking, albeit with

21

half a mind to turn back. She'd never felt so torn. Her cellhip glowed 9:15pm. She looked through her messages and crossed over the square, heading towards the taxi rank that she'd noticed on her way in. She stood shivering whilst contemplating her next move.

It didn't take long for her to decide that she needed the comfort of her warm hotel. The lure of the relaxed atmosphere of the bar and a large Disarrono certainly made it more appealing, given that it was New Year's Eve. She walked towards the taxi at the front of the line. As she drew near, the window wound down placidly and the familiar face of the taxi driver peered out at her.

"Hello. Fancy seeing you here."

Why not make today even more peculiar.

"The Montcalm in the Old Brewery?"

Ama turned her instruction into a question, in case he hadn't heard of her destination. However just like during their first journey across London, he seemed almost catatonic and unperturbed by anything.

"No problem. Been there a thousand times. It's a yank favourite. I guess that's where you're from, being with that orchestra from New York and all that." Ama opened the rear door before she responded.

"Yes and no. I'm a yank yet the USA no longer exists. Anyway my father's family was from Holland and my mother was from Nigeria." The driver completed a 180 degree turn, headed off round Sloane Square and back towards the river avoiding Victoria. "So apart from my accent, I don't know where I'm from." Ama muttered almost as an afterthought.

"You look like you've just seen a ghost."

"I'm sorry. I don't want to discuss it. I want to be left alone."

"Don't worry; I'm sure everything will be alright." The taxi driver, having noticed her pallor, continued with what he thought was an upbeat conversation, "There are strange things going on out there; rare news about life out there..." Ama interrupted,

"Please, I mean no disrespect but I'm tired."

"You're the boss. I'll get you there, no more questions asked."

With that Ama sank back into her seat and breathed a sigh of relief. She was overwhelmed by the day's events. Her mind was awash with the connections; the myriad little pieces that seemed woven together by nothing more than just fate. She needed to forget, even just for a minute. She didn't want to think of her father; her mother; the fear that they must have felt. She wanted to forget about all the news; the stories that carried any hope; any meaning. She wanted peace. The only release she had was her music. Working those keys into a frenzy when she was feeling especially wound up; letting those keys blend into her finger tips when she was feeling especially serene. The piano was her instrument. Hal's was quite obviously his canvas. She resented the fact that by pure chance they were now linked. She didn't like herself for liking him either.

He's cute too. That's just so unfair. I wish he weren't. I'll just spend the rest of my evening thinking about him. Ama looked out of the window and this time stared at the majestic mix of buildings that overlooked the Thames as the car raced along the embankment.

Following the brief interchange earlier, the cabdriver had noticeably changed his driving style, no doubt in deference to his charge. Within minutes they had crossed over Parliament Square Park, the memorial to the old capital, and were speeding along towards Blackfriars Tower. The tower had once been the largest single residential complex in the world but since the Oil Wars most of the blocks were now occupied by squatters and groups of Twentys. However it was also the most vibrant part of London's nightclub scene. Ama had heard some of the stories that had passed into folk lore of famous DJ's and Rapoet's who were 'born, bred and dead' there.

The taxi pulled into the turning circle a few moments later. Ama couldn't have felt more relieved. She didn't know what to make of London; no doubt due to her confusion over the evening's events. This time she hurriedly paid her driver, tipping far too much, she still hadn't got used to the Eurafrican way of dissention, and headed through the welcoming doors of her hotel.

She felt a stranger in a foreign land; a city that was still living on former glories. New York had a legacy of human struggle but it had never been subjected to the same conflicts that were resultant of the 40 years of war waged out of Cairo.

Ama, for a fleeting moment, understood Hal's message. His art contained the secrets to a brighter future based on a perfect past. If only mankind had held it. Like her thought; it was fleeting and gone.

She made her way to the bar as the sound system softly played out the chimes of bells, reminiscent of the former Elizabeth Tower or Big Ben, as it had been affectionately known. It was 10:00pm.

Two hours to go and I'm in no mood for celebrating. I guess I have to see it in, no matter what. It's almost become a superstition for us all. Why are we all so goddamn superstitious? It's just witchcraft. I need that Disarrono anyway.

She found herself drawn into the bar, made her way to the far end and perched on a stool. She ordered a drink from the attentive barman, as a haze of smoke rose up towards the ceiling, until it was caught up in the purifier's blast and disappeared. Ama did not smoke but liked the smell of a freshly lit cigarette. She understood what drove the urge. Two young men approached the bar close to her and Ama looked them both up and down, as if to warn them off from doing the same. She was in no mood to talk, especially to a couple of Fiftys looking for some New Year's Eve affection. The pianist missed a note, skipped another and then caught up with himself. Ama couldn't help but notice his fleshband slipping around his wrist as he began to perspire. She laughed to herself quietly and sipped her drink, lost in a whirlwind of thoughts.

No doubt I'll be the only one at morning rehearsal tomorrow; apart from Voegel. It'll be my chance to quiz him about the Laurence family. He'll know for sure. This music is beginning to grate and I'm just not in the mood. There's no point staying here, I'm sure with a good night's rest I'll be clearer in the morning. Hansel Laurence; a name at least that I'll never forget.

With that she finished her drink gracefully, rested the glass on the coaster provided, swiveled round and headed off in the direction of her suite.

Chapter 5

Towards the most eastern point of the Serpentine, snow had begun to settle on the lower branches of the sycamore trees. Hyde Park was white, brilliant; rare in its expanse. Sauntering up a path, Hal pondered on the preceding few days. His whole world had been turned upside down and he felt spent already. He'd been contacted by so many people, all vying for attention. This wouldn't have been all bad, if it weren't for the fact that he hadn't yet fully awoken from his stupor, of both revelry and unrequited wanton desire. Wishing to neither do his benefactor a disservice nor be caught off guard, he'd bounced all these off with a casual thought of *another day, another issue*, except, contrary to his gait; he didn't feel casual at all.

He had promised Laozi he'd attend a concert that evening, on the proviso they'd have dinner afterwards, discuss the future and what was to be expected of him, from here on in. His reasoned vision of the world, its constructs, its factions and its fictions, was at times juxta-posed with an overbearing lack of self confidence, as it was with most artists. He would disappear into a cave of self loathing, especially when tired. Today was one of those days. He would have to mask his fear and subconscious quest for superficiality during the course of the evening. He reached the exit of the park and turned left into the underpass, taking him to the entrance of 22 Park Lane.

"I'm here to see Mr. Veda." Hal informed the porter as he headed into the lobby waiting area.

"He's on his way now." The response was smooth and knowing.

They're so responsive, well informed and rehearsed. I guess you get what you pay for; highly likely that they are well trained duplicates. Hal thought to himself only a moment longer as, if on cue, Laozi walked out of the lift bank and into the lobby.

"Hansel Laurence, not only is it a pleasure but also high time that we both did something escapist, even if it is a little educational."

His beaming smile and bear hug put Hal immediately at ease. Laozi's time at Oxford University had stuck with him. He was able to adopt the sound and mannerisms of an old school English gent, whenever he wanted to; even if it was merely to put someone at ease. Hal's fatigued thoughts flittered away.

"Laozi, you must tell me the real reason for this evening. You're surely aware by now that I know little about this style of music. Other than you being a bored lonely old man, looking for an uncomplicated cheap date for the evening, I can't see why we have to go to this concert."

"Hal, my friend, as with all things in life, there is an ulterior motive, one that will no doubt reveal itself. However, until that point, might I suggest that we get on with our journey, as we only have a few moments before curtain up and I, like you no doubt, would like a refreshment or two."

"Lead the way, sir, lead the way." Hal made the mocking gesture of a slight bow and followed closely behind Laozi, as they made their way to the car.

Traffic was light and they arrived at the Barbican Centre in good time. Laozi had acquired two centre seats in the stalls, in the thick of the action. They made their way to the new private member's bar on the 1st floor, which just so happened to be managed by a Vedas Corp subsidiary. Hal checked his cellhip and switched it off. It was only 7pm. He couldn't rid his mind of the girl. Since that evening of his exhibition, he'd not been able to concentrate for more than a few seconds, without returning to the same thought pattern. *Who was she? Why was she there? How do I find out?*

He already knew the answer to the last question; Analucia. However he didn't want to risk the expectant nature of their working relationship. Hal was dismissively aware of Analucia's hopeful feelings towards him, but felt that they were best served from a distance, in support of her boss, and in turn his career. He also had no desire to ask Laozi directly, as since Alicia's death he was unsure as to Laozi's view about his private life.

The champagne was served in coupes, providing a retro elegance to the evening. The decor of the member's bar harked back to the 1930's and Hal couldn't help but notice a number of the female clientele were dressed in halter backless dresses, made fashionable in that era.

"Loving the scenery."

"This will be an evening not to forget in a hurry, Hal. We'll discuss the future over dinner but, in the meantime, I want to thank you for giving an old friend a chance to escape, from the real world. I do mean what I say, and I'm not speaking of tonight. You've created a vision of peace and understanding, which has been missing for many, many years. Knowing what I have to endure most days, I see little hope. Thank you for giving all of us some."

Hal toyed with the retro concert programme, casually bouncing the booklet between his palms, rested it on the table in front of him and took a sip from his glass, pausing for a breath before responding.

"Rare praise indeed Laozi, I guess you've got something up your sleeve, so you're softening the blow, but thanks all the same."

"Do you know much about the New York Philharmonic?" Laozi moved the conversation on without a flicker of mischief.

"A little, in so much that they've been on a world tour for the last year. I know that we are here to listen to their rendition of Hans Werner Henze's Piano Concerto No: 2; albeit that his Fifth Symphony is the main feature. I guessed that's why there's a Regency feel to the place, however this is slightly out of synch, given that Leonard Bernstein premiered the symphony in 1963."

Laozi broke out into a broad grin.

"You never cease to amaze me, profound one minute, evasive the next, all of a sudden you appear knowledgeable upon a subject you claim to know little about. Did you know that a new piano soloist joined them last year? A rare talent I hear."

"I didn't Laozi, but now that I do, I'm intrigued. Maybe this part of the evening hasn't been a waste after all." Hal sat back into his chair, not even thinking to look through the concert programme.

A moment later the 5 minute gong sounded, reminding everyone to take their seats. Hal and Laozi finished their drinks and made their way to the stalls on the ground floor. They were one of the last to file in and sit down. Muffled whispers gave way to pregnant pause, as the conductor, Benedikt Voegel, stood motionless in front of the audience. With a raise of his right arm, the auditorium fell completely silent.

The spotlight cast its beams, illuminating her; unblemished, mid tones shimmering, hands poised to begin. Her Tavernier blue silk dress was raised slightly above the right knee, showing the cusp of her thigh. Hal was transfixed.

They opened with Henze's piano concerto and she was the main attraction. As she lightly skipped from note to note adding variations of weight and depth, to the ever approaching wave of climax, Hal was sure that she looked in his direction. He sat motionless, willing her to connect with him, willing her to offer him a glance, a smile, a flicker of recognition; nothing. The concerto evolved from a solo piece into a full blown orchestral score. Hal recognised the Telemanniana from his childhood. It was ever the more engaging because of the soloist. 50 minutes passed and he'd had hardly moved. He felt a nudge in his ribs and realised that the music had stopped and people were making their way to the exits. It was the interval.

"So, what did you make of that?" a rhetorical Laozi prodded, as Hal stood up, looking at him like he'd been punched in the solar plexus, whilst being administered pure oxygen.

"You know her? You knew that she was playing?"

"Don't think for a minute I didn't notice a complete lack of focus, mid way through your speech the other night. I was relieved but also genuinely impressed by how well you held it together."

"I never mentioned her, nor asked for her name. How did you know?"

"It's simple really. Benedikt Voegel, her music director, is an old acquaintance from Oxford and I recently attended a meeting, on an entirely different matter, where he and I realised we had a lot more in common than just our alma mater. He let me know that he'd taken a girl with a rare talent under his wing."

"So thoughts of Alicia are to be pushed to one side and I'm to have a new conquest? I'm not sure how to take this Laozi?" A sardonic grin cut across his face.

"I wouldn't worry too much about what everyone else thinks Hal. It really doesn't matter whether your former in-laws, your mother or even your friends think ill of you. In this case, I know they couldn't care less. For one so at peace with the world, you're so at war with yourself." Laozi tut-tutted as he played along.

They reached the member's bar on the 1st floor and sat back in the same seats as before. Two more coupes arrived. Hal took out his pack of No 5's, tapped on its left shoulder, with a cigarette popping up on command. He took it out with the tips of his thumb and forefinger, rolling the filter over between them, while he pondered Laozi's words. His response was earnest and off-kilter.

"Have you ever been in love Laozi? I mean no disrespect to your ex-wife but truly, anyone? Do you know what it's like to be in the thrall of the chase?" Hal looked at his benefactor, imploring him to unlock some wisdom that could quell the growing storm in his heart.

"I was; once. However that time is no more. I made some decisions a long time ago for good reason. I've stuck by them and will continue to do so. That's it. I want no more on the subject."

Hal lit his cigarette and blew a plume of smoke into the purifier above them, as Laozi deflected any further intrusion on his past.

"You'll have to introduce me to her; properly and this evening."

"I will, after this. They've fleshed out the running time with a couple of concertos. Drink up."

The next 45 minutes passed by in a slow and painful blur. Hal willed each second to pass quicker than it could. He constantly checked in her direction to see if she had seen him, but he couldn't raise a smile or even a glance. To keep himself occupied, he stared at the ceiling and allowed the music to wash over him. Failing that, he tried to remain focused by looking through the programme again and again. He didn't know what to make of the situation. His rational self struggled with his romantic self. *Maybe this is the war Laozi is talking about.*

"Follow me." Laozi stood up and slowly made his way out of the row of seats into the aisle. The end couldn't have come soon enough for Hal but he tried to maintain a languid and respectable air about him. He had no background on her. No position of strength.

"Laozi, prior preparation prevents piss poor performance. Give me something to work with. What's her story and not the one in the programme notes that I've read over 10 times now?"

"I know very little except that her parents were killed in the most tragic of circumstances, over a year ago. She's 28 years old, from Flatbush, New York and as you know she's exceptionally talented; however she isn't aware, how much; one of her many qualities. Benedikt is extremely protective of her and it took a lot to get her to your exhibition in the first place."

"Fine. I get it. You're in two minds about which Hal should turn up, aren't you?"

"Of course. Out of loyalty to Benedikt I want the worldly artist to be in attendance, not the voracious beast with 7 years to live. You should also be warned that Benedikt is of Prussian stock and makes Christian references at any chance he gets."

With that they arrived at a door backstage, which looked firmly shut. Laozi raised his hand to knock, only for it to squeak open before he connected with the wood panelling. Behind the door there was a bustle and energy with musicians talking animatedly, while stagehands moved boxes from one place to another. The collective noise drowned out any potential private conversations. Hal was relieved. Passing the wind section, they turned a false corner in the room and Laozi spotted the music director.

"Benedikt, so good of you to welcome us back here. It always seems so few and far between, our meeting like this."

"I'm always happy to accommodate you Laozi." He paused and turned to Hal, as if he knew him and added "and you must be Hansel, I've heard so much about you from his eminence, that I'm not sure whether I should be joining your church or setting fire to it."

"Herr Voegel, kind words I'm sure, however please let me congratulate you. This evening has been exhilarating." Hal had barely finished before he was brushed aside by a figure in a grey tracksuit, leaning over into a large suitcase. Long, untied, wavy hair cascaded over the shoulders, down onto the undoubted feminine curves beneath the clothes. The girl scratched around at the bottom of the case, until she found what she was looking for. She looked up, papers in hand. It was her, the girl with the almond eyes.

That moment would have passed by in a blink of an eye, yet time stood still for both of them, while they studied each other's face, waiting for the other to speak.

"Hal Laurence, very pleased to meet you." Hal offered her his hand to pull her to her feet, at the same time shaking it in greeting. She rose elegantly, without a word, fixing her eyes on his. Hal pressed on, "I can't pretend that this is a chance meeting, I've engineered my way back here. I saw you at my exhibition and have been thinking of pretty much nothing else since that moment." He thought he'd overstepped with his candour, as there was a brief pause, but her hand gently squeezed his.

"Unfortunately it looks like I have the same complaint. Ama Pepper Clark, happy to make your acquaintance." Hal was lost for words. Her voice was lyrical, educated, masking tones of a harder accent; a lilt, softening a more throaty rasp. It matched her exterior; unblemished, vulnerable yet bold, hardened by the world; beautiful. He became aware that both Laozi and Benedikt were silently studying the pair of them.

"I think it best if we continue another time. Would you allow me the pleasure of your company over dinner, this coming Friday? We could meet at L' Escargot on Greek St in Soho, at say 8pm?"

"That suits me fine, she exclaimed quickly and without hesitation. "Just to let you know, I'll be flat out exhausted, as the director gives us little time off for good behaviour. However I have no other plans. In any case I want to quiz you on a load of things." She stopped, looked at Laozi and the music director and turned, so that they could not read her lips. In a barely audible whisper, adding to the intrigue, she continued, "but I guess we'll have to wait, until we're away from prying eyes."

Hal couldn't help but notice that her tonal inflections and insinuation mirrored his own. Laozi and Benedikt started talking in animated hushed voices, out of earshot. Hal strained to hear them, whilst maintaining his gaze on her. He realised that he was still holding her hand. *Or is she holding mine?* He let go with a broad confident smile.

"Till then Ama."

"Farewell."

Not wanting to break the intoxicating spell that he was now under, Hal backed away with a nod and turned to Laozi with a look of *let's get out of here* and proceeded around the partition, where he waited for Laozi to say his goodbyes and catch up. Hal waited for what seemed like an eternity, but which in fact was only a matter of minutes, until Laozi came sidling up to him.

"Get what you came for?"

"I did thank you."

"Well, let's get out of here." The driver picked them up outside the main entrance on Silk Street and headed for a new Panamerican restaurant that had opened up on Mount Street, near Laozi's place in Mayfair.

"I know little about where we are going but the head porter, Patrick, says that it comes highly recommended. Apparently it specialises in Argentinean beef, Californian wine and New York high society. Quite apt I'd say." Laozi added, as they settled into the back of his car.

The journey from east to west across London conjured up a myriad of possibilities for Hal. Life had extraordinary twists and no matter which way he turned; he'd be presented with opportunity or reprisal. This chance meeting with Ama hadn't been chance at all, but it had thrown his chosen path completely off track. He had his short future planned: expression, social commentary, notoriety, philanthropy, change. There was no place for romantic notions, no matter how farfetched or obtainable they were. He didn't have the time. Society had evolved to the same reasoning. If you didn't have the time you didn't get involved. She was a Ninety, he could tell by her wrist; but he hadn't hidden his.

The mean streets around the Barbican gave way to brighter, more hopeful, parts of Holborn. The car bumped along the wearing tarmac but mistakenly turned into an area cordoned off by the police.

30

"Apologies Mr. Veda, sir. I'll get us out of here as soon as possible." Solomon looked concerned as he turned to reverse the car away from the blockade.

Unfortunately the car behind hadn't noticed either and they were now stuck in a jam of their own. Out of the corner of his eye, Hal saw a hooded figure climb up over the barricade and beat his chest in defiance. He wasn't sure if it was actually in victory, but what came next was far more startling, as a hoard of hooded Thirtys climbed up over the top and started throwing missiles in their direction. Some were ethanol-bombs, some were bricks, some were bits of debris but all of it was intended for their car. The first one hit the right front wheel spraying ethanol all over the bonnet. The flames burst alive and licked up the side towards the driver's door.

"Solomon, get us out of here." Laozi exclaimed, but it was little use as they were stuck front and back. Next a brick hit the window beside Hal and bounced back into the direction from where it came.

"Hold on." Solomon ordered, as he pulled his index finger hard on the accelerator paddle, without concern for the damage to the rear of the car. Their car rammed the vehicle behind, pushing it out of the way. As they gathered momentum, Solomon flicked the gear paddle forward and spun the car at a right angle, setting off along the pavement towards the street corner and away from the now chasing faction. As they motored away he set the bonnet washers on forward and sprayed the front of the car with foam, quelling the flames until they disappeared.

"That was close." Hal exhaled in awe. "I hope those behind us got away."

"I wouldn't be so sure that they weren't part of it Hal. In any case, it's not as if they know who we are. I'm sure it was the car. It reeks of aging wealth. I keep telling myself that there's little point in having decent things, as they only attract the wrong attention. Yet, I just can't rid myself of a few of these comforts." Laozi tried to put a sense of calm in his voice.

"No matter how much I feel a part of the world and our plight, I just wish it could be different. Don't they realise that it's the same for all of us, regardless of our allotted lifespan? It is structure, leadership and a common voice that people are missing. Lack of belief has engineered its way into all of our consciousnesses."

"Quite right and given tomorrow's broadcast, there is no time like the present for us to make a change."

Not too long after they had ventured into that brief but unsettling foray, they arrived at Pampas. Hal used his cellhip to establish that it was the one of the few restaurants in the northern hemisphere that sold genuine beef.

"It is rare these days. I thought that most producers had attached such high premiums, that no restaurant bothered to serve it anymore. In any case, I thought your organisation had helped with the shortage?" Hal added sardonically.

Laozi responded in typical fashion, "As you know meat from cloned cows

31

tastes better, but unfortunately the side effects of its consumption stopped production pretty early on Hal. You should know better than to trouble me, especially over such a contentious issue. I'll put it down to hunger, I'm famished." This could have been taken either way, but Hal was too far locked into his own thoughts to care.

They were seated beside the private rose garden and heat emanated from the walls and the floor, keeping winter at bay. The decor was ultra-modern, clean and with a hint of Eurafrican flair.

It has to be the dark wood, fused with glass balustrades. The maitre d' made it very clear to all of his staff that they were to be well looked after. Laozi was pleasantly surprised that the fuss was not for his benefit, as it soon became apparent that no one had a clue nor cared about who he was.

"Analucia's obviously been doing her magic. I noted that there was an open copy of The Standard in the waiting area, the page, needless to say, was open on the 'Who's Who' of yesterday. The picture of you is actually quite good."

"Hey thanks. I like the article; it's a necessary evil. I want notoriety, as I see it as my ticket on. That indelible mark on society seems closer now, more than ever before." Hal looked earnestly at his benefactor, as he headed onto an already well trodden path. "Laozi, words can't express my gratitude, nor my complete and utter amazement at being singled out by you." Hal stopped, paused, stroked his chin momentarily then continued, "That's a perfect moment for you to let me in on what's in store."

Before he had time to respond, the waiter proffered a 2139 bottle of Ambassador's 1953 from the Hanzell Vineyard. Laozi looked at the label, checked the bottle, nodded at the waiter to proceed and allowed him to pour. He then gently swirled the glass in front of him, allowing the oxygen to enhance the distinct whiff of Chardonnay. Hal noted that he didn't linger too long nor too demonstratively, as Laozi hated the pretentions that seemed to follow most modern wine drinkers. Its legs were obvious. He briefly put the glass to his nose but already knew that the wine was perfect. He put the glass down, pushing the stem away with his thumb and forefinger, towards the right of the tips of his knives. He nodded at the waiter and leant back, deep into his chair, as if this was the moment of truth.

"Hal, later this year, I would very much like it if you were to accompany me on a tour of the three capitals. Over the next few days I have some extremely important business to attend to, which isn't relevant to you, but after that, you will have my undivided attention. I think it high time that you are unveiled properly to the world. This tour will be your making. Analucia and the team have put together a programme of exhibitions, press junkets, interviews and media appearances in each city. She has all the details and if you are willing to do this, you'll need to be in Sao Luis on June 1st."

Laozi waited for his charge to respond. Not even a flicker of acknowledgement, so he pressed on,

"Until then I'd soak up the success of your break-out exhibition and please comply with the few appearances and bookings that you get offered. I know a lot of people want a piece of you right now but this pales in comparison to what's in store. You have to respond to these representatives Hal."

He got the desired reaction.

"How do you know I've been avoiding everyone?"

"You know I know everything. It's my job to know. Look, once Analucia's PR train gets going, you won't be able to stop it and you will have to be ready. It's akin to being a movie star from the 20th Century or a tech star from the 21st. You'll be the centre of attention, they'll hang on every word and you won't be able to hide. You mustn't hide. You're the modern man: the painter, the writer, the photographer, the poet. People need answers, people need hope and most of all people need to escape."

Laozi paused for dramatic effect, lightly touching the stem of his wine glass, before leaning forward towards Hal and continuing on in a hushed tone.

"There's been a shift in life's balance and it's been brewing for years. Man wants to feel whole again, we've been looking for a catalyst and I believe that you are it."

Hal stared at him in silence contemplating his next move, knowing that his response had to be worthy. Mind racing he sidestepped the compliment and locked in on the commercial aspects.

"Okay, so I say sign me up; get me on board, then what? Obviously I'm going to be creating new pieces, I have a plethora of ideas but what of these exhibitions? I can do the media bits, I can do most of the things that you ask, but then, what do you get out of it and where do I find the time to put together my pieces?"

"Put simply, you have an excellent back catalogue of material. I know it needs airing. Most of it fits into a 'Faces of Our Future' world tour. Any new pieces that you do over the coming months should be saved for a sequel. You won't have time to reflect on new ideas, while you're with the travelling circus. You'll be honing your already established and key messages. It seems that your career path has just widened Hal. Think of it as a precursor to a role in revolution. It's well known that anything outstanding and original in the way of creative thought is a stride towards change. There is a strong relationship between the arts and politics. Art takes on social dimensions, becoming itself a focus of controversy and a force of political as well as social change."

Laozi took a sip of wine, whilst remaining fixed on his train of thought.

"We share a common vision Hal, one that you can express far better than I. Through you I can touch the hearts of the people; through you I can affect the masses; man needs something to believe in, only pure thoughts and true peace can alter the evolutionary path that we have been allotted. You ask what's in all of this for me. You have your answer."

Hal shifted somewhat uncomfortably in his seat, wondering why his benefactor had come over so wistful all of a sudden. Intent on not getting bogged down in a conversation, one reserved for late nights or early mornings, he changed tack with a fresh line of questioning.

"I know that this seems on a tangent but I have a serious question to ask Laozi, so please answer truthfully. Seeing as Vedas Corp is in direct competition with Etihad Spaceways, who's really funded this trip to Kepler 3? How much more do you know, more than that which we are being sold by the media?"

"That's two questions and quite a digression Hal, but there is a link. I guess you know me well enough to have realised that I somehow must be involved."

"It doesn't take a rocket scientist to establish that the Chairman of Vedas Corp, one of the richest men on the planet, with his own space exploration business, is involved."

"Sure, understood, but with regards to this particular mission to Kepler 3, it was the World Council who successfully lobbied for Etihad Spaceways and Vedas Corp to bury the hatchet. We combined to deliver the space craft, the technology and the team to ensure safe passage to this newly discovered planet."

"OK, but how much more to this is there? I'm not buying it, that there's an international broadcast going out in two days time, just for the sake of discovering gas, water or even a few plants."

"You still haven't given me an answer to my question. Are you in?"

"Of course I'm in Laozi. I was in, in Singapore 15 years ago. However I've now got the bit between my teeth. What do you know that we don't? Why does the timing of this mission seem so linked to your plans with me?"

"Such an artist; always thinking that the world revolves around you." Laozi mocked. "Just because Vedas Corp has funded the programme, it doesn't mean that I have the full picture. My knowledge is limited but I smell opportunity. This news could change our world and that's where you come in. Let's order before I drink too much of this delicious wine."

They ordered their food and Hal chose a Pluribus 2126 from the Bond Estate. As the waiter poured the bold Cabernet, Laozi spoke serenely and quietly.

"The first thing I must iterate Hal is that this is extremely confidential and I am telling you because you are a friend but also you are someone who perhaps can use the truth wisely. To be forewarned is to be forearmed."

Laozi let the phrase hang in the air momentarily.

"The Kepler 30 solar system was first discovered in July 2012 and astrologists originally thought that it was similar to earth's own solar system. However in March 2024, the Kepler telescope discovered a second solar system behind Kepler 30, known as Kepler Real and its third planet, closest to its sun, was given the name Kepler 3. However for a culmination of

34

reasons, we have only recently been able to send an updated 'Rover' onto Kepler 3, and we've been deliberating over our findings ever since. We found life Hal, real life and not just a few plants, as you put it." Laozi leant forward and lowered his voice into a virtually inaudible whisper. "What's more they're like us."

Hal leant in, feeling in cahoots with his benefactor, for the first time in a long while. He allowed his mouth to drop a little, before quickly re-establishing his position.

"I knew it. I could tell that there was more to this than what everyone has been saying. I know that you wouldn't be telling me unless it was going to go public, but thank you all the same. This changes everything; do they know about us, do they want to know us? Have they wasted time with some of our ridiculous human concepts; perhaps an even more pertinent question is, do they have the mark?"

They both sat in silence for quite a while, contemplating the complexity of such a revelation, and after a while their food arrived. It wasn't until they had both finished eating that Laozi spoke once again.

"No doubt you'll know that the oldest recorded human being without the mark died of natural causes, on November 1st last year? She was 129 years old. She was born in Japan on December 14th 2014 at 7:59pm local time. Her twin sister was one of the first to be born with the mark and died at the age of 32. You can see where I'm going with this can't you?"

Hal nodded.

"There's a parable here between us and those on this planet of Kepler 3; did these twins get on? Did they care for each other when growing up? Considering that they were identical in every way except for one difference, one that was unique to them and them only, they couldn't have seen the world more differently. It's all about perspective and they were victims of time and circumstance. There are great lessons here that we should all learn. I'll connect you to her biography. There's plenty to inspire you."

Hal, pensive, looked on but added nothing further. He had nothing further to add, as his mind turned over on the implications of this new discovery. He momentarily forgot about Ama Pepper Clark and it wasn't until later, when he was back home, that the waves of emotion washed over him. He quietly slipped into a hallucinatory sleep, languidly wrestling with the real and the fantastic. As for Laozi, the whole of the evening had played out entirely as he had hoped.

Chapter 6

Laozi Veda woke with a start, furtively glancing around his room, sensing the being of his dreams was still present; watching, studying, crafting a response. When he realised he was alone, he sat back against his pillows and clicked his fingers twice for the news channel. The projection immediately beamed a selection of images to the foot of his bed. He flicked to the familiar station and exhaled deep and slow. He'd been suffering the same dream for the past few months, but he wasn't going to be sidelined as to its meaning; he knew his thoughts and knew his experiences. This was neither, yet it felt so real.

As a direct result of these frequent early morning visits, he would feel emboldened by the scenes that had played out in his head. He would wake conscious of having been out of his mind and be almost instantaneously awash with the prudence of peace. It would spur him on in the dark moments of the day. The dream had become his inspiration, guiding him ever onwards, towards his objective; the importance of which only seemed to increase with age.

He sidled out from under the covers and padded towards the bathroom. The soft glow of the morning light penetrated the room behind him, as the blackout blinds steadily rose up towards their source. He rubbed his eyes sleepily and stood in the doorway, looking at himself in the mirror. His dreams kept him young; his work did not. The daily toil and continual travelling had taken its toll on his body, where the leaner fitter days of his youth had now distinctly passed. His business was also leaving its mark. The skin was beginning to wrinkle around his eyes; the laughter lines were etched with sorrow and concern, the lung capacity seriously diminished. He had been so focused on his work that the only recent respite had been these dreams of his. Their subject could have been mistaken for an obsession. A fascination that he hoped would be sublimated into something far more substantial than just fiscal return. It had become his sole focus, the daily purpose, the essence of his being.

The running water was cool to the touch. He kept both his hands under the tap for more time than was necessary, as if lost in a trance or deep in meditation. Returning to reality, he calmly applied the liquid to his face. The skin absorbed the moisture immediately and after he'd wiped his face dry, with the hand towel beside him, he stepped towards the shower, pushing a button three times for hot water. He stood in its centre, contemplating the day ahead. The evening would be a delightful distraction, but his main appointment still vexed him. As the water washed over his head, down onto his back, tiny prickles of heat attacked his pores removing any remnants of his sweat filled reverie. There was limited time left before his team had to come up with a solution; they'd reached the point of no return. He had no issue with the financial implications, just the feasibility and the measures that they would all have to take to ensure a satisfactory conclusion.

He left his flat early, to take his morning tea at Claridges. Whenever he was in London, he'd follow breakfast, at his favourite hotel, by a brisk walk along Bond Street. He'd usually stop and see his friends at Hermes and share a joke with the proprietor at Boodles, before heading back to his apartment at 22 Park Lane. His flat doubled as one half of the control room to his empire. His study was one of the most celebrated work spaces in the world, with the parallel half residing in Singapore. In amongst the multitude of interactive screens, linking him to his executives' offices, across all of his businesses, were 2 large oversize, handmade, vintage, mahogany pedestal desks. It was here that he would spend most of his day.

This morning was no different to any of those days before, except that today had a little bit more significance to him. It was his daughter's birthday.

She's 24 today. He anxiously hummed to himself, as he thought of her stuck in Mumbai with her mother. *Cut off from her entirely, no communication, frustrating.*

Laozi had sent her a present a few days earlier, as he always did, hoping that she would receive it on her birthday. He hadn't talked to her in three years and hadn't seen her for many more than that. For all he knew her mother never let her accept his gifts.

Wasting little time on what might have been, he turned his attention to the waiter hovering near him.

"My eggs and pan fired bread please Stephen, cooked as I always have them; some grapefruit juice and my usual blend of earl grey and breakfast tea."

Stephen nodded in agreement. He needed little encouragement, as he knew Mr. Veda's habits well, having been breakfast manager at Claridges for the last 5 years. Mr. Veda's bi-monthly trips lasted for 6 days at a time and always ran like clockwork.

Laozi sat back and stared up at the vaulted ceiling marveling at the room's majesty and significance. The hotel had been witness to many great emperors and empresses, in fact many of the world's most prominent leaders and influencers throughout its 300 year history. It was here that he felt truly at home. It was from here that he had, over the years, met for breakfast with some of the world's leading financiers, scientists, developers, telecommunications giants and commodities traders.

Laozi's life hadn't always been spent in Claridges. Born in 2092, not long after the Oil Wars had come to a dramatic conclusion, he'd witnessed the rise of his father from humble property developer through to corporate owner, in one swift move. The world's population had more than halved; through war, concern and an oversupply of birth control products that had malfunctioned. However, no matter the reasons for a diminishing population, the wars' end acted as a catalyst in enhancing the budding tycoon's status. Through his Park Lane contracts, Laozi's father made some interesting connections, and the most prominent were a group of scientists from Shanghai, looking for funding.

Mankind was looking for a replacement for their lost children and these scientists had discovered a way to reproduce humans efficiently and above all, cheaply.

Laozi's father was in the enviable position of knowing the right bankers and alternative debt providers to facilitate the funds. However it was his knowledge of structuring property development deals that led to him incorporating his company, as the brand and master developer of the project. The system was in principle easy to govern and the World Council, contrary to public opinion, not only sanctioned the contract but provided part of the equity for its initiation. Government backed and with the right partners, Vedas Corp won the sole contract for the development of duplicates worldwide.

The negative impact of this decision was seen by December 2099, when the early January sales in most shopping malls, in every large conurbation, saw pop-up stores offering individuals a duplicate of their own for just ♩10,000. This was inexpensive given that there had been a re-basing of all currencies to worldcredits in 2093. Many saw this as an opportunity to make their lives easier. The obvious repercussions were swept under the carpet, in a tidal wave of euphoria. The ability to have children identical to the parent had gone mass-market and everyone loved Vedas Corp for it. It gave them the power to play at being divine.

Laozi had had firsthand experience with the rise and fall of a relationship with a duplicate; in his case, two. On his 18th Birthday, his father bequeathed to him a beautiful and ornate dark wooden box. He had unclasped the 24 carat gold catch and ceremoniously lifted its lid, revealing two miniature glass tubes, lying atop a bed of fine synthetic wool. At the foot of each one, a small handwritten place card was firmly pressed into the material. The left hand one read, Lao; the right, Zi.

Yet over the years duplicates had proven expensive to run, unreliable and, in an ever increasing number of circumstances, extremely dangerous. 28% of all existing developed duplicates had gone on to commit the act of patricide. The motives for these acts of murder were always based on petty jealousies, systemic abuse of the relationship or the lack of clarity over their origin which had been bestowed upon them by their parents.

The World Council decided to terminate the Vedas Corp contract and to outlaw all duplicate development in May 2019. The corporation was instructed to destroy all relevant technology. The known backstreet development shops were raided and shut down by local authorities. Whilst in most shopping malls, in every large conurbation, pop-up stores offered individuals the deconstruction of their own duplicate for just ⅺ20,000. Mankind had blatantly legalised and commercialised murder.

It was as if Lao and Zi had foreseen this. Laozi was not prepared for what came next. It wasn't a tale of pain and neglect; it wasn't a tale of murder and intrigue; just a case of misunderstanding, loss and regret. When the entire family had got together to celebrate the twins' birthday, they both ran; far far away. They took nothing with them, ensured that no trail was left and disappeared into the night; never to be seen or heard from again.

Laozi was awoken from his thoughts, as his eggs and pan fired bread were placed in front of him.

"Thank you Stephen." He took a sip of his grapefruit juice and caressed the cup of tea as if warming the tips of his fingers.

It was his parents' death that had acted as a catalyst for his transformation into a philanthropic businessman. His remorse was based on his own guilt, having not shown them that he was the son that she had hoped he would be. He had vowed from that day forward to give back to society. Circumstance had seen to it that he had been born into a life of privilege and he had also been given a brilliant mind to match this gift. It was part of his psyche; an explanation as to the cause of his drive and personality. His father had been a role model, a distant but inspirational figure who would appear in his dreams from time to time.

His decision to be so consumed by his current project was in honour of his father's memory; this and the nagging visions. Laozi had formulated his life plan; his philosophies; his views on the world. Human life had become hopeless. Human endeavour was based on hope. The world needed to change; structurally, materially, culturally and physically. He resolved to never stop, until he could affect that change.

Laozi looked at the pocket watch in front of him, resting neatly to the right of the selection of knives that formed part of the table setting. With a striking amount of zeal and vigour he leapt out of his chair, nodded in Stephen's direction and was helped into his overcoat. He headed out into the entrance hall, leaving swiftly through the revolving door, via the main entrance. This morning was different. He was late and his usual stroll along Bond Street would have to wait.

He hurriedly turned left, rather than right, left again and headed towards Berkeley Square. He rounded the corner and made his way to the entrance of his apartment building. The porter came out to greet him, doffing his cap in awkward reverence, backing away slightly, as Laozi's wide frame passed by. Another porter escorted him to the bank of lifts and opened up the doors with a mere nod at the panel marked Penthouse. The journey to the top, all 207 floors, took only 90 seconds and Laozi stepped out into his apartment, overheating but on time. He hated being late, even for board meetings.

As he took off his overcoat the projection screens in front of him flickered into life with a different location and time appearing on each one.

New York: 5am, São Luis: 7am, Cairo: 12pm, Mumbai: 3:30pm, Shanghai: 6pm, Singapore: 6pm

He approached the left hand desk, pulling a large dark green leather chair along with him. As he sat down each projection washed over to reveal a male or a female of similar age to Laozi, dressed in a similar style and in a similar pose; forward and forthright.

"Good day, everyone; rather than waste time with the usual pleasantries, as I trust that you are all fine, we must discuss these recent events as a matter of urgency. What we are being asked to do here is of absolute secrecy. We cannot afford to let anyone know the terms that have been agreed. We must also all be aware of the consequences if any of the designs were to fall into the wrong hands; let alone any of the information from our contact over there.

"If we cannot agree on the timings and the layouts over the next few days, the implications will be disastrous, if not catastrophic. So to proceed with any alternative, we need to be content with both risk and reward, we need to turn all the current negatives into positives and we need to be certain that it will not fail." Laozi fixed his gaze on the central screen and awaited a response.

The meeting lasted most of the day, with each screen coming alive at various intervals, covering a host of outcomes, where one person would provide an argument and another a counter. He felt perturbed by their lack of cohesion and their collective disharmony. By the time he wrapped the meeting up, there had been no formal finale, much to his distaste, however they did resolve to conclude this matter by the end of the week; reconvening in two days time.

Once he'd shut down his office for the day, he headed for his dressing room across the hallway and changed into dress trousers, white shirt and a blue silk Nehru jacket, which he left open ever so slightly at the collar. He placed his scarlet handkerchief strategically in the left breast pocket of the jacket, allowing it to billow out like a red rose in bloom. He took his black, custom made, woollen overcoat off the rack, inspected the back for static debris, realising that there was none, put it on, inspected his black shoes for scuff and shine, whistled in approval and headed for the lift.

As if it had a sixth sense, the lift arrived as he approached the doors. As he descended he tried not to let the day's events distract him from the evening ahead. He wanted to ensure that his guest would have everything that was required to see the job through. Laozi saw it as a personal crusade to make the masses listen. The world needed to change and he would affect this change.

He left via the main entrance this time. His car rolled up at the precise moment he stepped into the cold air outside. He tugged at his coat as a gust of wind blew right through him, forcing a shiver. Stepping slowly over the cobbled pathway, towards the turning circle, he reached the open rear door, used it as ballast and put one foot in and sat down. Hurriedly the driver shut the door, ensuring that the warmth stayed inside. Laozi, blissfully unaware, played out his intentions, over and over in his mind, changing inflection, procrastinating over syntax and adding further depth to his words.

He had been looking forward to this meeting for quite some time. Since his 18th birthday he'd not looked back once. He'd cut all ties with those friends who had been holding him back, many of whom had now passed on. He'd focused purely on making good on the intentions of his father and the corporation's early mission statement.

The company philosophy had been lost over time. Deep down Laozi knew that it was due to winning that government contract in 2092. Whilst this could be seen as a negative, it had made the company, and all its executives, richer than they could have ever possibly imagined. It had spawned businesses all over the world, in all sectors. The Vedas Corporation dominated retail, manufacturing, construction, information technology, space exploration and fuel development. They had even acquired the development rights to the moon. The issue over who owned earth's largest satellite had been settled in 2099, when the corporation paid)50bn to each of the three members of the World Council; Eurafrica, Panamerica and Asiana. Given the state of their respective economies, following the Oil Wars, which had ended in 2091, no one could argue with receipt of such a significant credit injection, amounting close to 25% of their respective GDP's.

Laozi's businesses kept him on course to effect his dream of change, but it was through his relations with the arts that he had found solace. The mark of man weighed heavily on him. None of his businesses had been able to find a solution or a cure for nature's death predictor. No amount of research, testing and scientific remodeling of the human body would alter that which was preordained. It was in the arts that imagination, thought and ideology resided. It was in the arts, that he felt through the resultant debate on the origin of the mark, that a hopeful solution could be found.

From as early as 30 years old he had attended lectures, incognito, all over the world. He had visited the old world churches, temples and synagogues. He had read the old scriptures, the Sutras, the Quran, the many sacred texts of Chinese and Tibetan Buddhists. He'd gone as far as exploring Druidism, the ancient texts of the Egyptian sun gods and even the failed Scientologist movement of the early 21st Century. The oldest living religion, Hinduism, offered some hope in its comprehensive belief system but provided no riposte to his ever increasing number of questions. The world of his ancestors had changed and the old world religions had been replaced by a cult of the mark; a new order based on time and credits; a society based on those who had them and those who did not.

Hector Laurence's last lecture before he died was held at the Royal Botanic Gardens in Kew, London. He hadn't told Hansel of his going, nor had he let on that it was he who had funded the tours, and the resultant books that followed. In truth, neither the father nor the son knew that their paths were so inextricably linked with Laozi's. Hal would never know that their fateful meeting in Singapore, 15 years previously, had more than a smattering of luck attached to it. Hector's final protestations, on the essence of being and man's inherent goodness, fell largely on deaf ears. However Laozi hadn't failed to notice a good number, of some very distinguished people, in attendance that day in July 2137. He made contact with all of those he recognised and many of those whom he didn't. Most of which were now either in his employ or acting with a similar mission in mind. Mankind had to have a future; the World Council was as good a place as any, to start creating one.

The car turned off Knightsbridge into Sloane Street, passing Mandarin Oriental's flagship hotel and residences, heading towards Sloane Square. Laozi looked onto the street outside, windswept, serenely lit and shimmering. This was still the playground for the rich but time had worn away at its radiance. War had sapped its energy and Mark's Day had snuffed out its vitality. People no longer looked nonchalant; they no longer had the casual air of spontaneity and freedom. In their place, regardless of which faction they were a member of, everybody carried the burden of the inevitable truth. Pandora's Box had been shut firmly.

Laozi had no further time to ponder, as the car pulled up beside the taxi rank and the door opened. He sucked in the cold air and pressed his right arm against the curve in the door, maneuvering his body to the pavement. He exhaled deeply, almost sighing and headed towards the entrance of the private government bunker, which occupied the old underground train station.

Chapter 7

A blended hum of vibration and repetitive beeps permeated the hotel room. Ama reached out from under her duvet, blindly searching for the off button. She realised almost immediately that there was no switch, so clapped her hands in a double tap format, exactly the way the bell hop had instructed. It was 7am. She rubbed her eyes in an effort to banish the fatigue, whilst adjusting to the light in her room. Her thoughts had kept her awake for the past two days, leaving her in a merciless state of insomnia. Her performance had been a huge success, garnering substantial praise from a number of Voegel's friends and acquaintances. She'd even been openly propositioned by two. Then, of course, there was Hal.

Her breathless excitement had given way to elements of self doubt where, the day before, she had sought counsel from Voegel. He had been helpful, up to a point. Music was his only true outlet of expression; these conversations were not his forte. Ama had not wanted to burden him but the evening had panned out in such a way that she was left alone with him at the bar. As he loosened up, her emotional conflict gave way to suspicions that Veda and Voegel, the two university acquaintances, were otherwise involved. She noticed a familiarity and knowledge of the Veda family that only a close ally, or someone in special circumstances, would know.

Not everyone would notice; call it female intuition but they're involved with each other a lot more than meets the eye.

Ama sat up, turned sideways and ensured that both pillows were plumped up and firmly pressed into the headboard. She sat back against her newly formed back rest and pressed the 'info' button on her cellhip. The hotel's interactive screen came alive with five choices; *schedule, communication, news, research and music.* She selected *communication* first and a list of script messages and voice calls jumped out at her. Rehearsal updates were the only new messages in her inbox, where she happily found that she had the afternoon off, as well as the whole of the next day.

She moved onto *news*, where her preselected favourites appeared in a 4 way split; CNN, VCN, EBS and INN. She preferred the independent station, on principle, but being away from home, she felt compelled to watch anything with a Panamerican slant to it. However and most probably because of recent events, she opted for the Vedas Communications Network.

Ama stared at the ticker scrolling along the top of the projection, like a beacon looking for lost souls. Ama was pleased, as she reasoned that the other options would have had a far more negative approach to the forthcoming presentations. She listened to the newsreader for a while, read the ticker twice more and pointed her right index finger at the screen, flicking back to her schedule and then to the days date. She spoke steadily ensuring the room's microscopic speakers picked up every syllable.

"10am – rehearsal; 1pm – hotel; 4pm – Space Exploration Feature; 5pm – Kepler 3 Broadcast; 8pm – Dinner L'Escargot."

She knew that she was being excessively organised. For some reason she felt compelled to be, as if today was important to everyone's future and not just her own. She decided to take it slow in the morning, have a light breakfast, a long shower and then head into rehearsal at 9:30am. She kept her afternoon free, so that she could watch the VCN features.

It was 8am. Ama pondered on what to wear and the evening ahead. By 9am she still hadn't moved. The lethargy brought on by her lack of sleep was eating away at her. Realising that she was going to be late, she hurriedly leapt out of bed, put on her sweatshirt and pants and headed for the door. Her date with Hal was at the forefront of her mind and by the time she arrived at rehearsal, on time, she was in a fluster. Voegel assessed the situation immediately and so let her sit out most of practice. With typical Prussian precision the session stopped at precisely 12pm and everyone moved to the canteen for debrief, before departing to enjoy their 36 hour holiday. When one of her colleagues stopped to ask her how she was finding life in London, Ama appeared vague and distracted.

The questions regarding Kepler 3 were on everyone's lips. There was a hum of background chatter, as small groups huddled together, caught up in deep conversation. She overheard one cellist cynically suggesting that the entire broadcast was a hoax, whilst berating the news channels for taking it so seriously. Another, a little bit more sincere, still hadn't quite appreciated the enormity of what was happening; in this case thinking that it was just another probe, landing on another far off star. There had been so much debate, over the years, in every walk of life, that many had become numb to yet more news of distant planets and possible signs of life.

Ama couldn't help but think that this broadcast was real, as it seemed to fit with the litany of coincidences that she had been caught up in. After all the CEO of Vedas Corp was her music director's friend. It was well documented that Vedas Corp were the principle drivers in space exploration programmes; not forgetting the coincidences vis à vis Hal, his art, the painting, her father, the taxi driver; she'd even chosen to watch VCN that afternoon.

She felt the waves of an epiphany ripple through her mind, as it dawned on her that if she delved deep enough, there were passages at play that linked her to so many other people. She felt quite dumfounded but put it down to tiredness.

She arrived back at her hotel at 1:45pm, later than scheduled, but she was still in good time to order room service, eat, sleep a little and hunker down for the rest of the afternoon. At 3:59pm her cellhip awoke her to the images from VCN popping out from the screen on the other side of the room. The narrator's voiceover commenced in unison with the title credits. Ama was fully awake in seconds; tuned in immediately.

VCN Exclusive – Space Exploration in the 22nd Century

In 2014, we found a way to compress air and created a mechanism that could store limitless energy. Wind, solar, wave and thermal power were our focus over the course of the 21st Century but, even here, we have been hindered by one common factor; lack of consistent availability in the locality. After over 40 years of war and the suffering from our previous mistakes, we vowed never to disregard earth's natural resources again.

In 2114 we realised that we could recycle our fuel and use it again and again. It was self perpetuating and a seemingly endless natural resource. We could compress it, develop it and need very little of it, therefore not harm the atmosphere. Its power was immense.

In 2133 and with renewed emphasis on space travel we discovered that these new cells, when used in space or a weightless environment, had the effect of being able to propel an object as fast as the speed of light.

In 2136 we tested our first 'light' vessel. Uncertain of its success, three duplicates loyal to the Etihad Spaceways space programme volunteered to 'man' the vessel, named Hyperion. The mission was, up to a point, a triumph. The vessel jumped to light speed on command but immediately ran into an asteroid belt and disintegrated upon impact.

Since then the Etihad Spaceways Hyperion light travel missions have been well documented and no one needs reminding of the successful manned mission of last year, where it took less than two hours to reach Mars.

Ama was glued to the images in front of her, as the narrator continued to take her on a journey through history and time. She couldn't help but marvel at the quality of the pictures from the sun scorched planet and noted that there seemed to be a lot of manmade structures in the background of these shots, more than she and the rest of Earth's population had ever been led to believe existed. Previous missions had obviously taken place, where communities aboard large vessels had been shipped out taking many years to get there. These people had colonised parts of the planet, living aboard the vessels like prisoners. Many of the original team would no doubt have died on their passage and it was their descendants who'd be living there now, thinking of Earth as a distant planet, populated by people with strange ideals. The narrator broke her thoughts.

We originally discovered the Kepler System in 2024 and subsequently Kepler 3 but due to the lack of technology and our own desire, we didn't have the ability to get there in any of our lifetimes, let alone our children's or even our grandchildren's. Throughout the 22nd Century we've known that there were signs of life on Kepler 3 but we just didn't know what it was or how to get there. Our new capabilities of light travel changed this perception. However one negative factor remained; we needed to create a clear pathway direct to the Kepler System, as any vessel travelling at the speed of light would be unable to avoid the many random objects and asteroids that would be caught up along its route.

In 2140 Etihad Corporation and Vedas Corp combined forces, where their best scientists achieved what no one had ever imagined possible until now. They created a hole in space; and in such a way that it didn't corrupt any of the planets alignment with the sun. By use of a gravitational drive, they managed to fold space and time, without putting our solar system or the Kepler Real system in danger, of being sucked into an unforeseen gravitational pull. The entrance was placed outside Mars, with its exit in the Kepler Real system, outside Kepler 4, their Mars equivalent. The distance mirrors that from Mars to Earth, depending on the date and time of the year, which averages out at 140 million miles.

Ama processed the information not stopping to pause the programme, as she wanted to watch it all in real time. She knew that there would be unlimited coverage over the coming days and that she'd be able to pore over everything at any moment. A ticker ran across the top of the projection.

'Tomorrow VCN will feature a guide to the technology behind our ability to survive light travel in real time. We will provide a forum for discussion over the use of gravitational, warp and hyper drives. Tune in at 4pm on January 6th for more information.'

The editing was simple and effective. The narrator continued on with a tone that was both uncompromising and melodic.

The first spacecraft, Nephthys, built to go through this gateway, set off from earth on 1st January 2141, at a speed similar to that of 40 times the speed of sound. The journey took less than 6 months. The plan was to send a 'rover' aboard the ship and test its capability of withstanding the journey. On reaching the other side the 'rover' would be deployed on its own towards Kepler 3. It would report back its findings to the Nephthys and, in turn, the team on our side of the gateway. A beneficial outcome of this mode of travel was that there was no need for 'light' speed, as the passage through the gateway would only take a matter of seconds, thus mitigating the danger of nefarious obstacles along the ship's course. On June 21st 2141 the Nephthys mission was a success. The ship is now acting as our space station on the other side of the gateway. 'Rover' has been beaming images to Earth since the beginning of 2142.

The results were astonishing. Our findings are a revelation. The World Council has used the last few years to ensure a successful presentation to the world, without causing mass hysteria and without creating interference or damage to their project. It has been with much restraint that we at VCN have not reported our conclusions before, however we implore you to tune in at 5pm (GMT) to hear the live broadcast from Kepler 3. We haven't hoped for so much, for so long.

Ama noticed that it was 4:46pm, which gave her 14 minutes before the broadcast. She didn't know what to do with herself. So much had been going on behind the public eye; so much had happened. Mark's Day had been the beginning. It had also blinded most to what was really out there. A future beset with a plethora of possibilities. She sat rooted to the spot willing the next few minutes by. They came soon enough and at 4:59pm she emptied her head of all her questions and studied the pictures in front of her, looking for the answers; waiting for the broadcast to give her some.

The image flickered into life and revealed a large hall, reminiscent of the nave in a cathedral. A blend of dark wood and stone, thrusts towards a ceiling, made Ama quiver with excitement. The hall was vast and silent. The camera did not move nor did the lens change its focus. Slowly figures began to pass by, serenely crossing towards what Ama made out as large wooden thrones, in the centre of the hall. The seats filled up with an assortment of people and Ama was unable to make out their origin. The picture came out in a soft focus, preventing her from distinguishing their height, clothes and colour; nor could she make out their key features, such as their eyes, nose and fingers. The music started, the lens pulled in and focused on an archaic lectern, in the centre of a stage, set along what would have been the crossing. The title zoomed out towards Ama, almost shocking her out of incredulity.

VCN Exclusive – First Contact – Broadcast from Kepler 3

The camera tracked a familiar man on his journey from his seat below the stage, towards the lectern. Ama realised that it was the ex-Councillor for Trade and Foreign Affairs. He had left his post in mysterious circumstances, 18 months earlier, much to the wonderment of the world's press. The World Council had immediately announced his replacement, throwing the new incumbent headlong into debate with the leaders of the duplicate stronghold, based out of New Zealand. The ex-councillor gripped the lectern, while clearing his throat. He looked fresh, healthier than before and animated by the news that he was about to impart.

For the sake of this broadcast and for the people of Earth, I stand here before you, the people of Kepler 3, as the eyes, the ears and the mouthpiece of our planet. I stand before you as a humble servant to this voyage of discovery; one which we are all about to embark upon.

To the right, and just behind the ex-councillor, stood a man of average build and height, mid-tone skin and of non-descript origin, as if he were a complete cocktail of Asian, European, African and American-Indian descent. He was dressed in layers of silk and cotton and had the air of a leader. Given the occasion, Ama assumed that he was the ex-councillor's counterpart from the new planet. The camera panned round to the audience and she started to establish those who were from Kepler 3 and those from Earth. It was not just their skin and build; it was their clothes as well. Her knowledge of fashion garnered at NYU could at last serve her well. The style was an extraordinary blend of traditional Chinese clothing and 19th Century European formal wear; suits made out of robes, almost.

The journey here started many, many years ago. Many of you back home will think that I am referring to our discovery of Kepler 3. However our journey didn't start there, nor did it start with the invention of the telescope, nor the invention of the wheel, or the invention of anything material for that matter. It goes much further, back to the dawn of time.

I am not standing here in front of the good people of Kepler 3 and imploring them to like us or even tolerate us. I am standing here willing both planets to co-exist and learn off each other. Since arriving here, we have all been treated with caution, but respect. We have been afforded the time to get to know our distant neighbours and have benefitted, from their substantial hospitality.

We can now present to you, the people on Earth, a world that is by no means a replica, by no means a mirror to ours. We present to you a different world, on an alternative trajectory through space and time.

Acknowledging the fact that most people, watching back on Earth, would have been aghast at this point, the ex-councillor paused and cleared his throat for further effect.

Our journey started 18 months ago, where the World Council put together a select group of leading scientists, philosophers, linguists and security personnel in order to handle 'first contact' with the people of Kepler 3. This team of 48 arrived a little over two months ago and has used a multitude of methods to communicate and ultimately reach, what we hope is an understanding. In this time, we have learnt a little of their evolution, history, language and natural habitat.

The purpose of this broadcast is to not only introduce you to our kind hosts but to inspire you all into action. It is to prove that with the right aspiration and genuine foresight, we might truly get the answers that we have all been searching for, for so long.

The camera cut away from the speaker's face and music replaced his words. The images of mountain peaks, valleys, deserts and seas were quite literally out of this world. Ama couldn't control herself any longer. She paused the presentation, got off the bed and headed for her mini-bar. *A strong short would be good.* She poured herself a whisky, acknowledging that desperate times required desperate measures and slugged it down with little trouble. She sat back on the bed.

Ama contemplated the impact this news would have around the globe. Determined by circumstance and life cycle, everyone's reaction would be different.

The camera refocused on the lectern and the man previously stood behind the ex-councillor approached. He stood very still with his hands clasped loosely in front of him. He waited a moment and then started speaking in a language that she had not heard before. Simultaneously another voice overrode his. The cellhip translation responder service obviously had no trouble working, even on Kepler 3. Ama recognised the dulcet tones of the VCN narrator from the earlier space exploration feature.

People of Earth this is a rare moment and one where reputations will be made or are broken. My first words to you will define your perception of us and so I must chose carefully. We know little of your history but we hope that, through a successful period of responsible tourism, the future will bear some fruit. In time to come we will be able to learn about each other and our differences. As a result of these labours, we look to a common future and one where we might further our collective being.

The syntax was stilted; the translation gave him a loose air of indifference. There were obvious limitations in the responder service and no doubt an absence of a like for like vocabulary and a bilingual operative. However Ama understood his message and agreed that Earth's first impression of him would stick whether good or bad.

She was acutely aware of how difficult it must have been for the Keplerian leader to know what to say to a world, full of people and cultures, that he had had no previous experience with nor, on reflection, probably any wish to. It had been imposed on him and his people after all. They had had no choice in this visit from these extra terrestrials. Ama certainly knew how the people of Earth would have behaved, if it had been the other way round. It would have been a very thinly veiled line of perceived protection and direct confrontation.

Our planet is made up of 90% water, where we predominantly live on one single continent. 9 kingdoms divide this continent into almost identical sized pieces. We have detailed charts and local information which have already been made available to your leaders. Our society and kingdoms are only divided due to nature's provision in each location. This map here in my hand will help you understand the topography.

We do not bear this mark that you so vehemently speak of. We have been made aware of its fruition over a hundred years ago. We do not want to suggest that we have the answers, as to its origins, but we are intrigued by you and know that there is much that we can learn from you.

If you afford us the time to study you and your ways, we will happily do the same. We are concerned but fascinated by you. We have faith that you will convert this hope that you speak of into belief in your people as a whole. To hope for the betterment of your own being in front of someone else is to have a lack of faith, to hope for the betterment of the collective being is to be divine.

With that the sound and images became corrupted and Ama was left staring at white noise floating at the foot of her bed. She felt as if she had been knocked sideways by a sledgehammer, unable to move, she weighed up the consequences of the afternoon's events.

When would have been the right time to announce to the world the existence of another planet like ours? What would be the right approach? Would we want to hear what their people had to say? Would it make any difference if we did? What's everyone going to think now? We don't have faith? Are they surprised? If they knew when they were going to die, wouldn't they lose hope? Perhaps they can help us understand the evolution of the mark. I've always thought of it as being nature's way of adjusting us.

Ama wearily picked her way out of her pillows and headed for the shower, she had less than an hour to get changed and head out to meet Hal.

Out of the frying pan and into the fire.

Chapter 8

The Vedas Corp logo popped out at him, as a billboard beckoned Hal to take a trip to the 'One Season on the Sea of Serenity'. The bus made its last turn into Piccadilly and stopped. Hal's journey from Fulham to the West End had been without consequence and aside from the overly amorous couple next to him; he tried to get his head round the Keplerian's speech. It was clear that it had been bold. The leader had risked being misunderstood and had no doubt strayed away from the pre-agreed address; one that the politicians from Earth had obviously tried to coerce him into making. Hal, via his cellhip, had played the last few beats to himself a number of times, over the course of his journey. He couldn't get the words out of his head; one comment in particular reverberated around his dome.

To hope for the betterment of your own being in front of someone else is to have a lack of faith, to hope for the betterment of the collective being is to be divine. This gave Hal an extra spring in his step; it was as if his father spoke to him beyond the mausoleum. 'The Faces of Our Future' had been Hal's first foray into a critique of the maudlin philosophy of the general public, the world over. This man from Kepler had, in a matter of moments, summed up a vision of mankind that had once existed but had now long since passed.

He knew that his rapport with Laozi would pay dividends in furthering his education, where his obvious excitement at the immediate future outweighed his apprehension for the dinner date that he was heading towards. He picked his way, through a seemingly listless crowd of people, down Shaftesbury Avenue. The gusty wind swirled round the buildings, gathered up the remnants of a preceding snowfall and deposited its light flecks on the lapels of his overcoat. He turned onto Greek Street in good time. He was going to be early. Hal was well aware of Ama's alienation to London life; it had been visible from the first moment he laid eyes on her. No matter how graceful and striking she was; her disaffection for the trappings of wealth and modern society was plain to see. He was not going to be late.

He arrived at exactly 8pm and was obviously the first to arrive, as the restaurant was empty except for an elderly couple. There was little doubt that the couple were from out of town and had been planning the visit for a long while. L'Escargot was the oldest restaurant in London, still serving French cuisine, having first opened in 1927. A lot of Eightys and Ninetys, who'd made it past their 80th birthday, would come back to London on short trips to old haunts. The much vaunted violence of the Twentys and Thirtys was directed at the young not the old. It had always been in the direction of those who had time on their hands not those who'd already spent it. Hal studied the couple carefully, thinking of his parents and whether if his father were alive, they'd have responded to the recent spate of marketing in the rural areas. Many restaurants, theatres and galleries had begun to entice the elderly back to London, to where they had been born, with special offers and the promise of safe passage to certain destinations.

The lack of bustle in the restaurant provided Hal with an opportunity. He persuaded the maitre d' to give him the banquette seating area, in the rear left corner of the room. This not only gave him the best opportunity to see her come in, but also gave them the most privacy. For they'd both be facing out towards the rest of the restaurant, with no table too close to listen in on their, much hoped for, poignant conversation. He made an effort to be clear about the occasion and that he wanted special attention, without it being over the top. He wanted to appear in the know but not well known. The maitre d' understood and, expecting to be rewarded accordingly, acquiesced to Hal's demands.

All of a sudden Hal was overcome with nerves. He sat at the table furtively looking at the menu, whilst nursing a sparkling water. A large group arrived and headed for the private dining room. Four media executives sauntered in and were seated nearby. Another elderly couple were ushered in by someone who could only have been a bodyguard. Hal checked his cellhip; she was 10 minutes late. More guests arrived and another 10 minutes passed by. The restaurant was nearly full and there was still no sign of her.

He began to retrace their conversation at the Barbican. He was certain that he had said 8pm and not 8:30pm. He was sure that she would have made contact if she were unable to come or was held up. Either way, she was late and his nerves were beginning to escalate into a fever. He noticed that he had started to jiggle his right foot, in the precise way that had made Alicia's blood curdle, whenever he was nervous. He stopped it at once and looked up towards the front door. Through the melee of waiters and guests being seated he suddenly caught sight of her neck, the hairline rising up over the ear, a long gold and turquoise earring. Her long dark hair was tied back. He saw her face and then her smile. She had arrived.

"No point making any excuse, I'm sorry I'm late. No point blaming it on the traffic, there was none; no point blaming it on the weather, there's no snow on the roads; I guess I'll put it down to nerves." Hal stood up as Ama approached and moved the table to one side, to kiss her hello. He couldn't thank her enough for breaking the ice, in such a way, that the conversation now had three rivers to flow down. He opted for the second.

"Let's blame it on the weather. It's an English tradition. You look absolutely stunning."

His face reddened as he made the first of, what he thought would be many compliments that evening. "It's been one strange day today. In fact it's been a strange week, accompanied by this freakishly cold weather."

A waiter helped her out of her overcoat as Hal spoke. Another pulled the table out to allow her to sidle in. Hal continued to stand whilst this swift exchange took place, marvelling at both the waiting staff's efficiency and Ama's grace. He sat down and the table was pushed back in, locking them together in the perfect position to people watch and talk openly but discreetly. Both Hal and Ama were visibly content.

"I'd like to compliment you again for Wednesday. If it hadn't been for Laozi's scheming, I wouldn't have been there in the first place."

"Hal, I have a million different questions to ask. Would it seem strange if I said that I feel like I ought to know you?"

"I feel the same. Don't ask me why. I just have that feeling. That once in a lifetime lightning bolt, of now or never."

"OK, here goes. Remember your exhibition a week ago?"

"Of course, how could I forget?"

"No, I don't mean it like that. Remember your exhibition, when we first connected. Did you feel strange? "

"I definitely felt something."

"Me too."

"Why have you got a picture of my father?" She threw it out there as quickly as she could, hoping that it was all a misunderstanding; a fluke. She couldn't carry the burden of the question any longer.

"I'm sorry, I don't understand. What do you mean?"

"'The Ballad of a Crying Man' I'm sure it's my father. Even the backdrop is of Manhattan."

"You're right, it is set in Manhattan. I lived there for a few years with my wife."

"OK, hold on, back up, we've clearly got a lot to get through here. You're married?"

"No, no, my wife Alicia died a few years ago. Sorry, I still refer to her as my wife. She was a Thirty, so it hardly came as a surprise. If you hadn't already guessed, I'm a Forty which made us a suitable match." Hal carefully laid his arms out on the table in front of him, allowing the sleeves of his jacket and shirt to ride up to his forearms. Ama made out just over 40 rings on the underside of his wrist.

"Before we get lost in a thousand and one conversations; let's look at the menu and at least order something to drink." The waiter appeared before Hal had even finished his sentence.

Ama and Hal barely glanced at their menus, eager to get on with the conversation and to learn more about each other. Time was already playing a wicked game with their hearts. In each other's company they both felt that it could go on forever, yet the clock was ticking. They had to make time count.

They ordered quickly and unfussily. The waiter brought a carafe of the house white wine over to the table. Hal looked at Ama and smiled.

"The food's great here. So, in answer of your question, the subject of the painting is a Panamerican guy, who I spent the day with, about 7 years ago. He must have been in his fifties and was an Eighty. He was definitely of Dutch descent, as he still had a soft looping accent. I don't know where he is now, as we never exchanged details. It was one of those things, we connected, we exchanged our views on the world and we parted company."

Hal paused to think a little before adding,

"I took a load of photos of him over the course of the day. We agreed that if I ever used one, I'd make it a key feature at an exhibition. He said that he used to work for the machine, as he called it, and was an analyst, but had given it all up to be with his family. He was a part time cellist."

"You've got to be kidding me right? Hal, I'm from New York, half Dutch, Papa was an Eighty, cellist. It has to be him. He always maintained that he worked for the corporation but fell out with the owners. My mother and I never pressed him further, happy to have him at home."

"I see. How strange. He did actually tell me that he had a daughter who was a pianist. She'd won a scholarship but he didn't say where to. He was immensely proud, yet, he didn't dwell on anything for too long. That's all I can really remember. I can't believe the coincidence. How is he?"

"That's the sad part. My parents were killed nearly 2 years ago."

"Of course, Sorry, I've already been informed. I'm still reeling."

"I have so few pictures of my father, could I get some of yours?"

"Of course, it's the least I could do; I'm not too sure what to say, except that our meeting now seems more and more pre-determined. I'm glad that we have met. "

"Me too."

Ama looked into Hal's eyes and held her gaze for a long time, searching for a flicker of malevolence or insincerity. There was none.

"Hal, there's something else that's troubling me and it's nothing to do with today's broadcast, at least I think not. I know that we've only just met but it seems that our lives are entwined somehow."

"I know, go on."

"How well do you know Laozi Veda?"

"Extremely well; he's one of my closest allies or at least an uncle to me."

"Is he into guys? The reason being that my music director, Benedikt Voegel seems to know details about him and his family, that I don't think even you know about."

"Laozi has certainly never led me to believe that he is that way inclined. I've pushed him on the question of love a few times, but he never lets slip. He was married for a while and has a daughter. Not that that counts for anything."

Hal pondered on her question for a moment longer. "I'm now concerned

54

with the fact that Voegel knows so much about him, as I thought that they were just acquaintances from Oxford. Has he said anything in particular?"

"No, not really, it's just a feeling I've got. I'm sure it's nothing but I thought I'd ask. I'll put it down to alcoholic exuberance."

Their food arrived, providing a natural break. Hal looked at Ama's terrine of foie gras and signalled to her approvingly. The waiter emptied the carafe into Ama's glass and disappeared as quickly as he had come. Ama was amazed at the service and how busy the restaurant was. Yet, in truth, they felt entirely on their own and untroubled. She wanted to launch into another line of questioning but, seeing that Hal was busying himself with the snails in front of him, thought otherwise. Hal ordered another carafe and finished by mopping up the garlic butter and parsley with some French bread.

"So, I guess we can't assume that we know each other; just because there's this connection?"

"OK, let's assume that this is the first time we've ever laid eyes on each other. What would you say to me?"

"That's unfair, you're the guy. You should be making the first move."

"That's so archaic but OK I'll give it a go... Hi there, it appears that I have one shot at this and so I'd like to make it count. I'm intrigued by you, and it's not just by your obvious good looks. Are you a musician by any chance? You have the hands of pianist." Hal took her hands gently in his, casually gazing at them before letting go.

"That's cheating. But go on." Ama laughed breathlessly.

"Where did you grow up?"

"Flatbush, Brooklyn in New York."

"Did you like it there?"

"Hey I was fine. It wasn't easy living in a heavily rundown area, living in constant fear of the world outside. My parents wanted to tackle everything head on; they were amazing; so positive and giving, yet they refused to be changed by the system and were one of the few Oldys to stay in the City. Most of the Seventys, Eightys and Ninetys had long since left Manhattan. My school wasn't any different to anywhere else. In that I mean, if you didn't have money and couldn't go to private school, what was the point in going? None of the Shortys went. There were only a few Oldys like me around. The rest had shipped out, living on inherited money. I learnt at home. Both my parents were musicians and they gave me everything they could."

"They sound incredibly brave."

"They were. It almost became a joke, there seemed to be mass executions every month, in our area. It was like the population was controlled by the Shortys and its growth was harnessed by these killings. Anyone with a life span over 50 would be on their hit list and in these areas very few reached past 40, regardless of their mark. It's the same in most cities I hear, but it was prevalent in New York."

"So growing up with all of this around you, didn't you fear for your life, didn't you fear for your parents?"

"Of course I did, I mean it's not easy living in a small space behind bolted doors but we adapted well, covered up and blended in. I guess it was because Mama and Papa made it past 50 and started to age that the Shortys took notice. The kids had been oblivious but time caught up with my parents. I guess it was inevitable; they were resolute in their decisions. At least I had that chance. Getting into NYU changed my life forever."

"So you went to NYU? What was that like?"

"Enough about me; give me something about you. I don't want anything from the magazines or interviews. I want the man behind the mask."

"You can tell already? That's damn quick. Of course I have to have a facade. It's easier that way. It's not great knowing that you only have a few years left to live and no amount of doctors can tell you why. No history of heart disease, liver malfunction, cancerous growths, nothing. On all accounts, I just drop dead in late 2151."

"So you're caught between a rock and a hard place right? Damned if you do, damned if you don't... the affliction of most Fortys and Fiftys... MidTermers we call them. You have to approach life as if it will be a full one but its cut short just as you get going."

"I sometimes think that the Shortys and the Oldys have it easier. But then again I reason with myself that this can't be the case. No one has it easy, as no matter what time you're given, having it predetermined only counts against you; it marginalises your perspective and alienates you from the rest of society."

"The factions are born out of necessity and self preservation; not just as some sick joke, right?"

"It's why I've dedicated my life to looking into our plight. Look, my childhood was spent on my parent's farm in Cornwall, idyllic and educational but it all changed when I was sent to London at 13 years old. I went to St Paul's School. It had history. It was founded in 1509, with a reputation for nurturing some of the best academics, as well as the best artists in Eurafrica. I went there because I'm a Forty. My brother Calvin couldn't go to school in London because he was a Seventy; he ended up at a boarding school in Somerset. It wasn't seriously academic but he excelled in sports and country pursuits. They only take Oldys in any case. They suited each other well. As for Lars, his twin, he was a Twenty and didn't go to school at all."

"So you went to private school. Aren't those the only real schools nowadays? State, public, academy, college; whatever you want to call them, they don't exist in the cities anymore."

"The problem with all of these institutions, no matter where and what type they are, they suffer from the same affliction. They are a microcosm of society. They replicate the reality of the world. Even the groups that are formed in the classroom are based on when you're going to die, rather than sport or academic achievement. Let alone such a wonderful thing as friendship." Hal added vehemently and sarcastically.

"Factions rule." The main course arrived interrupting Ama, who looked as if she had something inspiring to add to Hal's musings. Each plate was laid out perfectly in front of them.

"Bon appétit." Hal said lightheartedly, touched with a hint of sarcasm, as if to move the conversation into shallower waters. Ama noticeably wanted to continue along this vein.

"I've never felt like my life was on fast forward. In fact it's been the opposite; I'd always find myself wishing; wishing for less time, wishing to be like my friends. However as we grew up and became more aware of our differences, their number diminished and I began to long for the comfort of likeminded people. I naturally felt compelled to join a faction of my own. I found this with the philharmonic. We have Fortys amongst us but we've only had one Thirty in our history. It's strange but when we're playing none of it, is really of any consequence."

"Now we're talking. That's exactly how I feel when I paint. By searching for the truth, I forget. I lose myself when I create. Up and to when Alicia died I was on permanent fast forward, but I've slowed down now. I've mellowed, without becoming melancholic. I've actually started to produce material that really matters. Before, I didn't really care. Not really."

They both stared at each other and the table in front of them, toying with what next to say. Ama beat Hal to it.

"Life would be so very different..."

"... If we just didn't know."

As Hal finished her sentence he noticed the four media executives staring in their direction. They quickly averted their gaze as his eyes met theirs. Sensing that Ama was beginning to feel weighed down by the circumstances, Hal swiftly changed the subject adding a lighter tone to his voice.

"So subject change... How many of the people here are duplicates?"

"You could be one for all I know. You did instinctively show me your wrist so undeniably you aren't one."

Ama bought into Hal's game immediately and continued to survey the room.

"The four guys over there are definitely not, as they're too interested in what we're up to; the elderly couple to our right are too old, to have been a product of Vedas Corp technology; the individuals from the private dining room, who keep passing us to visit the restrooms, are all Fortys, they're wearing their marks like badges of honour; the three women in the middle of the room all look like they are expecting, so it can't be them; the guys are obviously their beaus, so that's them omitted; that leaves the three tables towards the door. I'm guessing that the two guys closest to the door are bodyguards and so it could be them. The two guys closest to us are in a relationship; it could be them. The other couple, in their late 50's; I don't know, I haven't even started on the waiters yet." Ama paused for breath and to take a sip of her wine. She felt quite animated. Hal jumped in.

"Well, I've counted three this evening. The couple in their late 50's is most definitely Eurafrican duplicates, who've managed to break free from their life of servitude. I am thoroughly surprised that the bodyguards are not, given their line of work. The only other is this wine waiter coming towards us now." Ama giggled nervously as the waiter approached their table. He looked at them oblivious to their conversation. Hal grinned at Ama and continued, "You know we haven't even talked about that huge elephant sitting in the room, just over there in the corner. We haven't mentioned him once."

"What do you mean? I've lost you." Ama stared at him incredulously, her tone changed down, this time more serious.

"The Kepler Broadcast. I mean that was seriously insane. I wish I could say out of this world, without a hint of irony, but, come on, that was just the most bizarre thing I've ever witnessed."

"I couldn't move. I was glued to the show. Nothing will be same, everything will be different now."

"Pandora's box Ama, Pandora's box."

"You're referring to hope right?"

Ama's question was rhetorical but Hal could sense that she had the answers already but similar to Laozi's conversation with him, he would have to gently draw it out of her. Allowing the waiter to break their conversation and remove the plates, they both leaned sideways, towards each other. Hal's right hand rested on the table alongside Ama's left hand. They were centimetres apart. The nervous energy burnt out of their fingertips, begging them to touch, even for a second, to ignite the spark.

"We could talk for hours about all the permutations and differing equations that are conjured up by this miraculous discovery, but seeing as these alien-humans or Keplerians have no mark, one question stands out above all; is theirs a paradise that mankind would like to regain?"

"The Keplerian leader's words were somewhat mistranslated, but the message cannot be misconstrued. There was a time when the population of earth could have followed a similar path, but this got lost along the way."

"Instead we're stuck with duplicate uprisings, a fractured population and conflicts across the globe, based on when we are going to die. Do you ever think that we were just unlucky?"

"I think we got our just deserts, but it goes further than that. My father was a Sixty, perfectly poised, in the epicentre of the factions and life's cycle. He believed that man's evolution to the mark was a necessary step taken by nature, to eradicate the unnecessary human conflicts and their natural antipathy, based on race, colour and creed. It's obvious that Kepler 3 is the key."

Hal shifted himself a little closer and Ama responded.

"You think Mr. Veda's involved, don't you?"

"How did you guess that? I would like to think that he's intrinsically involved, as he so often is, but I still don't think that he has any more answers than you or me. He's been striving to find an answer since he was a young man. He'll die trying. That's why he's backed me so far..." Hal paused, realising that the mood needed lifting. He smiled and continued, "On a lighter note, what are you doing this weekend?"

"Well being a gal from New York City, in a strange town with strange ways, not a lot. I have tomorrow off. It's my final performance on Sunday night. I'm then foot loose and fancy free for a while."

"Well that's all I need to hear; as if I need encouragement." Hal looked up to see the media executives leave their table and head for the door. He felt the intensity subside and thought that it would be wise to relax, as he sat back into the banquette, staring intently at Ama. "That wasn't bad for five minutes of speed dating was it?"

"It was a lot longer than originally promised. You're better at this than you led me to believe. I feel like I've travelled the world with you already. Not even in an evening, we've only just finished dinner."

"It's getting late and now most of the duplicates have gone." Hal allowed a slight wink to pass in her direction as he asked, "What have a couple of strangers to do, on a cold night such as this?" Realising how this could be misconstrued, he backtracked quickly, "Before you feel compelled to answer, there is only a hint of wickedness in that question." Ama laughed and made no comment, just held her gaze.

Part of Hal's deal with the Maitre d' was for there to be no mention of the bill, nor insinuation that they would have to leave at the end of the evening. He had given them access to his creditry, via his cellhip, and agreed a tip if all had gone according to plan; which it had. His cellhip buzzed once and he noted out of the corner of his eye that it came to))85.06. He tapped a side button and the bill was paid plus 20%. The waiters focused on the last few tables, leaving Hal and Ama to fend for themselves. Hal toyed with a number of scenarios not knowing which one to play. Finally he took a stand.

"Would you allow me to take you back to your hotel. We can talk more in the car and perhaps we can meet tomorrow at the Hurlingham Club at noon?"

"I'd like that Hal. Where is it?"

"It's in Fulham, by the river, close to Putney Bridge. It's a great retreat away from the real world. I'm sure we'll benefit from its quiet atmosphere. You'll love it."

"Sure thing, let's go."

Chapter 9

1st July 2146 – Morning – The Asianaian Sea

The aircraft ducked down out of the stream of cirrus, cruising at 30,000 feet above sea level. The passenger felt no turbulence from the manoeuvre. He checked his watch, confirming his time of arrival. It wasn't as if he couldn't tell already; he'd made the journey to Singapore a thousand times and with the slightest command the projection in front of him, could have given him any amount of information. His watch was a force of habit; a fashion accessory from a bygone era. He looked out onto the scenery below, making out an old fishing vessel heading towards what must have been the islands of Southern Asiana.

The boat had a long journey ahead, past Australia's east coast and into the furthest part of the Southern Ocean. The old Chinese fishing fleet, which had become defunct soon after the oil wars had ended, had been commandeered during the first uprisings. Most of the vessels were now used by the duplicates fleeing Asiana, seeking refuge in New Zealand. These journeys were always carefully monitored by the council for immigration and duplicate control. If one of the boats strayed from its agreed course, safe passage was never guaranteed. The pirates of the Solomon Islands were notorious, having captured and enslaved thousands in the last ten years.

The passenger's assistant interrupted his thoughts. She let him know that they'd be reaching their destination in 20 minutes. Routinely he checked his watch again, sighing gently, and noted that the flight from London had taken just under two hours. He looked back out of the window, where the fishing vessel had now disappeared. Somehow he felt personally responsible for the predicament of the passengers aboard those ships.

Yet it wasn't his responsibility that the oil wars wiped out almost half the world's population. Nor was it his fault that New Zealand had been host to the last known accessible oil fields and therefore had become the final frontier to the wars. He wasn't liable for most of the natural born islanders either, being killed in the conflict or from fleeing the country before its ultimate demise.

It wasn't as if he'd single handedly initiated the process. For that matter neither he, nor his parents before him, were alive at the start of what had become the longest and most destructive war in mankind's history. This was not what was troubling him. The problem was that, no matter which way he looked at it, he was inadvertently responsible for those islands becoming a duplicate stronghold.

The guilt weighed heavily, as he watched a private intelligence report on the projection in his cabin. After all it was his company that had profiteered from duplicate production. He was well aware that it hadn't been his decision to make. He was only a young boy when it had all begun. However it was he who had benefitted and built on the legacy, that which had been bestowed upon him. It made him weary; especially given that he was going through a report on the very matter. A passing fishing vessel happened to evoke painful memories. It didn't help either as the crux of the piece, focused on the new duplicate stronghold, built on the remains of Auckland where, in order to prevent attack, their leader had undertaken some serious counter-measures. They were supposedly stockpiling weapons of total destruction. *So intent on protecting their brave new world, this couldn't have been better timed.* Laozi winced in sarcasm, as he looked at the pictures of the duplicate leader and his troupe.

However the report delivered a message that sent a lightning bolt to his brain. The duplicates were duplicating themselves. Laozi let out an exasperated and frustrated sigh, as he clenched his fist, gesticulating at the projection in front of him. They had managed to lay their hands on his relevant technology. They were developing duplicates with no duplication signature, with no idea of their own duplication. Being unable to create children naturally had not become an obstacle in becoming a parent.

Laozi's usual air of calm and joviality vanished. He was not only shocked but also furious. A fear welled up in him, as he thought of the power that the duplicates now had. If they weren't aware of their own duplication, were unable to breed and thought that they were human, they now had the ability to pass around amongst everyone and destroy mankind from within. A pungent blend of anger, fear and lamentation, far outweighed any emotional attachment or guilt that he might previously have had.

His obvious incandescent fury had to be suppressed. It wasn't Analucia's doing. He wasn't the type of character to vent his spleen, over matters not only beyond his control, but also that weren't the responsibility, of those around him. This didn't stop Analucia from seeing the pain in his face.

"We'll be there in 10 minutes Laozi. I suggest you switch off, as Dr. Aris Fleming is arriving almost immediately. You need to be focused on what he has to say. These unfortunate events will just have to wait."

Laozi sighed again and pointedly flicked his right index finger from the imaginary centre of the projection, towards the top right hand corner; closing it down. He knew that he would have said the same thing; if the shoe was on the other foot. He leant back, closed his eyes and willed the aircraft to land so that he could move on and begin the day in earnest. He liked returning home; Singapore was native soil; at least that had never changed.

As the plane landed there was a flash of lightning, reminding him of broader horizons, rather than just fleeting thoughts. The rain lashed down on the steps, as he and Analucia fought their way to the waiting car, in the hangar across the tarmac. Once inside the relative calm of his long wheel based Lexus Mirai, Laozi quizzed Analucia in regards to his schedule. Staring almost nostalgically out of the window through the persistent deluge and beyond, his anger subsided and thoughts of an imminent threat momentarily disappeared.

The downpour was short lived. The first rays of the morning sun poked through the dispersing clouds, as they made the short journey from Changi Airport to Marina Bay. The area had been subject to significant development during the previous century, where it had become renowned as an international lifestyle hub playing host to some of the most remarkable office buildings, residences and hotels in the world. Laozi had made the area his base, selling the Sentosa Cove family home for ₩49m in 2131.

His apartment doubled up as one half of the control room to his empire with the parallel half residing in London. In amongst the multitude of interactive screens were two large oversize, handmade, vintage mahogany pedestal desks, a mirror to those in London. In fact the offices were identical. However that is where the similarities ended; the rest of the apartment was an impressive mixture of 21st Century architecture and 22nd Century design.

Analucia walked with him to the entrance of his building. The sun pressed on his back. Its rays bounced off tiny speckles of granite, giving them both a radiance to take with them into their next appointments. Once they were inside the foyer Analucia bade him farewell, heading in the direction of the Central Business District and Vedas Corp's headquarters. Inside his apartment Laozi immediately sought out the dressing room. No matter how brief and comfortable the journey, out of habit, he'd always take a shower before starting the day. His meeting with Dr. Aris Fleming wasn't until 11:00am, which gave him an hour and a half to spruce up, take breakfast and read the analysis before their meeting.

His cellhip system pinged alive at 11:05am. He opted to answer through the receiver on his left desk. It was a throwback to a time long forgotten. By doing this he let himself believe that he wasn't succumbing to the latest fads and innovations that the masses were seduced by, on a daily basis; even when they were, in effect, his own creations. The screen above the left hand desk unveiled a be-suited man, not too dissimilar in age to Laozi, who was slight of build, bespectacled for affect, with wispy grey strands of hair, swept backwards over his thinning top.

"My apologies Mr. Veda but I've been held up at Parliament House. I'll be with you in less than 10 minutes."

"Aris, its Laozi and please don't forget it. I've been reading your observations; fascinating. I always think it better to meet in person, if we can. Projection conferences never leave me satisfied, as I can't smell the fear or the excitement in the room. In truth I need to taste the relief or the disappointment of my adversaries, let alone my allies. See you shortly."

He clicked off and returned his attention to the report. Dr. Aris Fleming, an extraordinary mix of Greek and Scottish blood, had been one of his chosen representatives on what had now been dubbed the 'Kepler Meeting'. He was the world's leading expert in mutation and genetics.

Laozi had ensured that he was well represented at the meeting, having provided 60% of the funds for the expedition. He had grown tired of being asked as to why he did not go himself; his response had always been the same; he needed to stay behind and engineer his changes. Leaving would have scuppered his modus operandi. His preference was to be the puppet master, rather than having his strings pulled; he'd maintained that he was of far more use on Earth, rather than charging through the universe on a hopeful quest.

He continued reading the analysis, where Kepler 3 had taken on the more manageable name of just Kepler. He got caught up in a section which described the original resentment of the Keplerians. This was of little surprise, seeing as the Keplerians would have been naturally cautious of a group of extra terrestrials, who'd just landed on their planet and had, in a matter of weeks, gone on to suggest establishing a base on Kepler. Naturally this would lead to much debate over the threat of colonisation. The people of Kepler were obviously aware of how this could end; an unequal relationship between the proposed colonists and the indigenous population. The establishment of a base would surely lead to exploitation, further acquisition, maintenance and ultimate expansion.

The Ex-Councillor for Trade and Foreign Affairs, Akihiro Iso, had been Chief Executive of Vedas Corp for 11 years before being appointed to the World Council. It was he who had warned of the Keplerians being aware of the threat to their social structure, their government and to their economics. Earth's history had proven that colonialism and imperialism were much the same and those sent to Kepler easily recognised that both the concept and the practice were interchangeable. Iso's loyalty to Laozi was intrinsic to the mission, where he had been installed as the leader to ensure that all 48 of the scientists, philosophers, linguists and security personnel were well versed in the history of colonialism and its process. It was his intention to leave them all in absolute agreement, that they should neither be viewed as an empire, nor as a colonialist.

However the year long journey to Kepler had thrown up many questions as how best to approach the Meeting and that, in the past, colonialism had succeeded in bringing a multitude of diverse cultures, under the control of an imperial authority. Aside from the security personnel, the rest of the team was wholly in favour of steering away from any imperialistic or predatory behaviour. The lessons had been learnt from Ancient Rome. Laozi's stooge had been at pains to make the point clear; they were not the authority.

One of their many fears was that the Keplerians were not going to be as technologically advanced. It would therefore seem natural, for a team from Earth to act as a link between the natives and a perceived empire back home. In the past the advanced technology of the colonist in areas such as cartography, weaponry, shipbuilding, navigation, mining and agricultural productivity, was the key to the colonialists superiority; it transpired the Keplerians were well advanced in these areas, holding sway over their own planet and culture.

Whilst Vedas Corp was the epitome of pure capitalism, for it could be seen as exploitative at any point in its timeline, Laozi and, more importantly, the World Council did not want to make this mission into one of new investment opportunities or the search for raw materials. This mission was a spiritual one; one that could affect mankind's future irrevocably, rather than acting as a brief foray in the pursuit of financial gain.

Laozi sat back in his chair pondering on Aris's observations.

Power is the fundamental determinant in social order. It infers the capacity to preserve one's interests; if necessary to enforce one's command by any method available. It all comes down to negotiation; how much one group respects the interests of the other. Kepler must survive as a physical and cultural entity. We are not to colonise, we must integrate. Enslavement, unequal social relations; language change and technological advancement are all byproducts of colonisation. It is a question of our morality. Our downfall hinges upon a failure to integrate. I don't want to be the mastermind, behind a reversal of fortune in honour of my forefathers. We have evolved far beyond brinkmanship.

A ping sounded; Aris had arrived. He got up from his chair and made his way over to the soft seating area, in front of the floor to ceiling windows, looking out over the marina and towards the sea. He sat down and stared out on a surfeit of shiny surfaces reflecting the sun's morning rays. The sound of approaching footsteps grew stronger.

"Laozi, my apologies again, you know how these things go at Parliament House. The World Council is a difficult group to appease."

"Aris, you actually gave me time to unwind and to focus on your observations. I heard the dreadful news this morning. So the duplicates are self-duplicating?"

"Unfortunately, so; in fact, it was the reason for my delay. I was mid presentation in regards to Keplerian DNA, which I would like to add is the carbon copy of ours, and I was inexplicably stopped by our revered leader. The speaker of the house read out the same report, which I felt was not meant for my ears. A victim of circumstance as you will."

"I suspect they feel that all 41, who returned, are now part of the bigger picture, in any case; as if you all have a knowledge far superior, to the over-abundance of councilors around the world. Forgive me but I've done away with the staff for the day, to ensure our privacy. What would you like; tea, coffee or perhaps something stronger?"

"After my extended stay on Kepler I've actually become rather accustomed to green tea."

"I'm a true believer in the powers of Shizuokan. No matter what our mark bares, it does certainly slow down the appearance of ageing. I have a pot brewing already, please sit and settle in, before we begin."

Laozi leant forward, towards a minimalist white coffee table. He pressed his right index finger on its side panel, the centre retracted and a lazy susan complete with tea pot, cups, saucers and an assortment of fruit and vegetable slices appeared. Once the manoeuvre was complete he gently swung the wheel round in Aris's direction, where the tea pot stopped precisely in front of his guest.

"Please, help yourself. I imagine that there is a lot to tell. We have plenty of time and I have a number of questions that I need answering first hand. As I said before, I like to sense the thoughts of my colleagues. This can only be done in person, not by projection conferencing."

"Thank you. I'm not too sure where you would like me to begin; given that you've had my analysis for the past month. Would you like to have a chronological account or should I move to the highlighted areas of concern, brought up in our last conversation?"

"Let's skip to the main topics, as I know my propensity to deviate from the point. How about you warm up by telling me a bit about the arrival, just the facts mind, we haven't got time for your full account."

Aris leant forward and looked earnestly at Laozi, searching for a flicker of mischief, benevolence; anything to put him at ease. He received a blank look and so hesitantly proceeded.

"Well, as you know it was a surprisingly safe passage. It took us just over 11 months from leaving the base outside Shanghai, to making our first steps onto Kepler. It was the strangest experience, where no amount of training, image revision or discussion with our group of philosophers had quite prepared me for the reception when we stepped out of the landing craft for the first time.

"There was a welcoming committee, if that's what you call it, made up of Keplerians who'd been warned of our impending arrival by the 'Rover', which had, the year before, deposited a huge and immovable box that was set to open upon the touch of a humanoid palm print. The box contained a number of pictures, drawings and photos describing our people and planet. It also delivered a message. It proposed a landing at the exact same spot, at the exact same point, in their lunar cycle. They'd clearly interpreted our intentions as the news of us, the box and its contents had spread across the whole of their planet. There were 126 Keplerians waiting when we arrived 12 months later.

"The Keplerians had arranged themselves in a triangle around the landing site, far enough away from the landing craft. What we weren't aware of was how advanced they were, nor the makeup of their society. Interestingly it was as if they had done this before. They had placed 14 thrones, each 14 metres apart from the other, forming an imaginary line. There was another space of 28 metres before another line of 14 thrones, 14 metres apart and so on. On one side there were three of these lines in a row. On another side there was the same and on another the same again. They had formed this perimeter as an equilateral triangle."

"So who spoke first? Did their leader rise and walk towards Akihiro Iso or did he have to make his way to one of them?"

"The way we had agreed to approach first contact was as per the World Council's instructions. The security personnel concealed small 21st Century handguns, armed with rubber bullets, in their jackets and everyone wore light weight body armour under their clothes. Iso and his lieutenants formed the first wave of people to leave the landing craft. They did this slowly and ceremoniously. Ensuring a sense of calm surrounded them, so as not to cause panic amongst the Keplerians.

"Once in the clearing everyone stopped but Iso continued walking steadily for almost another 50 metres before reaching the tall immovable box. He pressed his palm against it; it opened, demonstrating to the Keplerians that we were similar to them. When he touched it again, it closed. At this moment nine Keplerians from each side of the triangle, rose up from their respective thrones and walked towards the box in a similar languid style as to that of Iso and his team. When they were 14 metres away from the box they formed a triangle similar to the one encasing the landing craft.

"From a distance there was no way of telling them apart but in hindsight, and up close, it is easy to distinguish them, in respect to their laughter lines, smiles and weather ravaged faces. They're extraordinary looking; beautiful and knowing; ancient yet youthful. Once the small triangle around the box had been formed, the Keplerian from the northern tip of the triangle stepped forward and walked towards Iso. Once they were a foot apart Iso bowed in a modest fashion and the Keplerian stopped and mimicked his bow. He took Iso's right hand with his left, placed the palm on his right hand for a moment or two and relaxed both his arms by his side. Iso did the same. He spoke in the most beautiful tongue which to the untrained ear sounded as if he was softly singing a form of Sanskrit."

"I have heard this account from a number of sources, but yours I like the most. Every time I hear it, I get a sense of wonder and a vision of a better future for us all. I'm already digressing, my apologies. So what of the initial communication, how did you converse?

"It was simple really. After what had obviously been a Keplerian induction ceremony, they asked all of us back to their nearest village where we initially conversed through pictures and sign language. It followed that music and art were the best form of communication while a group of our linguists learnt their language. It turned out that four of them were redundant, given that the language was indeed similar to a form of Sanskrit, only more lyrical, and they had no background knowledge of the Kepler tongue. The others were more than able and it took them a matter of days to work out a basic form of communication."

"To be fair, I'm well versed in their language and its evolution, so perhaps you could tell me a bit about the village, its construction and layout. Perhaps practical things, like transport and food. I have heard a lot of accounts Aris, but I want yours first hand. I want to feel every detail."

Laozi leaned forward and poured himself another cup of tea. He helped himself to a couple of slices of apple and sat back with a beaming smile. He had the look of an expectant child about to be given a long and hoped for birthday present.

"We had our landing buggies available which, in reverence to our new hosts, we neither suggested nor used. We were instructed to get into beautifully ornate and large horse drawn wagons. These wagons were so large that they made the stagecoaches of our past look extremely small by comparison. An anomaly was that each one had a driver's cabin at the front, below the seat, where we would expect the stagecoach driver and a companion riding shotgun to sit. In the cabin was a large secured and comfortable armchair, a steering wheel and an assortment of levers, which we later found out to be brakes. There was one for each wheel, which incidentally where made of rubber and filled with pressurised air. There was a handbrake to use on all four simultaneously.

"Each wagon was pulled by 14 horses and had three drivers; two to hold the reins controlling seven horses each and one to steer. What was even more astounding was that their roads were covered with a similar but springier substance to that of tarmac. Even their horses' hooves had ample protection. They used a special type of spring steel which they put in the horseshoes, as well as part of each wagon's suspension. This fantastic combination of the steering, tyres, reins, brakes, hooves, horsepower and roads enabled these wagons to travel up to 50 miles per hour and very comfortably.

"Although each wagon could fit a load more, they were express in their command that no more than 21 people should travel on the wagon at any one time. Each wagon was decked out like an old Bedouin tent, with drapes, handmade rugs, cushions and mattresses, all set within the wooden base of the wagon. There was a coarse goat hair canopy protecting us from the elements. There was food laid out on small tables, in various sections of the wagon; even a secured wood burner in the centre, with its flue thrust up into the atmosphere through the canopy."

"Truly extraordinary: a complete blend of our time and evolution."

"Indeed; we made our journey to the nearest village. Buildings loomed on the horizon, which gradually got bigger as we approached. We passed an assortment of paddy fields that gave way to arable land that gave way to cattle farms. There were some amongst us who spotted something immediately; the machinery, the organisation and the type of produce were reminiscent of our 1890's; as a blend of old world styles."

"This is remarkable; what about the village? What were their homes like? What of their shops, their hotels, their restaurants? Did they have the need of offices?"

"Are you sure you want me to go into that much detail? It was a sight to behold I assure you. You've seen countless pictures and recordings, so you no doubt have a better idea than me."

"On the contrary, I haven't seen as much as you might think. Please Aris do not be swayed by my position or my involvement in this expedition; I never tire of hearing about it. I warned you about my propensity to digress, humour me."

"Ok. As we approached we saw two signposts on either side of the road, similar to those boards we have on the outskirts of our towns and villages, with a word that none of us understood in an unfamiliar font, front and back. Further on down the road, the magnificent tall buildings that we had seen in the distance now towered over us on either side of the road. We've since learnt that these structures were predominantly made from steel girders and limestone panels, giving them a look of small skyscrapers from early New York.

"We've since learnt that there are 14 roads leading in and out of each village and the perimeter of each village is shaped like an equilateral triangle, protected by these blocks of mini skyscrapers. As an aside, each building had four dwellings on each floor amounting to 28 in total. We therefore calculated 10,976 dwellings in the perimeter of the village. Now who's digressing?"

Aris took a sip of his tea, obviously animated by recounting his story, the cup shaking slightly in his bony adrenaline fuelled fingers. Laozi smiled at him but added nothing in response, willing him to continue by his lack of movement.

"There was no one around except for the people in the wagons, which gave it an eerie silence, as we serenely made our way. We ventured on and the buildings changed, the next block was the same in number to the first, but the buildings were solely made of stone, resembling giant Greek temples, with floors and windows capped off by triangular roofs pointing towards the sky.

"Each of these blocks was long and wide. Each one formed a perimeter fence smaller than the one before it. Where our cities seem to have the tallest buildings in the centre, theirs were the reverse. We finally came to a halt and were faced by a multitude of luxuriously green, tall and elaborate trees, lining the perimeter of a huge meadow. Facing out towards us were long and wide single storey stone cottages, reminiscent of those found in Scotland; close to my heart I know; and this time there were 28 of them in what appeared to be one long line."

Aris paused for breath, stealing a quick glance at Laozi.

"We had finally come to the centre, which we subsequently found out was 196 acres of grassland and a perfect triangle. Bear in mind that most of the journey was in silence, as there was little communication going on between our respective groups, especially because our team were sincerely dumbstruck. This is when we realised a peculiarity. We'd seen no retail outlets, in fact no commercial buildings at all. We understood that perhaps no one was there because of our arrival but we couldn't understand how the villages worked. As we had now reached the end of the road, we were faced with an old farm gate. This opened as if unmanned and we continued on into the centre of the field and stopped. We were invited to get out of the wagon, stretch our legs and look around. From the centre it looked entirely different. It was awe inspiring. Looking around, stood on lush green grass and encased by rich dark green trees, you couldn't help but get a sense of wonder.

"But even more so when you looked out on the horizon, in any direction. The buildings rose in height, the further you looked. I know that our cities, towns and villages no longer follow any particular pattern, yet this scene, coupled with the effect of a setting sun bouncing off the skyscrapers giving out a sweltering hue, saw to it that we were truly in paradise.

"We learnt that in all of the kingdoms, the meadow would act as the centre for community, where they would hold weekly festivals for the entire local population to park their wagons and interact."

"What of the commercial side Aris? Where did they get things made, where did they buy their food, where did they work, what about their recreation?"

"Well I did mention the farms and these were heavily relied upon to support the local area. What was most interesting though is that they'd set up the commercial centres, completely separately to the residential villages. All the markets, offices, workshops and entertainment areas were situated in the same location, seven miles away from the outskirts of the village. As far as entertainment, bars, restaurants, shops, offices and hotels were concerned; they are all located in these large commercial centres.

"What about their calendar, you mention weekly, what about money?"

"They have an exchange system similar to our own; bartering is common amongst all Keplerians; however they do it in a relaxed and gracious way, perhaps just out of ritual rather than to negotiate the best price. They use coins made out of a number of different materials giving them their respective value. As far as their calendar is concerned I do not have the answers, however I'm sure you know already. I use weekly in reference to a similar lunar cycle.

"I think, in summary, the one thing that I took away from the many weeks of dialogue that we all had to endure, in order to understand a little of each other's society, is that our DNA may be the same but their minds are entirely alien to our own."

"Aris thank you for this. It must have been extraordinary for you. You are kind to whet my appetite with these tales. Now let's take a few moments. We should get to the real point of your visit; The Repertega."

Laozi got up from his chair and moved over to the windows. He held his hands behind his back walking slowly, as if mimicking Iso's first steps on Kepler; no doubt playing the scene over in his mind. Dressed all in white, he had an air of divinity shrouding him. Aris sat still until beckoned by Laozi to follow him into the dining suite. An assortment of fish, meat, vegetables and rice were laid out on trays on a side table.

"Please help yourself Aris. I prefer taking lunch this way, all the fussing of staff is only really necessary when we have too many guests. Would you like some wine?"

"A little white would be nice. Thank you."

After filling up their plates and glasses, they sat down in silence and proceeded to eat. Not a word passed either of their lips, until Laozi broke the silence almost ten minutes later.

"So what is the news of the ship? Last I heard is that they'd made it to the Kepler Real system."

"That's correct. In fact they're a matter of days away from touching down."

"This has to work, for all our sakes. The risks are extremely high given my fears; the backlash will be monstrous if we get it wrong."

"Absolutely but remember we laid the foundations for this when we arrived the first time. It took our greatest diplomats to get them to agree to it in the first place. Every detail has been checked and checked again. It cannot fail."

"On another note, can you confirm that she is aboard the ship?"

"She is. She blames you; that won't change. She unfortunately can't abide Voegel, partly because she has to see him on a daily basis but otherwise, Ama is happy."

Chapter 10

4th July 2146 – Early Morning – London

To die is to sleep, to sleep is to dream, to dream is to live evermore. Hal's eyes flickered. The last of his thoughts drifted into the subconscious, as the sound of sirens teased him from his reverie. His state morphed from delusion to reality, with an unacceptable ease, where he awoke violently, sat up drenched in a cold sweat; near out of breath, shocked by the power of the vision. He took a deep lungful of air and surveyed his surroundings; at least he was at home. *Home is where the heart is; mine sure isn't here.* He pushed a retro button to the side of the head board and the curtains drew apart. The morning sunlight cast its rays onto the centre of the bed.

Hal, aghast, quietly caught his breath, whilst staring out on a picture of complete and utter mayhem. His newly acquired converted Kensington penthouse, formerly part of the Roof Gardens Hotel, was one of four apartments set around a magnificent courtyard, above a tall office building.

There was a blast of noise as a collection of rotor blades hovered precariously close to the eastern wall of glass. A repetitive thud reverberated through each pane, around the bedroom, as the waves of air were shifted in his direction. It was 7am and already there was trouble. For as long as Hal was aware, there were few known cases of ultra violence committed by Shortys in Kensington. The area was a relative oasis for Mid-Termers, who'd made it out of the quagmire of adversity, achieving a certain peace, in regards to their pre-determined mortality. There was a hedonistic air, mixed with casualness, only afforded by the inherently wealthy, or those few who were a success in the arts.

He looked out into the apartment block opposite him. Below one storey, directly in front of him, a scene played out like an old 21st Century movie, where he saw a nude man, firmly pressed up against the glass window of the apartment. He peered past the man as there was quite obviously an altercation of some sort, between a group of aggressors and the inhabitants of the apartment. Suddenly the residents joined the man at the window, all in various states of undress. Three unmarked helicopters appeared. They slowed, suspended mid-air, in front of him. Each one carried an assortment of mercenaries which added finesse to the sinister affair. They pointed an array of weapons in the direction of the offending group. Suddenly each one let a round off where the glass shattered on impact, leaving the group teetering on the edge of the apartment. The noise intensified. Hal looked down. The sickness he'd felt waking up had disappeared. In its place, an empathetic nausea welled up in his head, as if it were he tottering on the brink of his own demise.

Not knowing what to do next, nor knowing who the assailants represented, he was fixed in his position. The first to jump was a lady of no more than 30 years old; the second was the original naked man, but this time Hal noticed that he hadn't opted to jump; he'd been shot in the back. The tragic sequence of events culminated in all of the residents either jumping, being shot, or falling to their death, down below. Once the intruders had established their success they disappeared momentarily from the apartment, only to reappear on the roof above seconds later. Each helicopter picked up two of the assassins and disappeared as quickly as they had arrived.

Hal threw on his nearest clothes and raced to the lift bank outside his apartment. The lift took no time at all to reach the ground floor. He raced outside onto the street in search of answers. When he arrived at the mangled body of the girl he found it hard to look. The sight of mashed brains and blood splattered tarmac only added to his nausea. He fought back any inkling of sickness and looked at her left arm draped over her head.

He rose gently and backed away whilst still surveying the scene. He knew better than to get involved. Any number of circumstances could have been the cause of this group's downfall. They all had similar colouring and features albeit that they were all of different ages. Other than the naked man the two women were fully undressed; however the three middle aged or younger men appeared to have got dressed in a hurry with sheets or ladies skirts acting as cover for their lower halves. However one thing was for sure; all of them were duplicates. It had to have been a hit on one family. No doubt they were still carrying the burden of a violent altercation, from a not too distant past, or it had at least been a rich family member, discontinuing their entire line of duplicates.

Even if it were something more sinister, Hal knew that there was no point in getting involved. The police certainly wouldn't, as the question of morality, in discontinuing a duplicate was still very much one for the World Council. Trying to take on the local constabulary, local council and the majority of the residents in speaking out against these killings would only lead to disaster. Laozi had always warned him that his profession would make the necessary statements therefore the Vedas Corp PR machine would protect him, rather than wasting time waging personal vendettas against local pro-discontinuation groups and their sympathisers.

He reached the lobby of his apartment building, called a lift and ascended back to the relative peace and calm of his flat. It still didn't feel like home. It had been over a year since he'd officially moved in. It'd been over a year since Ama left. On the one hand the last year had been a whirlwind of press junkets, handshakes and public speaking; on the other it had been a desolate wasteland of remorse and lamented memories.

Hal's tour of the three capitals had been an enormous success. He had achieved the notoriety that he had so craved. It had given him the perfect platform to present, with authority, his views on society and the need for change. This time his message was clear and this time he had found a receptive audience. He had been amazed that whilst his earlier musings had fallen on deaf ears, with a little help in PR, presentation and performance, he had suddenly become an influential figure. The timing was perfect given recent events; the world had woken up to old thoughts, dressed up as new ideas.

Era to era we've fooled ourselves over religion, deification and idolatry. If only we'd thought of the future, whilst listening to our past. We would, most probably, never have evolved to the mark. There is no longer a need for religion or personal god. For thousands of years, mankind has wasted time over dogma and theology. What is needed is an acceptance of the natural, the universal and the collective energy. Through our struggle with religion we lost faith. The mark is our teacher. Kepler is the key.

However, for all his musings, the past year had also come at a great cost. A woeful emptiness had run along with him, bringing each day to a forlorn close, no matter where he was. The five months that he had shared with Ama had been the most fulfilling of his short life. The timing of her departure couldn't have been more apt; the manner of her departure couldn't have been more heartbreaking.

They had met the day after their first date. They'd met the day after that; the one after that as well. Within a week, she had moved into his small apartment in Fulham. They had stayed there until Ama went on tour to Vienna. Hal, having had no real commitments until his own tour commenced in June, joined her. After a few weeks she applied for leave and it was granted. They returned to London for two months of what turned out to be the most blissful honeymoon period.

Their idyllic life became complete when on 21st March, Ama's birthday, Hal had given her a Russian wolfhound puppy, which they named Borzoi; Boy for short. By Hal's birthday, two weeks later, they'd become so comfortable in each other's company that they'd already contemplated marriage, children and their future together. Ama was not bothered by his relatively short lifespan and appeared content with their uncomplicated life in London. They'd openly discussed a joint future with Voegel and even went as far as suggesting Ama quit the orchestra and travel with Hal.

However this had been met with resistance and Laozi had been called in to aid Voegel in his resistance. The arguments from both sides were logical but it was Hal who took the moral high ground, suggesting that Ama return to the orchestra in June, on the Russian leg of their Eurafrican tour. She would join them in Moscow. It wasn't as if money was now hard to come by either; he reasoned with her, that they'd never be more than a two hour flight away from each other. Besides she'd only be away a few weeks at a time. They agreed to leave Boy at home, where he'd be with one of them most of the time. For any overlap, they agreed to leave him with Hal's cousins who remained in London.

By the time May arrived, they had pushed to cram in as much life together as humanly possible. The energy between them was intoxicating and no matter whether it was a long walk, a visit to the theatre or dinner with old or new friends, they provided the world around them with positivity and calm. They knew that it would change; after all they were reasonable and responsible adults. Unfortunately, Hal wasn't prepared for how much he would have to face. Having found peace, after so many years of trying; it was torn from him that fateful day early in June.

He'd taken a direct flight to the Panamerican capital, Sao Luis, on Tuesday the 1st, early in the morning, leaving her to return to the flat and catch the late afternoon flight to Moscow. When he landed he had called her cellhip. Surprisingly she didn't answer. She would always answer, no matter who was calling. He tried an hour later; still to no avail. An hour before her flight was due to take off for Moscow he tried again; this time it went to voicemail. He left an agitated message, which he would later regret and called his cousins, to see if Boy had been dropped off at theirs. He hadn't. In fact they hadn't heard from Ama at all. Hal was understandably concerned.

His next port of call was Voegel, given that it would be the middle of the night in Moscow; he had decided to wait until early morning. When he rang him the next day, he got no response either. The number had been disconnected. Laozi was his last resort. He called him, but the response hinged on focus, reality and fulfillment. After a lot of pressing, even he couldn't answer Hal's one true question; her whereabouts.

He'd thought quickly and decidedly, knowing that he would not be able to focus on his work without answers, so he jumped on a plane to London late that Wednesday. He went to look for her himself and get the police involved if he had to. He arrived at his flat on the Thursday morning, to find it locked and empty of all her personal items; Boy was missing; all his things had vanished. It was as if they had never existed. Looking around the bedroom one last time, he'd noticed a piece of paper, poking out from under the pillow on his side of the bed.

It was short and uncharacteristic but the message was clear, 'Forget me. I am lost to this world. Do not look for me. I will always love you.'

She had left him and did not want to be contacted, Hal decided not to take it up with the police. This was not a case of a missing person. This was a case of a person who did not wish to be found. Dejected and broken, he turned around and headed back to the airport and another flight to Sao Luis.

When he finally reached Singapore, after a grueling press schedule, he sold his flat and bought a new residence remotely and site unseen. He only returned on the day of completion, to orchestrate the removals from one place to the other. With no reason to stay, he headed on to Cairo and the last leg of his tour. Having been away for almost six months, his feet had barely touched the ground. Returning to London had been an earth shattering restoration of normalcy. However the London he had left was an entirely different place to the one on his return. His apartment had changed; his life had changed; he had changed.

He'd now been back for more than six months and his new abode felt strange. He looked around at all the paintings, pictures, books and ornaments; even with those it felt Spartan and cold. There was no positive energy, he had no energy left. Nowhere felt like home.

Hal wearily got up from the sofa, upon which he was pensively perched, and dragged himself to the bathroom. All the memories of Ama and her departure had flooded back, drowning him in longing, and the cold sweat of his dreams had turned into a clammy chill, in need of invigoration. The blasts of a belting hot shower, combined with a blended fruit cocktail and a hint of rum, would surely rouse him, from the melancholic atmosphere. He gently tapped the button beside the shower, tapping thrice for hot water only, allowing the steam to fill the chamber.

He looked at his reflection in the mirror and knew that he had let himself go over the preceding few months. His usual swagger and elegance had been replaced with sorrow and mourning. He knew that this had to be addressed as he had a new found responsibility, one that far outweighed his personal circumstances.

Sacrifices have to be made; to realise one's dreams; it's just the not knowing that is driving me insane.

He knew that if he had an answer, any answer, he'd be reasonable. It was the abrupt nature of their parting, the finality of it all, that was so unreasonable.

Having shaved and put on his monotone informal wear, Hal walked towards the kitchen in search of the fruit cocktail, when his home media system emanated a sound, reserved for one caller only. He clicked his fingers and stopped in his tracks. Out of his hallway mirror, a stereogram image of Laozi popped out. Hal spoke sarcastically, away from him, averting his gaze.

"Morning, I take it that I've either missed a meeting, or, failed to respond to one of your many contacts; then again, it's not Analucia calling, so for what do I owe this huge pleasure?"

"None of the above, Mr. Laurence, I'm calling with some rather unexpected news and also some that was entirely expected. Would you like the expected or the unexpected first?"

"Given that the unexpected turned out to be the expected, this morning, I'll go for the former. However I would like you to know that I'm in a foul mood today. I've just seen an entire family of duplicates wiped out, by some bastard's hit squad. Not one of yours Laozi?"

"The resentment in your voice betrays you. I know you better than that. A bad night again, I take it. This news I have might, go some way to, alleviate your pain. I'm hoping that it will, for all our sakes; the last few months haven't been good to any of us Hal, especially when the 'voice of the people' has now gone mute."

"Hit me with it, it can't be worse than another day listening to VCN's 'news in brief' whilst trying to conjure up miracles with a canvass. I've lost my spark, my raison d'être, my muse."

"One of the committees working within the World Council, the Royal Court of Asiana, has requested your presence, in Shanghai, tomorrow. They want an audience, as they have a serious commission to discuss with you. I guess it is expected, in that I suspected they'd come calling, it was only a matter of time. However the actual contents of the brief are extremely secret, so much so, that I haven't even been fully briefed. If I find out more I'll be sure to let you know, but honestly I don't think I will. The Royal Court is an entirely different animal to the governing body. I have limited eyes and ears within their organisation."

"So I'm just to turn up on their doorstep within 24 hours, be given a lucrative commission and that's that, no questions asked? Come on Laozi, I need more than that, especially in light of the circumstances. I don't trust anyone."

"I'll be joining you. I'm in Singapore now but I'll get Analucia to arrange it that, we arrive at Hongqiao International at the same time. All I know is that they need me to be there to give you the peace of mind, that this is more than just an offer of further prosperity. They know that you have little regard for financial matters. They have instructed me to tell you that they can aid in your quest for revolution."

"Sounds like fluff to me. If they want you to be there, surely you know the real reason. It's hardly like one of the most influential men in the world, will just leap at their beck and call. Pull the other one."

"I hear you. Honestly I do but this time trust me when I say perhaps I know a little more than I am able to let on over the airwaves. I can't talk about this now. Yet believe me I don't have the entire picture or otherwise we would have been discussing this weeks ago. I can sense the bitterness in your voice. I can only say that the unexpected news will go some way to helping you trust me again. I am not to blame Hal. I never have been."

"Well you and Voegel were always in cahoots, so you must have known that their simultaneous disappearance smacked of intrigue."

"I grant you that. This is true. However I have always maintained that I've known what he is up to and where he is and that I couldn't tell you. However I have never been privy to Ama's decisions or her whereabouts; that is, until now."

"You've got to be kidding me, right? This is the unexpected news? Next you're going to tell me that she was actually not who she said she was at all and that I've wasted 18 months of my very short life on a figment of my imagination."

"I'm not, I assure you. In fact it's similar to your theories last year. Remember when you and I were in that restaurant in Sao Luis and you were highly emotive and angry at her, me, Voegel, in fact anyone who was in your way?"

"Much like now. Yes."

"You hit on the fact that there must be more to the one mission, amounting to the 'Kepler Meeting'; that there had to be something else. Mankind wasn't going to just wave his flag, say hello and get back into his ship and sail home. Those were your words Hal. Do you remember? I told you that you were right and that there was a second ship, with an assortment of specialists, venturing out on a voyage of discovery."

"Yes but we agreed that Ama wasn't a part of that. She would have told me. We agreed that she had nothing to do with it as she never showed any signs of anything but wide eyed wonder at the entire prospect of Kepler; nothing but total wonder."

"This is true and do you remember that we had agreed to leave the subject alone. She made her choice to leave you, regardless of whom and what she was with. Till now I have never had confirmation. I have always been under the impression that she had returned to New York and her life there; but Hal, this is not the case. She is most definitely on that ship."

"I went six months ago, looked over her old address and visited the places that she talked so spiritedly about. She'd never returned. Who gave you that impression in the first place? Voegel? What's wrong with you all; lying then, liars now; the lot of you. "

Hal spun round staring venomously at the projection of Laozi.

"Well, whatever you want to believe, the truth is that she is on that ship. I can tell you more about it when I see you. It's called the Repertega and is most probably landing on Kepler as we speak."

"I'll call you back."

Hal's subconscious had always accepted it as a half truth. He didn't know whether to laugh or lash out. He just wished that he'd been told outright; by her, by Laozi or even Voegel. This left him far angrier. He felt let down. It was no surprise that his art had been suffering; his voice was dying; his confidence in his own thoughts had taken a battering; his belief was wavering.

No one likes being taken for a mug. What does Laozi expect? Just roll over like a puppy and play nice; because he says so? How dare he keep me in the dark like this? Calling himself a true friend; he's no better than that piece of shit from Prussia.

He straightened himself up in front of the mirror, giving himself the mental fortitude to return his benefactor's call. Underneath it all he was a rational man. It didn't take long for him to realise that the entire situation had been played out with, both his and her, best intentions in mind. The clean break was exactly what was had been required at the time; for both of them to survive without the other. He could see that she was the ideal candidate; after all she was an orphan with a rare talent in music. The Keplerians would have no doubt appreciated this, far more than guns and threats. Her life cycle suited too. His did not. He could understand the secrecy of a mission and even how they might go about approaching a candidate, yet he would never be able to trust Laozi again. He missed Ama more than ever. He stepped towards the mirror once again.

"Laozi – Singapore" The line rang for two beats and his benefactor's face replaced his reflection.

"Has the battle of your two selves been engaged? Who won?"

"Alright Laozi, I get it. I understand. So what time tomorrow?"

They agreed to meet at midday, Asianian Northern Time. Laozi was visibly relieved. Hal replaced his anger with candour. He was genuinely excited about the opportunity in Shanghai and felt a sense of purpose which had been missing for many months return. By the end of their conversation it felt like business had resumed. For all intents and purposes it had.

After they had finished speaking and Hal was once again left to his own devices, he sensed that the trip was going to be a long one and so immediately headed for his dressing room, in search of the right attire. A while later when packed and ready for the next day, Analucia called with the details of his transfer, flight and pick up at the other end. She was naturally curious as to his better emotional state, given that he had been a varied mix of highs and lows over the past six months. She put it down to his return to London. He had never fully explained the extent of his longing for Ama, unsurprisingly, given that she would only be hurt by the reality. She confirmed that she wouldn't be there tomorrow and that it would just be Laozi that he would be meeting at the airport. With a frustrated sigh she signed off leaving Hal staring at the mirror, reflecting on the strange morning that he'd had. He'd built up a serious hunger and so headed outdoors.

There were few shops left in the cities as all transactions were done via cellhip, media system and warehouse. It was only the ostentatious high brands who felt it necessary to peddle their wares at street level. In their place stood coffeebanks, restaurants, wineclubs and popup stores on weekly leases. Hal crossed the street, realising what a beautiful day it was. The sun streamed past an assortment of buildings to the South, as he headed up the high street towards Hyde Park. He decided on taking a walk and grabbing a sandwich down by the Serpentine. The day had given him the perfect opportunity to take in his surroundings before he moved on yet again. The bustle of the city permeated every corner. People passed by oblivious to each other; each on a separate mission to their destination.

He carved his way eastwards and approached the park. The road rose slightly, following the original hill track carved out in the 1600's. This sort of nuance was the exact reason why he liked London so much; it was its charm and place in the past that gave it its character. Most modern cities had been flattened or built to a plan. London had been neither. Not forgetting the troubles the world over; the mark, Shortys and duplication; the people made the city. It was a true emblem of greatness; steeped in history, innovation, style and culture.

It was July and the trees were out in full bloom. Picking his way through the pedestrians he arrived at the eastern gate on the south side of the park. He took a deep breath as he entered. The air was rich and oxygenated. There was minimal pollution since the advent of air fuel cells. This compounded with the lack of noise, as the multitude of vehicles ran quietly along the roads, made Hyde Park a relative oasis from frenetic city life.

He headed in the direction of the Serpentine Gallery Cafe. He knew the place well; he'd had an exhibition there, not too many years before. He found himself a table and ordered a blended fruit cocktail and a chicken broth. He sat staring out; people coming and going, talking and laughing, exercising or dawdling.

It's times like these that one can forget the mark and feel truly inspired. Humans can be so blissful, unaware and caught up in the moment - if only it were true.

Afterwards he got up and went for a stroll around the lake, taking in the assortment of exercise and recreation groups. He watched the families aboard rowing boats and the swans drifting along beside them. He sat on a bench beside the lake and started to write. Out of nowhere he began to collect his thoughts for a sequel to his world tour; 'The Faces of Our Future II'. It was built upon an image of Kepler, through the everyman's eyes. He set out to provide an idealistic view of life on the other planet. He viewed it as a response to the many programmes he had watched; the library worth of information that he had processed since the Kepler Meeting.

He pictured himself aboard the Repertega, adrift, cruising to another world. He let his mind wander into the psyche of the Keplerian leader and pictured himself as Akihiro Iso, meeting the Keplerians for the first time. What he would do with an opportunity to meet them; what he would do with walking on Kepler; what he would do with understanding their world. He had to admit it, he was envious of Ama. He would have given his right arm to be one of the original team, let alone being on that second ship. A limited lifespan hadn't helped; a year's travel had put paid to that.

He sat quietly on the park bench until the white of the midday sun, aged into a reddening sky. He'd never had so many thoughts and ideas stream out of his consciousness at such a rate as this. By the time he stood up and looked around, breathing a sigh of relief, he had enough material to build an entirely new campaign.

Early the next morning, rejuvenated and refreshed, a Vedas Corp driver arrived at his front door, picked up his bags and left to deposit them in the car. Hal got a rush of euphoria as it felt like at last he was moving on. He could focus on his art, now that Ama's existence had been finally laid to rest.

He was happy for her, so long as she was content. His feelings for her had never wavered.

Laozi knew the bigger picture and his previous mutterings in reference to focus, reality and fulfillment were now being unveiled. For all Hal's empathy for the world, he was in many ways unaware of his own mind. It was Laozi who saw in him an energy; a life force which, if mixed with the right opposite, would create a balance.

He took a final walk around his flat, ensuring that the electrical mains supply was turned off, and that the fridge and freezer had alternated to the backup supply. He straightened out a picture in the hallway and took one last look at his rich blue silk Moroccan carpet. He knew he was leaving for a long time. It was as if there were new beginnings. *Give them the truth and you shall set them free.* The sense of trepidation was there but he had been set on an alternate course, casually readjusted by some overdue news. He shut the door behind him and as he slowly padded towards the lift, he knew he was going to miss this place; the irony of it all, for now it felt like home.

Chapter 11

4th July 2146 – Late Morning – Southern Kepler

A blue mist encased the outer window. Ama peered outwards into the void. She lingered in a form of congenial anticipation whilst the polar regions, flanked by glorious expanses of ocean, drew ever nearer. Between them the single continent with its large plains of lush vegetation stretched out as far as the eye could see. The light of an electrical storm flashed in the distance.

The Repertega had spent the past six months approaching, relatively slowly, from the outer regions of the Kepler Real system. Many times Ama had gazed out from the viewing deck far into the distance. As they had drawn nearer she had observed that Kepler's land mass replicated that of an oversized Panamerica, in shape, latitude and form. She'd noticed that the mountainous regions stretched over a latitude parallel to its equator and that the unbroken ranges of gigantic craggy and snowy peaks were similar to those found in Northern Asiana.

Suddenly the ship noticeably dropped through patches of inconsistent cloud and the mist receded. Ama was bathed in the warm glow of sunlight. The view was spectacular drawing in a myriad of rivers, meadows, hills and wetlands. Pockets of villages, a few towns and a large city loomed in the distance. Ama was not alone. 2,141 similar souls accompanied her, staring out from their own cabins or quarters; wherever they were.

The ship had been designed as a landing craft, albeit of colossal proportions, with the purpose of becoming Earth's only access point in and out of Kepler. When she had first stepped aboard she had learned that The Repertega was an ark on a voyage of discovery and peace. Its purpose was to establish a base, let its passengers acclimatise in a controlled environment and under the negotiated terms integrate into Keplerian society.

Everyone had been handpicked following an intensive selection process which had taken two years, for many, without them even knowing. Some were principal practitioners in medicine, construction or science, others in history, art or design. There were those who were leaders of language, literature or music and those who were philosophers, economists or diplomats. Lawyers, sportspeople and even the military were represented, but only as a precaution. Among these people, known as specialists, men and women were divided equally, aged between 25 years and 55 years old. All of them were Lifers, as they had become affectionately known, with more than 70 concentric rings adorning their wrists. There were no married couples, no divorcees and no one had been in an obvious relationship with any other person on board, prior to making the journey. In addition the ship carried the male and the female, species permitting, of all known creatures and plants from earth. Even one household pet per passenger had been allowed. Ama wouldn't have survived without Boy.

The Council for Keplerian Integration had placed heads of specific departments, known as chiefs, aboard the Repertega, who had continually briefed the specialists of their roles, the mission and the guidelines towards peaceful integration. Transporting and introducing a multitude of diverse cultures to a planet, with an apparently singular cultural background, was grandiose by design. The chiefs were aware of this from the outset and had also been carefully selected, due to their own lack of imperialistic or predatory natures. They were free-thinkers, who embraced diverse cultures and religious practices; they had no wish to be an authority. They were there to learn.

The ship dropped through another patch of stratus, dispersing the liquid droplets and Ama at last could see the landing site. It had been clearly marked by a multitude of large fires and torches, forming a triangle, the size of a small town or village. She had spent the past year studying a brief history of Kepler and its people. Although the information was limited, knowing a little about them had put her, and her colleagues, at ease. She was excited about hearing the Keplerian tongue first hand; she was intrigued about their language, given that it had a lyrical quality to its delivery. She had learnt that they had a singular common tongue, alike to an early form of Magadhi, an old indo-aryan language that was last used on Earth in the Indian region of Asiana thousands of years before. She hoped that she would, in time, be able to understand and speak the language fluently. She hoped to be able to differentiate between the minor dialect differentials depending on where and in which of the nine kingdoms one was in.

She held the map of Kepler in her hands eager to absorb the information by osmosis. The kingdoms were named in relation to their position from North to South but also in reference to being a specific part of a tree. The two most northerly kingdoms were named Agra and Uttara, for Summit and North respectively. This followed down to Utsima for Head and Amalaka, Fruit. The words intrigued her, like she was already learning a song and applying them to a piece of music: Garbha, Centre; Anga, Body; Ganda, Stem; Daksina, South; Adhara, Foot and the beautifully named free states of Arnava, The Sea and Maharnava, The Ocean. Yet Avasya and Karkara, the polar regions to the north and south, conjured up a fear based upon nothing more than a subconscious throwback to her late night discussions with Hal. His many animated references to Tartarus and the dungeon of torment obviously still resonated.

As the ship slowed to an almost stationary state, descending towards the patchwork fields of green and brown below she thought of their society, its constructs and whether there were any similarities between the two planets.

Nine High-Ministers sat on the Kepler Council, each one presiding over a specific kingdom. In addition to the kingdoms there were four other states that were not included in government or involved in direct regulation. They had been described to her as either, independent, free or controlled, depending on whom and how one spoke of them. Either way, the islands in the oceans were known as the Free States and the polar regions were known as the Prison States.

These areas were of particular fascination to Ama, where she had hoped that she would one day be privy to the entire planet and its history. During the many forums and classes she had attended on board the Repertega, she had felt that the information she and her colleagues had received was not complete. There had been little reference in regards to the islands or prison states. She sensed that at some point her curiosity would get the better of her and lead her there.

Each High-Minister was elected democratically and supervised for only nine years. There were neither mid-term elections nor the possibility to challenge the leadership. The following leader would have to be of no relation historically, physically or politically to the previous incumbent. This in itself appeared to Ama that the Keplerians had achieved an order to their society which those on Earth were still trying to manufacture. It appeared that there were similarities between the two planets but that there had also been a divergence in evolution. At a certain point in Keplerian history or perhaps it was Earth's; it depended on the way the question was approached. She could also see that they had the advantage in being one continent but then again Earth had been one once.

Earth's supercontinent, Pangaea, had broken up over 200 million years before. Ama's education extended far enough to know that the great apes didn't walk the Earth until well after the supercontinent had long since ruptured. However to explore a divergence she went on the basis of both planets being the same age as each other. She therefore knew that it wasn't possible for it to have been then that the two planets' evolutionary cycles had diverged. The genus of homo only came into being two million years before she took her own first steps. It seemed logical that the mark was a result of a divergence in the mind; therefore a possible reaction to the friction between the multitude of varying cultures and religions; not a direct result of fractured plates and shifting sands.

From the outset it seemed that Earth had evolved faster through its cultural communications. Yet through its inception of the World Council and the creation of the three regions of Eurafrica, Panamerica and Asiana, her theory, that the continents were closing in again, not physically but through technology and the blending of colour and culture, had some legs to it. A supercontinent of planetary proportions was not so far away. Perhaps Earth was light years behind Kepler not centuries in front.

Ama already understood that mankind had lost its faith; that they had little meaning for the word. Religion had been the cause of its destruction and the mark had been the messenger. Kepler held many secrets and for all the forums, focus groups and classes that she had attended nothing resonated more with her than the Keplerian leader's speech during that original broadcast. This only furthered her eagerness to get there.

The ship hovered above the site for what seemed like an age. The towns and villages that she had been able to make out in the distance had now disappeared from view. Outside was empty, without a living thing in sight. The design was so specific and the pilot had to be so exact that it was of little surprise that the landing was one of caution and precision.

They were to set down in the outer reaches of Adhara, a site negotiated by the original team at the time of the Kepler Meeting. One of Ama's new friends was a cosmologist, called Yakov Safronov. He had been highly skeptical of that meeting given that the ship had been designed with Keplerian society in mind. He let their tight knit group know that the size, shape and intricate details of the Repertega were mirrored on Kepler; it had nine departments for a start, of which Ama was not surprised to have been attached to the Department for Art & Music.

Yakov had proffered the cynicism, on occasion, that it would have taken years to construct, such a carefully considered and colossal ship. Ama had fallen silent at those times, as, given her knowledge of Vedas Corp and the power behind it; she couldn't help but suspect the same. It was common knowledge that the base of the ship was an equilateral triangle. They were also aware that there were a number of unused and sealed exit tunnels, placed strategically around its perimeter. The group was split on the timing of its original design, but all were agreed that it was more than coincidental that this appeared to mirror the shape and size of the landing site, precisely.

The journey had taken just over a year where Ama had been put through a surfeit of sentiments right from the start. The heart wrenching beginning in leaving Hal under such covert circumstances had left her initially resistant to the opportunity that she had been given. It had taken many months of persistent badgering from her new found friends and colleagues, to coax her out of what had been a bewildered state. It hadn't helped that Voegel was also on board and chief of her department. It hadn't helped that he was the reason for her selection in the first place.

She had understood the criteria and her inclusion but no amount of persuasive reasoning had managed to include Hal in the final 2,744. She'd argued consistently that he was the finest candidate capable of comprehending their mission. Being a Forty shouldn't have had any bearing on the process.

She knew that Voegel was only a spokesperson for his superiors but it was he who had let the committee know of their relationship while they were being monitored for selection. It was for this reason Ama resented Voegel since day one of being on board. He had originally tried to placate her with numerous counter arguments and alternative points of view but none had sat easily with her.

Before she had left she'd contemplated approaching Laozi Veda but accepted that she did not know him well enough to trust him with her views. She'd signed a contract of silence and so lived in fear of making the mission public during her final few months on Earth. Her responsibility extended further than just to this contract; it was to the calling, a promise of helping mankind; it was this burden that had weighed heavy leaving her unable to communicate anything to Hal.

Yet while they had been together their relationship had escalated into a romantic dream; into an illusion which both had conspired to create for their own independent reasons; both being inadvertent victims of time and circumstance.

From the window in her quarters she gazed onto the fields outside. She couldn't see a single animal, only a few trees on a hill in the distance swaying in what could only be a hot breeze. She had felt that she had been in mourning for the first half of her journey, juxtaposed with the sensation of being one of a privileged few. It was only the presence of Boy and watching him evolve from skittish puppy to brave young protector which had kept her sane.

Once they had reached Mars and passed through the gateway into the Kepler Real system, she'd undergone a transformation almost instantaneously. Another of her new friends, an Asianian historian, Ban Qian had joked that it must have been something in the air which had appealed to Ama's re-found sense of humour. Yakov, Ban and Ama had formed a close bond over those months drifting ever closer to their destination. The initial feelings of lamenting the lost had been replaced by the Keplerian reality glistening in the dark; day after day. They were surreptitiously surrendering themselves to a new and brighter future.

As they passed through the gateway, visually nothing had changed. The planet to their left had no atmosphere, similar to the one that they had only just left. Over the course of millions of years, the system's solar wind had gradually eroded it away. To most on board the gateway had been a waypoint, a point of no return. The experience, apart from a gong emanating round the ship to express their successful passage, had been minimal and there was little change outside. It was there that they were flung into the system's magnetic field, drifting along in a continuous stream of charged particles which had formed a heliosphere. Further on they encountered similar beads of luminosity which mimicked phytoplankton, in their absorption of light, whilst floating along in the solar wind as if it were the ocean.

From the viewing deck Ama had looked out into a new universe and stared incredulously. She took in each planet's magnetosphere with its long tear drop shaped tail extending outward and behind. She was wise to the solar wind and how it created glorious luminescent belts of radiation. But it was the moments when the sun's rays hit these belts, conjuring up beams of red, blue and yellow which would penetrate her very core. They had passed meteors and other organic molecules caught up in the slipstream of the passing ship. They had cut through cosmic rays, rich in colour, fleeting in existence, all conjured up by an array of subatomic elements and ionised atomic nuclei. Everything had a familiarity to it but a difference was felt by everybody.

Ama had spent most of her time either in class studying the ways of the new planet or socialising with friends in one of the many restaurants, wineclubs or coffeebanks situated in the main atrium at the rear of the ship. The Atrium was dome shaped. Made up entirely of a new form of transparent aluminum; entirely see through with a magnifying effect to draw the distant planets and the surrounding space in closer. On its many levels there were large viewing decks like seating areas in shopping malls, upon which many would sit discussing the countless permutations of their mission beyond whilst whiling away their days, or nights, looking out. On occasion there would be light shows and planetary exposés where the transalum would be used as a far reaching telescope, focusing in on one particular outer planet that they would never have had the chance to visit. Each event would be hosted by one of the many astrologists or cosmologists that they had on board.

Yakov had been the most entertaining with his vivid description of the many moons of Jupiter. Given that it was neither day nor night at any point, time ran to a 24 hour clock which had been set to Greenwich Mean Time on departure from their base in China. Ama would while away any of her free days on her favourite viewing deck, Level 9. This had been initially a place for remorse and fits of melancholy but recently it had transformed into one for glad reminiscence. The deck happened to be situated by Les Grenouilles, a French restaurant, which more than resembled L'Escargot in both layout and design.

Any other spare time that she had had was spent in practice or performing ensemble with the other musicians in her department. There were four theatres around the Atrium which could be found on Level 3. In fact the Atrium was the epicentre of life aboard the ship as if it were mimicking the Keplerian commercial centres that she had heard so much about.

Boy had needed a lot of exercise and thankfully there were a number of parks and recreation areas on Level 2. Ama had spent many a time jogging around these green open spaces whilst looking at cosmic rays crisscrossing above and beside her. It had an extraordinary effect on them all as if they were caught in a glorious purgatory. Boy's coat was now dusty blond, the hair becoming thick and coarse and in constant need of grooming. Ama had done her best to train him but thought it better to enlist the help of some more qualified people on a number of occasions. The results had been impressive where he had grown into an obedient and loving dog with the superior quality of sensing any threat to Ama's wellbeing. She felt protected at all times.

Conversely, there was one pressing problem that needed attention and Ama was unsure as to how address it; the unwelcome advances of one of her colleagues. Unbeknownst to her from the very beginning, she'd caught the eye of Jabir Ibn Al-Zarqali, the son of the head of the Eurafrican Council. He was a biologist and his life had been dedicated to the study of the formation of the mark. Although he had not made his intentions clear, prior to passing through the gateway, it was as if the very fact of travelling through folded space had given him a new lease of life. Since then he had hounded her with requests for study sessions and dinner dates. Ama had tried to be polite on every occasion but he hadn't fully got the message; she was not available.

She had however allowed him to join her circle of friends and to be involved in their pastimes as well as their profound discussions. He was amusing, intelligent and also good looking; just not her type. She had thought that Ban Qian and he would hit it off but it appeared that he only had eyes for her. Ban had quipped that something didn't ring true with him, for all his pleasantries and good intentions there were sinister undertones. Ama could see her point as he would constantly bare his mark. He would thrust his wrist forward and proudly proclaim that he was a Centurian with 126 years bestowed upon him as if he was some form of deity. At times he made them laugh but at others he made them wary. Boy had even made his views clear, growling whenever he was near. She had decided to let him down gently, emphatically, once and for all as soon as she was able.

The agreed terms resulting from the Kepler Meeting had astounded her. She could barely fathom the layers of detail which would have been meticulously fought over by both sides. Having set down on their landing site the 2,142 were to be allotted kingdoms and in two weeks time integrated into their respective societies. They would be given a dwelling, a modest income and the opportunity to watch and learn the ways of that particular kingdom and its people. In turn, they were to act as a consultant to the local council as an advisor on Earth's customs. The idea that had been sold to all of the specialists was that this process of integration would pave the way for Kepler to catch up with those from Earth.

However she and her friends saw it entirely as an opportunity for those from Earth to learn about Keplerian behaviour and the fundamental basis of their cosmology. Whichever way it was viewed the process of integration was to be phased and controlled. They were already fitted with microchips which acted as electronic tags to ensure that none of them went astray but more importantly for their own safety. The idea of being one of only 2,142

Earth people, walking around an entirely new and alien planet suddenly filled Ama with a huge amount of fear and trepidation.

During their time aboard one of the many colloquialisms attributed to the vessel itself, was an abbreviated version of its full name where it had become affectionately known as simply, Tega. The name gave it more of a grounded feel as if it were a country or a planet of its own. Ama couldn't have thought of anything more apt or pertinent, yet her thoughts continued to nag away at her.

She still awaited confirmation as to which kingdom she would be joining. Yakov believed that they hadn't been told in order for everyone to become acquainted with the entire continent and not just their allotted village, town or local area. She had initially thought that this had been a good idea. Now standing there looking out from the window in her quarters, she wasn't so sure. The thought of her next port of call conjured up images of spectres and ghouls which, whilst no doubt unlikely, were all the same alien to her and ominous.

The ship's gong sounded. A deep rich boom comparable to a fog horn reverberated through the network of passages and corridors, permeating the walls of each cabin, quarter or department centre. It rolled through into the Atrium, up each level, past each viewing deck until it reached the transalum ceiling, washing back on itself. Ama stood staring onto the field outside and a tear gently rolled down the left side of her face. They had arrived.

Boy approached sensing something was wrong and brushed up against her right flank. He nuzzled his nose into the cup of her right hand, pushing into her. Ama wasn't sad; remorseful but not sad. She wondered what Hal would be doing at that very moment. She wondered if he knew of her whereabouts, whether the news of the Repertega was even common knowledge back home on Earth. She had been told, as part of the original terms, no one would be informed of their arrival until the mission was a year old. She hoped that Laozi would have made him aware at some point, just for his own peace of mind.

If only she could once, just to let him know of her love and the crisis of circumstance that she suffered all those months ago. Supposedly the Department for Security had a system that enabled them to speak to the base in China. But everyone had taken a vow of silence. She knew that they wouldn't make special allowances. The gong had instructed them to proceed to their departments but Ama remained fixed in her position as the tears welled up from deep inside. She felt that this moment by the window in her quarters was the perfect place to wave goodbye to Hal and their time together. She cupped Boy's chin and patted his side, reflecting on the past one last time. With a sigh and a step she sidled away from the window to face her future.

The hallway was crowded with excitement. A variety of people rushed out of their quarters in anticipation of being informed of where they had been assigned to. Ama couldn't help but get caught up in the commotion. She picked up her pace towards the lift bank. Once she'd arrived in the large auditorium she sat in her usual seat. Two acquaintances jumped in beside her.

"Eerie wasn't it? I wasn't expecting that, but then again I didn't know what to expect." The girl whispered quietly to Ama, expecting an immediate response. She received a hesitant smile but nothing else in return. The other broke the silence,

"The electrical storm closed in on the capital of Adhara. I could see its towers reflecting the flashes; something I'll never forget. I hope we're all assigned to the same place." As she tailed off the auditorium fell silent. Voegel approached the centre of the stage, in front of where Ama was sitting. A large projection behind him appeared, showing the map of Kepler, complete with lakes, mountains and rivers. He turned to his audience and waited for a moment until there was absolute silence.

"Welcome everyone. Today is a day that will forever be remembered as a beginning as well as an end. Today marks the beginning of our journey but perhaps the end to our plight. Amongst all the excitement and intrigue, let's not forget the reason for why we are all here. Three people made this day a reality. We owe a debt of gratitude for their forbearance in bringing this plan together.

"We are, as I'm sure you would all agree, eternally grateful for the opportunity that they have bestowed upon us. Most of you will never have the chance of meeting them but you will surely know to whom I refer. The first is Akihiro Iso who has returned to Earth as head of the World Council. The second has since stepped down as leader of the Keplerians and retired from office. The third however you will know as the chairman of the Vedas Corporation, Laozi Veda. Without these brilliant minds and their tense negotiations, we wouldn't be here today".

Ama shuddered at the mention of Laozi's name. Voegel looked in her direction and she made an effort to recede from view. Perhaps he had looked unintentionally or subliminally, either way she pretended not to notice.

"We have spent more than a year aboard Tega. We have meticulously planned our journey. We have endeavoured to set in motion a chain of events which will aid us in understanding the mark, its origin and whether there is a cure. I do not need to remind you of your responsibility towards each other, the communities that you join and above all to those that you have left behind. I can now impart the finer details of the operation. The projection behind will assist with the logistics, so please bear with me."

Voegel delicately tapped on the top of a long thin object, reminiscent of a biro from the 20th Century. As he did this a table replaced the map of Kepler. He clicked the top of the pen, revealing figures as he spoke.

"Each kingdom has 126 villages, 42 towns and a capital city. Each village has the same number of individual dwellings; a town has three times as many as the village and the city almost triple that of the towns. We now know something of the commercial centres, we have studied the mechanics of their society but until now you have been not been made aware of where you will be assigned. This is that moment. It has been decreed that the Department for Art & Music will be assigned to the Kingdom of Amalaka which the linguists amongst you will no doubt know to be the fruit of the tree." Voegel paused for dramatic effect. It worked. There was a murmur of excitement before he carried on.

"This table gives you all a firsthand glance at the numbers aboard Tega and how we are divided. As you will see in each department there are 238 specialists. There are 588 members of the departments for Security and Psychology who also double up as Tega's crew. The Captain, Pilots and Flight Officers will not leave Tega. They will never set foot on Kepler.

"I am now permitted to tell you that you will not all be together. Some of you will be many miles from any other earth human for long periods of time. Do not be afraid, this is for your own good. In short, each department is to be assigned to a kingdom where one specialist will be placed in each village, two in a specific town and 28 in the city." This time Ama leant into the girl and whispered,

"I guess it had to happen, we have to immerse ourselves properly; although I'm feeling a little green now." The girl shook her head, looking almost white as a sheet. Across the auditorium smiles had been replaced with looks of trepidation.

"This may seem strange to you, perhaps a little daunting but I have been instructed to assure you that after the first few weeks you will feel at home and will have forgotten your old way of life entirely. I am sure some of you have friends in other departments," again he looked in Ama's direction but perhaps she was imagining it, "I can tell you that the Department for History & Politics have been assigned to Agra, Science & Technology to Uttara, Cosmology & Philosophy to Utsima, Industry & Construction to Garbha, Sport & Leisure to Anga, Finance & Trade to Ganda, Exploration & Marine Studies to Daksina and Agriculture & Farming to Adhara. The two other departments of Psychology and Security have been assigned to Arnava & Maharnava and Avasya & Karkara respectively and will remain on Tega for the time being."

There was complete stunned silence. The waiting was now over. No one could have fully prepared for what they were hearing. They sat for what seemed like an age processing the information before Voegel continued from memory,

"We have a further two weeks aboard Tega to acclimatise, further our language skills and mentally prepare for our futures. Our mission remains the same; to watch, listen and learn. You will keep a daily record of everything that goes on in your location. You will report back to me every three months with your findings. You will be assigned your village, town or city when you leave; for your own wellbeing.

"I expect there to be a lot of questions but I'm afraid I can't give you any answers, so please save them for when we next meet in a few months time. Remember that you have all been chosen because of your virtues and not just your talents. If there is a cure to this mark then you are part of that medicine; an intrinsic part. I bid you all farewell and good luck."

Voegel shuffled away from the centre of the stage and headed towards the exit, carefully avoiding eye contact with anyone on the lower level. He managed to escape before the barrage of questions was hurled in his direction. It would have been an understatement, to suggest, that there was a concoction of bewildered feeling present. It was no doubt the same, in every corner of the ship.

Ama sat silently until the theatre was empty. She picked herself up from her chair and made her way to the exit. She hadn't even got off the ship and was already looking forward to returning. She remembered Boy and appreciated that she would have his company in her new home wherever that was. She knew that good communication would be the best asset to a successful integration. She made a mental note to book another round of intensive Magadhi lessons. She could practice with Boy, he was a good listener.

Chapter 12

My heart is beating fast; I'm falling, twisting through the air, spiraling out of control with every breath, a furnace, fuelled by confusion wells up deep inside. I'm drifting through time and space; I've been drawn to a sun in another place. There are beams that glow bright beside me, as shafts of light particles coil around my face. Darkness pervades; I'm no longer outside, I'm no longer looking in.

I open my eyes and listen to the woman in front of me. She's speaking fast, in notes from a song of a distant past. I could sit here all day as she teaches me the old ways. She draws me out of my unilateral state; with consummate ease she changes my mind. For in her I find a solace, where no amount of reason can dissipate my fear of losing touch with my reality. The veracity of my realism is a construct of my idealism. I am at the mercy of the room; I am lost in time; I know that I will surrender to this place.

I study her features, dwelling on the face. It is weathered and knowing, giving me time and space. It is as it always has been, ever present and never to be replaced. I ask her my question and get the same languid response; it's as if I am the messenger, surrendering to anything she wants. Her skin is brown, her features refined; a blend or a mix, it never has been defined. She tells me of our journey so very far ahead. I look at her enquiringly as to what I should do next. She sings me a harmonious poem; gives me the code to unlock the door; I'm recalcitrant, weightless, persistent but otherwise perplexed.

The room is cold, the corners dark; the candle flickers, I catch my breath. I repose and ask again; she draws the air inward and recites her version of events. This time I understand the meaning, our willful journey to its satisfactory end. We will have to wait until that time; try as we might, it is a message that I must send. Her face is etched in beauty; a timelessness of calm. Her face is carved in knowledge; an embodiment of reason; an incarnation of time. She takes my right hand and places its palm on hers; we drop our arms to our sides and my heart beats still as I make a solitary wish. I am left with thoughts consistent and without boundary. I am now left alone with no fear, buoyant, willing and in a perpetual state of motion.

Hal's eye lids pulsed as a tap grew firmer and firmer until it was a prod. The repetition pressed into his left arm between the bicep and the bone, guiding him from slumber to observance. A sweet natured voice lulled him to his senses where upon he found a pair of entrancing blue eyes peering into his.

"We're landing in 10 minutes, Mr. Laurence. I thought about waking you when we were serving our morning snack almost half an hour ago."

"We're nearly there? I must have dropped off as soon as I got into my seat."

"You were in so deep that I thought I'd let you rest. You were deliriously repeating the word 'face' which I hoped was in reference to me. I just love your work."

Her voice tailed off, finishing poignantly on the final word. She was tall, blonde, tanned and extremely fit for her late forties. Hal couldn't help notice the lustful way she was looking at him. He smiled sleepily up at her. Unable to think of anything quick or witty to respond with, he decided to remain silent until she ventured further.

"I wonder if I might take a shot of you. Would you sign it? My mother would be so excited to hear who I was attending to. She's been to every one of your Eurafrican exhibitions, tirelessly reading up on your exploits, wherever you go. You'll make an elderly woman very happy."

Hal nodded trying to remain ambivalent. She pointed her cellhip in his direction and smiled for him as she took a picture. She presented him with her stylo whilst thrusting her left wrist in his direction.

"What's your mother's name?"

"Gwen. Oh sorry that's mine. My mother's is Stacey." He hurriedly scrawled a note on the face of her cellhip and signed underneath.

"Well Gwen thank you for being as attentive as I'm sure you were even when I was asleep."

"Are you staying long in Shanghai? Is this a business trip Mr. Laurence?"

"Please call me Hal and yes it is business. How long I'll be here is a different question. I'm not sure."

"Well I hope that it's a success. We're back and forth all the time so if you're ever in need of some Eurafrican banter you know where to look me up." She leaned in and whispered, "I'm on 'noticeable' by the way."

Hal silently acknowledged her overtures with a faint smile and pretended to busy himself with the seatbelt, subconsciously ensuring a safe landing.

The plane taxied across the runway towards the gate. He noticed some storm clouds brewing in the distance. Hoping that this was not a sign of things to come, he busied himself with his cellhip notebook continuing to toss around the ideas that he'd come up with in the park the day before.

He dragged the stylo from left to right, top to bottom toying with the running order of his fledgling creation. He mulled over the photos and paintings already in his collection and the new ideas that he'd recently jotted down. He focused on man's journey through time; from blissful tribesman to confused servant through to conscious statesman. He decided that the timing couldn't have been more pertinent; especially with what he now knew of the second ship and their mission. Man's journey back to the state of being a blissful tribesman held the answer to their survival.

The mark we have today is a burden of our devotion; we remain lost, conflicted and confused until we restore our conviction.

He was one of the first to leave the plane and at the front of the queue heading towards passport control. He was still coming to terms with travelling Daraja whenever he was at the mercy of Analucia and her organisation skills. He wasn't complaining, it was just that he never truly felt worthy of such lavish attention. His ideas and growing political popularity may well have been successful in increasing his notoriety and his balance with his creditry but he still remembered his origins.

As he passed through to the baggage reclaim area he received a call on his cellhip; expecting it to be Laozi, Hal launched into a tirade.

"The airport's virtually empty. Where is everybody? I've got here and it's like a ghost town. You persuade me to come all this way on another one of your flights of fancy…"

"…Hal, it's Analucia, just in case you were about to start using my name in vain. There's been a mix up and I've sent you to the wrong airport. Laozi arrived at Hongqiao an hour ago and you've landed at Pudong over 27 miles away. It's entirely my fault and this meeting is most definitely real. Laozi will meet you at the Royal Court's headquarters. I've sent a driver to pick you up. He should be with you once you clear customs."

"OK, don't worry; it is partly a game with him, you know. He deserves it now and then. The amount of sycophants that swarm around him makes him appreciate those people; those more candid."

"You're right. I guess we all try and stand our ground with him in our own very different ways. Thanks for your understanding. The driver will have your usual placard."

It had almost become a ritual with its format and formality. Hal passed through customs without any further complication and entered the arrival hall. The area was teaming with locals, quite different to baggage reclaim. It was oppressive and disorientating. He couldn't help but notice one group where each individual was the spitting image of the other. Ama had mentioned the over abundance of duplicates in Shanghai and the unabashed way that they had been developed and treated. This only added fuel to his fire. As he sifted through the multitude of screaming people he spotted his name in amongst the placards. The driver niftily took his bags whilst he took a few shots of the ever encroaching throng.

It depends on luck as to their usefulness; but then again sometimes the most rudimentary are the most revealing.

The drive to the Royal Court of Asiana was uneventful but it did give him a chance to look over the photos. One of which was of the 'family' of duplicates, leaning into each other, excitedly smiling. He knew he could use this as a corner piece to his next campaign.

There's enough material in that one shot to provide a litany of grievances against the current regime.

Coupled with his stylo musings the end result was clear in his mind. The revolution was gathering pace once more. He was beginning to enjoy himself again and that could only mean one thing; productivity.

They arrived and penetrated the outer ramparts of the Royal Court's compound. Hal provided the requisite documentation to clear the many levels of security that were deemed necessary. They pulled up outside the main entrance. The austere grey washed walls of the building threatened. He got out of the car unhurriedly. The driver attended to the bags leaving him to make his way to the meeting.

There were two armed guards standing up the steps, either side of a large virtual barrier. He sensed that there was an electrical current sealing the entrance. He made his way up the steps and as he approached it visibly subsided. There was little else in the way of foliage or decoration as he crossed over casually, stepping into the building not wanting to give off any air of concern. A long thin red carpet led him around a huge courtyard towards the other side of the building. He heard the low tones of hushed voices. As he rounded the corner the murmur grew louder, gradually extending into a discussion.

"Hal, glad you could join us; it's about time everyone got to meet you." Laozi stepped back away from the huddle, turning to welcome him with a smile. Given the circumstances and location, Hal merely nodded in his direction.

"Gentlemen, it is an honour to be here, however I am still very much in the dark as to the real reason as I'm certain that it has little to do with my day job."

A small, slightly built man of Chinese origin, besuited and well groomed stepped away from the group.

"May I introduce you to the Secretary of State for China, Hu Taolang?" Laozi jumped in maintaining the formalities. Taolang turned to face Hal, nodding gently, acknowledging his presence. He allowed a moment of silence to pass before he spoke ensuring that he maintained the upper hand using pure unbroken English, no doubt learned at a university not too dissimilar to Laozi's.

"In answer to your statement, yes and no; put plainly, your vision is what attracted us to you. Your benefactor has played a keen part in doing so. The commission we have in mind should be of great interest. But first, we should all meet properly in less formal surroundings, to see if what Mr. Veda says is true."

Hal nodded in response but remained silent. He appreciated the situation. A few of the other dignitaries spoke in hushed tones to each other. The group disbanded leaving Laozi and Hal standing on the red carpet.

"Walk with me." Laozi beckoned him with his hand, heading for the main archway into the courtyard. "I'm sorry that I wasn't at the airport, yet it turned out to be quite fortuitous as it happens. I got here in good time to discuss a number of things before your arrival. You know how I hate projection conferencing."

"I guessed as much. It came as no surprise; the clandestine meetings, withheld candour, hushed voices; sums up the usual amount of intrigue I expect from you, these days."

"You'll be in the dark no longer Hal. It is only light that I hope to shed. A little more patience and we'll get there. I am certain of it."

"The semanticist speaks. It's like taking the tour of an obscure crypt with you. However you'll be pleased to know that the knowledge of Ama's safety has set me free."

He allowed a smile to escape his lips.

"That is exceptionally good news. However you need to focus on this commission. I suggest you follow that member of staff and be shown to your room. Your bags will already be there. Freshen up and we'll resume in an hour over dinner."

Laozi pointed in the direction of a man dressed in black trousers and a white jacket, standing in the north east archway. Without any further riposte they headed in opposite directions. A selection of nightjars hummed the first notes of a chorus, almost in time with their footsteps. Hal serenely followed the man out of the main chamber and towards a lift bank. Not a word passed between them.

Once they reached the fourth floor they turned right and followed another dark red carpet, passing door after door; differing in style, shape and age. They continued on through what felt like a maze. With each twist and turn the experience felt more and more surreal as if he was being put to the test by some hidden group.

Abruptly they stopped. They stood still for a while staring at a large dark red wooden door. Hal was about to say something when the door opened. A prism of the evening's last rays was cast into the hallway, engulfing the two men. Without a word the man motioned for him to enter. Hal obeyed the silent instruction and proceeded into the room. The door closed behind him.

Inside he was welcomed by one of the most luxurious and high concept guest rooms he had ever stayed in. It was as if he was in a hotel that had been designed for him, by him. It was a suite of magnificent proportions with a terrace looking out onto yet another internal garden within the compound. Every detail had been thought of with its blend of dark woods from England, the minimalism of Denmark and the Italian soft furnishings. Hal was taken aback. They were obviously trying to impress him; to win him over. For what exactly, he was not so sure. The commission intrigued him more than ever given that they had gone to such great lengths. The art on the walls, the books on the shelves, the ultra modern technology courtesy of Vedas Corporation; it was more than a fleeting visit that they had planned.

He sat back on a huge bed covered in Egyptian cotton and looked up at the ceiling. There was a huge glass dome in the middle giving unlimited access to the sky and beyond. Transfixed by the firmament above, he forgot his meeting momentarily and leant back against the pillow to watch the dark shades of night wrap their cloak over the sun's final few flashes.

As he lay there night fell and the stars became brilliant almost instantaneously. He noticed the magnificent power of the glass above him. Whichever direction he focused in on, he found that he was able to zoom in naturally as if the glass was responding to his gaze. While he looked upon constellation after constellation the corresponding information in regards to its name, longitude and latitude would spring up on the ceiling above. There were even artists' impression of its shape and reference. Once he'd locked in on the constellation of Taurus, it dawned on him as to the purpose of the room and why he had been chosen. Mars loomed in the distance. The dome provided him with the omniscience of an all-seeing eye.

Realising the time, he jumped up from the bed and grabbed his wash bag from his suitcase. In the bathroom he set the shower to lukewarm to stir him from his trance. Once refreshed and clean clothed he left his room with five minutes to spare.

The man was outside as if he had not moved an inch since Hal had first stepped inside. He was glad as there would have no way that he would have been able to pick his way out of the maze. Turning left they reached a lift bank almost immediately, entered and then descended to the ground floor. They appeared in the main lobby which confused him even more.

The main section of the building was a different place to the one that he had left an hour earlier. Excited scurrying members of staff headed in many directions and the amber glow of the evening lights beckoned him into the uncovered walking area. He thought it prudent that he wait to be called. He stood earnestly looking at the assortment of trees and plants which had been growing for hundreds, if not thousands, of years. It wasn't long before he was again joined by Laozi, who looked resplendent, all in white.

"I don't know what's going on here. It's extremely surreal; like I'm caught up in a beautiful nightmare. I don't suppose for one second that you're going to help with proceedings."

"They've taken a lot of care in making you feel at home. You should at least be thankful that your hosts have gone to such great lengths to ensure your stay is successful, no matter how fleeting or protracted."

"Fleeting? Protracted? What have they in store Laozi?"

"All in good time; all in good time."

A few minutes later Hu Taolang and three others joined them in the courtyard. Each person covertly approached in unison from a different section of the garden. Laozi reintroduced him to Taolang and formally presented him to the Secretary for Scientific Affairs from the World Council and then to a quantum physicist at Vedas Corp. The other person, a woman, seemed to hang back and not wish to be introduced. Hal was immediately fascinated by this little scenario. Almost forgetting the importance of whom and why he was there.

The group stood posturing only a few seconds as a member of staff quietly crept up on them. They were ushered towards a corpulent and empty space which had the appearance of a banqueting hall. Everyone followed except for the Vedas Corp scientist who disappeared. In the far corner there was a raised dais and a table laid out in the form of a circular booth. The five of them proceeded through the join of the banquette and shuffled round, two either side. The silent woman slipped in behind Hal and to his left.

"Well now that we are all here and not wishing to make our guest any more disorientated than he already is, we should get to the point as quickly as we can." Laozi led the way trying to carve a route to the punch.

"How do you like your room? Is it to your liking?" The lady from the World Council spoke first.

"It's fantastic, out of this world, but cutting to the chase, I need to know a little more about what is going on here. So far I've been led along a thin red line which becomes more and more convoluted every way I turn."

"The secrecy of this meeting had to be absolute." The silent woman abruptly interrupted. "No one can ever know what we are about to tell you. We have made special provision against you being followed. From here on in you are to have no communication with the outside world. Not until we are certain of your suitability. Do you have your cellhip on you?"

"I do."

"Do you have any other components in your room?"

"Just my notebook and stylo."

The woman beckoned a member of staff over and whispered into his ear. He listened intently for a few seconds and then scurried off.

"We will need those. Please." She thrust out the upside of her palm and flicked her fingers towards herself, in a clinical demonstration of power and control. Hal immediately responded with a slight glance at Laozi, searching for an intervention. He reached into his pocket, took out his cellhip and placed it on the table in front of her. He flicked his head towards his left shoulder and took out the responder from his left ear. Afterwards he rested his hands back on the table in front of him.

He was a willing listener. It certainly wasn't the usual commission briefing. Although one could have viewed the meeting as having sinister undertones, Hal accepted that there were none. He had already suspected that this was a political play, not a social one. There was silence for a minute or so. The member of staff returned with his notebook and stylo. They were placed on the table in front of the woman, next to his cellhip. She picked each one up and ensured that they were all switched off. She looked at everyone else around the table. They all nodded.

Taolang broke into a smile for the first time.

"Gentlemen, now that we are all in cahoots we are able to bring Mr. Laurence up to speed."

Everyone at the table visibly relaxed. He turned to look directly at Hal and continued.

"May I call you Hal? You can call me Hu and the lady to my left Kalpana; you know Laozi well enough and the woman to your left is known as Winifred."

"Nice to meet you all properly, at last." Hal paid particular attention to stress the end of his sentence in Winifred's direction. Hu moved on quickly.

"Good. We understand that Laozi has divulged a certain amount of information. Some of which has entered the public domain and some of which has not."

"You're referring to the Kepler Meeting and the Repertega I take it."

"We are. No doubt you are thinking what this all has to do with you."

"That is correct."

"Well this is no ordinary commission. We are not sat here because we want you to put together a show on behalf of the Royal Court, if that is what you are thinking."

"Yet that was the pretence with which I was brought here under."

"This meeting is to ascertain your suitability for a project. You might be the final piece in a jigsaw which we started putting together a long time ago. You have been under surveillance for quite some time. Please treat the next questions with a certain degree of understanding as we need to ensure that you are who you say you are. Every one of us has been through similar tests, in similar circumstances. Over to you Winifred."

"2nd April 2110, where were you born?

"Truro, Cornwall but on Monday 1st April 2109."

"Your father, Hector Laurence, the famous historian and stoic was committed to exploring the origin of our mark."

"He was."

"His final lecture, on the subject of cosmic philosophy hung on what principle?"

"That ignorance is bliss, where mankind has spent too much time thinking, reasoning and deliberating over who is right and wrong; resulting in thousands of years wasted fighting the nature of divinity whilst destroying our natural resources instead of giving in to nature and our natural instincts."

"Your mother is originally from Denmark. Where exactly?

"She was actually born in Cuxhaven in Northern Germany to Danish parents. They moved to Copenhagen when she was 3 years old."

"Have you ever duplicated?"

"Never."

"Have you ever slept with a duplicate?"

"Not to my knowledge."

"Can you think of any reason as to why you might have been duplicated without your consent?"

"None at all. I am a Mid-Termer with limited physical attributes and an inquisitive mind. I am neither ignorant nor blissful. Not a good subject for duplication; too many questions; too much creativity."

"You have political persuasions and your output reflects that. What is your understanding of Kepler and its importance to us here on Earth?"

"Kepler is Earth only light years away. It is neither forward nor backwards in time. They are a people, a collective that have no mark. I am of the opinion that they are hiding something. You have sent a ship, the Repertega to find out."

"You are an artist primarily but it is through your commentary as a social scientist that we find ourselves drawn into your world. Putting mankind's evolution to the mark to one side, where do you think we will find our cure?"

"There is no obvious explanation and the answer lies within all of us not just on Kepler. If it means travelling to Kepler to get answers, so be it, but mankind needs to look within not outwards for a solution."

"Do you know anyone on the Repertega?"

"I haven't seen a list, so I have no idea. How many people are aboard? I know little about the mission only that Laozi referred to a second ship yesterday." Winifred sat back and looked in the Secretary of State's direction. "I think it best if you take it from here Hu."

Taolang leaned forward and spoke directly to him.

"We will give you the full details later but Laozi has already confirmed that you know a Benedikt Voegel and no one else."

"If he says so, without seeing a roster I can't say either way."

"The Repertega is a ship containing over 2,000 people from Earth with the sole intention of facilitating peaceful integration into Keplerian society. The people aboard are to study the customs and lives of everyone and everything on the planet. They touched down yesterday."

"What does this have to do with me?"

"We have an offer for you; one which we think would be hard for you to refuse. Laozi has briefed us on your background, interests and ideas. We have followed your work closely for some time. We also know that being 37 years old and with less than five years to live you have a burgeoning desire to do something extraordinary; something that could change our course forever."

Hu looked at Hal for a while. Finally he turned to his left.

"Kalpana, would you care to explain to him what it is exactly that we have created. Please keep it succinct."

Kalpana took over swiftly and in a manner that was well rehearsed.

"I take it that you understand the mechanics behind space travel? How we have been able to reach Kepler within a year?"

"I do. Ever since the Kepler Broadcast, it has rarely been from my mind."

"We purposely built a ship that fitted to Keplerian requirements."

"Interesting. So were you contacted by them a long time ago?"

"It wasn't only a few years ago, if that's what you are thinking."

"So I'm meant to keep this to myself?"

"That is correct. Moving on; with five years left to live, we wouldn't imagine that you would like to waste a year travelling."

"To be honest if it was to get to Kepler, I would be all for it."

Everyone at the table all looked at each other and smiled. *I must have passed the test by now.* Hal thought to himself and relaxed a little, settling into the conversation. Kalpana continued.

"As I've already made clear we built a ship to Keplerian standards. This gave way to our decision that if they are holding back information given that they must have done this before, we should withhold a little information as well."

"Go on."

"We needed someone we could trust with little to lose but who understood the reasons for our mission entirely. We did not want a gung-ho military type nor a science professional. The Repertega contains a number of very talented souls but they have one missing link; belief."

"How have I shown myself to be any different? I've only commented on society today and how we all must change, me included."

"It was Laozi who brought it to our attention. You may not remember but we were all in attendance at your break out exhibition in London. It was plain to see in your vision and creativity but most of all in your words. We have followed your career studiously, sticking to Laozi's wise guidance."

"That's extremely flattering. However I'm still in the dark as to what you require of me."

"To put it bluntly we've created a portal to Tega. This is the secret that we have been hiding from the Keplerians. If they were to discover its existence our entire mission would be ruined. They have categorically defined the terms of our integration, based on one ship in and one ship out. No other methods allowed. We have adhered to their instructions to the letter, except for this minor detail."

"A portal? Isn't that dangerous, on so many levels? What if it fell into the wrong hands?"

"How glad we are to hear you say that. Your primary concerns are Security, Secrecy and Sensitivity. Your sensitivity towards other people and cultures is well documented, you have proven to Laozi your ability in keeping secrets and now we know of your interest in security. Your true worth and value is plain to see. Thank you."

Hu, Kalpana and Winifred all looked at each other smiling, leaving Hal little option but to realise that he had now passed the test. Laozi at last broke his silence.

"Well done. To follow up on your question and without getting technical,

101

Vedas Corp developed the portal technology a few years ago. Since then we have been successful in transporting duplicates, rats, mice and other animate objects to all corners of the globe. The stipulation being that there is a receiver at the other end and that it is stationary."

"So you haven't been able to test it in space given that space is in perpetual motion."

"Correct, you catch on quick for a creative." Laozi winked at Hal. "The sending station or transmitter, known as Reper, is here on the fourth floor of this building, close to your suite. However we haven't tested the receiver on a natural human before nor have we sent one from one part of the universe to another."

Silence descended on everyone as they thought about the prospect. Laozi paused contemplatively in unison and then continued.

"However a question burns, one that we have no way of telling the outcome. It is the issue of whether one's soul is transferred along with the body when you step through that portal."

Hal winced at the thought.

"We know that the technology works but we've never been in this position before. We need the right person willing to give it a go; who, if successful, can be trusted on the other side to ensure its secrecy. Benedikt Voegel is the only person on board who knows of its existence and holds the receiver key. The code is his mark, ensuring no one else can activate it from the other side."

Hal shifted uncomfortably in his seat and responded.

"Right. OK. Hmm... Please allow me to digest for a moment... Perhaps if I take a walk around the gardens to clear the mind, I'll come back with some pertinent questions rather than pure anxiety."

Laozi again spoke for the others.

"Of course take your time. How about 30 minutes respite?"

"No problem. I'll return in good time and thank you all for this interesting opportunity."

Winifred moved out of the banquette allowing Hal to pass. He didn't look at any of them nor even glance at his cellhip devices. He walked steadily towards the archway and out of the banqueting hall until he reached the courtyard. He crossed over to the gardens where the nightjars were still singing along to the dark sky. He looked upwards searching for the resolve to give them a definitive response. He had minutes to come up with his questions; to which he already had more than one answer.

Chapter 13

So it's never been tested on a human before. It needs to be stationary. Voegel, the prick, is the only one who holds the key.

I could die in the process. That would be interesting. Would I know? What do I do when I get there? Nothing of Ama has been mentioned. I presume Laozi wants it kept that way. They are certainly unaware of any ulterior motive on my part.

Will I ever return? Like choosing certain death now, rather than when it has been predetermined. The promise of a short afterlife is interesting, very interesting. What of my commitments?

How ironic. I might have to die to live. Dying is a part of life. If I leave here and go somewhere else my life carries on but just in an altered state; a higher state of consciousness perhaps? Surely as energy grows in one part of the universe, it diminishes elsewhere. It's infinitely finite.

If I'm conscious, I'm alive. If I'm not conscious but dreaming then I'm still alive. So we're alive when dead. The afterlife is just a dream. I guess there's only one way to find out. At least I'd be the first to try.

Standing in the courtyard, mind racing, Hal found it difficult to focus. The proposition played over and over. He could hardly hear himself think. Pacing up and down the gardens, he zeroed in on the practical things such as leaving his family and friends without as much as a goodbye. He thought of his exhibitions, commissions and intended lectures; everything that he was booked in to make. He hated letting anyone down.

In the end there was an air of inevitability but he still had questions that needed answering. He took out a pack of Marlboro No. 5's and tapped the top side of the box in his familiar style. A member of staff appeared out of the shadows and lit the cigarette. He drew in deeply, blowing out the first plumes of smoke in the direction of the stars.

Moments later he approached the raised dais and stepped up in between the banquette. He leant into the booth maintaining an ambivalent air.

"Send me to my maker."

Hu Taolang was the first to respond.

"The look on your face doesn't give anything away. Does this mean that you accept?"

"Yes."

Laozi clapped his hands together in satisfaction.

"However, as you might well have guessed, I come armed with a consignment of questions."

"Fire away." Laozi jumped in, unable to hide his approval.

"Focusing on the practical; why exactly do you need me to go through the portal, what is my role and how do I explain myself to be aboard Tega?"

"Pertinent points, I think Laozi is best placed to handle these." Hu deferred.

"The timing is perfect. You will arrive just as those aboard leave for their allotted kingdoms. They should have been made aware of their intended new homes by now. They are currently acclimatising to their new surroundings within the confines of Tega. Rather than pore over the details, the specialists onboard are divided into nine departments; of which Voegel is the head of the Department for Art & Music."

Laozi looked at Hal defying him to interrupt with a mention of Ama, but he was equal to the task and remained silent.

"The chiefs, as they are known, will be the last to leave as they will assign each specialist to a town or village within their allotted kingdom on the final day. Reasons for which, I don't have time to expand on right now. The quarantine period lasts for two weeks. This gives you the same amount of time to read up, train with our linguists and prepare for your journey; albeit that your passage will be instantaneous. Voegel will unlock the portal before he departs."

Laozi flippantly added,

"A philosopher from the Department of Cosmology & Philosophy mysteriously never made it on board the Repertega. We have ensured that no one has been made aware of his absence. You will take his place. Your name is Liam Self."

Without batting an eyelid, Hal dove straight in,

"OK. That seems logical. But really, come on all of you, other than being a guinea pig, why me? What's my real mission? You wouldn't have gone to so much trouble just to test a portal unless you had something specific planned."

Laozi continued, unfazed.

"It's twofold really. The first part is to fit in and assume your new identity. You'll be assigned to a town in the kingdom of Utsima. You'll consider local Keplerian customs. Your background knowledge and ideas will serve you well. Meanwhile there will be research conducted by everyone into the origin of our mark with a view to finding a cure."

"That I understand. It makes sense; a little sinister, given that I've been watched for so long, without knowing, but satisfying all the same; yet why the portal?"

"It's insurance for the safety of the entire population of Tega. However I suspect that that will not suffice in an argument with you. There is no point hiding the fact that this device has been designed to ensure the safe and speedy delivery of a cure to the mark. If we are correct that the cure is not physical but a mental therapy then we need a vessel of the right mind to carry it back to earth."

"I see."

"A lot to take in I imagine." Winifred joined in, "Due to the sensitivity of this information we are buying into the trust that you and Laozi have built up over a long period of time. If the transmission is successful, you will be the one person on Kepler in possession of all the facts. You will be crucial to the safety of the entire mission. Once you are on Tega, a second key will be activated to access the portal in the future. This will be your breath extracted from one full exhale. Voegel will not be informed of the alternative key."

"It all makes perfect sense to me. How will I communicate with you once I'm on the other side?"

"The Department for Security has a patching system. However it is under heavy surveillance and is only there as a last resort. You will travel with a specially designed self charging cellhip which has a signal that works within a radius of 14,000 miles of Tega. This will bypass the Department for Security's receivers and use the mainframe as a transmitter to the space station at the gateway. All text and voice messages will be encrypted."

"Fine; well that leaves only one query left. Where I think the question should at least be begged, given that I am about to put my own mortality to the test; can I contact my family and close friends prior to departure?"

Kalpana, Hu and Winifred all looked to Laozi.

"Unfortunately this will not be possible. Those aboard the Repertega all went through a similar scenario a year ago."

Laozi looked at him with added sincerity so that no one else could understand about what he was implying.

"I will have to notify your family of your disappearance the day after your departure. If the transmission is not successful, we will obviously report back your premature death to your mother and brother as a result of an accident here in Shanghai. If your body neither makes it through nor is left behind we will attribute it to a plane crash out at sea.

He pressed on, changing tack with a more upbeat tempo.

"However when the transmission is successful and you have made it through intact you will report back to me. Your cellhip will only have two accessible contacts - me and Winifred. I would like a weekly call and monthly reports, no exceptions. Winifred is there as added security should anything happen to me. Kalpana and Hu are the only other two who know the exact details of this mission. This will remain so. If you are successful and return to a changed world but with neither Winifred nor I here, you know who to look up."

The table fell silent. Hal digested whilst everyone else sat still, contemplating his reaction. After a while it was he who broke the peace.

"Well everyone, I think that is plenty enough for one evening. I don't know about you but I'm exhausted. I certainly have a lot to think about. One thing is for sure I feel well informed and that is a seismic difference to the last 18 months; it's damn good to be involved."

He got up from his seat and gave a slight bow to his audience. He backed away bidding them all a good night. As he stepped down the dais he heard Laozi tell him that they would have breakfast on Hal's terrace in the morning.

At 7am there was a light rap on the door. He was already awake, washed and dressed; ready for the day ahead. In fact he had been most of the night. With the aid of the telescopic glass he'd stared upon the constellation of Scorpius, his mind racing. It had been relentless.

"Come." Hal ventured in a commanding voice. There was a moment or two of silence and the door opened. Laozi breezed in as if it was still the night before.

"Good morning; a very good morning indeed. I hope you managed to get some rest. It must have been some evening. I'm sorry that I couldn't brief you before. We now only have your successful passage through the portal, the peaceful integration of the specialists and the research and possible exposé left to carry out."

"No pressure then."

"You have 12 days left to ensure that you are ready. Your crash course in Keplerian starts this afternoon. I have a head start on you. When I was a child I studied Sanskrit. Strange how life comes round to revisit you."

"Laozi I'd like to clear one thing up before we go any further. I realise now that I have misdirected my anger and suspicions. Being in possession of all the facts is not only very liberating but also empowering. Thank you for your belief in me as I owe you everything."

The emotional circumstances seemed to get the better of both of them. Laozi walked over and squeezed his arm in an affectionate manner.

"I had faith in you from the start. It was only a matter of time. Now that we are on our own, I want to talk to you about Ama."

"I'm glad you brought her up. I'm not to mention her or our relationship to anyone right?"

"Correct. Only Benedikt knows. We spent most of last year trying to cover it up"

"Understood."

With that they walked out onto the terrace. They sat down at a large wooden table, already laid ready for a breakfast that would soon be forthcoming. The morning sun slowly descended the inside of the western wall of the compound. The uninspiring grey wash appeared bright white in its brilliance.

"Have you heard of Ra?" Laozi asked as he pulled a napkin off the table, placing it carefully about his midriff.

"Did the glare make you think of that?"

"It did. It's applicable bearing in mind what you are about to go through."

"If it's of any consolation, I've already given my intended journey much thought. Most of the night in truth; one of my biggest quandaries is centred around the sun. Ra was a god, if not the most important god to the ancient Egyptians over 4,000 years ago. He was the creator of life and naturally represented light, warmth and growth. Forgetting his many offspring for a minute, the Egyptians believed that he was self created. So using this theory Ra is the sun and is God. He is the beginning, the middle and the end."

"Go on."

"The Kepler Real system has its own sun and so do the countless other solar systems that make up the universe. If that's the case then the sun is not the creator but an intrinsic part of a pack of creators who all fall under one superior being - the universe. So if I were to go along with this theory then it'd follow suit the universe is female, the sun female and the planets male."

"How on Earth did you get to there?"

"Simple really; the universe is a giant womb; the suns are the ovaries and the planets the sperm. There's only one living planet in each solar system that we know of which is the strongest surviving spermatozoon and so therefore the solar system is in actual fact the gamete, otherwise known as the product of fertilization. Any other solar systems with more suns or living planets, or both, are simply either monozygotic or dizygotic gametes."

"Interesting theory; drink much coffee this morning?"

"No need. The prospect of losing one's soul is a natural amphetamine. If this is the case, isn't there something bigger carrying the universe; marsupials have multiple wombs, don't they? Seriously, it's more likely to be a tree or a plant on an even larger planet in an entirely larger universe and so on. The crux is that the superior being or God is at the top of the tree as there is an infinitely finite point where universe within plant within uterus and so on stops. I could get lost out there forever."

"I see where you are going with this. I understand your nerves. It's makes absolute sense for you to have fear. You're on to something quite unfathomable but you need to rein it in. Once you're on Kepler, I'm sure that the answers will be forthcoming. They've had far more experience."

"What makes you so sure?"

"Just take it from me that that is the case. Surely the fact that we built the Repertega to Keplerian standards must give some bearing to the magnitude of their existence?"

"Sure. So when do I get to see Reper?"

"It's hard to keep up with you sometimes."

They finished breakfast and then the training began. After his first day he was exhausted, passing out fully clothed face down on his bed without even enough energy to dream. The next day he began his study of the people of Kepler, the kingdoms, culture, interests and their history. He became increasingly aware that the Keplerians were holding back a lot of information; if they weren't then they were centuries behind Earth, rather than ahead, which did not corroborate with their obvious lack of surprise when initially contacted via a large rectangular box from outer space.

The daily routine had been mapped out for him where he easily absorbed the nature of the Keplerians; picking up on their points of reference in regards to their evolution as a culture and as a collective. He was never late for his date with the language doctor. Histories and scientific theories paled in comparison to being able to converse directly with the Keplerians. As the excitement of reaching his decision subsided and the information overload became more fathomable he started to feel apprehensive. He was itching to see Ama and to pick up from where they had left off. Albeit that he knew it wouldn't be quite so simple.

By the Wednesday of the second week he felt far better prepared than he would have hoped for. His language skills had increased dramatically. Laozi was due to return to the compound the next day and Hal decided that he would miss his next language class and take dinner with him in the banqueting hall instead.

That evening Laozi appeared in the courtyard accompanied by a scientist.

"May I properly introduce you to Kal Aryabhatta? Kal will be the one taking you through your last few days of training where he will introduce you to the wonderful world of quantum physics. "

Hal took his hand and shook it firmly whilst maintaining eye contact for perhaps a little too long.

"So you're the man in charge of Reper; the executioner or soul destroyer. You do look very familiar. Have we met before?"

"You may find it strange to begin with but I am in fact Kalpana's duplicate. I have been in charge of Vedas Corp's Space Science Division for seven years."

Hal endeavoured to act unsurprised. The mind raced while the lips moved.

"My apologies for not noticing but then again what's my apology worth? I'm intrigued to hear more about Reper and what it is going to do to my body as I'm transported"

Kal zeroed in on the game in hand.

"Your body is the easy part; it is your mind that you have to take care of. More on that later but I'm glad that we have been formerly introduced. I'll start by giving you an introduction to the study of the physical phenomena of microscopic scales. I will take you through the process of passing through the portal. I will describe the interactions of energy and matter which will take place within your body."

"You mention it as easily as eating a bowl of muesli. I'm a creative so the facts will probably get seriously merged with fiction. However I do have my own theories on matter and energy. You will have a willing audience."

"Good. I'll leave you both now. I look forward to seeing you again - tomorrow at 9am."

With that Kal took Hal's right hand with his left, placing the palm on his right hand for a moment or two then relaxed both his arms by his side. He gave a slight bow and left. Hal's lessons on Keplerian customs had obviously sunk in as this entire exchange was done seamlessly without provocation from either party.

Hal and Laozi proceeded to the banqueting hall. The raised dais had gone and the large open space was full of vigour and life. The entire hall was packed with small circular booths. They approached the entrance and a member of staff dressed in a royal blue jacket and trousers showed them to their table. The booth was in the far corner by the window. As they sat down Hal spoke tentatively trying out his Keplerian for the first time. Whenever he either failed with his vocabulary or if there wasn't a word that corresponded in the first place, he used the English word to fill in the gaps.

"I have a few questions for you; some of which will be rhetorical but at least it will start our conversation off in the right direction."

"Of course, please go ahead."

"I would like to explore the significance of the timing of my departure. In precisely four days time Mars will be passing through the Constellation of Aries for the first time in two years. I am an Aries born on the 1st April. You have referred to me as a messenger; a vessel to transport the cure back to Earth. Aries was viewed by many as a messenger. Isn't it apt that Mars is the ruler of Aries in old world mythology, seeing as I am to venture past Mars and beyond?"

"The significance has not been lost on us. It is entirely by design."

"I'm intrigued by the history of the Kepler Real System. We have not been provided with information as to when the planet came into being.

Laozi responded fluently and in a manner that demonstrated a mother tongue, rather than one that had been learned in a short space of time.

"I can't give answers to things that I do not know but I can tell you that Kepler's angle of tilt, towards their sun is that of 28 degrees rather than the 23.4 degrees of Earth's obliquity. This gives rise to far more temperate seasons with longer summer and shorter winter days in the higher latitudes. What's more, their moon is half the size of ours."

"OK, so like George Darwin's theory that Earth and the moon had once been one body. The planet that collided with Kepler in its early stages of formation broke up without destroying it. So in a similar way to our formation, the gravitational pull of the planet's rotation around the sun, sucked in the fragments of this other planet, forming the moon in an elliptical shape similar to ours. I see, so if their moon is smaller, the planet that originally collided with Kepler was smaller than Theia which collided with ours."

"I would counter as for their obliquity to be more pronounced then surely their 'Theia' would have had to have been larger, given that they are a larger planet than Earth and their tilt is more pronounced?"

Hal smiled, realising that he was onto something.

"OK, One final thing before we order and revert back to English. I note that the Keplerians are stuck in an equivalent late 19th Century for a reason. It must be out of choice."

Laozi responded in English.

"Correct. Your Keplerian isn't that bad either. I am impressed."

"Thank you. Can we order? I'm starving."

The food came and went while the discussion oscillated between light joviality and seriousness; none more so than when they discussed Ama and what Hal was allowed to and not to do. He reluctantly agreed with Laozi that he wouldn't make contact with her. As they finished the last of the wine Laozi became rueful and nostalgic. He reflected on their past together; the arguments and their many successes. They both knew that this would most probably be the last time that they would see each other. Standing up in unison, they walked towards the courtyard. Hal broke the silence.

"It's like I'm on death row heading for my final exit."

"A strange feeling indeed, like I'm losing a very dear nephew. I have faith in you. You have nothing to fear."

"Laozi, you have guided me through the dark times, elevated me through the lean times and sustained me through the bleak times. It is now my turn to repay the favour. I will gladly go through with this."

"Keep your countenance at all times and find a solution to our problem here on Earth. Good luck and let's speak when you're on the other side."

With that Laozi turned and retreated to the shadows of the garden leaving him full of apprehension. He made his way back to his suite seeking out a piece of paper. Finding one, he sat and wrote a letter to his mother by hand; something that he hadn't done since he was young boy. He made no mention of his intended journey or his role in a scheme of such grand design. He simply wrote from the depths of his heart regarding his family, past and present, and most of all the importance of her to him.

When he finished, he folded the paper over and wrote out her address with the reference 'by hand'. He knew that it would find its way to her via Laozi. He slept soundly.

As the sun rose on his final morning three days later he was already awake and petrified. His debrief with Hu, Kalpana and Winifred the evening before had added to his disquiet, as they jostled to get across their one sided points of view. It had been exhausting. He got out of bed, dressing in the dark blue cotton garments that had been laid out for him. His backpack was already crammed full and sitting near the door. He'd spent the best part of the day before ensuring that his sea, mountain and jungle gear were all in order. He was going to wear his beloved lace up Chameau's.

He killed the hours of the morning by putting the finishing touches to a painting which he'd started two weeks before; 'Duplication: The Necessary Twin'. He stood it up against the wall on his bed. The family of Asianians stared back at him as if saying farewell but not goodbye.

He arrived in the Reper station precisely as Kal had stipulated. He was not to step through the portal until exactly 1400 hrs. He had no desire to be late. As he stepped into the room his fear was palpable and Kal endeavoured to keep him calm by repeating the scientific facts based around the transmission. Their banter over the preceding few days had grown into a warm friendship. As the clock ticked ever closer Kal advised,

"Your body will endure a dramatic and instantaneous transition. So will all of your accessories. You must keep a clear mind and remain constant."

Hal stepped nervously towards the portal, furtively looking at the clock. It was 2pm. It was time. He stepped inside. As he did so, he grabbed Kal's arm, flipping it over to look at the mark.

"How can you know what it is like to do such a thing? For all your design you will never know. Your fancy chat in respect to everything being inherently random; that it is physically impossible to know both the position and the momentum of a particle at the same time, is all fair and well, but unfortunately it doesn't help me with what I am about to do. I stand by my view that when energy grows in one part of the universe, it diminishes somewhere else. That it is infinitely finite."

"It has been an honour knowing you Hansel Laurence. Good luck and I hope that we meet again."

Reper stirred into action, encasing him in a white-blue light. For a split second Hal felt completely at one with the Universe. Then, just like that moment, he was gone.

If I'm conscious I'm alive. If I'm not conscious but dreaming, I'm still alive. So we're alive when dead and the afterlife is just a dream. The mark is the embodiment of mankind's consciousness. So we need to return to our past to get to our future.

Chapter 14

The reporting system had been clinically designed. Each chief had been given a self charging cellhip notebook which linked only with the Department for Security's server. Although the knowledge had been kept quiet on board Tega, the chiefs had also all been assigned to the capital city of their respective kingdom. The system dictated that every one of the specialists would put together a brief monthly report based on their discoveries, no matter how obscure. Every month these would be posted and delivered to the main council buildings in the capital city of their respective kingdoms. Thereafter the chiefs would analyse, write and image record a summary of these reports sending them back to Laozi via Tega and the main computer.

Back on Earth, Laozi had assumed the role of a consultant to the World Council acting as the Secretary for Keplerian Affairs; on the proviso that he would not be coerced into having to make decisions on international policies nor fit within the brief of their regime. He had stipulated from the outset that he would only take on the role for a short period; only as a matter of courtesy. His view was that the World Council needed to be kept abreast of new developments in order for them not to interfere with any new developments. It was a ruse to keep them at an arm's length from anything that was actually going on. He was to feed them only the information of little consequence. His belief was because he held the majority stake in the expedition he also had the most to lose. He had no desire for politics to get in the way of such a sensitive mission.

One of the main pieces of information which he had shared with the World Council at their last meeting was that a common language had been found between the visitors and the people of Kepler. Many of the words that didn't exist in Keplerian now existed in a bastardised version based on a mixture of the nearest two corresponding words and the English phrasing. One of these colloquialisms was that an Earth human was now known as a Prithvian. It had a ring to it and once everyone had started to adopt the local clothes and customs, many of the specialists appeared no different to their hosts. Their height, skin, hair colour and even their mannerisms were very similar. It was only the mark that set them apart.

A message pinged as it hit the in-tray rousing Laozi from his daydream.

He'd been waiting for this report for quite some time, so breathed a sigh of relief. The anticipation of getting word from Kepler had far outweighed the importance of a lunch meeting with Akihiro Iso. With its arrival he could now make alternative plans.

Ever since the specialists had all set off for their respective kingdoms little news of note had been returned. There had been no reported problems with the Prithvians. There had been no real intelligence as to how they were settling in to their respective homes. In fact there hadn't been reports of political or social unrest from any of the nine kingdoms. Laozi was surprised given that it had been over three months since the Repertega had landed. However his monthly reports had kept on coming through in one format or another. Today was no different; except for the fact that the sender was purporting to have found a cure and that the messenger was not one of his usual nine. He looked at the projection above him in excitement.

October – Uttara, Kepler

Last week came with the sad news of a Prithvian passing. Apparently she was involved in an accident in Adhara; something to do with faulty farm machinery. We cannot be certain due to the fact that news travels slowly on Kepler. The sheer size of the continent and the relatively under populated kingdoms, coupled with the notion that we still bizarrely only use their modes of transport means that life remains at a constant but un-frenetic pace. However we all paid our respects at the allotted time; apparently this was the same for every village, town and city across every kingdom. Everyone gathered in the meadow in the centre where what can only be described as a festival of life takes place on the last Friday of every month.

As you know I am in the town of Maya and it was no different to what I hear happens everywhere across the land. All 48 million people turned and faced due west at their respective sunsets. The crowd chanted the most beautiful song I'd ever heard in the direction of the descending sun. When the reflection had made its final descent down the sides of the buildings and cascaded through the trees, turning their leaves from lime to dark green and the last rays of light had disappeared for another day, they placed their arms beside them in a similar fashion as to how they finish their greeting then stopped singing.

The elders of the community, all former leaders, languidly unfurled a huge scroll and placed it on a large stone table in the centre of the meadow. Apparently the scroll is a list containing the names of those who had passed away over the preceding month. The crowd turned to their leader who paused for dramatic effect. She curled the list back up and placed it in, what can only be described as, a cross between an enormous Chinese lantern and a hot air balloon.

She lit a giant candle within its bellows and let the lantern rise up into the sky, taking the scroll with it in an attached under basket. Once it reached a certain point it stopped as it was attached to a guide rope; it tightened to a full strain. The leader lit the bottom of the rope and the chanting began again in earnest. Flames licked upwards increasing in ferocity and speed as they drew closer to the under basket. Once they'd reached their intended destination the entire balloon was engulfed and the chanting stopped once again. There was a pause highlighted by an expectant hush. Suddenly the most dramatic and enchanting firework display emanated from the exploding basket beneath the balloon. It lasted only for a while but will forever be etched on my memory.

The opening of the report bore no relevance to what he was expecting and so he hurried through the sections, scrolling further and further until he could find a piece that actually dealt with the mark and its possible cure. The messenger dwelt with too much candour on his own interaction with the locals and his unnecessary study of the Prithvians. It hadn't gone unnoticed that he was more interested in himself and his situation than that of those around him. It began to dawn on Laozi that he was unlikely to glean anything useful from the report as it was more of a social study than what was required. His interest was beginning to wane when suddenly he stumbled upon a section, towards the end of the piece, which jumped out at him in bold lettering forcing him to stop, settle back and read on.

<u>*Probable cause leading to possible cure*</u>

Over these past few months I have been principally concerned with Prithvian physiology and their Keplerian counterparts. I have analysed the mechanical, physical and biochemical functions of the Keplerians. In short I have used the studies of Prithvian organs, comprising the cells of which they are composed and compared them to the results of my tests on the people of Maya. Put simply and using up to date physiological biometrics; Keplerian anatomy is the same, their physiology is the same, their DNA is the same. This I know is not news but what these tests did succeed in doing is to persuade me to focus on the psychology of the people and in turn to study the grey matter.

I think it relevant to point out here that all humanoids on Earth have this mark including duplicates, which is strange given that man should have set himself apart in the first instance. I guess he determined from the outset that if he were to be burdened with mark, then so too should his creation. Restoring his servant to one's own former glory would be far too magnanimous.

The Prithvian and Keplerian brain has the same general structure to that of other mammals. It is also larger than any other animal, proportionate to body size. Much of the expansion comes from the part of the brain called the cerebral cortex. In there you find the frontal lobes which are associated with executive functions such as self control, planning, reasoning, and abstract thought. This is where I have turned my focus and attention; to abstract thought and reasoning.

The human cerebral cortex is a thick layer of neural tissue that covers most of the brain. In most Prithvians the left hand side of the cortex or left hemisphere is dominant for language and the right hemisphere is dominant for spatiotemporal reasoning. However my focus has been on comparing the remaining parts of the cortex in both the Keplerian and Prithvian brain. These association areas, as they are known, receive input from the sensory areas and are involved in the complex process that is described as perception, thought and decision making.

Perceptual psychology and the study of the association areas of the cortex look at the way that people experience reality. Prithvians and Keplerians see the sun set in the west and marvel at the sight of a firework display in foreign lands. They experience the same rush of fear when attacked from the shadows by a rabid beast. Yet each individual has their own likes and dislikes, abilities and disabilities where some can introspect, yet others cannot see in depth.

It therefore stands to reason that if the brain differs between two individuals, the conscious experience cannot be the same either. The defining feature of consciousness in Prithvians is self awareness. This is no different in Keplerians. However I should point out at this stage that self awareness is absent in non primates, where a dog wouldn't worry about why its tail is wagging or a cat wouldn't worry about whether it'll be fed the next day; the key word here is worry, I am not referring to their instincts.

I have conducted meta-cognition tests on Prithvians as well as Keplerians. This is the science behind 'thinking about thinking' and the results that came back were both varied and very revealing. I managed to measure the variability of introspection and discovered that this measure correlates with the variability in the volume of matter in the right anterior prefrontal cortex. Put simply the more neurons that one has in this region, the better their introspection.

Judging by our records of the human brain and its evolution this part of the neocortex has expanded more than any other region in the Prithvian brain over the last 150 years, in comparison to its Keplerian counterpart. In fact the Keplerian neocortex seems to be waning in size.

In short the irony in all of this is that after such tests, the only conclusion that can be drawn is that the mark is indeed manmade. Prithvian brains have conjured up the mark and it stems from mankind's evolution of consciousness.

What I have discovered is that by altering the Prithvian mental state for a sustained period of time should change the shape and size of the neocortex. By understanding Keplerian evolution and psychology, man will get closer to the cause. If he captures the cause, he will have the cure.

As I have always maintained, it is my primary mission to protect the safety of any such discovery and I, Jabir Ibn Al-Zarqali, remain your loyal servant.

Laozi sighed at the screen in frustration. This wasn't a cure but just further evidence that mankind was to blame. It also threw up more questions than the ones it answered. It certainly didn't explain why all humans had been so unbearably blessed with the mark. He looked at the projection and pointed his right index finger at the screen adjacent to it, flicking through his files, stopping when the image and professional background of Jabir appeared in front of him.

Jabir's father Mohammed Al-Zarqali, the former head of the Eurafrican Council was one of Laozi's greatest influences and had been instrumental in getting his son selected. However it was also Mohammed's express desire that Jabir be given direct access to Laozi. He had no qualms about this as it had only added weight to his position. Knowledge was power after all; with nine chiefs and two covert operatives reporting into him on a monthly basis, he was certainly well informed.

He continued to flick through the projection and settled on another of Jabir's reports from the month before. Halfway through Laozi stopped and stared at the projection unable to believe his eyes. In amongst the reams of words was a large, fresh image of Ama and her dog, Boy. His heart jumped. He hadn't seen her for over a year. She was dressed in local robes. Her hair hung loose and wavy in the carefree manner of the Keplerians. Boy had grown fully, looking both playful and strong. Laozi couldn't have agreed more with the phrase 'a picture is worth a thousand words' as she looked happy, content and not at all as how he had imagined. However this still didn't relay the reason for the image in the first place. He scrolled upwards and settled on an earlier paragraph to give some lead in time.

It makes more sense in my travelling from kingdom to kingdom, conducting my research in a more expansive manner. I know that this is not part of the plan but I could not stay in the same place for too long. Three weeks ago I decided to travel to Amalaka incognito. The journey taught me a lot about the people and the culture; much more perhaps than residing in just one place. I dressed as a traveler. Once there I stayed in the large commercial centre outside their capital city.

Laozi felt obliged to read on. Although this was Jabir's report the focus was Ama. She was enjoying her new surroundings immensely. She had settled in, having become one of the main attractions at the Friday night festival. She had taken on an apprenticeship with a guitar and piano manufacturer, working in the commercial centre. At lunch times she entertained the locals and the travelers passing through with renditions of music of a not too distant past. Laozi scrolled to the next section, skipping over further irreverent detail, settling on a paragraph underneath an image of Ama and Boy smiling back at him.

Ama on more than one occasion refused to allow me to accompany her back to her residence on the outskirts of the city. She was clear on sticking to mission protocol but she was also mindful of the rumour of a more severe punishment for those Prithvians who had children born with the mark. The rumour had originated from a local council meeting in Utsima. The theory and resultant debate had been presented by a specialist whom no one remembered from Tega. However those in the Department for Cosmology & Philosophy had heard of him but none had ever actually met him. Apparently he'd spent most of his time infirmed in his quarters. They knew his name to be Liam Self.

The concept presented by Self is that the Keplerians are thousands of years older than the Prithvians; as in the civilisation and the resulting culture not the genus of homo. However the people of Kepler and their corresponding technology have not evolved over this time. Self certified that this was entirely by design. Self proposed that on Kepler the elderly would die, accidents would happen and that children were born in the usual human way but the population remained proportionately constant. As technology remained at a level akin to the late 1800's, human life expectancy followed suit. So life and death naturally controlled the numbers.

He proposed that every millennium, Kepler would be visited by similar beings to themselves from distant solar systems in far flung galaxies, many light years away. He suggested that first contact would always be initiated by the visitors; decreeing that the existing community on Kepler would not have firsthand experience of a visit as their life span mimics a Prithvian's.

Self suspected that the people of Kepler had the tools to understand the visitors from outer space as he suggested that the Keplerian Council kept a book locked away in its tombs. How he had established this is anyone's guess but he expanded on his declaration by suggesting that, the Keplerians kept a book so large and so heavy that it required all nine high ministers to open it. He also proposed that it would take many more years to read it in order to extract all of the relevant information. The knowledge of the book's existence is said to have been passed down from generation to cohort, from council member to high-minister until it is required. The book apparently contains plans, maps and histories of every town, village and city on Kepler. But more importantly it contains every plan and map of every visiting spacecraft and the history of the people, plants and animals that it carries to Kepler.

Laozi sat at his desk head in his hands not understanding as to how he could have missed this piece. It was over a month old. None of the chiefs had mentioned the theory in their reports nor could he understand why it would be lost amongst the willful ramblings of a necessary security measure. He read on with vigour and interest.

Self went on to expound that the Universe is shaped in a similar way to that of a tree and that there are nine parts. The visitor is instructed to set down in the kingdom, representative of their part within the Universe. In the case of the Prithvians, Earth is from the foot of the Universe; Adhara. Going further back in time the first visitors to Kepler all arrived from the nine parts of the universe at the same time. Each of their ships' footprints was an equilateral triangle and exactly 1,764 acres. This was not a coincidence but a universal design. The principle beings were all similar to humans with two eyes, two ears, ten fingers, ten toes, two legs, two arms and so on, but there were a number of extreme variants too.

He volunteered that the variants were that each of these human beings represented a different height, colour, creed and culture. He suggested that the parameters would have been from perhaps three feet to nine feet tall, from black to white and everything in between, from monotheist to polytheist, from capitalist to communist and patriarchal to matriarchal. He proposed that the original visitors from the Adhara region of the universe were six foot tall, olive skinned, pantheist, liberal and were guided by the principles of equality in a matriarchal form. He also anticipated that all the living beings on the original ships had one thing in common; the mark.

The design of the Universe was to communicate with all of the respective leaders of the respective planets, by way of their dreams or collective consciousness. They had attained the ability to travel through space and were now ready to make their journey. The Universe contrived to call them to Kepler through their conscience. So the leaders of the regions met and decided to divide Kepler into the kingdoms, giving each one the exact same amount of land as the other. What's more Self suggested that each of the ships had come from planets similar to Earth but that they were nine times the size and population.

As each millennium passed a new visitor from a planet similar to Earth would arrive in similar circumstances to the ones before; all humans were adorned with a mark similar to the Prithvian one of today. The living Keplerians who would make first contact with a device, such as the box delivered by Rover, would not necessarily know what to expect. The stories of ancient visitors would have been lost in time and would have become only legend and folklore. However the news would work its way back to the high-minister who would have been educated in the truth when they were inaugurated by the previous incumbent. This is when the Kepler Council would have convened and drawn up the instructions for the visitors and their landing such as they did with the Prithvian arrival.

Each meadow in each village and town, depending on its representative planet's size, is actually the original landing site for the one visiting ship of that particular millennium. For instance Earth is one of the smaller planets to have visited hence Tega having a footprint of 196 acres. There are two sizes small or large; village or town. The cities existed from the beginning.

Self determined that by there being 169 residential areas in each kingdom and that each kingdom started off with just a city then the process would have spanned 1,512,000 years. So by virtue and design the Keplerians have existed for 1.5million years, which is more than nine times that of the Prithvians.

He also went on to say that none of the ships remained on Kepler for more than a number of years. He made an established guess of it being no less than three and no more than nine. This meant that each visitor left their cargo on

Kepler and disappeared once they had got the cure that they so needed. This stands to reason given the fantastically rich and varied amount of different species of plants, birds and animals that populate the various kingdoms. It comes as no surprise given our experiences since we arrived in Uttara.

It is plain to see that Self's theory of the animal and plant kingdom evolving over time is true. The evidence is everywhere. This can also be said of the people. This is the root of Self's point. The integration of the specialists from previous millennia was undertaken in exactly the same format as the Prithvians now find themselves. By being separated and integrated into all of the kingdoms this allowed for the complete introduction of the new visitors and provided the chance of further racial inter connection, creating a comprehensive spread of human evolution whilst remaining technologically at a standstill.

The book decreed that they remain at a standstill. The high-ministers were sworn to protect Kepler; to maintain its current technological state. Self said that since human life was first established on Kepler, all of the visitors from the 1,512 planets had all arrived for a reason; their mark. They were seeking out answers to the questions that nature on their planet had posed. The Universe had tested them and called for them.

Self determined that for each visiting ship to leave after such a relatively short period of time, meant that the interest in Kepler and therefore the cure was something spiritual not physical, otherwise the visitors would have still been there, plundering the ground beneath them. His idea that the process of integration and equal distribution of the specialists does make sense; the visitor would come into physical contact with a Keplerian of the opposite sex, return to his or her base of origin and create a family with no mark therefore adding to the perfection of the people of Kepler.

However, this led to Self's final thought and to the rumour that Ama was referring to; concerning the Free and Prison States. The reason why no one is allowed access to or information in regards to Maharnava, Arnava, Karkara and Avasya is because the people that inhabit these areas are the descendents of those who have not acclimatised or evolved for one reason or another.

The Free States were occupied by the descendents of mixed race unions, Keplerian and Visitor but who still had the mark. He went on further to add that those in the Prison States were the 100% bloodline of the visitors who still carried the mark; meaning their forefathers had not mixed with the indigenous population but had instead procreated with one of their own kind. Self guessed that anyone born in the Free States without the mark would be allowed to rejoin the mainland society or remain where they were; hence the name. However those in the Prison States were being punished for their forefathers having never conjugated with a Keplerian and for not having returned home in the first place.

At first it had all seemed extremely farfetched but Self's theory reached *every kingdom and none of the leaders or councils denied his thoughts. So the rumours extrapolated from there. Once Ama had explained her lack of desire to be sent to one of the Prison States, I finally accepted there were more sinister reasons for why nobody aboard the Repertega was allowed to be in a relationship. I decided to focus my attention to the definitive cure of the Prithvian mark and returned to the kingdom of Uttara. I certainly wasn't going to tell Ama the doctors had declared me infertile years ago. I doubt she would have seen me as anything more than self serving in any case.*

As I have always maintained it is my primary mission to protect the safety of any such discovery and I, Jabir Ibn Al-Zarqali remain your loyal servant.

Laozi sat motionless staring at the projection. Hal had cracked it. He had nailed the truth. Without any prompting or guidance it had only taken him a few months to get under the skin of Kepler. He felt vindicated, proud even. Shaking with adrenaline he remembered his first visitation.

He had first been approached on his 18th birthday. He'd gone to bed resolute and determined to correct the error of his teenage ways. He'd not long been asleep before the first of many dreams came. The ensuing vision was so powerful, in its clarity and precision that he was able to recollect, the morning after, every intrinsic detail as well as every peripheral element. It didn't stop there as that same vision visited him on the evening of every birthday until he was finally in a position to act on its behest.

On the day of his 49th birthday he had slipped into a trance whilst sat at his desk in London. Under the influence of the vision he wrote out the instructions and the terms of Kepler's command. He understood why the Universe had only contrived to call at that very moment. The people needed belief to survive but they wouldn't be able to believe without tasting reprisal. They needed to feel damned, judged and hopeless before they gave into the simple laws of Nature.

No one knew of Kepler's communication with him. He had felt like Siddhartha on a spiritual quest where as a teenager, dissatisfied with the daily ritual and religious upbringing, he renounced the pleasures of the world in favour of spiritual enlightenment. Nevertheless as a young man he had left that quest behind. He had embraced the pleasures of the material world and capitalised on the riches that Vedas Corp had brought him. Yet since that birthday he had become wholly disillusioned with the decadence of his life and, again, focused his search for spiritual enlightenment.

Belief was the cure but it just needed the perfect messenger; one who was unwittingly brilliant; a rising star with a conscience. Hal had cracked it indeed; mankind's technological advancements and scientific research into the meaning of life had got them to a point of no return. Science had proven religion to be wrong. Laozi knew that he wasn't the proverbial ferryman yet another significant step had been made in man's journey. Man had to leap forward to leap back again; this was their salvation. This was the function of Kepler. This was Nature's design.

Chapter 15

The breeze rushed through the valley, down the sides of the foothills and across the tightly bunched exposed trees into the almond fields below, before finally sweeping up along the lower plains towards the capital city of Kumudam. Wrapping its arctic daggers around the sides of the towering skyscrapers it burst through onto the streets. It whipped up dormant dust and conjured up a frenzy, swirling around and attacking any of the city's inhabitants on their way to work.

Ama stepped onto the street and the chill wind enveloped her, delving deep into her bones. It was most definitely winter; no different to her native New York; she fastened her over robes, firmly drawing on each side, making sure that she was fully enclosed. Her apartment building towered over her, brilliant. The wind may well have been biting but the rising sun of the east cut through the cold as it radiated off the tops of the towers nearby.

City life was really no different for her. All the residential areas across the continent had running water and electricity. They were fully insulated and even had the use of a telephone in the reception of every apartment block. The telephone had become a Prithvian lifeline and was manned by the hall porter. Ama had immediately connected with hers, a lady called Kinvara, whose ancestors had originally been from Adhara but had moved to Kumudam nearly a thousand years before.

Ama had become used to Keplerian way of referring to time and genealogy as if a thousand years were of little consequence and a mere blip in the grand scheme. She preferred it that way. She, like all the other specialists, had slipped into a common language with her hosts as effortlessly as it had been hard to learn. Kinvara was a wealth of information on local customs, history and gossip where she had become a close confident, especially after recent events.

The Self Debates were the topic of conversation across most kingdoms. Ban Qian, who was in a village called Tarasvin in Agra, had called Ama with further details of Self's supposition. She confirmed it had reached the Northern most tip of the continent, sending shockwaves around her community.

Yakov, who'd been assigned to the town of Caitanya in Utsima, was equally dumfounded by the depth of Self's interpretation of the planet's secret history. He had called Ama to let her know that he was travelling to

Utsima's capital city to listen to a presentation being made by Self and the High-Minister of Utsima. He'd told Ama that Self's philosophy had paved the way for everyone to be respected and accepted into their respective communities; most probably far quicker than any other visitors before them. Ama had, at the time, agreed and said that she wanted to personally thank Self for uncovering the truth as quickly as he had. It had given them all a little bit of credence amongst the population as the knowledge enriched everyone. Yakov had also informed her that Self was to be accepted onto the Council for Utsima; the first time in Keplerian history that a visitor would make it onto a kingdom's council within the first nine years of arriving on Kepler, let alone their first.

However a cure to the mark had not been realised nor was it likely to be any time in the near future. The belief which Self had talked about still had to manifest itself in all of the Prithvians. This could not happen instantaneously. It would take time and that was just regarding the specialists actually integrated within Keplerian society. Convincing the Departments for Psychology and Security to change their views on science, nature, space, time; in fact their entire perception of reality, would take some doing. She understood why the Prison States were deemed necessary.

However two questions still burnt in the back of her mind; firstly how a cure would get back to Earth if those who believed remained on Kepler and secondly why non-believers would remain and risk being ostracised from an otherwise welcoming and peaceful society.

However Ama parked these seemingly unanswerable questions for another time. She was now a different person. Not only more laid back, she was positively introspective and outwardly confident. The subconscious vision of her which had previously been buried away in the recesses of her mind had now moved to the fore; she had nothing to lose and everything to gain.

As she made her way along the road towards the wagon stop, Boy tracked behind her. It was Wednesday. She had two days to prepare for her Friday night gig in the meadow. However she had to visit the doctor first; only to redress the wounds and check for any sign of infection. She did not dare look under the bandages. The wagon was rarely late and the drop in centre was on the way to work. Arriving at her stop she heard the even rhythm of running asvahs, Keplerian horses, in the distance. The sound grew louder as the canter slowed to a lope and finally it trotted to a standstill.

Boy brushed past her legs and jumped up the side steps and into the wagon. She followed slowly and with a little bit more care than usual, not wanting to catch her arm on the balustrades. She took her customary place towards the back of the carriage. Everyone asked after her health and wellbeing as she settled into her usual spot, with her back resting on the gunwales behind her. They were all aware of the brutal attack on her. The news had spread quickly.

Ama had taken up writing music where she had found special solace in the hills, especially at sunrise. Back on Earth she had always dreamed of being a popular musician; a singer and a songwriter. She had aspired to be in a band but her talent for classical music had led her on a different path. Being on Kepler had given her a new lease of life; a sense of freedom. She had nothing to lose and so had established a routine for every Saturday where she would wake well before anyone else and seek out inspiration.

The morning after the music festivals would always be tardy affairs as the amount of naturally sourced highs, indigenous to the area and culture, were stupefying. Stalls packed full of concoctions made from the blends of natural substances akin to marijuana, poppy flower and coco leaf were lined up in the meadow every Friday evening after sunset. The myriad colours, overabundance of options and the frenetic pulse was reminiscent of the Jamaa el Fna in Marrakech of yesteryear. However the hand-outs differed in that they were definitely more herb than spice. Although it was now winter and a new light settled on the meadow the offerings and festivals continued. The produce was passed around from family to family, couple to couple, person to person and the results were inspirational.

Because there were no manmade chemicals incorporated in the production process nor had there been any scientific tinkering with the herbs or plants prior to processing, most of the yield was reasonably mild and was proven not to cause unnecessary damage to the brain or body. Pastes, powder and solutions were handed out liberally, dissolved in hot water and served in a similar fashion to that of the Prithvian ritual of taking tea. The servings were routinely accompanied by an assortment of cakes and biscuits which were administered as the first notes of the evening's entertainment sounded. Teenagers were allowed to join in; whilst their younger siblings and friends knew that their time would come as part of a grand initiation process.

Ama had at first been wary of her own initiation but was now a firm believer in the long term benefits and remedies of these plants and herbs. She had been able to unlock parts of her brain that she had no idea existed, increasing her ability to think, understand and also write music. With no fear of reprisal and no fear of addiction, the Keplerians had the ability to travel through their senses once a week and in moderation. They were able to visit other realities, mine the depths of their minds and return stronger, brighter and more intelligent than when they had started. This process was cathartic, healthy and what the planet's natural produce was designed to do.

Keplerians were incredulous at the Prithvians stories of how mankind had set about recreational pharmacology over the centuries. In a similar way to their approach to religion, Prithvians had used the produce to affect power, control and financial gain. By thrusting themselves into the production process, creating manmade super strength substances, they had developed sordid and malevolent end products. Ama now realised that by lifting the veil of inhibition she had allowed her mind to expand and grasp concepts that those on Earth had been sheltered from for so long.

She had risen early on the morning of the attack and had got dressed quietly and quickly. With Boy accompanying her she had weaved her way through the streets until she had come to most eastern point of the city. Facing up at the foothills of the valley she proceeded along the path. She picked her way through the patchwork fields of various cover crop which were regenerating the soil for the next season. Boy alternated between a tracking position and that of point, instinctively searching for any potential threats to her wellbeing.

They followed the path until they arrived at a copse of trees, not too dissimilar to the yew of Northern Eurafrica. They were all 28 metres tall with trunks of three metres in diameter; their bark thin, scaly brown and flaking at the stem. They had dark green, flat leaves which were arranged spirally upon the stem. She had been warned that most parts of the tree were toxic except for the bright red aril surrounding the seed. Legend had it that they were the oldest trees on the entire continent and were brought by the first Amalakian ship. The original visitors had held the yew tree aloft as the link with their land, ancestors and their ancient society.

Ama and Boy continued zig zagging up the side of the hill, past the copse until they reached a clearing. At the other end there was a viewing deck with far reaching views to the West over the city. It was early morning and she had wanted to catch the sun as it rose up from the horizon in the East; so dog and mistress had carried on as the first rays of light stroked the sky, leaving Kepler's moon gleaming in the distance.

Boy ran ahead and they passed through the last of a thicket, up out onto the brow of the hill. It was then that it hit her. It came at her from behind, fast, low and ferociously quick. At the time she had had no idea what it was and was knocked to the ground instantly. It stood menacingly over her; bright yellow eyes piercing deep into hers. Immediately on the defence, she had held up her left arm with her elbow bent in the attacker's direction. The animal snarled and growled with a deep rasping hiss producing a low sound, akin to a ghostly panther and it went in for the kill. It grabbed her by the arm, assuming it was a more vital part of her body and proceeded to drag her into the thicket, hoping to feast on its spoils.

The sheer surprise of the attack had left her stunned and unable to struggle free. Fighting for breath as the full force of the cat's weight had taken the wind out of her, she lay motionless in amongst the thorny brambles. In the blink of an eye her loyal protector appeared, ramming into the feline shape stood above her. Boy hit it with his full force, head down, low and sincere, knocking it sideways whilst her arm was still clamped within its jaws. Twisting onto her side in order to prevent her arm being broken, she watched as Boy unleashed all his fury upon her assailant. He bit down hard on the nape of the cat's neck, unlocking its jaws and then mauled it away, rolling over and over again until enough momentum had been built for him to release his foe down the side of the hill, off a small rocky cliff to the ground below. Successfully dispatched and maimed the large cat skulked off, back to the shadows from whence it came.

Ama, semi conscious, had lain wincing in pain oblivious to the ensuing moments of indecision that Boy had suffered. Instinctively he had gone in search of help but was immediately drawn back to her side in fear of another attack. Torn by this vacillation he had howled like he had never howled before. By pure chance Kinvara was paying her respects in the copse and had rushed up the hill to find out what was going on. Ama had passed out with the pain by the time she arrived. Ripping off her over robes and tearing one in two, Kinvara had made a tourniquet and wrapped it firmly above Ama's elbow. Luckily she was carrying a hip flask full of a blend of spring water, limeflowers, milk thistle and goatweed. It hadn't been her intention to use it for treating a wound but the potion turned out to be cleansing and inspired. Ama had been attacked by a citraka; to her it was akin to an overgrown snow leopard. The cat had wandered south from the icy wastelands of Southern Uttara.

Ama could tell that her strumming arm was not yet fully functional and the doctor confirmed that she would not be able to play the guitar for another month at least. This created a problem. She had won her slot as the support act for a touring band and was due to play her first solo set after sun down on Friday. She left the drop in centre where Boy joined her and they got onto the next available wagon heading to the familiar surroundings of Bhuva, the southern commercial centre. The wind jostled with the canopy, cavorting around with the cushions whilst Ama and Boy were the only passengers in the back.

If she couldn't play the guitar she would have to find someone to support her. She'd written the songs and would sing in any case. She had been playing the piano as part of an orchestra but had also been supporting other bands, building up quite a fan base. Everyone loved her style and dexterity. However she had wanted to do more. She had wanted to stun the city of Kumudam. She wanted to show off her own songs, those akin to the blended rock, pop and soul music of the early 21st Century.

Guitars, keyboards and drum kits existed albeit in varying degrees of the Prithvian modern form. However this hadn't been Ama's original concern; it was the reproduction of sound; how the possible lack of a stadium effect would affect her performance and the power of her ballads. However she had been relieved to learn early on that forms of electronic amplifiers existed and that they were known as tubes. Ama had been originally told by a friend in Uttara, after a particularly enthralling evening in the meadow, that they were based on valves, modulators and the flow of electrons along a grid. This had fallen on deaf ears but she was thankful all the same. Her dreams would be able to find an outlet.

When she and Boy finally reached the workshop quarter of Bhuva the arctic wind had disappeared. The courtyard was awash with the silence that meets the calm before a storm. Ama sensed a snowsquall brewing and beckoned Boy inside with her. The luthier that she was assigned to was on holiday, in the islands off the kingdom of Anga, so she had the workshop to herself for the whole week. This gave her the time to think about how she would get around her dilemma. She did not want to forgo the opportunity to appear on the undercard of the most revered group of musicians across Kepler.

Having shaken off the shackles of her classical training she had adopted the free spirited, care free attitude of a post, post-modern poprock chick. She made a few calls to her colleagues based in the city and was pleasantly surprised that she had no trouble in recruiting three others to form a band. Two visual artists, one male and one female, elected to play bass and lead guitar and would also double up as backing singers. A percussionist was not just an established drummer but also a revelation; it turned out that he was as obsessed with popular rock music as she was.

Seeing as she had already been billed to perform, the newly formed band agreed to let her name remain and the group Ama was born. They set about learning the songs from the reams of sheet music that she had produced and then practiced all through the nights of Wednesday and Thursday, agreeing that Ama would return as the rhythm guitarist when her arm had healed.

Ama woke on the Friday morning entirely focused on the evening ahead. The day then passed by unbearably slowly; so much so that she developed a horological fascination with time. As the winter sun disappeared for another day she shut up shop and returned to her apartment. The adrenaline started to kick in. The band had agreed to meet in the meadow in the area beside the enormous stage placed over the large stone table in the centre. The stage was a huge circular platform which had large tubes wrapped around its base, pointing in every direction. During the winter months the stage would be covered by a large circular canopy which was 784 metres in diameter and 49 metres high, complete with a hole seven metres in diameter at its centre allowing for a lantern to pass through when required.

The entire population of the city would set up large sleeping areas with central wood burners housed in vast tents, set around the perimeter. The tents were always laid out in the inverse of the residences. Those who lived in the stone cottages would pitch the largest tents up against the perimeter fence and furthest away. Those from the skyscrapers would pitch their smaller tents closest to the canopy and the stage. The rest would follow suit according to their block, street and district number. The canopy was designed to accommodate 180,000 people underneath however it had never been called into such extreme use, as everybody could still hear the music, theatre or oration via the sound system wherever they were.

Ama and Boy picked their way through the streets and the stage called out to her like a homing beacon. Her time had arrived. It had just gone 8pm and she was ready. There were still swathes of people arriving. Huge bonfires lit each gate highlighting the perimeter, providing heat for those in the immediate vicinity. The storm that Ama sensed had been brewing had still not arrived. The fires flickered and crackled, allowing the shadows to dance in the chill static air. They passed through the gate, past the first row of tents and into another clearing. As they went by, slowly taking in the awe inspiring scenes of colour and spice, the tents got smaller and smaller.

Reaching the perimeter of the canopy she was struck by its sheer magnificence; so all encompassing. Similar to the exits out of the meadow there were six huge open entrances; so large that a Prithvian aeroplane could have flown through without touching the sides. These entrance, exits were equally spaced around a circular wall of canvas. Huge effervescent bonfires stood sizzling and sparkling at either side; amounting to 12 in total, in the shape of a circle. The heat given out was immense. Once inside and under the covering she realised that if the covered area was full of people, it didn't matter what time of year it was; nor whether a snowsquall was on its way; in fact, it would only add to the occasion.

The area was reasonably empty as most were setting up, settling in or leaving their tents in search of their medicine. Ama noticed a group of children playing hide and seek on the other side. A few groups had already huddled together bringing flasks and rugs with them. They had moved close to the centre stage; obviously diehard fans of the main act. She spotted quite a few similar groups occupying symmetrical positions around the stage. They were most definitely the uncompromising Dipotsava devotees. She approached the enormous stage and spotting the drummer in their band signaled to him, almost shouting in excitement.

"Sorry I'm late. I hadn't fully appreciated this before. I've always been looking in or in a tent with the likes of you or our Keplerian counterparts."

"This is an entirely different experience. Isn't it? Everything has been laid out for us. We don't need to do anything except test just before we start."

"Where are the others?"

She climbed the steps up onto the stage leaving Boy sitting patiently on the ground below. He stared up at her with his lopsided, loving face tilted to one side; his tongue hanging out as usual.

"They've gone for a cup or two. They'll be back in a moment." He responded with a wink.

"I could do with one however I'm not sure now is the best time. I'm going to get this out of the way before I start meddling."

"You know visual artists."

They sat down on the stage with their backs to each other staring out in opposite directions, taking in their surroundings and discussing the crowds that began to drift in. The others returned joining them in a similar fashion. Their instruments and microphones sat close by whilst they absorbed the atmosphere. It must have been the cold as by 9pm Ama thought that there were at least 20,000 people who were now under the canopy. She had to focus to keep control of her nerves. She'd played in front of large audiences before; she'd even been a soloist; a very successful one at that.

Gradually a silence descended across the entire crowd forcing the band to their feet. Without looking at each other, all locked in their own thoughts, fighting to control their nerves, they took up their positions. The drummer was placed in the centre of the stone table. The three others surrounded him at the tips of an imaginary equilateral triangle, equally spaced out and pointing towards a different part of the audience. The microphones and leads connected to the tubes underneath, ready to blare out at the first opportunity.

"Testing, testing." Ama tapped away and then shook the adrenaline out of her arms.

"One two, one two." The lead guitarist countered.

The sound quality was unbelievable. There were a few, barely audible cheers from a group towards the back. The entire audience fell quiet again. Ama stood totally still. She felt her arm twinge with pain, absently massaging the bandaged area. She had an epiphany; she was a Keplerian. For a short time only while her lower left arm took time to heal, she had no mark or at least the forces of Kepler had contrived to keep it hidden. In the back of her mind she heard the sound of a ticking clock and it pushed her onwards until the bass guitarist picked up the beat of the first song. A few seconds later the drummer and lead guitarist joined in, leaving Ama standing locked inside her lyrics, listening for her cue. Her time to shine had come; at last.

The first song went by quickly, without a hitch. The audience was visibly entertained; they began to sway to the melody. A few stood up giving the newly formed band much needed confidence. For the second song, lead, bass and singer all moved round one to where the former had been positioned; on the next point of the imaginary triangle. They rotated after each song as the third, fourth and fifth increased in pace, whipping the crowd to a fever pitch.

The band couldn't believe their eyes or ears as more and more people began to join the already enthralled crowd; everyone was on their feet moving in time with the music. Ama had not expected such a reception nor had any of the others. They were overwhelmed. Rising to the occasion they belted out the sixth and final song with extended instrumental solos, showcasing each other's talent. They finished with the panache of a well rehearsed unit, rising to a crescendo of voice, drum and guitar, fading out to leave just Ama breathless, husky and worn; with a voice to match.

When they finished they stood still listening to the cheers and chants, soaking up the ambiance as if it were a dream. None of them had ever experienced anything quite like it. They wanted to milk the adulation for as long as they respectably could. As they made their way towards the steps at the side of the stage the crowd started chanting in earnest for more. It started out as a low hum, quickly gathering pace until it was a sustained shout of at least 40,000 voices in unison. They stood rooted to the spot just above the steps. Ama turned to the others and said,

"I have one more but it's not quite finished yet. You'll catch on pretty fast. It opens up with just me, after the first verse lead joins in; bass; you'll know when to come in; then bass and I; no lead or drums; you all come in together, creating the big finale. I'll give the nod."

The others looked at each other in a state of euphoria and then smiled. The drummer was the only one to respond.

"What have we got to lose?"

With that they swiveled on their heels and took up their positions again. Ama stood on the northern tip of the triangle with lead on west and bass on east. With their senses alleviated by the elixir being passed between them, the crowd was near to becoming a hysterical frenzy. Both bass and lead were visibly in a similar state. Ama admitted to herself that it was hard not to get caught up in its hypnotic power.

Her mind went still, the ambience dimmed. She entered into a zone of complete concentration. She allowed the heat and noise of the crowd to usher her into a mindset reserved by her dreams. The auditorium was vast, silent, waiting, watching, listening; expecting.

> *If I ever think about it, I'd let you know,*
> *If I ever dream about it, I'd let you know,*
> *If I can't go on without it, I'd let you know,*
> *Would you let me in or let me down?*
> *Would you let me sin or let me drown?*
> *I can't stand without it and that you know.*
> *Of all the things that are worth it, you I know,*
> *Of all the timings, this is perfect, yes you know,*
> *Of my indecision, it had to happen, I had to go,*
> *Would you let me in or let me down?*
> *Would you let me sin or let me drown?*
> *You would have been a gift and that I know.*
> *By the time you can reach me, I will be gone,*
> *By the tongue you speak to me, it is my song,*
> *By the light you are here for me, for so long,*
> *Would you let me in or let me down?*
> *Would you let me sin or let me drown?*
> *We could have been perfect and that we know.*
> *Would you let me in or let me down?*
> *Would you let me sin or let me drown?*
> *We would have been perfect and that I know.*

Chapter 16

He lay face down in the ice and rock; flat out exhausted. He'd been climbing the peaks of Utsima for a week, finally reaching the tip of the kingdom's highest with nothing but a pack and a board to keep him company. He'd headed into the Parvata region in search of some stimulation having taken a few days off to clear his head before his appointment. Back home, he'd been more than a good skier as he'd spent countless months trekking across the Alps of Eurafrica in his early twenties. During that time he'd also acquired a deep rooted passion for rock climbing.

He had been reading a book on the kingdom's peaks whilst sitting quietly in his apartment in Vitti a town 126 miles from Utsima's capital city, Samanya. The idea of testing his limits, pushing himself to venture out into the unknown alone, never seemed more relevant than at that precise moment. He had felt that he had nothing to lose and everything to gain, except for now when face down in the snow and doubled up in pain. The exertions of the past few days had seriously taken their toll on his knees.

Like most of the kingdoms, Utsima had a mountainous region in its centre where the highest peaks would reach as far as 14,000 feet above sea level. These weren't anything like the consistency or height of Kepler's foremost mountain range which like their Prithvian counterparts went by the name of the Himalayas. Those summits reached twice as high, acting as a wall between the North and the South with craggy impenetrable peaks sitting atop lush, tropical vegetation below. They were a formidable sight to behold, spread across the continent along the corridor of the equator from East to West. Routes through the lower parts had been plotted and carved many millennia before. However the summits had been left untouched by Keplerian hands.

This could not be said of the Vizala peak of the Parvata region. He was not the first nor would he be the last intrepid explorer to reach the pinnacle of this lesser range. Yet it was most certainly a very personal challenge given that he was unguided and alone.

Over a week before he'd crammed his backpack full of provisions, put on his mountain gear, complete with his beloved Chameau's and taken the first wagon out from Vitti. The route had taken him east towards the mountains. Once he'd arrived at the base of the Parvatas he'd immediately set off on foot, up to the back of the valley and beyond. He wasn't going to stop until he'd reached the summit. He felt that he had to sit atop their highest peak staring at the rising sun before he could truly take his place amongst the members of the council.

He did not want to carry skis or use skins to shimmy up the mountain side. He had been told of the ridges and faces that he would have to overcome on his way to the summit. However he had fashioned a board similar to the Prithvian snowboard which would, while hooked into his Chameau's, allow him to glide over the lower glacial surfaces down the circuitous routes of the descent. If only his knees weren't troubling him so. The ascent had been spectacular but extremely wearing.

The Vizala peak was 14,949 ft high and an isolated mountain. Set at the back of a long and steep valley it was not too dissimilar to the Matterhorn of Switzerland. It had four steep faces, rising above the surrounding glaciers which faced the four compass points of North, South, East and West. Because of its position as the kingdom's main watershed and because of its great height, it was exposed to rapid weather changes. This, combined with its steep faces and isolated location, made it prone to banner clouds creating vortices of air and condensation. The ridges and faces had been successfully ascended in all seasons but not without the aid of fixed ropes, pick axes and crampons.

He had ensured that he had enough kit to assist him with this undertaking. The inherent hazards of falling rocks, adverse weather conditions and climber inexperience, all amounted to a very clear and present danger. To add insult to potential injury, in a fit of pique he had decided to tackle the summit in the dead of a cold snap.

Not to be beaten he had progressed surely and steadily up the valley and towards the lone peak beckoning him in from a distance. It had taken him four days walking, climbing, camping and very little sleep to reach the foot of the mountain. It had taken him a further three to climb it; cold, alone, hungry, tired but completely exhilarated. This was his crowning achievement, personal and unlike anything that he had done before. Being on Kepler had given him a new lease of life, spurring him on to great things in such a short space of time. It was hard to fathom the extent of his erudition since the day he'd woken up, fully intact, on the floor of the receiver chamber on Tega. As soon as he had arrived, he'd fashioned an elaborate brown wrist bandage which he wore over his left forearm. It discreetly carried the cellhip, placed poignantly over his mark.

He rolled over onto his back and looked up into the pale azure of the dawn. Through all the icy wind, extreme temperatures, equipment failure and buckling limbs, he'd made it. Out of breath and exhausted, he realised that the wind had dropped to barely a whisper. The temperature was pushing to respond. With no wind chill it felt eerily temperate atop the tallest peak in Kepler's Northern Hemisphere. Liam Self had earned it; he'd earned this moment's respite. He sat up beating his gloved hands together to keep the cold at bay, looking out onto the horizon. It was awe inspiring; jaw dropping. If ever there was a time to feel closer to nature, this was that moment.

He pulled his pack off his back, unzipping it at the side. Reaching in he took out a non- registering thermometer which told him that it was still damn cold. Without the wind it felt a lot warmer. Something somewhere had to be smiling down on him. There was no other explanation for his good fortune in facing the elements whilst reaching the summit. He took out a vacuum container and unscrewed its top taking out a hot inner flask. Carefully placing it in between his legs he then took out a pack of his favourite Marlboro No. 5's. He had rationed himself to one cigarette a day until he would return to Tega and perhaps Earth. Except it didn't look like he would be returning to Earth, given that he was to become a member of the Council; or at least Liam Self was. Tapping the shoulder of the box in his familiar way, he took out a cigarette with his thumb and forefinger. The air was thin but at least breathable. He glanced at it and checked the time. It was 5:49am. The light of dawn hit the peak at the precise moment that he first inhaled.

Liam raised his flask in private celebration, acknowledging his new found home. He now felt ready to take his seat amongst the Keplerians in his own right and not as someone else. It was Liam Self that had achieved this, not his previous guise.

Not long after and when the adrenaline had subsided, the chill atmosphere started to bite into his extremities, leaving him with little option but to move on. Plotting his route back down was not going to be any easier than it was during the ascent. He recorded a 360 degree panoramic image on his cellhip and sent it to Laozi, before deleting it from his files, as he was still strung out on security, being cautious at every turn. He took a still of himself with the glorious expanse of over half of Utsima filling in as a backdrop. He sent it to Laozi and then deleted in customary fashion.

He looked out to the east, where the surprisingly tranquil surroundings that he found himself in were the complete reverse a few hundred miles away. A centre of low pressure was developing within the high pressure system. The opposing forces had begun to create such a wind that a large cumulonimbus, the size of a kingdom, ominously stretched far out in front of him.

With the added pressure of time, Liam packed his things away quickly and efficiently. If he could get off the summit before the storm arrived he fancied his chances. He could make it to the relative safety of the shelter, a day's trek away. Heading off the apex he was careful not to make any mistake as he picked his way down the North ridge to the glacier below. Where gravity acted as help on the ascent, it didn't help with his back to the wall and with no eyes in his feet. Yet he found the perfect rhythm between his left and right legs whilst using his upper body to maintain balance. His knees were severely sore and the descent proceeded to punish them further.

Just over three hours later he touched down, feet in the thick, unblemished powder which lay across the Vizala glacier. Without stopping for a moments rest, he whipped the pack off his back and unclipped the board. Returning the pack to its usual position he put his left foot on the board, strapped it in and pressed down fastening the bindings. Once secured, he pushed off with his right foot, gathering pace as the gradient steepened. The momentum picked up, so he put his right foot into the straps at the back of the board and clipped in, in a similar fashion as before. He was now at the mercy of the terrain.

The sun beat down as he carved his way down the crest of an enormous wave of snow and ice. The deepening contrast of blue and white glared back at him. In any other circumstances he would have stopped to collect a thousand images. This was not such a moment as the threat of pursuing cloud led him further, fearless and faster down the mountain. He continued for what seemed like an age, weaving in and out, picking his way through each crevasse until he had to stop abruptly as he came to what had to be the edge.

Over its seemingly eternal life the glacier had accumulated a vast amount of debris by plucking at the rocks as it carved its own path through the valley. The river of ice had caused gargantuan abrasions along its route, pushing the loose rock to the front and spitting it out as terminal moraine. Because of the glaciers apparent longevity, it was truly an awe inspiring sight with a billion years worth of deposits lying in a heap below.

Liam bent down and unclipped his right foot. He quickly glanced in every direction, ascertaining his route to safety. The best option was to move to the side and climb the ridge to the east, away from the oncoming storm. With fresh snow from the night before, he established that he would be able to continue his journey by board. The next half an hour was exhausting as he almost ran up the side of the ridge. The impact on his knees was unequivocal to anything that he'd experienced before. At the top he stared down along the glacier. He hastily retrieved some raw footage of his route as the sky began to take on a murderous hue. The wind whipped up in his face. With a deep breath he disappeared over the other side and towards the safety of the refuge.

A few days later a bedraggled but buoyant Liam returned to Vitti in one piece. It had been a great test of nerve and skill to avoid the storm; one that had spread from the eastern seaboard of Amalaka all the way to its counterpart in the west. He stepped down out of the wagon and headed for his apartment. His home was on the first floor of a building, reminiscent of an ancient Greek temple except for the huge windows on either side. Once he stepped through his front door he slumped fully clothed into his chair with one hand still holding onto the strap of his backpack and fell fast asleep. It wasn't much of a home coming.

He woke up the next day still fully clothed in a similar position to the day before. He took a shower, freshened up and put a clean set of robes on and made his way out of the apartment. He crossed the landing, reaching the other side and rapped lightly on the door with the tips of his fingers. He momentarily heard a shuffling and the languid pad of a considered approach as she drew up close on the other side. He closed his eyes and took a deep breath. She spoke softly through the door.

"Liam, I assume that it is you. I've not been expecting anyone else for quite some time."

"It is indeed Attika."

She opened up and stared at him with an inquisitive look, imparted by her weathered and knowing lines. He was overcome with a rush of déjà vu as he stared at the woman in front of him. He almost forgot about his well rehearsed dialogue which he had practiced countless times over the preceding few days.

"You have some questions for me."

She closed the door and stood in her entrance hall, waiting patiently until he spoke.

"The Keplerian calendar is similar to that of Prithvi yet there aren't special holidays based on religious celebrations. There is no Christmas, Eid al-Fitr or Vesak. I know each village, town and city has a Formation Day commemorated separately and once a year. I know that each one holds the festival of life on the last Friday of every month but as far as I know there are no other special days. For instance does anyone celebrate their birthday on Kepler?"

"There are no other special holidays. We do not celebrate birth in the same way as you Prithvians do. The nature of being exists eternally whether you are born on Kepler, Prithvi or anywhere else. It does not mean that you have come into existence for the first or last time. By virtue, death is more of a celebration than life. Your death means that you have moved into another existence, far greater than the one you are experiencing right now. That is what the festival of life commemorates. It is in fact a festival for death; in honour of the enduring energy of each being striving forwards onto the next part of their journey.

"Tell me, if someone in the Prison States was born without the mark, wouldn't they be allowed to leave?"

"The Prison States are numbered by those that still bear the mark of their planet. However it is impossible for any of their progeny to be cured as they are not privy to nor are part of the collective consciousness that exists on the continent. I would also like to highlight that the nine kingdoms are not some utopian ideal yet I sense that your question is rhetorical and that you already know the answer but I will divulge all that I can.

"For every yin there has to be a yang. At its heart is the ancient philosophy of the two poles of existence. They are opposite but complimentary. The two opposing forces, flow in a natural cycle always seeking a balance. As two aspects of a single reality they create a dynamic system. Shadow cannot exist without light. However the perception that yin and yang corresponds to evil and good is universally misconceived. Yin-yang is an indivisible whole as dichotomous moral judgments are perceptual, not real. Good and evil become each other through the constant flow of the universe therefore becoming indeterminable.

"In any case, who is to say that the Prison States are as you envisage? By the mere use of the term prison you would have conjured up dark, repressed and horrific images of pain, torture and sacrifice. What if these states where there for the protection of those within it not the other way round?"

"That is as I thought. Here on the continent, there seems to be little mention of those that don't procreate and of those attracted to the same sex."

"Due to our ancestors' foresight and by their design we have been unable to trade property. We have been strictly anti-capitalist since our time began. Marriage and the laws that surround it, concerning the sharing of assets, are redundant here. So consequently there is little need to distinguish between a homosexual and a childless person. We don't use the Prithvian technology that can create a child for a childless individual. Only the union of a man and a woman creates a child, the rest is unnatural.

"The physical union of the same sex is overlooked and not an issue. They will have no progeny and so therefore it makes little difference in conjunction with their beliefs. If they have the mark they would find themselves in the Prison States or are the progeny of a mixed union and are born to the Free States just the same as everyone else."

"Attika, thank you; my recent journey provided me with some much needed solace but it has also afforded me the time to clear up any misgivings that I still had about the structure of your society. You have only guided me further."

"Liam, there are many reasons for you being here - many reasons for what it is that you are about to do. Before you move on there is one final thought that we should share; however I'd prefer it if we didn't stand here. I'd like you to follow me."

With that she turned around and ushered him into a room that was dark, cold and quite a contrast to the warm, welcoming entrance hall. She pointed to the far corner with both her hands. He sat down in a large comfortable chair, listening with intent as she spoke fast, using a more melodic and ancient dialect; one that he had only heard, once before. He studied her features, dwelling on her face. He asked her the question, the one which had been burning in the recess of his psyche for as long as he could remember.

Her speech slowed and Liam already knew the answer. The candle in the corner flickered as she gave him her version of events. When she had finished, she took his right hand and placed the palm on hers. They stood, bowed and dropped their arms to their sides. Liam now felt certain that he was correct in taking up his position on the Council.

The next day he woke with a clear head and a strong sense of purpose. He put on his over robes, picked up his bag and closed the door behind him. He slowly descended the wide sweeping staircase down to the ground floor. His knees still ached, limiting his movement. He bade farewell to the porter and stepped outside onto the tree lined street as a chill wind enveloped him. It was most definitely still winter; no different to his native London; he fastened his over robes, ensuring he was fully covered and headed for the wagon stop.

Many of his neighbours and recent acquaintances had foregone their usual route to work in order to be present for his departure. As he'd suspected a group of people were congregating nearby. They immediately saw him coming. The wagon had been waiting for a while. The asvahs were shuffling their hooves in anticipation. A few of the crowd walked steadily towards him smiling whilst others stood still waiting. All of them wished him well and not to forget them, now that he was to become a Samanyan.

Using the Keplerian short farewell gesture of placing his right palm on their upturned right palm and simultaneously his left palm onto his own heart, he bade farewell to the gathering. He climbed the steps of the wagon turning one last time to see a sea of upturned faces smiling back at him. He waved and the wagon moved on and at pace. He sat back into a selection of cushions beside the wood burner, closing his eyes momentarily.

An hour later he woke to find the weather and surrounding landscape had changed dramatically from the cold austere town that he'd left behind. The fields were alive with greens, yellows, pinks and blues. The full bloom of spring was underway where giant insects buzzed around in one direction or another. The patchwork fields of the lowlands gave way to the extensive coastline of Utsima with its many inlets, peninsulas and offshore islands that had once been a part of the mainland. The wagon rattled south-west into an intensifying heat and sea breeze. His basic understanding of prevailing winds, marine currents and other climatic influences ensured that he understood the environment to be a fragile but dynamic ecosystem. The Keplerian's had removed little vegetation throughout their history. They had not touched the surrounding area except for implementing and maintaining the roads to include the enormous commercial centre outside of Samanya.

The prevention of trading property had stunted any plans to develop, commercialise and ultimately mar the land. This hadn't escaped his attention as this was one of the main factors in the Prithvian demise. Ownership of real estate, the rights to land and the laws surrounding it had all paved the way to crusades; personal and territorial; rights issues, sectarian conflicts, greed, avarice and malevolence; these things were absent on Kepler. It was small wonder that their society blossomed without it.

He noticed the overabundance of birds jostling for position in the sky and along the coastline. He saw little penguins on the sand, shearwaters along the steeper headlands and countless other sea birds looking for their home, in and amongst the surrounding beaches. In either direction there were reptiles, mammals, the Samanyan seal and the Keplerian kangaroo. He even heard a varied assortment of whales out at sea as the wagon rolled on. He felt the sun's radiance permeate his body through the canopy.

After a few hours they entered the city passing familiar buildings on either side where each one was three times the size of those in Vitti. The wagon finally pulled up outside a stone cottage. A beautifully overgrown but well manicured hedge was tree lined with lush greens, browns and yellows. In precise and symmetrical positions each tree soared up into the sky marking the back and centre of the plot housing each stone cottage. Liam's was close to the centre of the south district. The sea breeze gently swayed the tops of the trees making them wave in honour of his arrival. It was just before midday and the city, surreal in contrast to the Prithvian metropolises, was tranquil.

It was obvious that the purpose of the Keplerian existence was to explore nature, energy and the cosmos. It was to accept their fate, surrendering to the power of the universe. They were not there to compare themselves to others or to be better off than their neighbour. The original visitors or settlers as Liam had come to name them had decided on every detail of Keplerian society on the basis that their own worlds had become defunct due to their overzealous approach to the all encompassing ideal. It hadn't mattered which part of the universe they had come from they were all called to Kepler at the same time with the same mark.

Their planets had been mined, drilled, developed and fought over for too long while their minds and technology had advanced at such an alarming rate that it had threatened the very core of their existence and the sentient spirit. Attika's wise words rang through Liam's head. He knew what the cure was but he was still failing to understand how it would be best delivered and how long it would take to restore the balance back on Earth. This was the Prithvian dilemma.

His inauguration was in a matter of days and he needed to prepare a speech. A speech that would not only present the Prithvian plight in the simplest of terms but also one that would prove him worthy of the honour bestowed upon him.

Keplerian was one principle, one rule, one ideal. Prithvian was a multitude of malicious and self serving doctrines bundled together, creating power and control for those at the top of the tree. The Keplerian tree was the sum of all its parts. The nine kingdoms were all equal in direct contrast to the warring factions of Earth divided into age, colour, creed, race and gender groups. He knew what he had to say would be explosive. He just wasn't sure that it would be any different to what their ancestors had heard before.

Liam stepped down out of the wagon to find an array of important figures from the district there to greet him. Milling through the merry throng, he performed a series of short gestures with a number of dignitaries before being shown to the door of his cottage. He walked up the front garden path, turning one more time to wave at the remnants of the welcoming entourage and then entered. The dwelling was clean, comfortable and unpretentious. He immediately felt at home.

Chapter 17

They entered through a gate of giant yew trees, reaching the council buildings in good time before the ceremony was due to begin. Large, overhanging branches sprouted out of short bulky stems and formed an archway, providing a natural tunnel with only one possible destination. Ornate and huge, the stone building waited patiently for him. His wagon drew up and he was ushered out into a rapturous crowd.

The steps were clean, cream and enormous; even by Prithvian standards. It was obvious to him that the original settlers were taller than Prithvians. Any adept human would have been able to climb them but it still required a good deal of lower body strength and a large stride. A form of wheel chair ramp snaked round the border and up to the main doors. Most inhabitants used this easier route on a weekly basis but not he; not today. Liam decided to take the line of most resistance ascending the traditional way given that it was his first day as a genuine part of their society. The stair may have been daunting yet it paled in comparison with what he was about to do. After a brief look around he climbed purposefully.

The edifice, Doric in design, had vertical shafts fluted with 28 parallel concave grooves standing directly on the stone floor below. It was reminiscent of the former Lincoln Memorial in Panamerica. Like the Parthenon before it the columns were topped with traditional metopes and triglyphs which provided the historic carvings of Utsima's visitors over many millennia. In so doing the settlers had created a beautiful and ornate roof laid out as an entablature, forming a frieze reminiscent of the Bayeux tapestry for all its story telling and intricate detail.

The imposing entrance was merely the tip of another equilateral triangle as the seemingly immeasurable walls ran on endlessly at 45 degrees in either direction. It was certainly an imposing sight. Once he had reached the top step he turned and looked through the trees down the road. There was no turning back now; this was his ultimate moment and the people of Samanya had come to bear witness.

Inside the building the crowd of onlookers filed away upstairs, heading towards the viewing gallery. Once seated their expectant voices wilted into a hushed murmur as they waited for the council to enter and the ceremony to begin. Liam at the same time was ushered into a council room to the side of the main chamber where he was given his new robes and instructed to wait with the middle-minister. They went through the procedure one last time and he stood ready, waiting for the bell to sound.

The last time that he had felt this agitated was before his speech at the Saatchi Gallery. That moment seemed an eternity away. It wasn't the distance he'd travelled but how far he had come; on an evolutionary path of the mind and spirit. He took stock, feeling his mental fortitude grow at exactly the right moment, leaving him with nothing but the strength and conviction of his own words.

As the clock struck noon the bell sounded and the doors to the side chamber opened simultaneously. A procession of ministers passed languidly in front, heading for the main chamber. Timed to perfection, Liam followed the middle-minister and joined the line towards the rear, keeping in step with the others. He bowed slightly. The hood of his enormous royal blue robes covered his head and concealed his face. He was to remain unnoticeable until he was asked to come forward and speak for the first time as a part of his unveiling.

Inside the inner chamber, there was a large open floor spanning the entire width and breadth of the room, leaving a row of benches on all four sides of a rectangle. Simply known as Sabha, the area was an amalgamation of many Prithvian debating rooms. The open space reminded Liam of the Roman Senate. The wood paneling on the walls was reminiscent of the now defunct House of Commons in London. The viewing gallery on the floor above was almost identical in design to the senate of the now disbanded United States of America. It was packed full of bodies.

The procession reached the middle of the floor. Liam kept his head bowed with his eyes focused on the back of the person in front of him. The bell sounded another time. Each councilor turned, facing the section of bench nearest to them and walked serenely towards their station. A few moments later the bell sounded again. The middle-minister sat to the right of Liam and after a moment's respite rose, approaching the centre of the floor. Shuffling serenely to his position he then made the short greeting to each side of the rectangle, turning full circle until facing back at Liam.

"Brethren today is auspicious because of whom we are about to receive into the fold. Propitious because of what we expect him to divulge and more importantly, fortunate for all of those from Prithvi here and afar. We expect today to be the founding stone in a clearing of their conscience. I know that many of you will be thinking why a man from so far away, should be accepted onto our council in such a short space of time. Yet we are of the mind that not only the Prithvian people will benefit but more importantly we will eternally reap the rewards. It is absolutely necessary to help the Prithvians eradicate their mark. With that in mind and without any further ceremony, it is our great pleasure to welcome him among us today. Brethren, I give you Liam Self."

Liam rose slowly, naturally fitting in with what was required. He kept his head bowed with the hood covering his face. He stepped towards the centre and once in the imaginary circle he stood still. He raised his head, lifting his hood gently backwards whilst smiling coyly up at the viewing galleries. He tried to establish if there were any Prithvians in the audience but the time that he had been afforded allowed for little examination. He mimicked the middle-minister's gestures to each section of the room, finally turning to face the high-minister and her counterparts on the other side. With the air of someone born to the task he spoke for the first time.

"Rather than trying to give you a full account of human history, of Prithvian culture or our journey to the mark, I have decided to give you a snapshot of our existence since it first appeared. Whether it was our distinct lack of conviction in the world around us that caused the mark to first appear or whether it was a direct result of its appearance that we lost faith remains to be seen but there is no doubt that the mark caused our loss of belief in nature, in ourselves and our very existence.

"I am not standing here before you to provide a damning critique of mankind. Whilst I might paint a dystopian view of Prithvi I am most certainly not entertaining the idea that we cannot be saved. I will champion the cause of any man, woman or creature from any of the nine regions of the universe who believes in themselves, has faith in others and their future in this world or the next.

"132 years ago, on the 14th December 2014 at 2pm in East Africa, the mark first appeared. It took root and spread across the entire planet affecting every single new born human. Mankind's reaction to this was extraordinary. We went through periods of denial, anger, bargaining and depression; all the while, trying to accept our fate. These stages came in no particular sequence and have been ever present for over a century. In our defence we have had to come to terms with being faced by the reality of our own impending death. The resulting years have been about this conflict and our inability to gravitate towards an acceptance; until possibly now.

"For all the advancement in technology and science, Prithvi is many years behind Kepler, in regards to the human condition, our culture and our own perception of reality. Both worlds have distinct similarities but are divided by conscience. Over the last millennia Prithvians have chosen to put themselves into the context of the divine. Where it has allowed them to perhaps progress further technologically, it has torn a gaping hole in their consciousness.

"The Prithvian 21st Century brought about a sea change in the creative power of humanity. We had poor nations pitted against the rich; big business against environmentalists who raged over the effect mankind had on our climate and natural resources. The financial crisis of the first two decades played a role of a pathogen, an agent of disease, which spread like wildfire around the globe threatening mankind's very existence. During the succeeding decades we suffered many global disasters which brought about total globalisation. Our population became endangered by rapid economic growth and technological integration.

"The latter part of the 21st Century ushered in widespread reforms where the original group of seven having been constrained by debt problems and lack of leadership were absorbed into the three world powers that exist today. The final act of rebasing to world credits led to a dramatic shift in focus; to the greater integration of our species. New institutions such as Vedas Corp grew, phoenix like, out of the ashes of our Oil Wars and simultaneously empowered individuals with positive and more benevolent aims. Yet through benevolence we still bred malice; duplication was at first deemed necessary to rebuild our society and population but it had only one sorry ending; a frightening one that all Prithvians still face today.

"With technological advancement and raised standards of living the very essence of being should not have changed. However it seems to me that we Prithvians have chosen the wrong path; when is a focus for further debate but I can see points in our history where we had the opportunity to take another route and where we did not. Junctions in the past are easy to spot in hindsight but if only we had had the foresight to see where it was that we went wrong. The simple ways afford a happy life as so clearly demonstrated on Kepler; if only we had chosen the same path when we could have done.

"We had intricate systems of welfare where our governments played key roles in the protection and promotion of the economic and social well being of our people. The welfare state was based on the principles of equality of opportunity, equitable distribution of wealth and public responsibility for those unable to avail themselves of the minimal provisions for a good life. These ideas may well be alien to a culture that has no use for money and astounding to one which has suppressed any form of capitalism but you must understand that due to an inefficient system and with a plethora of opposing theories and ideals, Prithvian culture has had very little opportunity in recent years to alter its evolutionary course.

"Attitudes have changed in recent times, where our World Council focused no doubt by the harbinger of our existence has sought an alternative to the communist or capitalist vision of their predecessors; trying to cover the entire population with a basic form of free, social and economic services. However old age pensions, healthcare and unemployment benefits have been rendered pretty useless, since the advent of the mark and the new social groups that have emerged.

"Over the course of our centuries, the labourers, the servants, the working class, born out of the trauma of the industrial revolution morphed into the middle class where they were aided and abetted by a technological revolution. In the social aftermath of urbanisation, industrialisation and technologicalisation, collective social groups such as the middle classes grew into the largest group of like minded individuals on our planet. The poor had access to credit and grew accustomed to material possessions. The rich were no longer those with inherited wealth, title and status. Our social order was in upheaval.

"Where many philosophers, economists and social scientists saw the middle classes as the tool to end all class division with an end of days revolution; what they got so wrong was the idea of ever-accelerating extremes between the top and the bottom; instead we saw the enlargement of the middle class and a collective loss of sensibility; none so prevalent, than when a generation of people were more interested in social networking sites, online shopping and virtual reality TV programmes. The middle classes continued to evolve, incorporating anyone who lived in a capitalist society; those who were able to create businesses out of their living rooms. This wiped out any other social order. At the turn of our last century, we saw duplicates, slaves to you and me, available to anyone and everyone on our planet.

"One shining light in the den of iniquity was that the mark eradicated religion, our hackneyed beliefs in fictitious ideals, creating yet another change in our social order. Factions developed based on the death dates and ages pre-determined by nature herself. Those who had years were afforded the time to live if they kept out of the city; those without used the cities as their battleground.

"During the early days of transplanting organs, limbs, blood and tissue we found that the only thing that we could not transplant was the grey matter. If the mark and the brain are irrevocably intertwined there is no way that anyone could beat what was pre-ordained. The mark predicts when the brain dies out, the energy, the life force of our being, not the function of the heart, lungs or limbs that support us. Fate still has a role to play in our existence but the Prithvian has been trying to cheat death ever since he first came into being.

"Duplication started with the very significant, constructive and necessary development of the in vitro fertilisation process which led to a twin epidemic at first. Yet it is now a pandemic and a very real threat to Prithvian existence, exacerbated with the advent of duplicates duplicating themselves. The ethics of duplication have been argued for well over a century but the practice persists. Morality has been called into question and faith in nature has been exposed. It stands to reason that the mark was nature's way of telling us to alter our course but instead we chose to carry on. It is no surprise that we find ourselves here before you, seeking answers or perhaps judgment for our crimes against humanity and the universe.

"Morality on Kepler is seen as the collection of beliefs as to what constitutes a good life. Yet on Prithvi, through centuries of growth and expansion, Gnosticism gave way to religion and material possessions. These religions initially provided our regulations for a perceived ideal life but morality became confused with these religious precepts. It is clear to me that

Keplerian moral codes are based upon well-defined value systems, governed by codes of your culture rather than being part of a religion. Prithvian codes such as the Noble Eightfold Path of Buddhism, the Ten Commandments of Judaism, the Quran of Islam and the Yamas of the Hindi all provided the morals upon which we built our society. Yet for while we have become truly globalised and are heading towards a single state, we have left little room for us to change, adapt and reverse the damage caused by conflicting ideals and our loss of morality.

"Your principles demonstrate that it would be foolish for any man, woman or otherwise to believe that they were created in the image of God; that their route to God is better than their fellow being. Prithvian cultures created a heaven and a hell, the good and the evil, the black and the white. Keplerians by virtue cannot fathom such views. It is therefore no surprise that nature, therefore the divine, has found a way to try and eradicate these manmade myths. The universe does not concern itself with the fates and actions of human beings.

"Prithvians must learn that intelligibility is the simple fruit of evolution; that after this, there is no need to rise above it by posing problems and asking questions. They must learn that the laws of natural selection and cosmic evolution do not require such questions as it is simply nature, the universe and therefore divine. They have to understand that everything is just as it is and that being just as it is, they should not question their existence in such a deterministic way.

"Your planet, your world, your culture is a beacon of hope for a land of despair. For Prithvians to be saved they must change their ideals, their principles, their ethics; their moral code. They must continue to do away with class distinction and religious orders; they must eradicate the factions, believe in natural welfare and a true singular system benefitting all. They must believe in themselves, the future; in life after death; the essence of being, energy, matter and the journey. They must forget material possession, technological advancement and their obsession with power. They must believe in the concept of the divine. The driving force, behind our sense of loss, is our loss of faith."

Liam looked down for the first time, realising that he had hardly drawn breath apart from pausing for dramatic effect. He looked around at the audience, above and below, but could not tell if they agreed, disagreed or simply had not understood. He felt the adrenaline surge out of his fingertips as he waited for someone to respond. The high-minister was the first to get to her feet. As she rose, everyone else in the chamber rose with her. A low note, similar to a guttural hum, resonated around the building and he realised that this was the Keplerian tradition during an inauguration. He looked at her then at the others beside her.

"The mark is a burden that is currently ours to bear but your ancestors once bore it and they were saved; acceptance will, no doubt, be our saviour."

The high-minister stepped forward and walked slowly towards him. In similar fashion she made the greeting to all sides of the chamber, turned to him, bowed and placed her right palm on his upturned right palm. Everyone in the chamber sat back down in their seats. She stepped back, speaking in the direction of the middle-minister and those to his side.

"The only real unity is the universe."

She stopped, pausing to look at Liam before sweeping her head round to all the corners of the chamber. Her voice carried through the silence, echoing off the rafters as everyone listened intently to her words of wisdom.

"Keplerians believe that the matter or energy of which we know we consist was in existence, every atom of it and every element of force, before we were born and will survive our apparent death. The same is true of every other mode of apparently separate or finite existence. Therefore no birth of a new world, a new star or a new being ever adds a grain of matter or an impulse of new energy to the universe. And the final decease of any or all of the infinite solar systems will not make a difference whatever to the infinite balance of forces of which we know the eternal all to consist."

No-one stirred. Keplerians and Prithvians alike were transfixed. None of them had ever been privy in their lifetime to such a discussion before. The high-minister ventured on giving an answer that Liam and all of Prithvi were looking for.

"With the correct understanding the mark will be cured. However this takes time and is not an automatic fix. The period of integration on Kepler is in direct correlation to the Prithvian capacity of acceptance."

Pausing again to ensure everyone had heard, she continued.

"We as a people have become one; through time we have become neither giant nor dwarf; neither black nor white; neither rich nor poor; neither corpulent nor emaciated; neither progressive nor regressive; neither monotheistic nor polytheistic. Your mark is readying you for your transformation."

There was a silence. Moments later, Liam cut in.

"It is clear what our mark represents. For as long as we can remember trees have been used as our oracles. This stems from every walk of life, across every era, culture, race and history. The Ancient Greeks believed in the Tree of Life, the Oubangui people of West Africa planted trees whenever a child was born. Through all our ages trees have been viewed as a link from the underworld to Prithvi pointing towards heaven. However we have needed time to adapt to a changed world; Prithvi's religions originated in times very different to those that exist on my planet today. Those times were of ill-education and limited scientific exploration; they were times of wars and epidemics where life was short and death quick.

"Our people are more intelligent; education is no longer the backbone of the elite. Some people on Prithvi would claim your way of thinking to be a philosophy, others would claim it to be a religion. Some would claim it to be

Stoicism and others would claim it as Buddhism. Your ideology deals with philosophy but also those spiritual concerns which are innately religious. You explore the emotional relationship between humans and nature. You approach ethics, rights and the environment in exactly the same way; a way that is inherently peaceful and scientific; a way that looks at the present as the most important time in our lives; that life is not better after death but that it is a continuous stream of energy, on a constant journey through space and time.

"The mark of the nine kingdoms, the mark of the one tree, the mark of the universe; whichever way we choose to see it, it is truly the mark of man."

Liam stood tall, taking strength from his convictions, realising that the inauguration was drawing to a close. The middle-minister rose up accompanied by the entire crowd. The deep humming tone returned. The two of them made a short gesture towards each other before returning to their benches on opposite sides of the room. Liam sat down next to the middle-minister who nodded approvingly in his direction.

Chapter 18

24th August 2147 – Morning – Samanya, Utsima, Kepler

"So we're all meant to simply surrender our existence and leave? We've been here a year; everyone has now been fully integrated. So do tell me, what's so important for us to give up our lives and return?"

Liam listened intently to the concealed cellhip, pressing his left wrist firmly to his ear whilst standing in the centre of the enormous living room. His cottage had taken on an air of familiarity where the ornaments and soft furnishings were reminiscent of those in his home back on Earth. The caller's words cut through his senses. He paused contemplating a worthy response.

"So how's everyone going to get back? There are 2,141 of us. We're spread out across the continent in over a thousand different locations. Next you are going to tell me that you have portals everywhere."

He paused again as he listened to the response and nodded in agreement.

"Alright, I'll go along with it for now but bear in mind, mine are Keplerian concerns. I'll meet the others and we'll be ready. We wait for them to arrive - until then."

For all the distractions he'd succumbed to since his arrival, Liam had meticulously maintained his mission, keeping to his correspondence whilst never revealing the nature of his true identity to anyone. He was in no mood for this to change. He had found his niche. He tapped his bandage and cleared the cellhip's contents; removing any trace of the conversation.

The house telephone immediately started to ring. He hurried into the hallway and picked up the handset, pausing momentarily before placing it to his ear.

"Hello, Liam here."

"It's Alb - I'll get straight to the point; we've been recalled to Tega. I don't know why exactly but it's a directive that includes all specialists, no matter how their lives have evolved."

"News indeed," he bluffed, "no point in me asking too many questions as I'm sure you've got a lot to deal with; who have you told so far? Can I be of any assistance?"

Alb Stein was chief of his department and also stationed in Samanya. They had become good friends since his inauguration. After Stein's initial scepticism which had hinged on the fact that he had never met him personally, they had built up a solid rapport.

146

"I've got a serious job on my hands as I can't make contact with everyone; it'd simply take too long. Every specialist in Utsima needs to get to the Samanyan meadow within 48 hours. The same is happening in every kingdom with everyone from Prithvi being called to their respective capital. We're being picked up by an aircraft from the Department for Security. The target is to have everyone back on Tega within 96 hours."

"Well there's obviously been a grave security breach for these measures to have been taken. There's no record of anything like this happening before. Do you need me to contact some of them?"

"I'm glad you ask. I've divided the kingdom into quadrants, which leaves you with 42 residential areas. I've allotted myself the rest of those in Samanya and the North-East quadrant. I've already instructed two others from here to do the same."

Liam listened intently into the receiver and scribbled on the note pad in front of him.

"Unfortunately there is little that we are allowed to say to everyone. We have been instructed not to cause concern amongst the locals. The idea is to make this appear as if it was intentional, similar to our first year audit of our original plan; on par with what was agreed between both councils. I'm sure you knew that this was coming up in any event."

"I did but it's not for me to say as I'm on the council for Utsimian affairs and not privy to Prithvian politics. In any case I'm here to help, give me the list and my quadrant. I'll do the rest."

"Thanks Liam, I knew I could count on you."

The rest of the morning was spent calling every Prithvian within his quadrant. The 48 hour window was to ensure that everyone had enough time to make it to their respective capital from the furthest reaches of their kingdom. The second 48 hours were obviously a contingency for those who were unreachable.

By the afternoon he had managed to speak with 37 of his 42. Three were on holiday and two were missing. By nightfall four of them had been located and were on their way back immediately to collect their things. This left just one cosmologist called Yakov Safronov still missing. No one had a clue as to his whereabouts. It turned out that he had been missing for more than two weeks.

That evening Liam received a call from one of Caitanya's elders who apologised profusely for not making anyone aware of the cosmologist's disappearance. They had hoped for his imminent return because he was such an integral part of their community. Having paced up and down his living room for almost an hour, Liam decided to ring Stein to update him on the situation.

"Alb, there's a problem. The bottom line is that I've got hold of everyone except for a man based in Caitanya. He has literally disappeared without a trace. The rest are all on their way to Samanya as we speak."

"Strange, we have news of a similar problem from the other kingdoms where there's one person missing with no trace of where or why they have left; all are pillars of their community and are respected specialists in their field. I've spoken to my counterparts in Amalaka, Uttara and Agra and they've confirmed that they have one unaccounted for, missing and presumed dead. The coincidence, of course, leads us all to believe that this is not the case. Each one left their community just over two weeks ago and hasn't been seen or heard from since."

"Haven't the tracking devices been activated?"

"They must have been but that's now out of our hands. I'll see you in the meadow in 36 hours."

Liam put down the receiver, thinking long and hard about his next steps. It was now late at night or the early hours of the morning, depending on how one looked at it. Laozi was in London; it would be the same time for him given that Keplerian Northern Hemisphere time corresponded to Greenwich Mean Time. There was no other solution he had to call him. The intrigue behind the disappearance of the nine vexed him tremendously.

"Laozi, it's me." He let the silence pan out until the breathing on the end of the line was audible. "I'm sure you are aware of the fact that nine specialists have gone missing. However what's strange is that it amounts to one from each kingdom all at the same time. No doubt you've got them tracked?"

"Of course we have. Every single one of our specialists, including you, has been fitted with a tracking device. It's spliced with your blood so you can't sense it. We know where you all are."

"Ok, so forgetting the reasons for the recall to Tega for a minute - have they gone after the original seven?"

"You know about them? No-one has ever mentioned them before. We have kept their identities hidden and never reported their disappearance. How do you know?"

"Come off it Laozi, I maybe on the council and concerned with Keplerian affairs but you can't pull the wool over my eyes. I don't know who they are but I was certain that a few would have been left behind after the initial Kepler Meeting. It was only after the events of today that my suspicions were confirmed. Does anyone else know about this?"

"No and yes."

"So let me guess, Mr. Cryptic, none of the Keplerians belonging to the nine kingdoms know but those in the Free or Prison States do. Am I correct?"

"You are."

"So who's where and what have they gone to do?"

"It wasn't our plan; we never gave a directive for any of them to leave their kingdoms but the cosmologist Yakov Safronov got wind of the fact that seven had remained behind. He'd obviously worked this out long before he'd arrived. He put a scheme into action involving a select group. We know that he was their leader because we have a source; one of his wider circle of friends."

"What have they gone to do? Why didn't you stop them? Tell me Laozi, is Ama one of them?"

"Those questions aren't so simple to answer in one breath but yes, Ama is one of them."

"Why didn't you tell me before? Where is she?"

"We were going to handle the process of extracting the seven in a few months time but now that a further nine have joined them we need to act fast. We do not want any of the Keplerians to find out as we are in enough bother as it is considering the situation back here on Earth. The recall to Tega has actually presented us with good cover in being able to fly our aircraft across the continent without causing any alarm."

"Ok, but you haven't answered my question yet - are they all in one place, what are they doing?"

"The original seven were left behind to explore the Free and Prison States, reporting back whether the Keplerians were telling the truth or hiding something. We had trackers on them from the get go, where they had covertly got to the free state of Maharnava by the time the Repertega landed. They all stopped reporting in. However we are still completely in the dark as to what it is exactly that they have found. We know that they have since split up as there are two of them in each state except for one alone in Karkara."

"If you knew so much, why did you allow this plan to go ahead?"

"Because we wanted to get to them in the first place; the only question is; do they want us to get them out of there?"

"I see; and you now want me to clear up your mess."

"Unfortunately so; this situation needs to be cleared up quickly and effectively, in less than 84 hours. The Kepler Council must know nothing of it and it must remain that way. You are not to mention this to any of your new found friends in high places."

"Upon this I will ponder, what are your intentions?"

"The specialists have split up and gone to each of the Free and Prison states in search of their Prithvian counterparts. Ama is in Arnava."

"On her own?"

"No, there are others with her. With the aid of one of our soldiers from the Department for Security, you will go to Karkara to rescue the two Prithvians that are now there."

"What of Ama?"

"One of our biologists, Jabir Ibn Al-Zarqali, knows her well; seeing as we do not want to blow your cover in any way, I'd suggest that he go to Arnava. The other two states will be covered by a team similar to yours; one local Prithvian and one security personnel. You'll return with the other specialists to Tega so as not to arouse suspicion, link up with your counterpart and be dropped just outside Karkara's walls.

He paused contemplatively for a minute before carrying on,

"We must prove to the Keplerians that all the specialists are on Tega within 84 hours. Time will be of the essence. You have the trackers; you can get to everyone easily. It's the extraction that will be the interesting part."

"OK; nothing like something out of the ordinary to play havoc with one's wits."

"We better not talk until you are back safe with mission completed; so until then."

"Until then Laozi."

Liam tapped his bandage, once for off and once again to delete the conversation log.

At noon the next day the aircraft arrived, touching down on the sandstone of Samanya's meadow. As he walked towards the steps at the side of the plane; his senses were wild and alive. He knew that there was a distinct possibility of him seeing Ama again; yet he wasn't certain if she would remember or even care. Once Laozi had divulged that she was in Arnava he had been less perturbed for the islands were a safe haven. He suspected that she was attracted to their ideas and the intrigue surrounding those mythical atolls.

However he knew little of the Prison States. Attika had told him that nothing was as it seemed. So perhaps it was true that the continent was shut out from the states to their north and south for their own protection; not the other way round. However he had also been warned him that once anyone found themselves on the other side of the wall they would disappear never to be seen again. This only added fuel to his fire.

He chose a seat near the front by a window. He stowed his backpack away in the overhead locker, stuffing it in to the tight space as best he could. He wasn't the only one who'd brought too much luggage with him as the other 236 Utsimian specialists were all taking their time to get to their seats. The pressing nature of their departure was not apparent and Stein wanted it to remain that way. The flight to Adhara would only take just over an hour in any case, so they had little cause for alarm.

Sitting back, he looked onto the stone meadow outside. A woman who'd been based in the North-West sat in the aisle seat, leaving a space between them. After a brief exchange, they reverted to their own thoughts and waited for takeoff. Once everyone had secured their things in the hold the plane took off.

The scenery that was unveiled was truly remarkable. They reached 36,000 feet quickly. There wasn't a strip of cloud in the sky, allowing them to see as far as the eye could see. He had always wondered what the shoreline looked like from the air; in fact the entire continent; the Himalayas, the beaches, the fields, cliffs, rainforest. They were now privy to it all. They swooped over the highest Keplerian peak, known as Dhavalagiri or Dhava for short. Once they'd crossed over into the southern hemisphere, passing quickly over the glorious expanse of rainforests, the lush greens of Utsima's summer were a distant memory. They were confronted by the barren wastelands of Garbha ravaged by a long winter, the myriad colours of the patchwork fields of Ganda and finally the frozen deserts of Adhara which were waiting for a long hot summer of their own.

An hour later, they touched down with a lot of shell shocked people aboard, all carrying a sense of foreboding and the unwanted feelings of one's first day back at an institution. Having spent a year away, Tega would now feel like a prison. Very few got up to leave as the doors opened. It was left to Liam to make the first move. He was on a different course, a separate mission where he had only a few hours to meet his counterpart from security and turn around and head for Karkara. He couldn't hurry fast enough.

With his backpack slung over his right shoulder, he leapt down the steps two at a time, holding onto the rail with his left hand. The only other time he'd walked across the landing site was when he'd joined the Department for Cosmology for the first time as they had headed for their wagon waiting in the far corner. That journey to Utsima had been arduous but very informative.

He made it into the entrance hall which funneled into the atrium of Tega. Lit up by the early evening's rays, it was deathly silent. He stealthily headed towards the Department for Security following the array of Keplerian signs that were laid out before him. The specialists obviously had been trained from the very beginning in both the language and the customs of the Keplerians. It is why their integration had been such a success; up and till now.

He arrived at the Department for Security and the camera domes blinked at him as they recorded every movement in the vicinity. There were two security guards standing post on either side of the double doors. One of them received a message and waved him in. A voice emanated from the walls.

"We've been expecting you. You leave in an hour. Proceed upstairs."

Before he had a chance to open his mouth his backpack was taken off his shoulder and he was being ushered towards an internal spiral staircase, sandwiched between two people dressed in white army fatigues. The sound of their feet against the hard metal flooring beat in time with his heart as the blood rushed through his veins in anticipation. They reached the top and he found himself in a small, clean and minimalist room with multiple exits. A middle aged, muscle bound man walked towards him talking.

"The name's Robert Peel; I'm chief of department and the leader of this mission. This is Jabir Ibn Al-Zarqali, who was based in Uttara, Ban Qian from Agra and Ines Pizzaro from Daksina."

Liam nodded in each of their direction and switched back to Peel who continued with his brief.

"There is precious little time to make conversation so I would suggest that I get to the point quickly and that you listen carefully. In short, you must infiltrate the community at your intended destination and you must persuade your Prithvian counterparts to join you back on Tega. Jabir you are going to Arnava, Ban to Avasya, Liam to Karkara and Ines to Maharnava."

He looked at each of them briefly before continuing,

"By the time you land outside your destination, you will have only 42 hours to get them onto that plane and bring them back here. We want no one to be harmed. You have been assigned a military specialist each who will act as your partner in this mission. You'll be introduced on your journey. Avasya is the furthest away so Ban, you will be leaving in 15 minutes; then you Ines; Jabir after that and Liam, in an hour. Your best negotiation skills will be needed. Understood?"

They all looked at one another but remained silent.

"Good - Ban if you follow me, I can walk and talk, while we head for your aircraft."

With that they were gone, leaving Liam, Jabir and Ines alone. They remained silent, lost in their own thoughts, before Peel appeared again and took Jabir off. Not long after that Peel returned. When he and Ines left, Liam was left stood in the circular room, alone. He was intrigued to know who it was that he would be rescuing or more likely coaxing to return. Why it was all so clandestine was beyond him. A few moments later Peel arrived to escort him to his transport.

"Robert; who's in Karkara?"

Peel turned to him as they walked side by side,

"Yakov took two others to Avasya to rescue two of the seven. Ban was approached by him to join them a long time ago. She refused and so therefore is ideal to bring him back. Jabir knows the three that went to Arnava, the same goes for Ines and his mission to Maharnava, leaving you with one original and one other to bring back. Just because there will be only two of them doesn't make this an easy task; yours will be the hardest given where you are going and who you will be up against. I guess that's why you've been put forward for this task."

"Do you care to shed any light on who I'm actually meeting?"

"Karkara is a mystery to all of us and given your status amongst the Keplerians, we should be looking to you for answers. We have no information and all our covert efforts to ascertain what lies behind the walls have failed over the past year. It's like there are defences above and below ground, in the air and all around repelling any advances. The other prison state was not so difficult to access where we have been able to record the lives of their people and the topography in secret since day one. Avasya is an unattractive place to be and I don't envisage Ban having too many problems extricating the others from there.

Liam looked at Peel waiting for an answer to his question. Noticing his impatience, Peel pressed on, trying to find the right line.

"Karkara is an entirely different story. With no information we have little to work with and so you are going in blind. What's more the member of

Yakov's team who's already there is our chief of the Department for Finance & Trade where he was stationed in the Kingdom of Ganda and goes by the name of Krugman. We do know that he serves the original who's been there for almost 18 months. There is little hope in either of them leaving let alone within 42 hours. Yet we need a clean slate with the Keplerians in order to return to Earth with a clear conscience."

Liam looked at Peel intently, studying his face as they walked down another corridor.

"So who is this original person that Krugman serves?"

"He goes by the name of JPK, a mathematical genius; apparently a force to be reckoned with. He was originally a Vedas Corp operative before he gave it all up to be with his family. He stayed behind after the Kepler Broadcast as he was dead to Prithvi or so it was said."

They crossed over the threshold, stepping into the cabin of the aircraft.

"Surely there is more on him to work with."

"Unfortunately no; all records of the seven were destroyed as a security measure when they were first left on Kepler. The only reference we have to them is their tracker and their initials."

"Alright, here goes nothing – see you anon."

Liam shook his hand before making his way to a seat. The cabin was small but extremely comfortable, laid out in a similar style to the private jets of the 20th Century with six leather covered chairs, providing ample leg room and sleeping space. His backpack was lying on the floor, in front of what he took as his appropriate seat. He sat back thinking fast. JPK's identity may not be such a mystery after all.

Liam's partner in crime arrived a minute later. They looked at each other for a moment before he spoke in English with a thick North African accent.

"Moshe Elazar."

"Liam Self."

Short, stocky with a shaved head, he was the exact opposite to Liam in every sense of the word. Pugnacious, dogmatic and determined the soldier looked at his perspicacious, pragmatic and positive counterpart.

"So do you know what we are up against?"

"I can safely say that I have no idea what but I suspect I know whom. Rest assured Moshe, I think we have the measure of our quarry."

They couldn't have been better suited and they both recognised it immediately. Where Liam understood that he would have to take great care in educating his companion in the ways of a world without violence, Moshe knew that he could rely on Liam's wit to extract them from any potential war of words.

The aircraft took off immediately after they had sat down opposite each other. It was dark outside and Liam realised that it was only going to get darker as they headed due south towards the borders of Karkara. His climbing gear would no doubt come in useful as he envisaged the two of them having to scale icy walls and ramparts whilst trying to penetrate the hostile perimeter in the dead of night.

The feeling of pressing on into the unknown was exhilarating. Moshe detected no fear in Liam's eyes, leaving him content that his partner had a plan, no matter how outlandish.

The aircraft set down on the ice, 45 minutes later. The pilot stepped out of the cockpit and told them that they were a few miles from Karkara's known border. He informed them that his orders were to remain in situ for 42 hours awaiting their return. The aircraft rocked as it was blasted by a severe gust of wind outside. Moshe thanked the pilot. When they were both ready with their packs firmly strapped to their backs he reached for the release button at the side of the plane and the door fizzed open, letting a chute unfurl to the ground, providing their exit.

The next three miles were to be tackled on foot where they estimated that they'd be at the gates within the hour. Without another word, Liam dropped down out of the plane with a casual wave at the pilot and was gone. Moshe followed quickly after.

Once on the ice, the chute curled back up retreating into the warmth of the plane. The door closed ominously shut. Nature was at her most extreme in these parts and they were now at her mercy. Moshe led the way as they took up a brisk pace, battling the elements, making their way towards the arctic fortifications looming in the distance.

The pace never slackened. Moshe was pleasantly surprised at Liam's fitness and athletic ability. Little did he know that Liam was at his most comfortable when faced by situations such as these; he was in his element. They continued to jog whilst the wind drove hard at their sides forcing them off line every other step. The swirling top snow rushed, restlessly across the ice and through the darkness Liam made out a deep blue glow far off across the expanse.

Half an hour in Moshe slowed to a halt, holding up his right hand at 90 degrees with his fist clenched in true military fashion. Liam stopped immediately, closing in towards Moshe so that they could hear each other through the howling gale that enveloped them. They crouched down at exactly the same time as Moshe spoke in forced but hushed tones.

"Over there. It comes and goes like a pulse, a beacon calling us in. There it is again."

"The gates are beckoning."

"Can you see the darkness of the perimeter walls?"

"Like clouds across the void. The moonlight is pushing through the snow swirl; I reckon we're only half a kilometre away."

"Any ideas on what's on the other side?"

"Expect nothing Moshe; nothing will be as it seems. Those walls may be of ice and snow but its gates will be anything but. I have a feeling that they already know that we are here and the pulse is for our benefit."

"I guess we should play ball and head directly for it. No time to waste if we are going to complete this mission."

"Absolutely, lead the way."

The beacon burned brighter, pulse increasing in speed as they approached. When they were only a hundred metres away the wind dropped surreptitiously, dissipating the snow which allowed the dominance of the walls to be revealed. Standing two miles high and running 24 miles in either direction, it was supreme in its enormity. The pulse quickened until they stood opposite what had to be the gates.

The beacon disappeared, leaving the moonlight to dance on the doors before them. Liam succumbed to their magnificence. Sheer and luminous they were majestic in their splendour. Two sheets of frosted glass stood 64 metres high and 24 metres wide in front of them. Firmly shut and with no apparent intention of opening they were left to marvel at the intricate and ornate carvings in the glass. An entire list of mathematic symbols decorated the doors. Liam made out the signs for summation, product, Dirac delta, pi, selection and transpose but it was the formulae dancing around the symbols that sucked him truly in.

Momentarily forgetting the reason for their arrival Liam gazed upon each one, mouth wide open, trying to unpick the reasons for their relevance. In amongst the formulae could only have been Einstein's field equation, Newton's laws of motion and Johannes Kepler's equation or at least the Keplerian version.

Kepler's laws of planetary motion were the principles that governed both planets, the fundamental philosophy that every Prithvian had built his or her scientific understanding of the universe. Liam's preparatory school teacher's words rang sharp in his ears 'the square of the orbital period of a planet is directly proportional to the cube of the cube of the semi-major axis of its orbit'. He remembered that Kepler's third law captured the relationship between the distance of the planets from the sun and their orbital periods; noticing that here on these doors the symbols of P and A were interspersed with indices. Again he recollected that Kepler had described his laws as the 'music of the spheres', where Prithvians had affectionately given it the moniker of the harmonic law.

He gazed intently upon the symbols, searching for anything that could assist them in their quest. The inscriptions obviously held the secrets of what lay behind the doors but he was intent in being forearmed before they were sucked into whatever it was the Keplerians had been hiding. Moshe looked at him questioningly, hoping to be guided in an area alien to his instincts. They stepped in, close up against the glass, almost trying to peer in but to no avail. The water vapor in their breath condensed in the still cold air, rising up against the sheer sheets of glass that towered above them.

A blast hit them, knocking them sideways. Again another blast hit them, this time resembling a fog horn. Moshe and Liam cupped their ears, for the deep rich tones dug deep where they were afraid that the bass vibrations would shake the flesh off their bones. The sound gave up with one final boom before shards of light cast long lines out into the abyss behind them.

The beams brilliant in their radiance grew as the doors slowly retreated into the ground below. There was now nothing between them and their mission. They looked at each other and back into the white light before them; neither able to make the first move. The two lost souls were momentarily motionless, captivated, floundering in the grip of the gates of Karkara.

Chapter 19

24th August 2147 – Evening – Arnava, Kepler

Ama awoke, alone in the dark. The crackling sound of a newly engaged fire broke her reverie. The dense smoke of damp wood burning through its moisture wafted around her. She'd fallen asleep under a palm tree whilst the melodic tones of the lapping water had lulled her into a dreamless haven of peace and serenity. It had not taken long to settle into her new habitat along a stretch of beach in the north west of Arnava's main island, Zuddhi. She, Boy and her two traveling companions had been welcomed into the local community with open arms, like prodigal children making their gloriously strategic return.

Yakov's quest had been driven by reason; however hers was a secret desire to go along with the plan purely to get a taste of life off the continent giving her options, enabling her to produce better material with more rounded and worldly testimonies.

She woke rubbing her eyes in hope of clearing the listless fog that had descended. The laid back and unsophisticated lifestyle had already coaxed her body clock into a new regime. Her siesta had lasted a lot longer than she had originally intended where a quick rest had turned into a couple of hours. The moonlit ocean invited her in and she was drawn to its tune. Rising up steadily she eased the dress off her shoulders allowing it to fall to ground. Naked and uninhibited she headed towards the sea.

A group of people scurried around behind a coppice, tirelessly setting up for the evening meal. She skipped on into the shallows, entranced by the bioluminescence generated by microscopic organisms reacting with the oxygen in the water. The sea of light was a genuine thing of beauty where each small wave lit up like a sheet of lightning as it lapped at the shoreline.

The islands of Arnava were a tropical paradise. Within her first few days of being there she had befriended one of the two originals, Arwald who'd been handfasted in style to Fairuza, a girl originally from Anga. Ama had left her co-specialists to their own devices whilst her hosts had shown her around.

Arnavian society was conducted upon a set of clear principles which were exacted by their rituals and forms of worship. She had never once felt confused by their beliefs as it was clear to her that they had chosen a pagan existence yet shared the fundamental principles of their more exalted continental counterparts. For Arnavians considered themselves as stewards of the environment and caretakers of their islands.

She swam out until she could no longer touch the bottom and far enough so she could see both corners of the bay. The fire in the centre of the coppice had burned through the wet wood and was now radiating heat and flame. It danced in the moonlight as she trod water lapping up the scenes. It had been over a year since the Repertega had landed. They had all ventured out into the relative unknown. Earth was a diminishing memory but she still maintained a loyalty to her kind; to the memory of her family, friends and great loves of the past.

The year had offered up little romance but again this was more likely by design, rather than a lack of interested parties. She hadn't shaken off her sense of loss as she had thought she would have done. The loss of her parents, the loss of her life on Earth and her one true love, Hansel Laurence had forced her to change, to become more distant and retreat from making any real connection with anybody. She thought at times that the people on the continent for all their rituals and blissful ideals were timeless, existing in world without progression which was, for all the problems with Prithvian society, contrary to human nature.

She liked her new life and was content. Yet she felt like there was something more that her existence was truly lacking substance. Self's explanations and the resultant debates were absolutely necessary but they still couldn't quite fill the void. The void of feeling, the void of presence, the void of existence; she wanted more answers, more reason, more sentiment.

She needed love and it was only when she found love again that she would be truly happy. She knew that she would return to Amalaka after a brief sojourn in a primitive paradise but it was absolutely crucial that she explore the islands and perhaps the Prison States before she settled down entirely. She had plenty of time; she was a Ninety after all.

Arnavian society observed the solar cycle with the two solstices and the two equinoxes occurring over the course of a year. A small difference to the Prithvian calendar was that the solstice and equinox months of June, December, March and September all lasted for only 28 days and the others lasted for 32 days, except for February which was akin to a Prithvian leap year. All Arnavians performed rituals on the nights of the new and full moons in reverence of the ovulation and menstruation. Self had determined the universe to be a womb.

She continued to stare back incredulously at her surrounding environment. Originally she had thought that she had been sent on a voyage of discovery for the purpose of bringing new worlds and ideas back to Earth but it had in fact been a very personal journey where she'd learnt more in a year about her own reality than she would have ever learnt back on Earth; in such a fractured, dystopian modern society.

The Arnavians had taken a further step back in time to a place where they recognised nature as sacred, divine and deserving of human respect. At its purest it could be described as a natural mysticism where they exalted the empirical, the measurable physical cosmos far above spiritual concepts and beliefs. None of the Arnavians had heard of Liam Self, let alone the Great Book, so it came as no surprise that Arwald and his original counterpart, Baijika hadn't either. Ama was in no hurry to question their way of life or their views on reality.

Although warm, Ama sensed that it was time to return to dry land before the salt water turned her soft unblemished skin into a wrinkled prune. She took one last glance at the shoreline subconsciously humming to herself in a state of complete calm, devoid of any emotion, at peace with her environment. Transfixed by the luminescence floating alongside, she flipped her legs up from behind, forcing her head down under the surface and kicked for the sandy bottom of the sea bed.

The view above was glorious. The pale moonlight shimmered through the ripples and mixed with the plankton providing pearl drops of light which swayed forwards and backwards in the current. Before her breath gave out she swam towards the surface, catapulting herself out of the sea like a dolphin during playtime. By this time she was not far from the shore and so stood up covering her modesty, in case anyone happened to be passing by. Some Prithvian habits still remained. However it seemed that she was all alone and away from prying eyes. She hurried along towards her dress and shoes, slipping them on effortlessly and headed for her hut to change for dinner.

She crept quietly through the coppice, along a sandy path that had been nurtured through the year until she reached a clearing where there was a row of 98 huts forming a giant circle. Because there was no beginning and no end Ama could not tell who was a descendent of an early settler or who was a relatively new arrival. She entered her un-fussily neat abode and was immediately confronted by her loyal protector. He'd quickly ascertained that there were no obvious threats to Ama's wellbeing so he spent most of his days scurrying around the kitchen areas and playing with the local children. She cupped his face in her hands, running her fingers softly over the long line of his nose and patted his side absent mindedly.

After a while she slipped her dress off once more and removed her shoes. The room smelt of fresh lavender, providing an ambience that becalmed anyone who entered. She took a look at her slim toned body as she rubbed herself down with a soft clean towel. Her skin was lithe but firm; there wasn't an ounce of fat on her. Her mind was pure and her body healthy.

She wanted the best of both worlds. No matter how often she tried to move on, she couldn't shake the thought of him; his spark, his essence, his joie de vivre. She wished that she could communicate with him, to let him know of what she was doing, how far she had come and to let him know of her enduring devotion. She knew that he only had a few years left but wished that they could have been spent with her. She would have had his child and would have brought it up on Kepler; in the Prison States if she had to.

Her hair had grown longer; the dark brown strands had begun to lighten. She tied it loosely in a plait allowing it to fall down the middle of her back. There was no electricity on the island. Everyone used gas lamps, burners and candles. Ama's hut contained an array of elaborate lights which blended the ambience of a witch's coven with a detoxifying retreat of the 21st Century. Her face had hardly changed at all, in fact she looked younger, healthier yet she was wiser, more knowing with a few scars to prove it. With nothing else needing doing she slipped on her shoes told Boy to stay and look after their home and made her way back towards the thicket and the community dining area.

Weaving her way through the palm trees along the path she came to another clearing drenched in the heat and light of a multitude of fires, arranged in a circle, acting as a perimeter fence. In the centre was one giant bonfire. It would be lit at sundown and wouldn't go out till sunrise. Enveloping this fire was an enormous, immovable circular stone table with heavy wooden stools placed in an organised symmetry, at equidistant of each other and on either side.

The most ubiquitous Arnavian symbol of all was the circle and this was not lost on Ama. The circle was a symbol of the feminine linked to the womb. To her it represented Earth and Kepler moving in a circular orbit around their respective suns. All Arnavian ceremonies were conducted in a circle, all their community gatherings were brought together this way and their living quarters followed suit. By there being no obvious beginning, middle or end; no top, middle of bottom, Ama knew that there was a universal rejection of hierarchy. The most peculiar part of their society was that it seemed as if the islanders, the caretakers had been waiting for Ama and her fellow Prithvians all along. She couldn't understand why there were enough seats and huts for all of them; no more, no less, exactly the right number.

Those, who hadn't been helping with the preparation, came out through the gaps in the hedges between the perimeter fires at precisely the same time as her, as if by force of habit. They all made their way towards their place around the table, standing quietly behind their stool. Everybody sat down at the same time as the last serving plate was carefully placed on its surface. They sat down in the same order as their homes. Baijika, Arwald's original counterpart was positioned directly opposite and so screened from view by the central fire. Everybody began to talk animatedly as soon as they'd helped themselves to the food and had passed it around. There was an assortment of vegetables, salads and fruits which were accompanied by a selection of rice.

After a while the conversations died down as most were concentrating on the plate in front of them. Ama turned to her right and looked directly at Arwald.

"Something's been troubling me for quite some time. Sorry to gun straight in but why did you not stay on the continent when you first arrived? How did you hear of this place? It wasn't exactly advertised."

"It's such a long time ago that I almost forget." He responded without a hint of irony. "But in truth we were told a little of the islands when we first arrived. When we met the Keplerian Council we were taken to a village not far from our landing site where we tried to communicate as best we could with the locals. You have talked of the broadcast and the message relayed back to Earth; much of it was representative of how it was back here. However it was subsequently agreed by Iso that the seven of us who looked most like we came from Kepler would remain without a word to the council.

"Not wanting to arouse suspicion and knowing a little about the Free States we decided to head for Maharnava which was the largest of the free communities. We had heard of their liberal attitude towards the codes and practices of the continent and thought that it was a good place to start. Baijika hasn't always been known as that, she was originally called Mary but took on a new spiritual path almost immediately when we arrived. She and I were interested in going back to our roots, finding a source to this modern pantheistic society and heard that Arnava was a replica of one its early forms. That's why we came to be here."

"If it wasn't for Yakov we wouldn't have even known. I imagine that he had a tip off from someone whilst onboard the Repertega but we are still unsure as to whom it could have been. There were no names, no records. So what of the others now?"

"We all disbanded. We were told of the Prison States but no one on the islands knew what they actually entailed. Three of us headed for the arctic nations, citing that they were already well versed in the ways of paganism. They wanted to see for themselves the customs of the prisoners before returning to Adhara and waiting for the Repertega to appear. Neither Baijika nor I knew that we would become so immersed in our new lifestyles that we would never return. That was not our original intention. We wanted to report back what we were learning but we soon felt like we were being unfaithful to our own people, spying on people that we had come to adore. We stopped almost immediately. You would have done the same."

"True. But what of your responsibility to your people? To your own kind?"

"As I said Ama these are my people now. I have no other kind. I'm sure my colleagues feel the same wherever they are."

"I guess we had a very different experience as we were all trained with a mission in mind, a purpose rather than being thrown into an alien environment with little to go by. We weren't exactly staying on an unknown planet with no motive or possibility of explaining why we were here. I guess that's easy to understand; so why not the continent?"

"I'm fearful of their system, it's too easy to corrupt; too hard to maintain."

"Yet why have they been able to keep it so for so long? Why have they been going for millennia after millennia, neither progressing nor regressing, on a constant path for all eternity?"

"I'm not sure of what you speak. What do you mean?"

"Arwald, you've missed out. A lot has changed. Everyone is aware of what is really going on within their society and also in the wider community. When we arrived no one talked freely about the free or prison states as they knew very little and it seemed natural to talk little of something that you did not know about. Rumours are dangerous and the positive karma generated by all of Kepler's people explains why none of them openly discuss things of which they are uninformed. One of us uncovered the truth of their existence extremely early on. It was an extraordinary feat but it worked. I've mentioned Liam Self to you before in passing but I think you should know more about what he determined as I think it might persuade you to come back with us."

"Nothing would sway my decision Ama, my mark exists and no amount of spiritual cleansing will eradicate its stain on my soul. I am closer to nature, my god, my goddess, my universe than I have ever been or ever will be."

"Understood but that is not my point. It's been done before Arwald and it'll be done again. Everything that we are doing is part of an immeasurable circle of life; let me explain."

Ama felt like a disciple. She drew on her experience of Earth, Kepler and what she had heard of in the Great Book. By the time she had finished Arwald was not the only one silent. Everyone within her community was looking at her astonished with the revelation. The last thing she had ever wanted was to become a cleric. In any case she was describing a philosophy, a way of life, a perspective not a set of rules or a religious code. Aware of a multitude of eyes gazing upon her she became self conscious and changed tack.

"My father was a free spirit of the true sense. His life was taken by a group of unfortunates, along with my mother's. His body was never found. My mother would have been happy to be wherever he was. All I can do is hope that they are still together singing the same tune along an endless stream of dust and dreams."

She fell silent. A multitude of minds reflected inwards. Suddenly there was the sharp crack of a breaking twig under foot and a rustling in the hedge beyond the perimeter. Everyone was visibly startled, looking in the direction of the sound. There was another crack, further rustle and before anyone had moved from their perch, Jabir and a very serious looking accomplice walked through into the clearing. Not a soul spoke. Jabir took up the reins.

"Sorry to crash in on this party but my colleague and I have important business. We must speak to the three known Prithvians in private."

Ama stood up, looking in the direction of Baijika and her two neighbours.

"Everyone this is Jabir; a friend. There's no cause for alarm. I'm sure it's nothing. We'll take this to the beach."

With that she got up and headed over towards Jabir and his accomplice. The two people sitting next to Baijika followed her lead, demonstrating their heritage. They returned back down the path whereupon Ama spoke quickly and decisively.

"Jabir, why have you come all this way? If it's in pursuit of me, why include my friends? I've told you before that you're barking up the wrong tree."

"Ama, I wish it were that simple. You've made quite a name for yourself on the continent. What exactly are you trying to achieve here?"

"The fact that we now have an audience hardly warrants any more candour. So cut to the chase and tell me why you are really here as it can't be just for me."

She looked at the member of security with venom in her eyes. Jabir responded,

"We've all been recalled to Tega. Reasons for which I'll explain later but our entire mission rests on your return; it is imperative. The originals can stay."

"You know of them? How? Your timing's impeccable. I was just making headway with Arwald. He could be persuaded to return to the continent. How can I trust you, especially when you have at least one obvious agenda?"

"Why would I know that they are here and also be with a woman from the Department for Security unless it was a very real directive?"

Jabir turned and looked at his accomplice who took it as her cue to join in the conversation.

"I can confirm to the positive. There has been a substantial breach in security and all 2,141 specialists have been recalled to base. No exceptions. Our orders are to bring you back against your will if we have to. However your overriding responsibility to the mission and towards those that brought you here should prevent any such force being necessary."

"Ok. What of the originals?"

Jabir took up from where he left off.

"It's simple really. You three need to come with us now and the two of them can either join us or stay where they are. The Keplerian Council is not aware of their existence and so it matters not whether they come or go. However I sense that you feel otherwise."

Ama backed off and turned to her two beleaguered colleagues and discussed the matter privately with them. They had overheard the bulk of the conversation and had certainly got the gist of what was being proposed. A few moments later she returned.

"We came here with the specific intention of bringing the originals back to the continent and would like to try to complete our own undertaking. How long have we got?

"That's the issue Ama. We don't have a few weeks or even a few days. It's a matter of hours before the Keplerian Council has to be informed. They will no doubt conduct their own examination to ascertain the success of our recall and so we need to be back within the next 24 hours."

"Cutting it fine aren't you?"

"Not us; you. We never accounted for nine loose cannons going off in search of a group of people who didn't wish to be found. Talk about being the proverbial fly in the ointment."

"The problem from the beginning has been the lack of real information available to any of us. If we were all in possession of the facts I sincerely doubt the originals would have even been here in the first place, let alone in the prison states. The continent is by far the most compelling place to be but how were we supposed to know?"

"Ama, I'm just another specialist just like you. I'm a biologist who became your friend. My concern is your safety, the mission's safety and my orders."

"Ok. The three of us will come gladly and that is not in question. However we want Arwald and Baijika, sorry Mary, to come back with us. Arwald is, in all intents and purposes, married and his wife is expecting a child. There is no way that we can turn this around in 24 hours. What can we do? What would you do?"

"As I said it's not my concern."

"Give us time to talk to those that we need to and to pack our things. We'll meet you back here in one hour Ok?"

Ama turned to her colleagues, spoke to them briefly and they disappeared in an opposite direction. Their discussion with Baijika would no doubt be more successful than her own with Arwald. She knew that there was only one possible outcome but she persevered in any event. She stuck to the perimeter path, circling the dining area and fed into another route heading towards the housing area. Arwald and Fairuza had always had the huts next door to each other ever since their separate arrival. Now that they were handfasted, hers had become their home and Arwald's had become his temporary meditation centre. This would be short lived as it was destined to become his child's in a few months. Ama knew that he would have returned to his solitude, especially after their earlier conversation. She approached the door and waited a moment before knocking.

"Welcome."

"We have to leave."

"You or me?"

"Both, me, I don't know."

"Slow down Ama, what's the story?"

"There has been a substantial breach in security. All of the specialists have been recalled to base. Unfortunately it's not something that can happen in time, it has to happen now or otherwise we jeopardise the entire mission. You know how we came to be here. We owe a debt of gratitude to those who made it happen. We have to leave within the hour. I think that you should come with us; if not to the base, at least to the continent for your child's sake, let alone Fairuza's. This is no long term life plan, its hiding away on a magical isle waiting for nature to take you away."

"If that's the way you want to look at it. What do you call the lifestyle on the mainland?"

"As I said before there's more to it than this. There are layers upon layers of evolution, advancement of consciousness, development of the physical; with a distinct lack of technological progression for the wellbeing of all. I don't have time to go into it again but your children will benefit from an existence akin to what you have here but one that is far more sophisticated. One that is a well developed philosophy which has taken thousands of years to be perfected."

"Shouldn't we wait until we can determine whether my children have the mark? What if one does and the other does not? What happens then? What if the eldest is freed from its burden but in the youngest the malevolence flourishes? What then Ama?"

"The mark is about you not your child. Perception is energy; energy needs to alter before matter evolves. Are you familiar with the phrase mind over matter? If your mindset changes, your body will too, manifesting in your child at the point of conception. Once the doors to perception have been opened they will never close. Trust me I have seen through them and so have all of those mainlanders, no matter their heritage."

"I am drawn to your words and want to taste this life on the continent. Fairuza talks of it as a benign place but where few of her own choices are made. As if she was awake but dreaming, never living. To live is to endure, to love, to lose, to understand."

"Points that no longer exist on Earth, all eradicated by our mark. Before Mark's Day there was talk of love, loss and understanding. Of course we have suffered, endured and fought but we have learnt little of ourselves. Life on Kepler has given us that chance. A chance to change, to change our destiny and this is what we need to initiate here before we return to Earth. Your conscience won't change on these islands Arwald. You'll be stuck in a blissful purgatory and your children after you and their children after them; never to return."

"That's a pretty damning critique from someone so naturally peaceful."

"It's not damning. On the contrary this place is a primitive paradise but look how un-evolved it is, how un-evolved its people are. Their principles, their ethics, their concepts of the divine all make sense but the continent uses these and pushes on to places that you can't yet comprehend. It's all about the evolution of the spirit and the Keplerians have transcended anything that we have ever been able to achieve up to this point in the Prithvian timeline."

"I will consider your words carefully. I cannot leave now nor come with you. I will wait till my child is born. I'll discuss it with Fairuza. Have you ever been in love Ama? I mean properly in love? I hadn't until I met Fairuza. It seems strange that I had to travel light years to find her."

"I'm the opposite. It's my greatest mistake. I travelled light years to leave my one true love far behind. I can't help but think that this entire world would have been his if he were here. He would have understood every inch, every facet of their life; their concepts and their beliefs. He was an exceptional artist with an uncanny ability to use his canvass as the window to his subject's soul. I've never met anyone past or present who has given me that sense of purpose, that warmth, that connection, that sense of being. I wish he were here with me, listening to me speak now. How I have changed. I am more like him than I ever thought I would be."

Ama put her head in her hands and sighed deeply, holding back the tears. She sat perched on the side of a table in the middle of the room. Arwald got up from his bed of cushions and walked over to her, placing an arm round her shoulder. She ventured on with breathless sentences.

"My biggest regret is not telling him everything; not allowing him to know the full story. If only I could turn back the tide of time, I would have done so much, so differently. If I continue down my current path, I'll end up settling for Jabir and a life in the Prison States."

"Ama neither will come to pass. You can live wherever you choose, with or without anyone, there is no correct path."

"I will return to base and whenever we are set free I will be part of the team that stays behind and sets up the Prithvian settlement in Adhara."

"Why won't you return to Earth and your long lost love?"

"He'll be dead by the time I'd get back. Besides I'm most probably dead to him already; the manner of my departure wasn't exactly honest."

"I promise to look you up in Adhara if we ever make it off these islands. It has been a truly memorable experience and I hope that we will always be friends, no matter where we are."

"No matter where we are."

With that they hugged and she left as quietly as she had arrived. She quickly went to her hut, grabbed her things and stuffed them into the same large travel bag that she had taken with her the day she had left Hal in London. There were memories of him wherever she turned. She ensured that she left nothing behind; not a trace. The pain of her loss only added to the weight of her baggage as she looked around her temporary home one last time and beckoned Boy to follow her as she blew out the candles. They walked slowly back down the path towards the beach as she reflected on the Arnavian principle that humanity is a part of nature, not above or outside.

She now recognised that no map was complete without a mapmaker, where human nature required as much attention to nature as it did to humanity. Nature imposed limitations on the experience of being human with the suffering, aging and loss as much as the joy, love and wellbeing. She could see that part of being human was to accept such limitations and the art was in finding the right balance between the two. Arnava offered up no reason for its existence, it offered no purpose. Yet to its credit it offered up no dogmatic idea of the eternal. Honour and virtue seemed to be the prevailing truth of its people as the islanders didn't merely exist to enjoy the bounty of the environment but they also lived to serve and protect their environment, for the benefit of nature herself, not just their children.

It had been a cathartic process. Ama felt cleansed, ready to return to the continent. She now saw why the Free States were necessary, why the settlers long ago had decided on their creation, for they were a place for those lost souls embarking on a spiritual journey that had long been forgotten. She on the other hand was not to be swayed. They followed the well trodden path towards the beach once more whereupon they met the others, accompanied by Mary, who filed into procession following Jabir along the beach towards a small landing craft tied up not far away. The journey back to Tega held no mystery nor intrigue just a nagging feeling of fear; for the mission; the specialists and for all mankind.

Chapter 20

The beams dazzling in their radiance grew as the doors slowly retreated into the ground below. Liam and Moshe looked at each other and back into the white light before them; neither able to make the first move. Blinded by vacillation, not knowing what was in front of them, they stood rooted to the spot in fear of stepping off a cliff into a brilliant abyss.

Unable to see anything clearly Liam cupped his eyes with his left hand creating a visor to cut out the glare. Moshe mimicking his actions gesticulated with his right hand in a forwards motion pointing towards the light. Liam nodded. Treading carefully across the thin layer of snow, they slowly made their way through the gates. With fear in their hearts and doubt in their minds they surrendered themselves to the mercy of Karkara and whatever she would behold.

A few steps in and this time from behind, a blast hit them, electronic with the familiar deep rich tones. With one final boom the beams retreated as the doors slowly ascended back. With the glare gone and the extreme elements shut out, no amount of imagination had quite prepared them for what was now revealed. A metropolis beyond the realms of possibility lay before them as if they had left Kansas and where now firmly in the enthrall of the Emerald City.

They were stood on a large and expansive glass highway which rolled over hill after hill into the distance, where a tower of impossible proportions pointed towards the sky. The firmament above was bright white but not dazzling, neither atmospheric nor natural and most definitely man made. They set off in the direction of the tower gradually picking up their pace. As they came over the brow of the first rise, they were met by a row of houses on either side. Sitting atop the perfect glass mound and running along in either direction, the houses formed what could only be described as a circle for as far as the eye could see.

There was no vegetation; there were no animals, no plants, no birds and no bees. It was deathly quiet. Aware of the time, without a word to each other they started to run. Towers on either side loomed in the distance, getting larger and larger as they covered the few miles to the next mound.

They slowed to a walk whilst taking in the unbelievable scenery around them. In the distance they saw vehicles moving along the road, to and from the central tower. It seemed frenetic, in direct contrast to the crisp, clear lines of the outer reaches. As they dipped down with the descending road, marveling at the row of towers flowing in either direction they became aware of being followed. Liam made out the hiss of an electric motor closing in on them. Unsure whether to venture on, a vehicle neared forcing them to stop and wait with baited breath. Within seconds it was alongside them, drawing to a halt.

The central part of the vehicle pulled apart revealing a passenger sat in one of eight luxurious seats. He gazed upon both of the visitors for a second or two before stepping out of the vehicle. Dressed in dazzling white robes he walked towards them with a beaming smile.

"The name is Krugman. Welcome to Karkara. Liam, we've been expecting you."

"You have? Krugman we're here for you."

"I know."

"This is Moshe by the way. We're here to take you back to Tega. We have a crisis on our hands and everyone needs to get back immediately before destruction of dystopian proportions is brought to this planet."

"Who's to say that it isn't already prevalent? I think you should come with me, there's a lot to discuss. Things are not as they seem; not at all."

Moshe nodded at Liam suggesting that they had little other option. They climbed into the vehicle sitting side by side in the front row. The outer shell closed, encasing them in a protective perspex wrapper. The vehicle slowly moved off with an almost inaudible hiss in the direction of the tower.

"So Krugman give us the tour, the potted history if you like; I'm more than intrigued."

"Well, I know why you are here. That's a start. I also know a lot about you. I'm so glad that you have come. It won't be me coming back with you; precisely the opposite in fact. That aside, I have only been here a short while. I feel that this is where I have truly come of age; a reincarnation perhaps. Wait until you meet JPK. He is a revelation, an enigma; so inspiring."

"I am aware of his existence. I need to talk to him immediately."

"All in good time, all in good time. Besides there is so much you need to know before you meet him; otherwise it'd be wasted breath."

"But that's just the point we don't have time. Our orders are to bring you back within 24 hours. Ideally both of you; I have something of the utmost importance to discuss with JPK privately."

"I am as much a part of this, as he. If you destroy the architect, you destroy the society. He cannot leave."

"Sounds ominous."

The vehicle kept to a constant speed as it cantered down the highway. Moshe remained silent; at a loss to the conversation. They entered an area indicated as Zone 1 where there were tower blocks twice as high as the one's before, laid out as a circle enveloping the central tower. Other vehicles headed in a multitude of directions, scurrying silently from one destination to another. Krugman animatedly broke the silence.

"Everyone has the mark here. No matter where they are from and no matter when their ancestors arrived. We are not one giant collective but a collection of variants. There are dwarves and giants, yellows and browns, whites and blacks. There are fat people, thin people, poor people and rich people. In many ways it is life as we know it and it tastes so good. I was tired of the contrived insouciance of the continent; it felt so unnatural."

"I beg to differ Krugman. Do you know who JPK was back on Earth?"

"No."

"Well I have my suspicions and you'd be no more surprised than I am right now as to how he finds himself the leader of a society which appears to be wholly subservient to technology."

"You don't seriously believe the technological revolution to be unnatural, do you? Do you really? The power of progression is what mankind is all about. The power to change, evolve, further ourselves in the eyes of the universe. You of all people should understand that."

"I know who you were Krugman. I can't fathom why a man of such intelligence is so blinded by science. Before this conversation goes any further, Moshe and I would like to get a steer on what exactly we are dealing with. Are you friend or foe?"

"I'm not sure what you mean. Let me tell you a little about the place and leave it up to you to decide – Karkara is 2,304 square miles. It is a perfect square along its outer walls. In the centre is a central tower, the Burj Bhavya, standing 7,104 metres tall. Its base is a perfect circle and the tower is used by the entire population as their commercial centre. Society is based upon a principle of eight. Each tower block in zone 1 is 888 metres high, in zone 2 they tower 512 metres above us and even the houses in zone 3 are 2,304 square metres each. There are 24 districts, eight routes from the centre to the perimeter and eight parks which no one uses except for holding real estate value. The population is 888,888, who spend their weekdays in the tower and their weekends in their homes.

"There is no outdoor leisure; there are no hotels and sights to see. All information, trade, exercise and relaxation is administered through one's own home or work station. It is a world of pure commerce, pure technology; a post-capitalist society with no alternative philosophy but to cut out the middle man. There are no agents, brokers, lawyers or bankers; there are no animals, pets, birds or trees. Karkara's people worship pure trade. With chips connected to their brain they pay a bit for everything that they do, see, smell, taste or interact with."

They arrived at the foot of the tower funneling into a queue behind hundreds of vehicles heading in the same direction, underground. Liam and Moshe knew that they were being taken on a particular route, specifically designed to give them enough time to hear Krugman's pitch as if he were selling a piece of prime beach front real estate. Krugman wasted little time in gunning in with his next gambit.

"On Earth, we moved away from the depersonalised world of institutional production and moved towards a new economy built on social connections and rewards. This became known as social structuring with new systems for producing goods but also for providing meaning, purpose and a greater good. However this led to abuse and inequities. The more necessary it became to acquire followers on our social networking sites; to trade friends and social connections, the more necessary it became for us to change materially and our system had to evolve with it."

"The idea was to bypass the central banks and governments by making all transactions peer to peer with no central clearing house. However our infrastructure couldn't cope, we had no way of regulating the entire population. We couldn't prevent the hackers from disrupting the system and changing the code. The idea of an un-forgeable, truly international digital currency, protected against inflation and interference from politicians and bankers had broad intellectual appeal but the biggest threat to it was the idea itself; other digital currencies."

"Karkara's system has been in place since Kepler's time began but JPK has added to it; upgraded it transcending all the early inherent problems that Earth faces today. JPK has created the new algorithms that our system is now wholly reliant upon."

Liam couldn't suppress his emotion any longer and had to interject.

"We went through all of this during our 21st Century. We have world credits, a single currency and only three recognised trade organisations in Eurafrica, Asiana and Panamerica."

Liam surprised himself with his vehement defence of the Prithvian system. However he was now witness to a world that was devoid of nature, wholly reliant on science and technology. He automatically slipped into the guise of the rescuer, positioning himself as the savant but not the scientist. He continued with his defence.

"If you are referring to Bitcoin and its descendants, the trading platforms were proven to be another challenge to our system, bringing power to a collection of new individuals who reverted to type and behaved in exactly the same way as those before them. For all its purity of principle, human nature remained the same. With great power comes great responsibility and the Bitcoin Billionaires were just the world's new upper class. Surely it is the same here? Post-Capitalism has been proven to be nothing but an upturning of social order, giving power to a few and coercing the masses; making them slaves to the coin. Tell me where in that is progress?"

They pulled up in a vast underground car park with a host of electronic loading bays. Each vehicle approached a specific recess according to their serial number and came to a halt. The front and back pulled apart as it had done before and they followed Krugman's lead and got out. Krugman momentarily looked at the vehicle as if in a daze where Liam noticed his eyes lost their sparkle and took on a sheen of pure white. It was like he was giving a command by thought alone. The vehicle was then collected by a stacking machine that filed it away in an orderly sequence along with the assembly of others that were in the vicinity.

"How did that happen?"

"I was chipped immediately on arrival. Through our synapses, our brains send signals through the chip and out to the super computer carrying out our instruction. Each action costs a certain amount of bits as does eating, sleeping, and talking, walking let alone buying, selling, trading or even breathing."

"What a frightening thought. What about the outside world, your existence? What about your conscience? Is this really a reality or aren't you now just a cog in a malevolent machine?"

"Is there any difference to what we have left behind? Isn't the world just one giant device playing us all off each other, challenging us to fit in, sidestep, trade, progress, further ourselves for the betterment of our own situation? At least it's all transparent here."

"Krugman, I'm speechless. Where's your hope for humanity, your wonderment of nature, your understanding of the universe and least of all your principles? I need to meet this JPK."

"Time you did indeed."

The three of them entered the building through the basement, heading into a circular lift bank with 64 ways of ascending the building. Taking lift number eight, Krugman again only had to merely look in the direction of an ultra blue dot in the wall and they set off for the 888th floor. When they arrived, the doors opened onto a large open expanse with frosted glass walls forming a circle. There was a chaise longue laid out to their left and a reception desk to the right with no one behind it. An ominous blue door lay diametrically opposed to where they were now standing. They walked over towards the desk and Krugman spoke once more.

"He is expecting you." He nodded in the direction of the door. "Moshe please wait here, the couch over there is most comfortable." With that he walked round the side of the desk and sat down staring at a projection out of view.

Liam stood momentarily at a loss for words. A terrible fear of failure welled up inside him. This was an impossible task and he now understood Peel's words; his relative lack of hope for their success. He approached the door, only for it to disappear into thin air. He took a deep breath and kept his wits about him. He crossed over the threshold and entered slowly into another circular room. Only for this time it was darker with a film of blue light coating the walls. The door reappeared behind him once inside.

"Liam Self I believe. We've heard so much but it's not until now that we meet the man from Earth who cracked their code."

172

The voice was whispered yet it echoed around the chamber, creating an eerie feeling of power and hostility. Liam stopped in his tracks, not moving another inch. A light hum resonated around the room as the walls receded into the ceiling, revealing floor to ceiling transalum windows encircling him.

"Let me guess, a perfect circle of 888 square metres with ceiling height of eight metres."

"Correct. But that is not why you came to see me, is it? Let me take a closer look at you."

JPK crossed the floor from his desk in the centre of the room. Liam couldn't yet see his face clearly but the memorable shape of the man drew closer. They walked towards each other and by the time they were a few feet apart, he looked upon the familiar visage of the estranged Prithvian and wondered if he too would be recognised. Suddenly he was uplifted by the fact that neither party wanted the other to know who each other truly were. JPK cut through his thoughts with a knife so sharp it left him cold.

"Joost Peper Klerk. It's been a long time Hal."

"I had my suspicions but seriously? You've been dead for years."

"I never forget a face and for once I never forgot your name. The up and coming artist, now quite the councilor; how times have changed."

"I think the change has been in you. I'm still the same person I ever was – but you – you were as disinterested in monetary systems as I was. What happened?"

"Now that is a long story which I'm sure is no more captivating than your own. So tell me was my death big news on Earth? Perhaps that's for another time; for now I want to revel in the moment. I knew there was more to this Liam Self than what everyone else supposed."

"Likewise, I knew there was more to JPK than a few initials. So here we are with precious little time to spare – so I'll cut to the chase. I need you to return with me to Tega; our lives depend on it."

"Don't you mean Keplerian lives? I have my sources too you know. The situation shouldn't be of concern to any of us here unless it is something that threatens the security of the Repertega. I'm guessing that you know exactly what that is as it is my guess that a man carrying the mark of a Forty wouldn't have got here by taking a trip on some glorified ark. He couldn't have spared the time."

"I fear that you know the answer already. Who's your source? What would they gain? Why are you here?"

"A lot of questions and so little time - I was an intrinsic part of the corporation you know – I had been for many years. I dropped out for reasons to my wellbeing that I kept from my wife and daughter. What followed was no lie; my wife and I were attacked and left for dead – only I knew the assailant. I was rescued by the corporation but it was too late to save her. The situation presented itself with an opportunity to escape with no questions asked. Our daughter returned home to find her mother's body and not mine.

We ensured that she found her way into care and that there were watchful eyes over her."

"It's Voegel isn't it?" Liam skirted the issue concerning Ama, choosing to play the white man until absolutely necessary.

"Regardless of who my informer is, I must say that I am impressed by your ability to adapt to the situation. You really would be useful here, better than you could possibly imagine; for we have a system that cannot fail, a perfect system based upon rules and mathematical principles that exist to further mankind's capabilities. This is a world of pure trade and eternal light."

"You must know how farcical that sounds. You don't really believe in all of this, do you? Surely you can see it for what it really is; another system providing the architects with the power and control, who use and abuse their position. Where is nature's design? What of the rhythm of the universe?"

"We've transcended such basic ideas. We are what we need to be. We are perfect humanoids. Everyone is a duplicate of their former self; only perfected. Apart from Krugman and I, who are first generation Karkarians, the rest have been here for thousands of years, constantly regenerating when their life cycle dies out. Our children aren't our children, they are ourselves. The only thing that we have been unable to change is the mark itself. The brain dies when the original parent's time was determined. We are therefore able to maintain a finite number of people within our walls with the population neither decreasing nor expanding dramatically at any one time. Yet part of the balance within our society is the quest for perfection; the perfect number."

"So, what if your perfect humanoid malfunctioned?" Liam questioned sardonically.

"It happens on occasion where the humanoid in question makes a break for the continent. We are all fitted with a chip which will terminate our life force if we were to cross the great divide. If we rip it out and survive the exercise our life force is lost with it and we wander in perpetual darkness. Not many have gone this way. We merely replace the person who goes missing with another one like them."

"I take it that by the great divide, you mean the vast sheets of ice and snow upon which we travelled to get here? But what of your soul? How can you transfer a soul from one generation to another? Souls aren't memories and you know that."

"We have no use for souls. Our system has been perfected."

"Interesting yet rumour has it on the continent that the mark has been known to disappear in Karkara."

"Sometimes it's absolutely necessary to retire a Karkarian altogether. It has been known on occasion for a fresh duplicate to lose their mark during the development process but they cannot procreate so our society is naturally

174

protected. I cannot over state the pun. We are not about death but ensuring eternal life."

"It makes perfect sense as to how you got here - how you came to be their leader, but why do you choose to stay?"

"It's simple. I would have died on Earth. There were people who wanted me dead yet here I can physically live forever maintaining a lifestyle that I never could have possibly imagined back home. I feel exhilarated, honoured and one of the chosen few."

"Don't you miss your daughter? Do you not wish to see her again? How can you live with yourself?"

"Of course I do. I originally came here to offer my services. The idea was to help evolve an already perfect system. The lure of a society based on pure trade was too much to turn down. I came, integrated and created. In many ways like you I found my niche and so have found it impossible to leave."

"I sense in you that there is a man with a brilliant mind who's lost direction; a man suffering a crisis of conscience; who will return to a more natural state if only he were able. Do you know of the ways of the Great Book? Why would a world full of people regenerating themselves into perpetuity be enticing? Isn't life about change, evolution and experience? Here there are none of these things."

"I evolved the algorithms, I changed the trading platforms and everyone's experience is the better for it."

"That is not what I meant and you know it. We have a plane on this side of the border which can take you direct to Tega where I'm sure your chip can be programmed to believe that it is still in Karkara. The computers could mimic the signals required to keep you alive."

"Tell me Liam, what good would that do? To live out my days in a prison, confined to my quarters. What of my daughter? How would I even communicate with her and what good would come of it? I've already left her; I abandoned her. I have since created a new world, for me and my latter selves."

"Isn't that a little short sighted? Surely Karkara is as much a prison as Tega without even a suggestion of real freedom?" Liam seized his chance while he had the opportunity. "What if I told you that you could see your daughter now rather than while away your days until your soulless resurrection?"

"Tell me - how is that possible?"

"You mean you don't know? For all the sources, for all the power that you say you have, you don't know that she is here?"

"Ama? On Kepler?"

Liam paused for a moment to catch his thoughts, pacing backwards and forwards as he rubbed his chin pensively.

"There is more to this whole situation than meets the eye." Liam muttered under his breath before continuing, "Joost we need to be entirely transparent with each other, otherwise we will end up enemies. You quite obviously know about the portal; you probably know about the imminent threat on Shanghai and so therefore Tega; you also accurately suspected that I in fact was Liam Self but then again you're not in on the whole scheme. Correct so far?"

"Yes." JPK responded visibly thrown. Liam ventured on.

"I suspect that we are both pawns in a much bigger game. Unfortunately we are currently sitting on opposite sides of the board. If Voegel is playing us, he is mere puppet. My question to you is; who is his master?"

"Voegel; the weasel. That wasn't the arrangement. She was to be looked after. She was to stay in his charge until he left. You've met her, haven't you?"

Liam kept his counsel a moment longer not giving anything further away while JPK stood silently stunned, arms folded and staring out of the window across the tower tops below; thinking fast. Finally Liam could resist no longer, the situation begged him to come clean if only to make it easier to persuade JPK to return with him.

"There's more to this story than you could possibly imagine, I for one am astounded by the intricate layers of intrigue that it. I said that I would be transparent with you and of what I am about to divulge my candour is a direct result of this pledge. I know your daughter and I know her well. What's even more surreal is that I created a story about you and encapsulated it in one of my feature pieces at my break out exhibition in London almost three years ago. Joost I've only met you once but standing here before you irrespective of where we are, you have to know that I am in love with your daughter. I have been since the day I first laid eyes on her."

Liam paused for what could have been construed as dramatic effect but which was entirely natural, for his mouth had gone dry and his breath had departed with the fleeing moisture. He had not spoken of Ama to anyone for so long that his feelings had been boxed up, left in a very personal safe. This moment required sensitive navigation. He ventured on leaving JPK with little doubt that he was deadly serious.

"She and I shared a moment, one lost in time which turned into more than anything that I have ever experienced or ever will again. It wasn't a temporary madness. Yes it burst forth like a volcano but it didn't subside, it only grew stronger. This was not a love born by breathless passion but a love that could stand forever with roots so strong that they'd sprout throughout eternity. It was torn asunder by greater forces and not by her own design. I would give anything to see her again, hold her, touch her face and promise never to leave her side. The burden of knowing that she is here within my grasp but yet so far away has been a heavy one, worn weary as each day has passed. You do not want that Joost, I have carried the thought of her for so long now and I wouldn't wish that on anyone, let alone her father."

"It now comes as no surprise that Voegel kept details of Ama's whereabouts hidden from me." He paced in frustration as he finished with the afterthought, "and of you entirely."

Liam looked at JPK, looking for a flicker of emotion, anything that he could work with but was in receipt of none. So he took another tack, focusing on the pertinent problem causing the most consternation; communication or the lack of it thereof.

"Joost, I'm working directly for Laozi Veda. I am here to bring you back to Tega and I think we have now found our reason. Yours is to settle a score with Voegel and to see your daughter. Mine is to talk to Laozi and find out the truth. If Voegel is not reporting to him, who is he getting his orders from?"

Liam tapped his disguised cellhip in frustration. JPK responded.

"No good trying that here. Karkara is cloaked by an electronic force field that gives us our perpetual daylight and energy. However it prevents any foreign device from functioning and I suspect your concealed cellhip will suffer the same fate. You have certainly given me much food for thought Liam as there are some substantial choices that we have to make, here and now."

"Would it help by telling you that Ama has more than flourished both here and on Earth? Not only had she become a soloist with her orchestra but she is also the lead singer of a band here on Kepler; one that is fast becoming the most popular on the entire continent. It is truly extraordinary. I saw her perform not so long ago but had to keep my distance. For what it's worth and of what I remember, she thinks of you and her mother every day and would give anything to see her father one last time."

"I need to assess my options. I am committed to Karkara in more ways than one. I am torn as you no doubt respect." JPK strummed his finger tips upon his forehead, forcing himself to act decisively. "You must return to the waiting room and to your security colleague. Knowing the constraints of time, I am left with little choice but to come back to you within the hour with a response."

"So be it but remember this, I would die for Ama to ensure her happiness and her safety. Would you?"

With that he moved towards the section of the room where he had first appeared. As he approached the walls and the blue door re-materialised whereupon the door disappeared again leaving him with his exit. Liam crossed over the threshold without once looking back. He was received by a very perturbed and watchful Moshe. There was no sign of Krugman.

"So? Who was he? Were you successful? This is insane. Krugman is mad."

"Depends on what you mean by successful? I have given JPK plenty to think about. Put it this way, he was who I thought he would be but not what I expected. We will be getting out of here, one way or another within the next few hours. So where is he?"

"Who? Krugman. Oh, he's had to leave on important business or so he said. Seems to me that the guy isn't the full ticket if you know what I mean?"

"I sure do. JPK is an entirely different animal and one that is far more useful to us back on Tega. More on that later but there is little we can now do but wait."

Liam slumped into the chaise longue with a weary sigh. He stared momentarily at the clean, curvaceous lines of the wall as Moshe continued to talk. JPK's words pinged back and forth until he could think of nothing else, causing him to block out anything that was being fired in his direction by his associate. Moshe gave up after a while and Liam prepared for the worst. He shut his eyes and thought of Ama, hoping that she was safely onboard her plane, heading back to Tega. He drifted off into a half-sleep.

A while later, the hum of a lift arriving at their floor broke the silence. The doors opened and Krugman stepped out with a look of absolute determination.

"Gentlemen, follow me."

Making no comment, Liam and Moshe followed him into the lift. They descended back down to the underground levels and the car park. Repeating the procedure of before but this time in reverse, they all got back into the vehicle and headed out of the tower and its confines. Once they were on the glass highway Liam broke the silence.

"So where are you taking us? We have precious little time and I have no desire to be sold further on your perfect system."

"Have no fear, much to my annoyance, I have been instructed to take you back to the gates and to let you go, no more questions asked."

"I was under the impression that we were meeting JPK again."

"Those are not my orders and I have strict instructions to leave you as you were on the other side of the gates."

"But we cannot leave without one of you."

"Yet we would be rendered pretty useless if we were to be forced to leave. Your companion is surplus to requirements here. We're dead to the outside world and you know it."

Liam thought quickly, resolving every permutation and possible sequence of events. He had a sneaking suspicion that there was more to this situation than met the eye and decided not to press Krugman any further.

Liam could sense that Moshe was preparing to strike, jumping in before his associate could make a huge mistake. He was mindful not to give his own suspicions away, signing to Moshe to remain calm and to stay silent. The vehicle progressed along the highway at high speed, hurtling away from the magnificent tower that was Karkara's centre piece. Moshe sat back and stared out of the enormous panoramic window contemplating his next move. Fields of towers gave way to plains of houses until they were once again back at the only known entrance to the prison of all prisons. The vehicle drew to a halt, pulling apart in customary fashion. The visitors and their host got out, standing opposed to each other. Liam was almost relieved to be leaving albeit empty handed.

"So how do you expect us to explain this to our superiors, let alone to the Kepler Council?"

"You're more than capable of letting them know that it was a fortuitous event. In any case I am only one of the nine, the others I am sure would have returned and they will remain none the wiser about the original seven."

"I'm not so sure Krugman but I am sure of one thing, that you have put us all under an insurmountable amount of pressure. We will all have to go back to Earth immediately, never to return, having failed in setting up a new community in Adhara; all because of your selfish and crass ideals. How can you live with yourself?"

"No point crying over spilt milk, I am no use to anybody on the outside. A man of your verbal dexterity should turn this on its head in no time."

The glacial blue gates receded into the electronic abyss below and the elements swirled in once more. As the wind engulfed them and the snowflakes flecked at their clothes, Liam turned to Krugman and fired a parting shot which was caught up in the breeze, lost to his associate who looked at the Karkarian with venom and disdain.

"You are but a shadow of the man that I thought you were."

With that they turned on their heels and headed once again through the gates, not speaking until the doors were firmly shut behind them. Moshe was the first to weigh in.

"So what are we to do now? Admit it, you've failed. I stupidly left it to you thinking that there was another plan. We can't go back empty handed. We'll do it my way this time. We need to go back and take Krugman, forcing him to return, in restraints if we have to."

"Moshe, relax, it's not that simple I'm afraid. JPK is not the type of man to abandon his daughter."

"His daughter? More insanity, what has his daughter got to do with anything?"

A figure appeared out of nowhere, his voice whistling with the wind.

"She is everything; to me and to him."

A well wrapped JPK, laden with a pack of his own stood behind them, appearing through the swirls of snow that were being kicked up by the increasing force of the gathering storm.

"We must hurry."

Liam turned to his old acquaintance giving him a look of feigned surprise and back at Moshe in a commanding manner, putting his companion firmly back in his box.

"Moshe, this is JPK or should I say Joost Peper Klerk; the former leader of Karkara and one of the original Prithvians."

He turned back to him with a broad smile and a raised fist of success.

"Let me guess, Krugman is on his way back to the Burj with strict instructions to leave you alone for 24 hours; which he will do without question. He'll miraculously find a file containing all the secrets to your algorithms and how to manage the current system."

"Correct. What's more the balance will be restored as he has a vial of my DNA to initiate the development of JPK mark two in 48 hours. Krugman is under strict instructions to put my duplicate in at the bottom rung of Karkarian society with no bits or favours to trade. He is to monitor my progress without aiding me once in progressing up the ladder. An interesting project I'm sure."

"For some; sounds like you are getting the best of both worlds"

"If you must call it that; however for now I do have the minor problem of keeping my brain alive."

"Moshe, can you call the pilot. Explain to him that we will be bringing a passenger aboard who needs the cabin to be hermetically sealed with an electric current so that his life force can be sustained."

Moshe stared incredulously at Liam for a moment before responding.

"I take it that there will be little more explanation as usual. Let's hope that works."

He turned to shelter his voice from the baying wind as he made the call. Liam turned to his former flame's father and pressed on with the plan for Karkara, now that their leader had absconded.

"So Krugman is to take your place as I suggested?"

"Absolutely, he'll be far better than I. I thought upon your prudence earlier and so long as we can keep up the appearance of normalcy the Keplerians should be none the wiser."

"Answer me one more thing before I drop the thought entirely; your duplicate is an extension of you but it's not you. Leaving memories and experiences aside, your duplicate has an entirely separate energy; so how can it have your soul?"

JPK ignored Liam's questions with a smile adding, "I fear that Karkara will become a fiercely different place under Krugman's stewardship."

With that the three of them set off at a brisk pace in the direction of the plane with the safety of Earth resting firmly on their shoulders.

Chapter 21

Liam lay staring at the ceiling in his quarters. The post extraction debrief was at an end. He was exhausted. They had been the last of the rescue teams to return. All had, for the time being, been successful.

JPK was to pose as Krugman to the outside world. They had added to his story where he'd picked up a rare and untreatable virus whilst stationed in the Kingdom of Ganda therefore confined to quarters, indefinitely. This provided them with the perfect opportunity to replicate the frequency used to energise the chip in his brain whilst limiting it to his lodgings suiting all concerned. JPK had agreed to keep his identity secret, even during potential exchanges between father and daughter; should they ever take place.

As the adrenalin subsided Liam was left with little to do but wait; the frustration had already begun to set in. Ama was now within touching distance yet seemed even further away than before.

What's more his cellhip had become corrupted during their time in Karkara with no possible way of being fixed. The system's defences were impregnable in more ways than one and he felt naked without his lifeline. With one fell swoop the security of knowledge and therefore his inner power had been taken from him. He felt ineffectual and unable to have a hand in determining events.

News reports played out on screens in every department which told the horrifying story of war on Earth. The extent of the conflict had been carefully chronicled by the media teams aboard where each programme informed everybody of the situation, starting from the day that they had departed for Kepler in 2145.

Liam was already aware of the earlier events, however his familiarity with the past 12 months had been limited to the clandestine conversations he'd had with Laozi; exchanges that he could no longer have.

Earth's circumstances had changed dramatically since the 3rd June 2147 where separate armies of duplicates simultaneously attacked all three capitals. They had been successful in taking control of Singapore but were unsuccessful in capturing Cairo. Eurafrica's capital had turned its internal turmoil into a strength combining the multitude of opposing cultures to focus on repelling one clear and present danger.

This could not be said however of Sao Luis where the Panamerican city was still under siege. A stalemate looked the most likely outcome. Pyrrhic victories aside Liam was not excessively concerned given his current location and identity but it was the subsequent decimation of Auckland and all of its inhabitants that had surprised him most. Mankind was now determined to rid themselves of their own creation.

The ceiling in his quarters carried no answers but acted as a decent sounding board as he had found no other in those first few hours of being back. He questioned the number of duplicates already out there on his home planet, marked, their parent dead, they in their stead; no different to Karkara. He thought of the collective responsibility of the early cloning pioneers and the consequences of not creating a visible sign of the duplicates being man made and to this end leaving them free of mankind.

What was even more shocking was that Reper Station and a direct portal to another world was now common knowledge and in duplicate hands. Their leaders had contrived to take up a position within the base outside Shanghai and to give their kin a route to safety in search of another life, devoid of slavery and persecution. Eight duplicates had falsified their documents, their appearance and had managed to get through Reper. To make matters worse they were now untracked amongst the specialists on Tega. All they needed was to take control of the portal and all hope would be lost.

Liam was perplexed as he was unsure as to which side of the fence he now sat. It was hardly the fault of the duplicates that they existed. However mankind's very existence was now under threat. He questioned the morality of his future actions knowing that his was a role integral to their ultimate demise or resurrection.

Prithvian duplicates had no place in the imperfect society of Karkara as the fortress was based on its quest for the perfect number. The potential hordes from one planet seeking refuge would overcrowd the system and bring it to its knees. On the other hand the Free States existed to instruct its inhabitants on the ways of the universe where they relied on procreation and the evolution of thought to resurrect man's mind; again this was no place for a glut from Prithvi. This left the continent itself, his domain where society dealt with finite numbers where the majority had the chance to locally procreate and therefore infuse their progeny's soul with the conscience and spirit to protect themselves.

His breath was a key to stop the advancement of the flocking duplicates and so was Voegel's mark. Perhaps there was another key, one that Laozi had kept from him. The choice seemed simple but was not his to make; they should deactivate the portal leaving the specialists with only one route back to Earth; The Repertega. He was not about to abandon his post nor did he have any reason to return to Earth. His choice was straightforward; protect Kepler at all costs, at the expense of duplicate lives; his people's future depended on it.

He rolled over onto his side. Lock down would be an endurance test. He would paint. He had scenes beyond Prithvian imagination that needed to be explored. If he was never to return to Earth at least his pictures could be enjoyed for all their brazen glory.

Naturally he was the go-between the two planets and so he'd made a statement to the representatives of the Keplerian Council before he'd returned to his quarters. At least those concerns were under control now that the nine were all accounted for. As far as they were concerned, Tega was on lock down for an internal audit of their peaceful integration programme just over a year after their arrival. This was a planned and approved event, all part of the Great Book's design. The troubles on Earth and the portal's existence were Prithvian problems and not for airing on the outside.

With a huge sigh and sagging eyes, Liam welcomed the sleep when it finally came.

He awoke with the dawn light, seeping through the window via the viewing booth. His quarters were functional, comfortable and spacious allowing him to compartmentalise a lot of his life aboard into areas for sleeping, eating, painting, writing, entertaining and so on. His were standard lodgings, no different to anyone else's. He felt rejuvenated and decided to head out to the atrium in order to get his bearings, acclimatising to his new environment. Having actually spent such little time on Tega, he felt it would be useful to see the entire base first hand rather than from a blueprint. Not wanting to run into Ama unprepared was his main priority. He made himself aware of her department's schedule. No one was purported to be around so he saw this as his opportunity to move about unnoticed. Voegel's duplicity was a grave concern and so he set about confronting him even if to simply stare into the whites of his eyes and get a gage on his motives.

He headed in the direction of the Department for Art & Music knowing the risks involved but threw caution to the wind as the moment warranted action. Contrary to what he thought he knew of their timetable, most of this section was teeming with life as specialists hurried from one destination to another. He pondered momentarily on everyone else's experiences, unable to second guess events in their respective lives. He wondered whether any of them had truly grasped the reasons for them being there. He passed through the corridors, heading for the communal living area. Not knowing the layout as well as he should have, he took a wrong turn and passed by the department's conference centre.

There were huge glass windows looking out onto a widened corridor. Smaller individual offices, adjacent to the main debating rooms sat atop a mezzanine level, splitting the panes of glass in two. He felt the cold of the air conditioning and shuddered softly. Each office was crammed full with people talking animatedly to each other and before he had time to react there she was. It couldn't possibly have been anyone else, it had to be her. With her back to him, back to the glass partition which looked out onto the corridor below, she stood gesticulating at none other than Benedikt Voegel.

He couldn't move; undecided as whether to hurry on or to retreat, he looked up and caught sight of Boy's furry mane and raised tail. Marvelling at how he had grown, he almost lost sight of the fact Boy had turned and was now facing him, looking inquisitively down, tongue out with a wagging tail.

Ama's temperature had risen dramatically; the conversation with Voegel had reached a very unsatisfactory conclusion, leaving her with little to work with. From hot to cold she shook violently as she stared at him, infuriated by what could only be construed as lies. Boy started to whine affectionately towards the glass partition. She reached out with her right hand to pat him whilst contemplating Voegel's words. The chief of the Department for Finance & Trade Krugman wanted to meet her because of their fellowship in being one of the nine. She couldn't understand why it was he who was delivering the message. Voegel had had no part to play in Yakov's grand plan nor had he been involved in their daring liberation. What's more, he was acting on Laozi's behalf whilst Mr Veda had no idea what it was like to actually be on Kepler. She was bewildered by Voegel's blind faith in a man, millions of light years away from them. Boy's whining reached fever pitch. She spun around enabling her to see what the commotion was about only to find an empty corridor and a now sated dog by her side.

She turned again to Voegel but he had gone, heading swiftly for the exit as if he had seen a ghost. She pondered on his words for a moment longer, deciding that she had little to lose in visiting Krugman whatever his motives. However she was not going to act on Voegel's request that she chair his conferences for the next few days whilst he looked after a group of specialists who had remained on Tega for the last year assigned to the Department for Psychology. His responsibilities lay with their department; he was their chief and not her; besides his argument smacked of fiction; his fear of being overheard, his furtive glances and his time checking seemed completely at odds with their open and honest familial relationship. Something had changed him and it most certainly wasn't Kepler. Whatever pressure Laozi Veda was putting him under, she didn't like it.

Ama took little time to cross the atrium and reach Krugman's department. The corridors were exactly the same as hers in layout and design, except for the walls being a light shade of salmon pink. Each department had a distinct colour code yet the rest was identical. This made it extremely easy to navigate and so his quarters were easy to find. The memories of the year spent hurtling through space came flooding back to her as she approached Krugman's door. She was suddenly overcome by a genuine source of trepidation where the all too familiar feeling in her stomach rose up through her body, hitting her throat at precisely the same time as she pressed the buzzer.

She waited quite a while contemplating leaving, having been sent on a foolhardy errand at the behest of an aging stranger who had once purported to be her guardian. Before she acted on her impulses the door sashayed to one side, leaving her stood on the threshold peering into darkness.

"Hello? Mr. Krugman? I've been told that you urgently requested my presence. My name is Ama Pepper Clark."

Ama remained confused whether she should enter or stay outside. Boy made the decision for her, bolting in and going quiet, adding to the intrigue. She followed her loyal protector, stepping in slowly not wanting to fall into a trap, aware that Voegel had changed and was no longer acting in her best interests. A few paces in, the darkness fazed into a soft light, allowing her to make out the figure of a man stooping to affectionately cup Boy's snout. The door closed behind her but she already felt safe as Boy was a true gage of any potential threat and she knew that here there was none.

She felt nothing but warmth and a congenial ambience as she stepped further towards the man at the other side of the room. The lights slowly brightened allowing her to see his legs, his arms, hair, cheeks, nose and finally his eyes. She stopped, unable to move any further. Confused and catatonic her mind was devoid of reason. The man before her was her father; older more frail but indeed her father.

"Ama, my beautiful..."

"This cannot be; impossible. You died Papa. Mama's with you. Is she here? Where am I? Is this real?"

Ama fell to the floor unable to stand. Her legs buckled out of bewilderment. Perplexed and uncertain she knew not how to continue, leaving the man before her to respond.

"Ama, mijn liefde, if only I had been able to tell you; if only I had known that you were here."

He walked over towards her and knelt down beside her. He took her in his arms as he had done on so many an occasion when she was a child. He knew that so much had changed and that the tables had indeed turned. However for that moment he was once again able to provide the cloak of protection, keeping the world's woes at bay.

JPK's strength was fading as the frequency connected to his Karkarian chip, albeit similar was not exact. The life force was slowly being sucked out of him and he knew that he had limited time left. Time that would be well spent repairing the damage of years spent alone and away from his family, his daughter; his one and only child. They rocked back and forth, Ama enveloped between her father's loving arms until the tears of joy, frustration and relief subsided.

After a while they sat and talked of their respective lives and experiences; sharing stories, reminiscing on their past. Boy nestled himself firmly at the feet of his mistress. Finally after most of the day had passed, their conversation began to draw to a close and her father talked of Liam Self's rescue mission and what an inspiring character he was. He was true to his word and never let slip his true identity. Ama noticeably regained strength whilst her father's visibly deteriorated. It was as if now he had seen her after so much time, he had surrendered his will to live; the circle now being complete.

Liam had moved swiftly away from the corridor on seeing Ama and Boy earlier in the day. He'd made his way back to his quarters, plotting his next move. After the morning hours had passed with increasing frustration for the lack of action, he went in search of a diversion, mid afternoon. He had wound up in a bar on level seven of the atrium, which reminded him of the opulence of the Mamounia Hotel in Marrakech for all its dark wood, gold leaf and scarlet drapery. Sat perched on a high stool close to the main bar he contemplated approaching Ama and tried to cover off every single, unforeseeable situation that would arise because of his intended actions.

Out of the corner of his eye he saw Jabir sitting comfortably in one of the low rise circular booths, close to the main seating area. He swung round to look at him quietly, ascertaining the company that he was keeping. Having both been part of a secret mission albeit to different locations, theirs was an unspoken camaraderie and he felt that now was the time to address it. Before he had managed to get up off his perch, Jabir had excused himself from his table and was already heading in his direction. He thought it only courteous to get up and walk towards his colleague.

"Jabir Ibn Al-Zarqali; pleased to meet you once again. Less unfortunate circumstances this time around."

"Liam Self; likewise."

"Would you like a drink? I'm buying. One good thing about Tega is the seemingly endless supply."

"Yes but a scarcity of cigarettes. I would have thought I'd have lost the cravings by now; nice to be back on board, right?"

"I was beginning to tire of being a humble researcher. I am the son of the great Mohammed Al-Zarqali, head of the Eurafrica Council, now deceased."

Jabir flicked his long wavy dark hair back over each shoulder and looked at Liam without a hint of irony, encapsulating the essence of an extremely spoiled son of a very wealthy man. This was contrary to his preconceptions. Jabir was one of Peel's chosen few and so he held him in high esteem, regardless of the frivolous way he was now acting.

"A whiskey and soda, it is. I had you down for a tea drinker not as a purveyor of barbarian tonics."

"Those times have long since passed. Keplerian wines have been the only things that have kept me going over the last year and I'm in no mood for changing; a bottle of French red?"

"I guess there is little else to do and now is as good a time as any to get to know someone from the home team."

They moved towards a more private section of the bar and sat down in a rectangular booth. Jabir looked at the table for a second or two then ran his finger over the surface, scrolling through the menu until he found what he was looking for. He pressed down on his selection allowing his fingerprint to be fully analysed. Moments later a bottle of Beaujolais ascended out of the box like stem of the table on his left hand side. Two crystalline white wine glasses stood beside their host and beckoned each of them to take them up and commence their conversation. Jabir broke the silence.

"Red wine glasses are rare on this ship. I've never actually thought to ask why. Judging by your expression you don't really seem to care."

"Jabir, it's been a while since I last had a taste of any red wine and seeing as you've ordered a smooth punch, I'm happy to use anything in order to get it down. But seriously, how did you come to be part of our covert operation?"

"I'm a biologist by trade and that's how I came to be here. However I should come clean in that I have been studying the origins of the mark for almost as long as you. I originally was conducting meta-cognition tests on Prithvians way before I got here. However it was only when I got to study the Keplerians and the size of their brains that I discovered that the Prithvian neocortex has expanded far more than theirs. My tests concluded that by altering the Prithvian mental state for a sustained period of time the neocortex will adapt. A cure to the mark can be found."

Jabir allowed Liam to see his mark as he finished his sentence almost challenging him to argue with his proclamation. It was obvious that Jabir was slightly in awe of being in his company. A silence returned, hanging over them until Liam thought he had left it long enough.

"So the scientist talks; the mark is not manmade but I see where you are coming from. What you are saying is that man's brain has evolved to the mark through thought and expression. This may be true but it is not over the last 150 years as we had already evolved. The preceding 100 years were intrinsic to our evolution with the catalyst applying her hand at the turn of the 20th Century. But that is another discussion, how did you come to be part of Peel's team?"

"I should ask you the same question. I know who you are and of your many achievements but why you? Where did you come from? I know so little about you it makes me uneasy."

"You first."

"I was friends with the group that went to Arnava and had served as a captain of the guards in the Eurafrican Liberation forces. It was natural to put myself forward for any exceptional circumstances and you?"

"I was sick for long periods on the journey over and whenever I felt strong enough to venture out I only visited Peel. He was my mentor back on Earth. I already had quite a few strong views about the Keplerians and the validity of their broadcast. I didn't want to cloud my judgement by making new friends only to leave them behind once on Kepler."

Jabir poured them both another glass.

"The similarities between us are easily recognisable but what of our differences?"

Liam saw through his cover story and suspected the same of his counterpart. Both decided to press each other no further, leaving him to switch tack and zero in on Jabir's mark, carefully keeping his arms hidden below the table.

"So you're a Centurian and a long timer; do you think that we'll lose the mark? Have you seen and learnt enough here to think that Earth's future generations will be blessed with the freedom of ignorance?"

"I'm of the view that it could disappear on a live human."

"How's that so?"

"The evolution of the brain."

"Yes but we can't physically reverse the process. The dinosaurs had their time and ours is now. We can stop our demise by listening to nature. It was only her way of telling us to respect the universe and not to believe that we are bigger or better than her. All the other living species on our planet are blissfully unaware of the turmoil that this mark has caused us. These creatures will survive because the knowledge doesn't harm them. I disagree with you but if man accepts who he is and stops playing at being divine, he will go a lot further than what nature currently has in store for him. Never play with nature. She will win."

"But that's exactly it. Human nature is derived from trying to cheat death."

"We are bent on prolonging our own individual lives. The further we push scientifically we'll no longer be human. It's all too relevant. I think we should leave that subject well alone; don't you?"

Jabir had already poured himself another glass and was nearly finished when he stopped talking. He toyed with the stem of his glass leaving a frosty silence between them. Jabir was visibly drunk and slurred his words.

"I'm not too sure what it is that you are referring to."

Jabir got up quickly and unsteadily from the table and left leaving Liam alone to ponder on their quick conversation. It was an odd exchange between two guarded people. With inhibitions lowered for a second, Jabir had provided him with the opportunity to assess his motives and whether he was someone that he could trust. Liam was at a loss as to whether it was possible. Perhaps it was the situation or the effects of the alcohol but his judgement felt askew. He knew that Jabir was hiding something but then again he was too. Jabir had skipped over the reasons for his being selected for the Arnava mission. He was quite obviously ex-military and so was a useful tool in the extraction but for him to go to Arnava there could be only one other area of interest to him and it had to be Ama. He sensed that this man was in love with her and posed a threat to his now burgeoning desire to rekindle their relationship. It made him uneasy.

He left the bar a few minutes later and ventured to the lift columns. He took a ride to level four and walked around the theatres, looking for inspiration and perhaps subconsciously hoping to run into her as if he was at the Barbican back home. He felt nervous for the first time in a long time. He had a competitor and this made him even more determined. Suddenly he ran into her interactive poster, teeth glistening back at him, standing tall outside Theatre three. Ama was giving a solo performance of Mozart's Symphony No. 41 in C Major K.551 ("Jupiter") the next evening; as if his day wasn't fantastic enough already.

Ama made her way to her quarters fighting back the tears. Her father was dying and wouldn't be able to leave Tega ever again. She knew that she was all he had to live for and she could think of nothing else, especially not being parted from him once again. She resigned herself to the fact that she wouldn't be able to go home to Amalaka but was comforted by the fact that she had had the chance to find inner peace.

Boy reached the door first, sniffing at its join with the wall before it opened. They went inside and headed for her bedroom. She wanted to rest, to wipe away the emotional exhaustion; most of all she wanted calm. As she took off her clothes, Boy started growling in the direction of the door. Knowing the signs of danger all too well, she slipped on a robe and headed to his side. Boy growled once more and the electronic rat-atat-tat of the buzzer sounded. She flicked the image responder on the wall to answer and was presented with the familiar face of Jabir.

"Ama, can I come in. We need to talk."

"Jabir there is nothing that I want to say to anyone right now. I've had a long day and the last thing I need is you stopping by."

"It's a matter of urgency, I need your help."

"I need to sleep and you are the last person I want to see. So long as it's not some ruse to get me into bed, I can talk through the intercom."

"I can't discuss it out in the corridor. After all we've...."

Ama pressed the screen on the wall and the door slid open. Jabir had a wild eyed expression of repressed rage written across his visage. She backed away into the living area and sat down in one of the long chairs.

"Keep it sweet please Jabir. I'm feeling more than a little delicate right now. What's happened?"

"I ran into Liam Self and then returned to my quarters to freshen up. I was then summoned to my department. I've since been cross examined by my chief and he suspects me of being in cahoots with eight duplicates who are now running around Tega."

"Slow down. Let's start with the first thing, Liam, what was he like?"

"He's nice enough but something doesn't add up."

"Many would say the same of you. Was he inspiring?"

"Anyway, we drank a bottle of wine and something reacted as I felt queasy and had to leave. I went to my quarters where I felt better after drinking some water and taking a cold shower."

"I really don't need a blow by blow account. So – the duplicates?"

"There's a rumour that they have somehow made it here and apparently I'm working with them. I need your help to back me up that these accusations are unfounded."

"Why are you telling me this? You're part of the security team, surely you should know?"

"I think he's one of them."

"Who? Your chief?"

"No. Liam Self."

"He couldn't be. He's the guy that's unlocked the secrets of the Prithvians and their relationship with the universe. I've really got nothing further to add Jabir. I don't know about these things."

"I've been with or near you for over two years now, surely you must know that I am the one to be trusted."

"Is this some fishing exercise just to see if I know something which you don't? Come on Jabir, what's the real reason for yet another of your impromptu visits? I'm going to have to ask you to leave."

Ama got up and walked hurriedly towards the door, Boy standing tall mirroring her now resolute posture.

"Please leave. I do not want to ask you again." Jabir stood still staring at Ama, "Jabir..."

Boy growled firmly and before she had time to finish he was gone.

Chapter 22

26th August 2147 – Evening – Tega, Kepler

The auditorium was bare and silent. Liam sat in the near darkness waiting for the crowd to file in. He had been there for most of the afternoon, biding his time until the evening's performance. His ruse was rudimentary but born out of necessity. He felt no loyalty to anyone except himself. Confronting Ama after her recital whilst in the company of strangers seemed the right thing to do. He sat motionless, full of emotion waiting for her audience.

The lights gradually grew to full and they started to arrive. The legend of the band Ama was undeniably a talking point amongst the specialists. The opportunity to see their lead singer performing a piano recital was still of major interest to most. He assumed that most of her department would show yet was pleasantly surprised to see the seats fill up almost to a maximum capacity. The burgeoning throng all whispered to each other excitedly as the lights faded out once again, throwing the theatre into expectant darkness. Murmur replaced chatter and then hush descended like a blanket covering them all.

They waited peering into the obscure void of black air. After a while footsteps slowly slinked across the boards, a chair leg creaked as it was caught in the grain of the floor. Finally sheet music was routinely unfolded and placed in its stand. Through the shadows he made out her graceful feminine figure. The darkness bounced off her as if it couldn't touch her. Suddenly the spotlight illuminated her. As if he were transported back to the Barbican he was entirely mesmerised. She looked radiant with her unblemished, caramel skin shimmering in its rays. Her scarlet maxi dress was raised slightly above the right knee, showing the cusp of her thigh as she perched on the stool.

The silence was broken by her graceful touch. The whispers of the keys turned into persuasive tones; everybody was in her thrall. She lightly skipped from note to note adding variations of weight and depth to an ever approaching wave of climax. As she threw her head back in time with the music, Liam was positive once again that she looked in his direction. He sat motionless, willing her to connect with him, willing her to offer him a glance, a smile, a flicker of recognition; nothing. The recital evolved from a solo piece into a full blown orchestral score which again he recognised from his childhood. No different to before, the soloist made it her own yet all he wanted was to be the music. He knew what he had to do and when to do it. It was only a matter of time.

Note after note she moved her audience, willing them onwards to its dramatic end. When she had finally laid her fingers to rest the rapturous crowd rose to their feet clapping and chanting her name, building up to a crescendo of their own. This had been her finest and most heartfelt performance and they knew it.

Liam waited not a moment longer, joining in the procession out of his row and into the aisle. Going against the tide he pushed through the people filing out towards the exit and headed backstage. He had already scoped out the area, plotting his route carefully. Once he reached the doors he was alone for a moment before he hurtled through the gap and into the restricted area reserved for the artist and her well wishers. He was greeted by wave after wave of people pressing forward in the same direction as he.

As he pushed through the crowd whilst trying to maintain a low profile, he saw Jabir standing still observing a group of people on the other side of the room. He stopped and thought of taking another route even if it was just to avoid being noticed by his strange competitor. But before he had the chance to alter his course Jabir had squeezed through the milling throng and was bearing on course for the huddle.

He surveyed each face desperately seeking Ama's eyes, exploring each one hoping that it would be hers looking back at him. He saw in whose direction Jabir was headed for. It was the last person that he expected to be there. For Laozi was furtively standing behind the group surveying the scene, looking for something or someone, he was not sure. Their eyes met briefly and he waved in his direction. He looked far healthier, stronger than when they had last seen each other over a year ago. He did not wave back nor even acknowledge his presence; instead he glanced intently in the direction of the incoming Jabir.

Liam set off to speak to his former guru, cursing the situation given what he had intended, pushing on through the madding crowd. By the time that he reached the other side of the room, avoiding the multitude of opportunities to trip and fall onto yet another of his Prithvian colleagues, Laozi and Jabir were both gone. Into thin air and via no apparent exit both of them had disappeared, leaving Liam now on the other side of the room and still no further in achieving his goal.

Returning to his original plan he scanned the room for Ama and any other familiar faces. Standing right next to him momentarily oblivious of each other stood one person that he wasn't going to forget in a hurry; Ban Qian, the Avasyian extraction leader. He looked around to check that no one could overhear.

"Ban, I wish we could catch up in less pressing circumstances but have you seen Ama?"

"Is everything OK Liam? You look intent on something."

"It's strange being back here. Anyway, do you know her?"

"Yes, I do. She's one of my only real friends."

"So where is she?"

"Why do you ask? She's quite popular right now as you can imagine. What do you need with her?"

"Nothing, just intrigued."

"Join the queue. She left with someone only moments ago. In fact you know him; Jabir."

"Jabir? Where did they go?"

"It's common knowledge that he's been after her, ever since we first stepped on board the ship. She's got major romantic issues. Apparently she had some boyfriend back on Earth, who she literally worshipped but left without saying as much as a goodbye. She's resented herself ever since. Simply hasn't been able to move on. Why am I telling you this? I'm sure you're not interested, me and my big mouth, why do you want to see her?"

"Nothing in particular but you wouldn't happen to know where they went; would you?"

He desperately tried to remain casual. Suddenly Ban noticeably clammed up, preventing him from gleaning anything further except for her own self interest.

"Unfortunately I don't know. However if you are at a loose end, we could perhaps go for a quick drink and go in search of them afterwards?"

"Thank you for the kind offer but I have a prior engagement; another time perhaps."

Seeing her in more exotic circumstances certainly accentuated her beauty, he wondered why she and Jabir had not made more of a connection. It would have certainly helped his cause if they had done so. He pressed on back, out through the auditorium into the atrium once again. Contrary to the day before the atrium was alive and buzzing with people fresh out of the recital and heading for one bar or another on the upper levels. Deciding to drown out his sorrows on yet another missed opportunity he joined a group heading for level nine.

The top level had the farthest reaching views of the surrounding countryside and also housed the best restaurant and bars. He solemnly made his way to SkyBar where the views were spectacular, regardless of the fact that it was dark outside. The transalum exterior lit and magnified the surrounding landscape as if it were bathed in a pale moonlight. He stood looking out for a while marvelling at the undulation of the fields below. With each glance the windows zeroed in on his point of focus, adding depth and clarity to his vision. Reminiscent of the ceiling in his suite in Shanghai, for a moment he wished that he had been aboard the Repertega whilst it had travelled through space. Everyone must have spent hours each day marvelling at the planets, stars and streams of gas that would have been lit up; all delivered to a close proximity as the ship hurtled towards her intended destination.

Prior to being sent through the portal and as part the preparation for his arrival, all systems had been programmed for him to take the place of Liam Self; including all retina, fingerprint and blood scans. For all intents and purposes he was Self on Tega. Using the self service station he ran his finger over the menu, copying Jabir's actions of the day before until he came to the whisky section. He selected an 18 year old Glenfiddich and opted for a sparkling water from Adhara. Both bottles materialised from within the station at the same time, accompanied with a bowl of ice and a tumbler. He put three cubes into the glass, poured the whisky until the cubes were floating and topped up with the local soda. He made his way over to the long chairs and sat down staring out into Prithvi's future kingdom.

Half an hour passed. He'd almost forgotten that he'd seen Laozi only a few moments before, such was his tunnel vision. Laozi indeed had a grand plan but as to how far it had strayed off course, he was not sure. He was frustrated with himself but furthermore with the situation. His competitor was now in the driving seat whilst he was out in the cold on an alien ship with nobody to relate to. The duplicates roaming free probably felt more at home than he did. This was not what he had envisioned.

What's more, Voegel had to be working with them as he was the only other person who could activate the portal or that was at least what he had been led to believe. Voegel had become extremely elusive, had avoided all contact with him and now Laozi had arrived. They were obviously working together. There had to be a reason for why one minute he was knight, next a pawn, in this galactic game of chess. He processed each incident from the very beginning. He sat staring out onto the landscape. The epiphany arrived like the morning sun.

The leaner version of Laozi isn't him at all. It's one of his duplicates. It's a little uncanny that my cellhip corrupted at a similar time to when all of this macabre business began.

Through Laozi's twins, they have access to an entire empire. They have the command of vast numbers back on Earth as well as on Tega. This is a potential disaster. What's real and who's true? I'm not as certain as I once was.

The only person who can possibly provide help is Peel. However there is always more to this than meets the eye; perhaps the portal is in fact a duplication device.

For all I know I am on Earth right now oblivious to my quest. I'm not me but actually my duplicate. I am purporting to be Liam Self. I didn't in fact travel at all. I've been positioned here by Vedas Corp as a security measure against my own kind. But I look, feel, smell the same. I think the same. If I'm not me, then who am I? I have my memories. I have my thoughts. I still care about one thing and one thing only; Ama.

He finished the last of his drink. With an affirmative clink of the now diminished ice cubes he rested the glass on the table. He stood up, confused but not compromised and headed for the lift bank on the other side. The Department for Security was easily accessed via the stern of the ship. A conversation with Peel was high on his agenda prior to dealing with Voegel and a case of misplaced loyalty.

There was an assortment of restaurants laid out in a row as he headed along the internal walk way surrounding the atrium. He hadn't eaten for quite a while yet was not hungry. He put it down to adrenalin, nerves and the alcohol. This heady concoction had left him determined, resolute but not without fear. As he strode purposefully along he shuddered slightly as he neared a French restaurant, reminiscent of L'Escargot back in Soho.

Wafts of garlic and slightly warmed bread hit him as he went past, beckoning him in. There was a faux-glass exterior allowing those inside to look out perfectly at head height. He stood momentarily looking in, balancing the thought of fine cuisine with the truth and the purpose of his mission. The sights and sounds screamed out at him but he remained on the periphery, undecided and thrown by a glorious wave of nostalgia. The decor was the same, even the table settings and lay out were similar. He peered through the window, contemplating steak frites and a glass of red when through the melee of waiters and guests being seated he caught sight of her neck, the hairline rising up over the ear, a long gold and scarlet earring, her hair tied back, her face and her smile.

For Ama, the evening was no different to the many that had gone on before except for the fact that she had been persuaded by Jabir to let bygones be bygones and to remain friends. He had promised to drop his jealous thoughts and personal designs. He swore to treat her respectfully. They were sat in the familiar surroundings of Les Grenouilles at her favourite table in the banquette seating area at the rear left corner of the room. She was buoyed up by the evening's performance and was caught up in a genial conversation with her companion. They were visibly enjoying each other's company basking in her achievements when suddenly she succumbed to a chill, startling her for a second.

Gathering herself momentarily she focused on the window facing onto the walkway outside. Through the glass pane a familiar figure appeared out of nowhere; she made out the outline of his head, his jaw and his face; facing towards her, eyes peering in captivating her once again. Jabir started to speak as she caught her breath. Not knowing what to do, she acted on impulse, gripping the table with both hands as she stood up. Ignoring her companion's remarks, she hastily meandered her way through the tables until she reached the entrance. Without another thought or regard for her surroundings, she rushed out onto the walkway and into his open arms.

With the remarkable story unfolding before his eyes, Jabir sat at the table looking out, not knowing whether to follow her or to sit tight and see who or what it was that she had suddenly seen. Once Ama made it past the last of the tables he noticed a beaming and expectant Liam standing just outside the entrance waiting open armed for his companion. He thought long and hard as to how the two of them could have known each other and especially in such a familiar way. He flashed back to the one time he had dismissively been privy to a picture of her boyfriend back on Earth. Of what he could remember this incarnation was leaner, fitter and had longer hair. In his own state of shock and surprise, Jabir realised that Liam Self was indeed Hansel Laurence, a new adversary made old. Realising that no matter whom or what this person was, he could not break that moment for his friend. He paid the bill and slipped away quietly, unnoticed.

Time stood still for them as it had always done; their worlds had collided once more. They held each other for an age, in fear of letting go. As the music in their minds subsided and the words began to form, they stood apart looking deep into each other's eyes. Simultaneously they expressed their emotion, Ama being the first to speak.

"Is it possible? Can it really be you? How did you get here? When did you get here? This is just so incredible, I don't know whether to laugh or cry. Perhaps I should do both. Are you just a figment of my imagination? Let me see your mark just to be sure I'm not dreaming."

"Aren't you sure enough already? For it's me, the one you left so suddenly without even so much as a goodbye. Look into my eyes once more; you'll sure as find that it's truly me."

Liam undid his wrist bandage, peeling off each layer, slowly, deliberately whilst maintaining controlled but candid eye contact with her. He reached the final part and was just about to reveal his mark when she jumped in.

"Stop, don't do it. I know it's you. You don't have to prove it to me. What am I asking? I'm sorry. I'd rather you knew that I believed you, rather than surrender to the suspicion of me doubting your integrity."

Liam stopped on the cusp of revelation, slowly, deliberately winding the brown linen cloth back round his left forearm, restoring it to it its former guise as part of his Keplerian identity.

"Ama, for you I'd do anything. For us to spend any time with each other; for a chance to recapture what we once had, I'd venture into the realms of the real and the unreal. I've seen things that you'd never believe were possible. I've done things that I couldn't possibly dream about; but this moment is by far the most real, the most genuine expression of my existence; one that I would never be likely to have again."

"Why have I had to wait so long? Why has it taken so much time? All I have wanted to do since the first moment that I left is come back and say to you that I am sorry. I never intended to leave you; I was certain that they wouldn't have made me go without you."

"But you were. Now, I understand. I didn't then."

"I have felt torn between two worlds. What is it with you? My peace of mind has already returned. Just being here now restores my wounded heart."

"I have spent so much time deliberating over you, not knowing what you were thinking, where you were or even how you pictured what we once had. How is it that you still appear to be mine as I am yours?"

"It was never ever in doubt; since the first day that we met. You remember right?

"Every second of it." He pulled her close.

She pressed her waist towards his.

"I guess I had to play by the rules."

"As have I; I've stuck to them by the letter."

He gently pressed his hand into the small of her back.

"So how is it that you are here? I've heard rumours of duplicates, is it true? Did you come with them?"

She almost appeared excited by the thought of the terrorists, if only if it were to bring him to her.

"No, I've been here for over a year now just like you."

"How's that possible? You weren't aboard the Repertega. I left you over two years ago... so there is a portal... which you used when we first arrived."

"Indeed. I came the same way as these duplicates have done. I came at the behest of one Laozi Veda."

"Where have you been? Have you been here on Tega all this time? With psychologists and security personnel for company, are you mad?"

"No, I've been in Utsima. Forget about me. What about you? Are you happy? I've a hundred questions; I don't know where to start."

"We have all the time in the world. I'm not going anywhere. In any case you're the one who's known that the other is here. I've been oblivious, ignorant if you like; my eyes are now open; so what's the story? You've been a specialist in Utsima and then what? How did you manage that? Whose place did you take?"

"Well first I was assigned to Vitti and then they moved me to Samanya. It's been a long journey. I've been involved in some strange goings on. One thing is for sure, you'll find it hard to believe what truly happened to me since we parted."

"Vitti? Samanya?"

Ama looked at him then looked away, pondering her own questions, piecing together the information that she had just gleaned so expertly. The penny dropped; when it clicked she turned back to her former lover and smiled an expansive grin, beaming back at him with all the pride, love and happiness that her heart would allow.

"You're Self; the infamous Liam Self."

Ama laughed a weighty, instinctive and emotional laugh allowing her core to release the tension of the preceding years. She'd never felt so relieved nor unable to suppress her joy. She jumped at Liam, throwing her arms around him once more as he stood solid, resolute on the walkway.

"My father's alive; what's more he's here but how can that surprise you as you were the one who brought him back to me. Thank you, thank you; I wish everyone could know who you are. I'm utterly speechless." Ama held onto him as she kissed him and whispered in his ear, "he's not in a good way, he's dying; I need to sit down."

"To SkyBar we go then - Judging by our audience, there's enough material here for an entire conference."

They spun round to see a number of prying faces peering out of the glass facades.

"On second thoughts, it would be wiser to head for Krugman's quarters. Seeing as the cat is out of the bag, I think we should get over to him as soon as possible. Was he visibly deteriorating whilst you were with him?"

Ama nodded unable to vocalise anything further. They held onto each other, neither willing the other to let go as they made their way to the lift bank. Their excitement quickly turned to a solemn dread as they neared Krugman's quarters. They arrived out of breath and were surprised to see that the door was open, the lights fully on. Liam quickly checked along the corridor for anything sinister or untoward. Ama ran in, in search of her father. The frequency pulsating through the walls of JPK's quarters wasn't part of the perfect system; replication wasn't the same as the original source thus this particularly fine tuned version was slowly rendering JPK's life force terminal. Liam couldn't help but notice the irony.

He sensed a putrid smell of disease, quickly realising that it was emanating from the bedroom. Ama had already made her way into the sleeping quarters as he checked the frequency level on the panel beside him. There was none. Reacting fast, he punched in the code. A barely audible hiss akin to the noise emanating from the Karkarian automobiles filled the walls, floors and the ceiling.

Liam hurried into the bedroom to find JPK barely conscious, lying prostrate on the bed as if he'd already been mounted onto a Viking long ship, ready for his journey to Valhalla. Boy on seeing him rushed over to his former master and pressed into the side of his legs whilst making a low pitched whine in appreciation of his return.

Ama sat on the side of the bed and took her father's hand in hers as he stood at its foot with Boy at his side. JPK opened his eyes and smiled. His lack of strength culminated in not even being able to muster the requisite amount of breath to speak properly, creating a moment of silence before Liam had cause to break it.

"Who's been here? Who did this to you?"

Ama put her ear to her father's mouth and listened intently as he whispered softly to her. Liam waited patiently before Ama spoke on his behalf.

"He did this to himself. He's been waiting patiently since I left him yesterday; willing that you and I meet regardless of the others; with no interference from any other party for our own good and his own ultimate salvation."

Liam bought into the process of using Ama as interpreter.

"Tell me, if no one was here, how did you switch off the frequency? Only Peel and I knew the code; for your own safety. Was he here?"

Summoning up the last of his strength JPK shook his head and determinedly spoke.

"It was only a matter of time. I'm already on my way." He looked at Liam and added, "As are you," and continued to them both "Promise me that you'll return to Earth. Promise me that you'll have children. Promise me that you will never be apart from one another again for as long as you shall live."

Ama spoke while Liam nodded at the old man.

"Of course Papa, we will do everything in our power to protect each other."

"My only child, mijn dochter, I can go safe in the knowledge that you have found him."

Ama touched her father's face with her free hand and gently stroked the lines of his cheeks.

"As can I; safe in the knowledge that you are here with me and leaving on your own terms. I hope you can see Mamma, she's waiting for you."

Liam watched in silence as Ama's father smiled a weary somewhat forlorn but poignant smile that turned his inner darkness into light once more before closing his eyes one final time. Ama held his hand and continued to stroke his face as Boy softly whined.

After a while and having kept their thoughts to themselves Ama, Liam and Boy returned to the living area and sat down, huddled close together. Words began to flow as if they were back in their old flat; as if time had stood still for the past two years; neither of them seemingly perturbed by how much had changed.

"We better notify the Department for Security. I know that it's still fresh Ama but judging by your resolve, you've already come to terms with the situation."

"I think the revelation of him being alive far outweighs the pain of his ultimate demise. The anguish that I felt in my parents passing left me when I was first bound for Kepler, replaced with the loss of you and our life together."

"I can't imagine your father would want to be buried on Kepler. Mind you there are no burials on the continent. Knowing what I know of the man I'd imagine that he'd have wanted to be cremated and scattered upon his birthing ground."

"That is true. Yet we are not back home so what do you suggest?"

Liam chose not to mention that JPK's DNA would have already made its way into a development chamber, courtesy of the real Krugman and that her father was to be reincarnated into perpetuity.

"I'd suggest his ashes are scattered in the slip stream of the solar wind, when the Repertega eventually travels back to Earth. He'll roam free throughout the universe for all eternity...."

"...on a continuous stream of energy, on a constant journey through space and time. Are we going to go back? You only have a few years left."

"Less than four, last time I checked."

"So why go back? We could remain here, live in the Free States and take our chances. Our children will carry the mark but is that so bad? Is it really? On Kepler it carries no meaning; it has no bearing on your soul."

"Keplerians view the present as the most important time in their lives; that life is not better after death but that it is, as you so succinctly put, a continuous stream of energy on a constant journey through space and time. I have to go back."

"Do we have to decide now? I'd go anywhere with you. That much I know."

"Nothing has been decided besides I fear there are a lot of ulterior motives and differing endgames in play right now with the Reper Station, Laozi Veda and Benedikt Voegel our main concerns. I'll explain all of this later but the crux is that we are stuck here until either the portal is destroyed or the Repertega leaves. Neither looks like happening any time soon."

"So what do we do until then?"

"Well we have to continue on with our lives and what is expected of us."

"What of us? Can Hansel Laurence and Ama Pepper Clark be together or will we be ostracised by our own?"

"There is no way that we're the only ones. Not everyone stays remember, only a select few. Remember the stone cottages in your capital city? Well the village of Tega will have 84 to begin with and will grow from there. It's quite simple really."

Ama smiled releasing the emotional drain of her father's death; visibly changing gear.

"So we won't be sent to Karkara any time soon?"

Liam, sensing that the easy manner of their previous relationship was fast approaching, joined in eagerly.

"Unfortunately no; having been there once already, I can safely say that the city is soulless and lacks character."

Chapter 23

"When do you think it'll all be over?"

Ama looked at him questioningly as they lay on their sides facing each other on the bed in her quarters.

"What exactly do you mean by that honey; lockdown or the mission?"

"Both; lockdown; the mission; just about everything; how about us getting out of here?"

She was frustrated by the lack of progress being made and Liam responded in as relaxed a manner as he could muster given the circumstances,

"Don't worry; it's only a matter of time. I'm sure everyone will be brought in for questioning once they've been captured. The net is closing in and soon we'll be able to resume our lives once again."

"But those lives are separated."

"I know. I'm working on a plan but it all depends on the terms negotiated."

"So how have your talks gone? Any sign of a truce?"

Self had been appointed as the specialists' representative acting as the mediator between the High-Ministers and their Prithvian counterparts. Most of his time over the past few weeks, had been taken up with trying to re-establish the trust which had previously existed between the two cultures. Unfortunately the Keplerians had found out about the group of originals soon after lockdown began. No one was certain of how the leak was sprung but he suspected that it had emanated from Arnava and the island of Zuddhi. He hadn't brought it up with Ama, not because he was in fear of reprisal but to the contrary, so that he didn't point any needless blame in her direction.

There was little that they could do, apart from damage limitation. The Prithvians were only just over a sixth of the way through their journey according to the Great Book. He knew that he would have to be highly persuasive to get the Kepler Council to agree to terms that were completely outside anything that had ever gone before.

However the threat of an army of duplicates making their way onto Kepler was still very much in his mind's eye. He had visited the heavily guarded portal chamber not long after JPK's death. He'd tried to test it, seeing if he could activate it but he had been left wandering around the dome feeling a little self conscious as he had breathed on anything that resembled a panel or activation unit. Nothing had worked.

As the ambassador between two worlds, Liam met with a representative of the Kepler Council on a weekly basis. They used the outdoor exercise area; an external part of Tega that had been contained by the Department for Security. Being in possession of some worrying facts he tried to engineer a Prithvian exit without giving away too many of the details. He presented the situation to the Keplerians as gross misconduct; as damage that the Prithvians would have to take great measures to repair. His fear of the portal and the danger it represented to both parties, far outweighed any loyalty he had towards Laozi and the bigger picture. He never said it outright but insinuated on more than one occasion that they were safer in letting the Prithvians leave.

The flipside to this was that the Prithvians did not want to depart. They were still no closer to eradicating the mark and felt that they had to remain until they had a clear indication as to the process of change that they would have to undertake. Time was most definitely a factor and they needed at least another five years. With no word from Laozi, Liam's only directives were coming from Peel on security issues. He had been thrown into a difficult position. He was now making decisions for the people of both civilisations. He kept most of his qualms secret and barely even let Ama know of them. His main concern was to prevent more duplicates arriving and any possible coup d'état.

"A truce? We're not even at the negotiation table yet. Taking you and I out of the equation, the Prithvians want to stay and the Keplerians know that it's safer if we leave. However the Keplerians won't act contrary to the Great Book and the Prithvians will only leave if they have a cure. I have to convince both sides to go against their instincts whilst we try to eradicate the threat of the duplicates, both on home and foreign soil. I need to speak to Laozi; I'm at a loss as to why he hasn't got in touch with me."

"What's the latest on Voegel?"

"We're on his tail."

"Why's he still in charge of my department?"

"We've been through this before. He is of far more use to us on the outside, rather than clammed up in chains."

"Can't all his devices be tapped and his every move be clearly monitored?"

"What do you think we're doing? He'll slip up at some point and lead us to whomever it is he's reporting to. We want a peaceful resolution remember?"

"I know but I think it has gone way past that now. Everyone is going stir crazy here and there'll be more problems to contend with, more than just a few extra bodies on Tega."

"You know it's more sinister than that. I'll forgive you this once."

He smiled playfully at her before continuing,

"It seems to me that this entire scenario has been cooked up by Laozi with Voegel's assistance; our meeting at the Barbican, our getting together in the first place and then you leaving in the manner that you did; even my selection as their lab rat. They knew that I would have no fear. They played on the fact that I would be able to work with the Keplerians as their mouthpiece. We are hostages to their intent and now is the time for all of that to change. But you know what, it's been a ride and worth it. I'm here with you after all."

"You make it sound so final. Are you going somewhere? Can I come with you?"

Ama playfully responded to his caresses as she teased him.

"So they've had over a month to find just eight people. In a place that can only be described as well contained and still they're missing?"

"Well I think that's the problem. They're duplicates who are demonstrating that they are very hard to find. No doubt you've heard the rumours of there being an assassin onboard. Everybody is hoping that whoever they are, they're successful so that we can all resume our lives and get out of here once and for all."

"No chance of you being the hired gun then? I guess we're in it for the long haul."

"I guess we are indeed."

With one hand resting between her thighs, he touched her face with the other. She laughed coquettishly as he pulled her towards him. Kissing her made anything seem possible. Lost in the moment they feverishly enjoyed each other until the noon rays splashed across her viewing platform.

Afterwards and as they lay back, looking out through the transalum, a strange ringing sound of an antique Prithvian telephone emanated all around them. Boy startled and unaccustomed to the noise, jumped up onto the bed as Liam looked around checking for its source.

"It's coming from your study area. What is it?"

"I've never heard it before. I have no idea."

Ama gave him a bewildered look as he grabbed his trousers covering his modesty in case they were to have visitors.

"I'll answer it once I've found out how. Put some clothes on. It must be an emergency."

He made his way to her desk and proceeded to push and prod every single vertical and horizontal part, yet the ringing remained persistent and increased in volume. After a while he sat back in the chair. He'd given up. As he sighed shrugging his shoulders at Ama who'd joined him, they were greeted with a flickering projection above the surface of the table.

Two large oversize, handmade, vintage mahogany pedestal desks appeared before them. No one was sat behind them. He instantly recognised his mentor's London office. It hadn't changed one iota. Everything was exactly as how he remembered it. Only this time he was looking down from one of the interactive screens and not up at them.

"Laozi? Are you there? It's me, are you there?"

The projection flickered, the reception quality was distorted. He suddenly got the sickening thought that Tega was definitely under threat as the message could have been caught up in a queuing system whilst the portal was inactive. This was a double edged sword and he was not sure which he preferred.

"Is anyone there? Hello?"

Ama stood behind him, resting her arms on his shoulders as they stared into the intermittent image spotted by static.

"Hello Ama. I haven't much time, so I will be as concise as I can be."

A concerned looking Laozi appeared from out of view. Ama tried to respond but Liam signed at her to remain quiet as he sensed that this was not going to be a two way conversation. He was immediately vindicated.

"Today's the 24th August 2147. Recent events have led me to take the drastic decision of providing you with intimate details in respect of the mission to Kepler and all that it has entailed. It may be too late by now but it is imperative that this information is shared with a trusted party before I fall into enemy hands or, worse still, am killed.

"You are my last resort in ensuring the success of our mission. My building in London has been overrun and it is only a matter of time, minutes even that my office is broken into and they do whatever it is that they have to do. They have already taken over our base outside Shanghai. I do not have much time..."

He looked over his shoulder and towards the door making his audience aware of the imminent danger. Liam realising that the message would have been routed via the Reper station bit his tongue as he was positive that this was a definite sign that there had been a security breach.

"You will have to fill in the missing pieces. What you need to know now is that Hal is on Kepler going under the guise of Liam Self. All the specialists have been made aware of the importance of Self but after what I am about to tell you, you will be privy to something that most would not have a clue as to what it is we are up against.

"Hal arrived on Tega just as all of you were leaving for your kingdoms. He arrived by a portal, one that we had not tested on a human before and one that had many inherent risks. The portal was designed for a specific purpose and one integral to the entire mission. It was built for all of us to come to Kepler; that is all who will be left of us; all of mankind after our war to end all wars with the duplicates. Our planet is overrun and we have destroyed ourselves in our pursuit of perfection.

"I have known of the ways of the Keplerians for quite some time and had purposefully chosen Hal to be our route to safety. However I am now uncertain as to whether he can be relied upon. The portal has corrupted him and I am positive that he has turned against us. I am no longer sure if he is who he says he is.

"Ama you have been chosen to be the founder of our settlement on Kepler. Your former beau was meant to ensure that everything was put in place for our survival. You were not meant to have a romance; you were meant to foster a close relationship between the Kepler Council and the new village of Tega when the time came. Since your arrival we have managed to keep you apart as your relationship has impacted on all of our futures and not just your own. With the impending lockdown on Tega, you two are in very close proximity and I need you to be aware of Hal's presence and your role in the grand scheme."

A thumping could be heard. Laozi seemed even more harassed. He looked in fear behind him then continued,

"I haven't got long before they get in but you need to know that Robert Peel is your friend and ally. As you will no doubt know by now our headquarters in Shanghai have been taken over. We need your help. You haven't always trusted me but I need you to now."

Laozi quickly glanced behind him and then returned to face the screen and continue.

"Hal is not one of us; the portal has changed him irreparably. I need you to track him down and, this is where it will get difficult, you must kill his imposter if necessary that is imperative. We cannot have you two getting back together. That would throw the entire plan into further jeopardy.

"Please Ama, I need you to do everything in your power to stop him and complete the mission.

The door behind Laozi started to glow red, ever intensifying as the assailants on the other side began to make headway into his office.

"If I am to die I want you to know that I have done everything in my power to help our people and to continue our existence. I pass this torch onto you and hope that you can carry the burden far better than I- one final thing - there is an assassin on board who is not to be trusted. He will kill anybody who gets in his way. He is the son of the former leader of Eurafrica and you know him as Jabir Ibn..."

As Laozi uttered the final words, a noise unlike anything that either of them had heard before shook his office and the projection died. Ama backed away and moved over to the window looking out onto the ground below.

Liam immediately cut in.

"That's a rare case of the outlaw becoming sheriff. Or should it be the other way round? It seems to me that no one is sure of anything, least of all Laozi. Everything has been put in place for our survival. It is being undone by the very thing that I came here by; the portal."

Having spent a while contemplating Laozi's strange words, Ama finally turned round and walked towards him as he stood calmly masking his frustration. She placated the situation with a warm soft smile.

"I want you to know that I do not doubt for one second that it is you. Our last month together has been idyllic. I wouldn't change it for anything in this world or our last. Laozi's concerns are not my own. However I am more perturbed by the future and our intended separation. I cannot live with the thought of losing you a second time. I can't let that happen."

Liam scratched his head,

"Perhaps we should return to Earth, take the portal away with the Repertega and take our chances."

Ama rose to the challenge,

"But you heard the man, we can't. Our lives are so far entwined with the Keplerians. Prithvian survival depends on it."

Now that he had her full attention he zeroed in on the situation,

"If we manage to keep a lid on the existence of a portal and suppress the duplicate uprising, the only hurdle that we have to overcome is the fact that we originally left seven Prithvians behind after the Kepler Meeting. The Keplerians are outraged by our underhand behaviour and I'm inclined to agree. I'm not suggesting for a minute that this is your father's fault as it goes higher up than that but the orders given out by Iso and his chief of staff were categorically wrong in every way. This was sanctioned by Laozi and even more likely to have been cooked up by him. Now we're paying for it. Their stupidity only means one thing; that they are planning something disastrous."

He paused to draw breath and then continued apace,

"These insinuations are completely off key. Yet I am not surprised. It's not as if this is the first time that something like this has happened. It corroborates the stories that I heard from Vitti's town elder, Attika, who herself was a former High-Minister of the Kepler Council. She told me of a passage in the Great Book that referred to a time many millennia ago when there were visitors who did not play by the rules of their society. These visitors tried to bring their people to Kepler on vast ships of planetary proportions. However the planet's natural defences, the atmosphere to you and I, would not let any of the ships through; most broke up on entry or were forced to turn around and head back to their world. The key was - that they had to be invited."

Ama thought for a second,

"Oh I see - you weren't invited. The originals were and a few stayed behind; everyone on the Repertega was but you weren't; so tell me - how did you get through?"

He walked over to the window, body mass growing as he gained in strength. The wisdom of the elders began to course through his veins.

"The Prison States are made up of all those duplicates from other worlds that made it through in similar circumstances; their progeny being those that exist there today."

"Oh, I see." She digested for a second. "Go on."

"This current crop of duplicates arrived on Tega and not directly on

Kepler and so somehow slipped through the net, regardless of whether they could have been detected. They have no soul which compounds my theory that those duplicates of the past who arrived in similar circumstances via portals from their other worlds went undetected until on Kepler for real."

Ama finished the sentence for him,

"And so were therefore banished to the Prison States. But what about you, if you aren't a duplicate then what are you?"

"That will have to wait – we haven't much time – what I can say is that I am neither dead nor is this the afterlife; of that I'm certain. I, we are very much alive, more than we ever were. Look at what we have all achieved since arriving here. The fact remains that I reached here undetected and uninvited yet my soul is somewhere out there waiting to be reclaimed and Kepler knows this; he feels it."

Liam was aware of the ticking clock of subterfuge taking place elsewhere on the ship. He was quick to progress the conversation.

"As for Jabir being the assassin; that comes as no surprise; now that the finger of blame doesn't need to be attributed to anyone here, perhaps we should spare a thought for Laozi. I am deeply concerned by this message. After all he is the architect of all of this; of everything that has happened to us. Something tells me that that was quite final."

Ama couldn't resist having a go at his former mentor.

"I know but I get the feeling he's been too clever for his own good. He's pushed things too far. Look what he did by introducing a portal in the first place; especially as he had the grand idea of bringing all Prithvians to Kepler, using you as the guinea pig."

Liam countered, almost agreeing with her,

"There is absolutely no way that I would have been part of any scheme to bring everyone here. We are here to unlock their secrets so that we can bring them back to Earth and change things there. We are here to save mankind, to reset the balance, not take over. I am surprised at him. His desire to save us has outweighed his good sense. It seems to me that he's fallen at the final hurdle; temptation to be our saviour has got the better of him; deluding him, lulling him into a false sense of true worth – there's more to this than meets the eye Ama."

They moved closer towards each other. Boy ran over to Liam pressing his muzzle into his master's cupped hand. With the bit between his teeth Liam pressed on with another concern.

"There has been a security breach and its most definitely connected to the portal. I have to go and check it out. I know that it's heavily guarded but I think it best all the same."

"Agreed; no time like the present. Take Boy, he's an excellent judge of character. He can tell if someone is truly who they say they are. It's why I've never ever had any doubt about you."

"You needed your dog to tell you that?"

"Oh I see; it's my dog now is it?"

Ama's eyes sparkled as he hurriedly put the rest of his clothes on. In a matter of minutes he was ready and focused on the job in hand. He laced up his Chameau's and kissed her on the cheek. Boy waited a moment. Ama gave her dog a maternal look before he followed swiftly after his master.

Once they were outside in the corridor, people were ambling along in either direction without as much as a care in the world. Liam and Boy headed for the atrium with the sole intention of reaching the portal chamber before anyone further and uninvited arrived. They reached the stern of the ship in no time at all given that Liam had mapped out the quickest route on a number of occasions in recent weeks; anticipating a moment like this. Whoever it was who'd activated the portal, they'd managed to slip the guards and were now most likely to be in the chamber waiting for an arrival.

As they entered the zone marked clearly for authorised personnel only the mood changed dramatically. The corridor blackened. A damp heat emanated from the walls. Liam dropped his right hand to his side, clicking his fingers softly for the canine to respond quietly and come to heel. Their movement was seamless as they crept towards the crossroads along their route. At one, they reached the outer chamber. The security guards had disappeared, leaving the perimeter empty and with only an eerie silence for company. He patted Boy on the head and clicked his fingers twice before putting his hand to the panel at the side of the door. The full body scan took seconds before the door disappeared into the floor below and they were presented with yet another empty chamber. It hadn't changed a bit since the first day he'd arrived. Dark, dank and decidedly hostile, the portal drew them in and the chamber door closed behind them. There wasn't a soul in sight.

As Liam walked around looking for any sign of life in the panels to the side of the portal, careful not to breathe on anything, a familiar bluish white light appeared in the centre of its frame. At first it began as a small spot, hovering three feet above the floor until it grew stretching outwards, equidistant in every direction until it encased the entire portal, reminiscent of when he'd first made his journey.

Thinking quickly he pressed his palm on the panel whilst breathing heavily on the receiver above. A projection with a dark blue hue popped up above and he pressed the imaginary button as speedily as he could. Breathless with fear, he hoped that he'd acted in time to stop whatever it was that was on its way and sank back down onto the floor under the panel. Boy sat down at his side whilst he wondered where everyone had got to and why the portal had been intermittently active. The most relevant question was answered by the sound of the door to the outer chamber being unlocked. Liam jumped up from his low position and sped over to the side, out of the line of sight of the incoming intruder. The door descended into the floor and a hasty, shifty Voegel stepped through the frame.

"Care to explain yourself Benedikt."

"Ah, Mr. Laurence, good of you to join us. I see that you have brought your trusty canine with you; a good idea, given who we have arriving. I suggest you prepare yourself as everybody will be here soon."

"I've already taken care of matters and switched off the receiver; no one is going to make it through."

Liam stepped in front of Voegel preventing him from moving any further towards the transporting device. The chamber door closed once again.

"I'd suggest that you get out of my way. You are only creating obstacles that are unwarranted. Everything is set to play out exactly as your benefactor planned. You have no power here."

"So why did it stop when I intervened only moments ago?"

"As it was supposed to; Security are on side, as is Peel, now is the time to bring the past to a close; everything has been sanctioned by mission control."

"That is a preposterous notion. Can't you see that what you are doing is aiding and abetting the wrong side?"

"The wrong side? I've been working in everyone's best interests since this entire operation began. I have been entrusted with the secrets of the whole scheme. It would be foolish to think otherwise. We have been through this before, only this time you must listen correctly. Do you not feel displaced and out of touch on a regular basis? Don't you feel alone, scared and then elated? Do you not have thoughts of misplaced anger and layers upon layers of ghastly mistrust? These feelings you have are quite common amongst your kind. You must understand what we are about to do is for you and your breed. Everything you have tried to do has been contrary to human nature."

"Everything that I've done? You are mad. I'm in possession of the facts; facts that will render your argument useless. Those who you act for are not who they say they are. The Laozi you work for is nothing but a scheming, immoral and spiteful fool."

"You speak ill of your maker, something that your type are wont to do."

"Laozi is not my maker but it would seem that he is my adversary. You are clearly my enemy and my instincts to do you harm have never been stronger - and that is very much a part of human nature."

As they stood facing each other Boy growled before the machine whirred back into life. Liam turned around to face the portal. The bluish white spot returned to its centre and increased in magnitude at a similar rate as before. He ran over to the panel and tried the same sequence he had used previously. The dark blue projection appeared above his head but this time the machine continued on with its sequence.

"It's no use, I've told you already, it is as he instructed. You are ineffectual within these four walls. I'd stand aside and let them join us. This is our future, we will prevail and there is nothing you can do to stop us."

"You're a deluded old man. It goes against reason to harm a frail weakling but I will have to if you don't stop this at once."

"Too late for that; everybody should be along soon to greet our new arrivals."

No sooner than had Voegel finished speaking the chamber door opened once again and Peel, Moshe and Ines Pizarro stepped through to join them. The light had fully extended and a noise of static saturated the chamber. Realising that there really was very little that he could actually do Liam altered his stance and patted Boy on the right flank in an effort to reassure his friend. He studied the three new entrants and realised that not one of them looked in any way surprised.

Unperturbed by the commotion Boy ran up to the portal, sniffing at the floor and howling in its direction. Liam looked at his adversaries whom appeared to be in a transient state of bliss, oblivious to his concerns and eager to meet who or whatever was about to come through the portal. The glare intensified until no one could look directly into its beams any longer; shielding their eyes and turning to their sides. The blast of static disappeared after a sound akin to a sonic boom signaled the end of the transmission. The whoosh was followed by a rush of air, so strong that it almost knocked Voegel off his feet, making him use Peel for ballast. There was a moment's silence and then the room was plunged into darkness.

Chapter 24

3ʳᵈ October 2147 – Evening – Tega, Kepler

The group stood huddled together in awe, peering through the obscurity. The memories of his fleeting journey flooded back. Everyone waited for a sound to confirm the success of the transmission. The lights flickered on, off, on and then off again; so quickly that the strobe effect created a surreal, sluggish charm to proceedings. Liam ventured forward slowly, accompanied by Boy. They staggered steadily in the darkness towards the familiar device.

The lights flickered on again and this time remained constant. Rising up from the floor stood three bodies dressed all in white; Laozi, Iso and Kal. The light of the portal regenerated, shimmering behind them, dazzling their audience. Contrary to his experience they seemed fortified by the trip. Laozi stepped out of the device, striding purposefully towards him with his arms outstretched, ready to take control of an extremely precarious situation.

"I see everyone is here, alive and well; step forward all of you, this is a momentous occasion."

Peel, Moshe, Pizarro and Voegel moved out of the shadows and were promptly bathed in rays of dazzling light. Their smiles radiated as if they were looking upon a benevolent god of the old world. Liam had no such ideas. His fear and loathing welled up deep inside until it burst forth like a torrent unleashed by a cracking dam. Boy voiced his agreement in time with his master.

"I will not let this farce continue any further. I sincerely doubt that your accomplices represent anyone's best interests let alone yours and there is no possible way that you are, who you say you are. The Laozi I knew was a very different man; a man who felt for the world; his world; his people. He had a duty of care to society, nature and the universe. Not an apparent perverse propensity to consume and destroy."

Laozi responded quickly,

"Can you be that blind? Are you that inflexible? We had you down for a protector of our species; a shining light in the den of iniquity."

Liam cut in,

"I am here out of duty; out of compassion. I am here out of love."

"So your duty to me is unstinting?"

"To a Laozi that is no more."

"Allow me to enlighten you; follow me."

Laozi brushed past everyone and headed for the door. He merely indicated to the panel and it disappeared. He proceeded out of the chamber and along the corridor with unwavering knowledge of the route. The group meekly followed behind with an intrigued Liam leading them forward. They crisscrossed along the passageways until they reached a serene but busy atrium. Akin to a sightseeing tour, they followed their leader in processional silence until they reached the lift bank.

They arrived moments later at an already familiar environment, SkyBar. They headed into a newly partitioned section which appeared to have been set up for the sole purpose of their meeting. With cream leather furnishings set amongst pine, the room was crisp, clean and secure. The transalum windows were no different than before, providing far reaching views across the valleys and plains of Adhara whilst taking in the ever encroaching evening sky. Once they were all inside, ring fenced and cut off from the outside world, Liam targeted their leader.

"I see that everything is going according to plan Laozi; if that's what you want us to call you." He turned to the rest of the group. "Peel, Voegel, seriously can you not tell that this is an imposter? I know of what he has planned but it won't work. Only a duplicate posing as my former mentor could be so deluded. I implore you to look beyond yourselves and see these three for who they really are."

Liam swept his hand in their direction but decided that it would be prudent to bide his time and hear Laozi out, even if it was just to unpick the truth of his benefactor's demise. The others ignored his comments and stood still as Laozi turned towards the sheets of transalum.

"Look out there in front of you; a large untapped world of limitless boundary. No conflict, no retroactive dogma; just peace. War is in our nature. It is without question that our evolution has been staged by war. It is without question war is waged in the pursuit of power; for the attainment of wealth, status and empires in the name of freedom. Freedom is what I have in store for all; freedom from a pre-determined life cycle; freedom from enslavement, freedom from false idols and most importantly freedom for ourselves."

As Laozi's voice rose with excitement Liam turned to face the windows outside, looking steadily out on the horizon. Unable to wait any longer he cut in.

"You speak like the greatest imposter of all. Only a duplicate can carry such pain. The lives of humans aren't pre-determined; their life cycle is simply demonstrated from inception. Nature conspired to kill hope by giving us the one piece of knowledge that we can't live with. It was not given with the intention of total extermination but borne out of her desire to save us. The universe has warned us that we must change our ways if we are to survive; for too long we have acted contrary to her laws, culminating in giving birth to our killer; you."

"Who are you to deny mankind their freedom? For the benefit of those unaware amongst us, it is not I who is the imposter but you Hansel Laurence."

"I am equal to the task of demonstrating the difference between you and I. Where you are one kind, I am another entirely. So tell me who are you to determine another's destruction?"

"We come in peace, in search of a new world for the human race."

"And then what? When will it stop? When finally Kepler has been raped and pillaged enough and you find yourself in need of another diversion?"

"Mankind's existence depends on us."

"Where you say mankind, I say replace it with your kind."

Visibly spitting Laozi raged on, becoming increasingly despotic and uncontrolled in his delivery.

"Before I was so rudely interrupted, I hadn't finished, so where was I? Ah yes, freedom - Human conflict started from when time began; it is our territorial basic instinct. We have a clear trajectory of violence. Violence begets violence. Cruelty begets cruelty. You must understand that there must be violence to end violence."

"My benefactor must be turning in his grave to hear you utter such words. We have always had competition within our species; for food, for a place to live or for a mate. These are implicit in the process of our evolution and thus intrinsic to our genetic makeup. But how could you possibly understand such things when you can neither procreate nor say that you are a product of natural selection?"

The others had been quiet for quite some time and Peel interrupted before anyone else could.

"We can all testify that this is indeed Laozi. He not only knows every intimate detail of the mission but also every single conversation that we have had since the first time that I ever met him."

Voegel nodded his agreement vehemently and shook his head at Liam in disgust. Unaware and un-swayed Liam pressed on as Boy stood glaring at the oppressors, challenging them to attack his master.

"Humans are social beings and like many other animals we have evolved our behaviour, adapting to our environment, making the subconscious effort to avoid the detrimental effects of violence within our social groups. The groups that we consider ourselves to be part of are critical to our understanding of ourselves. We are far more likely to empathise with those of our own and therefore dehumanise those from another group. This can be seen through our religious wars, through the dehumanisation of those who did not believe in our ideals. Too much conflict was borne out of such a terrible misappropriation of faith. I can understand why your kind sees Kepler as your salvation; why you have dehumanised the human race; yet I cannot stand by and watch our destruction through such blind belief in this false trinity."

Liam turned to look challengingly at the three new arrivals, pressing down on Boy's flank to settle him and then continued.

"If you are to have your way we will be destroyed and you and your kind can exist on both planets, redeveloping for all eternity. Laozi was captured and most probably killed by this imposter well over a month ago. I saw the projection only today. I'd imagine that you have been in contact with Voegel for a lot longer than that too."

Voegel spoke up for the first time since they'd arrived at the bar,

"That projection was entirely our design. We had to get you to leave your intimate sanctuary; you are no use to anyone if you deviate any further from your directive."

Laozi's imposter assumed control,

"Remind me Liam, what was it that you agreed to do when you last spoke to me in Shanghai?"

"To repay the favour you bestowed on me; that I will gladly go through with my journey where I had the opportunity to change so much, for so many."

"Yes and that is precisely what we are still asking of you."

"The problem is that the Laozi I knew and loved was a protector, a benefactor and a peaceful man. He did not talk of war, destruction or our need for territorial gain, whatever the cost. He viewed these factors as a malevolent force driving mankind to destruction. Only duplicates deal in such absolutes because of their unnatural position within our society. I will not be party to our destruction. My pledge to Laozi has not altered, I still have the opportunity to change so much for so many. I will not deviate from my mission. My intentions are my own."

Moshe and Pizarro were noticeably moved these protestations and shifted uneasily on their feet. Liam sensed that the time spent with Moshe would at last come in useful. The directive of the security team was to protect the specialists at all costs. If this indeed was not Laozi then they were surely protectors of everyone on the ship therefore inadvertently aiding him. Knowing this, he winked conspiringly at his counterpart and turned the screw,

"I know things about the portal that you perhaps are unaware. It has a power to transform, a power to cloak one's thoughts and hide one's true feelings, hiding its passenger from this planet's natural defences. You may well have downloaded all of Laozi's memories when you finally captured and killed him but it seems to me that you have one fatal flaw in your plan; me."

Liam turned round to face his wilting audience, slowly unwinding his bandage. He looked at Laozi, at Iso and finally at Voegel before voicing his instructions in an extremely controlled manner.

"Moshe, Pizarro please restrain them all including Peel for I think we have a rare case of insurrection from those who apparently are in command.

These three are all bearing one vital ingredient that makes them, them."

Liam pulled off the last of his bandage with such force that the malfunctioning cellhip was cast across the floor in the direction of the door, coming to rest against the leg of a chair. He held his left arm aloft and showed them a bare wrist devoid of any blemish, devoid of scars and most importantly devoid of his mark.

"The portal splices the human soul, leaving a human's roots on his home planet along with his mark. Only a duplicate would make it through with his manmade mark intact."

Moshe and Pizarro had concealed their weapons and drew them out immediately, pointing them at the others. He walked over to his benefactor's imposter and grabbed his arm, turning it over to find a mark.

"You didn't even think to check, did you? Without ever having used the portal before, how could you know? I suspected that Laozi had been replaced by one of his twins quite some time ago, months before your feigned attack on his office in London. The projection today only confirmed my suspicions. I am indeed vindicated."

Liam walked over to Iso and Kal, dragging his foe by the arm, not letting go and checked their wrists. They were both marked.

"Peel and Voegel while they are not forgiven, they have been greatly fooled by a plan that started quite some time ago."

Liam glanced at his two colleagues from Security and then back at Peel.

"Pizarro, when we have finished here, could you take these two to isolation and keep them under a watchful eye. They need to be properly debriefed so that we can work out how deep this fabric of lies goes."

Laozi's imposter tried to escape Liam's vice like grip, pulling in one direction and the other but was unable to get away. Realising that that there was little that he could do and being totally unprepared for this sequence of events, he was left spluttering protestations like a child.

"This is utterly preposterous. You are the duplicate. There is no other explanation. Peel, Voegel do something about this, unhand me at once."

"You forget that Kal was the portal engineer attending to my original journey. As for Iso, the real Iso wasn't even part of the Kepler Broadcast; I've worked out that much. And as for you, you may have his memories but you couldn't be further from him in spirit. Let me tell you something about this planet; something that until recently even I was unaware. Kepler has to invite you; Kepler has to want you, to allow you to visit him at any time. Only a duplicate can go through a portal and not be transformed as there is nothing unique about a duplicate, therefore there is nothing to transform, apart from matter. A human's soul is entirely exclusive and cannot be replicated. We become a splice and only reconnect when restored to our planet of origin. Part of the transformation is to lose the mark and therefore one's soul indicator.

"The Keplerians can read any human and more importantly they sense a duplicate immediately. I was uninvited yet they couldn't read me either way. It is why they see me as one of them; for they are descendents of people from other planets whose souls reside at their point of origin, thus linking them to the entire universe. The Prison States were created for all duplicates that made it to Kepler. A deal was struck with the first of them to arrive and they had a choice to either go to Karkara or face extinction, the choice was simple. As for your grand scheme, I see why you are in such a hurry." Liam paused for a second, "Moshe, follow me, we're taking these three to meet a new friend."

With that Liam turned on his heels and headed for the door, ready to take on anybody who got in his way. His next port of call was to enable him to find out what it was exactly that the terrorist group intended. With a sixth sense as to the situation, Boy waited until everyone had left the room. He growled at the passing Voegel, hurrying him up as he continued to make false protestations.

Once everyone was out, Boy swept the area ensuring they were not being tracked and they moved swiftly across the walkway back into the lift and down to level zero and the floor of the atrium. They crossed over to the other side and snaked along the corridors until they finally reached the entrance to the Department for Security.

They were met by two security guards, flanking the entrance and a sea of blue dots, scanning the surrounding area. Liam knew that they were being carefully watched and that the body scans were already underway. Moments later the doors opened and they were waved through. He led them into the familiar entrance hall and up the spiral staircase. The sound of their footsteps rattling brought back the memories of his first meeting with Peel which now seemed an age away. Once they were all stood in the circular room with its many passageways leading off in different directions, Liam gave Moshe instructions to stay with the triad of imposters whilst he and Boy went in search of the new incumbent in the seat of power.

Meandering down the corridor, he found himself drawn to an idea of resolving matters, once and for all; something that could only be facilitated by the absolute destruction of the portal. He knew that it would fall to him to carry out and so steeled himself for any potential battle with the terrorists still at large.

Finally they reached another circular room but this time with a large table, multiple projections sitting atop its surface and 14 high seats placed symmetrically around. There was one solitary figure sat opposite to where Liam had come in, sitting slumped face down over the table. His long black hair was sprawled across the surface accompanied by his outstretched arms. Liam coughed to signal his arrival and Jabir twitched mid-slumber in recognition.

"It's all getting pretty interesting out there. You should have been with us. I'm pleased to report that we've found the source to most of our woes."

Jabir raised his head sleepily, rubbing his eyes until fully focused. Realising that he had been off guard, he snapped back to reality quickly and responded.

"The last I saw of you was as you headed into the atrium as we intended. So the plan was successful?"

"It sure was. Leaving the chamber unguarded was the right thing to do and especially as it made Peel think that he was still in control. This entire business with Lao and Zi has created a whole world of confusion. We're proven to be right. Laozi hasn't been Laozi for quite some time. My guess is that he was captured as early as six months ago and has since been killed, once they'd downloaded all of his personal information. You and I have been dealing with Zi ever since; the reports, messages and even cellhip calls, they've all been fielded by his grand imposter."

"That explains Lao being the healthier version. Zi has had to impersonate Laozi for so long that he took on his girth and distinct mannerisms. Lao is obviously the fighter and Zi the thinker. At least I have the measure of my adversary as it seems did you."

"That faked message from Zi whilst it was a genuine surprise, played into our hands fortuitously. Thank you for leaving it to me to sort out. So that you are aware I have kept our recent collaboration completely under wraps. I haven't divulged a thing to Ama. I am still concerned for her safety and don't want her knowing too much, for her own sake, let alone ours."

"Understood; since we've been allies, I've not given her or your union one further thought. It makes sense and besides I have more grave concerns these days."

"I know and three of them are standing back there in the briefing room."

"Shouldn't we head there now?"

"You know what I have planned with the Keplerians, don't you?"

"That will not be put in jeopardy. I will however use any means necessary to extract what these usurpers had planned, so that we can catch the rest of them. I have a feeling that the weakest link is Kal, so that is as good a place as any to start. One final thing, the portal needs to be destroyed immediately."

"I hadn't forgotten. Moshe and I will head there now. Do whatever it is that you have to and cross-examine Peel or Voegel to glean anything from their side. Meet back here in three hours?"

"Till then."

Liam and Boy disappeared down another passageway, bypassing the briefing room, leaving them to Jabir's devices. He stopped at a communication station and waited for a while; Boy at his heel. All security specialists were fitted with communication devices that worked solely on Tega, the stations provided access to them at any time. Liam spoke briefly to Moshe, giving him his instructions and they agreed to meet in the atrium. He headed out immediately to Level 0 and the base's grand vestibule.

Moshe was already standing in the centre staring up at the ceiling, towering half a kilometre above. The night sky was illuminated by Kepler's moon. It blended with criss-crossing beams of starlight which were being sucked in by the transalum dome and created a clear spectrum with an epicentre just above where they were now stood. Liam couldn't help but feel that this was an auspicious moment; a turning point in all of their lives. The rays began to move and extend creating droplets of luminosity, each one forming a ball of radiance. The surreal charm made them both stand still, neither wanting to break its beauty.

"Moshe, I wish we had time for this but unfortunately we don't. Have you got the explosives?"

Liam got no response as Moshe continued to be transfixed by the beads pitching and falling above him.

"Moshe, the explosives?"

Moshe mutely tapped the pouch attached to the upper arm of his jacket and remained silent.

"Come on Moshe, its unlike you to be taken in by such things, it's only the trick of the transalum. We need to hurry."

Liam grabbed his arm trying to coax his friend along. Finally he acquiesced and the three of them moved off in the direction of the portal chamber. As they headed down the corridor Liam spoke with his friend properly for the first time in a while.

"So what was all that about? That was unlike you; you're not usually so caught up with these things."

"I'm not sure. I'm not that sure about anything the truth be known. First you're Liam Self then you're this guy Hal then I find myself acting against orders and going with my instincts."

"Is that a first for you?"

"I do know that what you say is true. We've been too far together for me not to believe you. That Zi character was an odd fish. He couldn't make his mind up whether he wanted to save or kill everyone."

"Insightful. Perhaps there's a place for you on Kepler after all."

"What's it like out there on the continent? I'm coming round to the idea of staying."

"Let's get this over with and I'll show you."

Meanwhile, back at Security, Jabir put his tools down and looked at his victim. Kal bleeding from most parts of his body sat slumped in a chair with his hands tied behind his back. The different measures that he and Liam had taken to expose their enemies were plain to be seen but both were equally as effective. It had taken no time at all to extract their plan. Jabir was mindful that Kal may not have been in possession of all the facts but was pleased that he had at least a framework to work from. His next port of call was Voegel who, according to Pizarro, had continued with his insistence that Zi was Laozi and that it was Liam who was not who he said he was.

Jabir had learned that there were over three million duplicates left alive on Earth. Most were still on the islands of New Zealand but no longer in Auckland, given the total decimation of the urban areas. The armies of a few hundred thousand stationed in Shanghai and outside Sao Luis were currently heading back. This was merely a ruse. They had taken control of the Reper Station and were set to transport the portal back to their new capital, near Queenstown, in two days time. The terrorist cell sent ahead of them was dispatched on a reconnaissance trip led by Zi's twin Lao to ensure that everything on Tega was as it seemed on Earth. Satisfied that everything was as it should have been Kal, Iso and Zi went ahead to take command of Tega and to initiate the process.

The idea was to enable Liam to get back onside with the Keplerians and for him to carry out their wishes as in to aid the transportation of all three million duplicates purporting to be humans through Tega and out onto Kepler for real, duping everyone in the process. Jabir laughed at the thought of it. Knowing what Liam had told him of not only the Great Book and the Keplerians but of the planet itself and its natural defences, it seemed incredible that they had truly believed that they could have got away with it.

He returned to the briefing room and then headed in a new direction, down one of the side passageways towards the isolation units. At the end of a tunnel he reached a set of cells with transalum frontage, soundproofed and all empty except for two. With Peel at one end and Voegel at the other, Jabir hoped that he could detain them long enough to ascertain the risk of releasing them back into the fold. He turned right towards Voegel's cell and when he was in front of the former Chief of Department he couldn't help but notice that the onslaught of self doubt was etched all over his face. Jabir ran his index finger over the transalum in a horizontal direction, opening up the pathway to speak.

"So Herr Voegel is there anything that you would care to say in your defence? Liam's views are far more lenient than mine."

"I don't know how you have come to be in your position but seeing as it is you, I can only apologise for my involvement. I have been serving my friend Laozi Veda for as long as I can remember. I even took in one of our own, Ama Pepper Clark, as if she were my daughter. Her father was on board fleetingly, you might remember him as Krugman."

"There's little use in grovelling to me and even less use in trying to appeal to my weaknesses. How could you have been so stupid? You are a crafty man Voegel and while you might doubt yourself now, you wouldn't have been duped for all this time unless you had willingly played your part. I need to know who else we are dealing with and how long you have been involved. I need to know the whole story from start to finish."

"I know very little. I have been acting for Laozi and only him."

"If I can't get a straight answer from you, I will have to walk you down the road that Kal has just taken. Let me remind you that it is a one way ticket and most definitely not first class."

"How can I divulge information of which I know little about?"

"Do you take me for a mug? A dim-witted grunt who knows little about human nature? You forget that I am a scientist."

"I had not forgotten, merely put it to one side, seeing as you are now the torturer."

"Whose fault is that? Your colleague at the end of the hall has had a similar amount of regard for the rest of us. I have a good mind to come in and tear it out of you but before I do I give you one last chance - when did you first notice the change in Laozi?"

As Jabir took on the wit of Voegel, his Prithvian colleagues were heading into a dangerous situation with great stealth. They were making good time in an effort to get to the portal chamber before anyone else. They had made it to the final corridor before the outer chamber when the hairs stood up on the back of Liam's neck. He tapped Moshe on the shoulder and led him and Boy into an alcove to catch their breath.

"What if Lao and the others have been alerted. What if they are already here?"

Before Moshe could answer, a booming but familiar voice came out of nowhere.

"What if they are?"

Having only just got rid of one, Liam now had to deal with the brutish other half.

Chapter 25

4th October 2147 – Early Morning – Tega, Kepler

From the corner of the recess, their adversary glowered as he spoke. Unlike Moshe, Liam was aware of what he was up against. Without turning round, he backed away. He sensed that the entire terrorist cell was also lurking in the shadows yet was baffled as to why Boy had not sensed their presence. Preparing to be struck from behind, he looked to one side and noticed his canine friend lying on the ground. He crouched down to feel Boy's pulse, realising that he must have been hit by some form of tranquiliser. When no blow came for him, he spoke unflinchingly.

"With a voice like that - you can only be the product of one family. Is this on what the future of our people now resides; a nefarious exchange between two great imposters?"

He gently stroked the back of Boy's head before rising up to his feet. As he did so the hidden group's anointed leader stepped out of the gloom.

"The time for decency and rhetoric is over. It is our time; the age of man has only just begun."

Lao urgently pushed past Moshe and circled Liam, standing tall. He was physically superior to his parent in every way. Liam couldn't help but wonder whether it was only nurture that had resulted in this magnificent transformation of his benefactor's genes. Lao sized Liam up in equal measure. They stood glaring at each other in pure hostility. Lao was the first to break the heated silence.

"No one will stand in our way and least of all you. My brother has wasted too much time allowing leniency. I have always been aware of the futility in reasoning with your kind."

He gesticulated to a few, till now unseen, members of his group.

"You two and yes, you Sirp, bring them with us, we have no time to lose."

Before he had a chance to argue, Liam's arms were whipped behind his back and forced into a vice like grip. Out of the corner of his eye, he witnessed the same thing happen to Moshe where there were too many aggressors for it to be a fair fight. He caught sight of the female who Lao had referred to as Sirp and tried to place where he knew her from. He and his security colleague were propelled forward and steered out of the alcove towards the portal chamber.

He was in no mood to rationalise what it was that had driven them to so much anger. Struggling against his captor, Zi's words *violence begets violence* rang loud in his ears. Liam knew that no matter what he had stood for before, only aggression and ferocity would win this fight. He felt confident that if he could somehow break free and with a little luck, he and Moshe could deal with all six of them. However with Boy out of action, they had no way of communicating with Jabir or any of his team.

They reached the outer chamber which Lao accessed easily using Laozi's scancodes. Everyone filed enthusiastically inside. Liam remembered where he'd seen the girl before as she was without question the duplicate of the famous Panamerican screen legend, Sirpica Ross. He had always found it more than a little strange that her career had lasted for over 70 years yet she had never looked a day over 30. Rather than make an untimely comment, he chose to remain silent. A mass transportation was out of the question. Neither Kepler nor the duplicates were ready for such a thing. As if he was reading his mind, Lao zoomed in on his thoughts, speaking loudly so that everyone could hear.

"We will take control of Tega without alerting the Keplerians. The portal can only transport three beings at a time and make only one transmission every hour. This gives us less than 60 days to complete the transmission of an alternative cast of specialists whilst employing the wit and guile of Liam Self in preparing the Keplerians for the return of our people to their respective kingdoms."

"Are you mad? You'll be found out and incarcerated in Karkara or Avasya before you know it. They do have the means to protect themselves. A power much greater than you or I could ever truly understand. If I could offer my counsel just one last time, think seriously on whether you want to do this; as regardless of it being 2,141 people or two million, you will be destroyed and we will all lose; everyone, including you. None of us here can remain uninvited."

"We will take our chances. All we need is the queen to your knight, to close out this immortal game once and for all."

Before he had time to finish the door opened and the missing two terrorists returned with the final piece in their grandiose scheme, Ama. Perturbed and petrified she looked at Liam, crestfallen and almost apologetic. He struggled to break free from his captors. Relenting he gave her a look of reassurance, trying to muster a smile given the circumstances. Lao's confidence swelled as he realised that he had played his rook at precisely the right moment, now having Liam firmly under his control.

"To initiate proceedings we need a declaration of peace to be drawn up between the Prithvians and the Keplerians. We need you to meet them as planned. You are to give them the names, descriptions and personal details of the seven originals and assist them in their search, deportation and possible extermination. You are to demonstrate that every single specialist is back on board and will be ready to return to their kingdom in 60 days time. You will agree that in a year's time the Repertega will leave for Earth.

Liam didn't even bother to interject.

"By then we would have successfully completed the transmission of our most prominent people to freedom and so, once we have taken the technology from the prison states, we will be in a position to repopulate the entire planet."

Liam could only wonder as to how Lao was in possession of such sensitive information. As the two terrorists returned to guard the entrance on the other side of the door, Lao looked at Ama, standing fragile against the oncoming verdict.

"To keep you focused, her welfare will be at the forefront of your mind but furthermore you will have the lives of 2,141 others, pending on your actions. If any of our plans are to be changed or if there is even a hint of duplicity in your dealings, everyone will be killed, including her."

Liam remained silent and calm yet his chief concern was Ama and how he could extricate her from these unfortunate circumstances. He and Moshe were maneuvered to one side, leaving Lao and Sirp standing in front of her as she stood trembling in their presence. Lao looked her up and down in a leering fashion before striking her across the cheek.

"Strip her down; let's show him that we are prepared to act upon our words."

Sirp appeared confused with the order as she was the only one free to do his bidding. It was clear to Liam that she and Lao were in some form of a relationship. After a moment's deliberation which was plain for everyone to see, she set about her conquest. Before she got close Liam interrupted her movement with one last attempt at quelling the affront.

"What do you expect by such a course of action? Leave her alone. I take you at your word and as long as she remains unharmed, I will carry out what you wish. Please don't insult my intelligence with threats, immaterial to proceedings."

Sirp stopped, glad for the intervention but Lao turned back to Ama and with all the venom of a duplicate poisoned by years of pain, struck her across the other cheek, this time drawing blood. Liam knew it was useless in pleading with their enraged leader.

"We take orders from no one except ourselves. We are free to make our own choices; of places we visit, wars we fight, people we screw and people we strike. Yet for us to be truly free we must work together to destroy the non believers. Sirp I will not ask again, remove her clothes."

She re-approached Ama with an apologetic look, intimating for her to undress. Lao turned his back on the unfolding scene and moved over to the corner of the chamber where Liam was now being held, fiercely eyeballing his adversary.

The room fell silent as both women whimpered for two entirely different reasons. Luckily for Ama the stars aligned perfectly at that precise moment, as the sound of bodies slumping to the floor in the corridor outside were drowned out by Sirp spinning round and screaming in the direction of her lover, as she took out a handgun and pointed it at her own temple.

"I can't take this any longer."

For the first time during this extraordinary exchange, Lao looked almost fearful. He hesitantly moved in Sirp's direction. Before he had a chance to prevent her from doing herself a damage she fired the weapon and splattered her brains across the floor. Her body collapsed with a thud and then the door to the outer chamber opened. A wave of fresher air rolled in and there was silence. The lights went out and whatever power that was left in the room was sucked away, leaving everyone standing in trepidation.

Lao was the first to move, signaling at the other four terrorists who'd been holding Moshe and Liam. In a quick well rehearsed move, they positioned themselves on either side of the door, waiting for the insurgents. None came.

Liam and Moshe drifted together, trying to untie each other's bonds but their efforts were useless. Liam checked Moshe's upper arm and set about getting free. As Lao and his team were fixed on the opening, waiting for an attack, he managed to wriggle his legs through his arms and take out the small pack of explosives from the pouch in Moshe's jacket. After a while there was still no movement from either side so Lao signed to two of his men to crouch down and venture into the next chamber. As the first made his move, within a nanosecond of flinching he was hit in the head, rolling sideways onto the floor. The other remained stock still for fear of the same thing happening.

A gas canister arrived. One of the Lao's men picked it up, threw it back but in the process was shot through the heart, leaving him stone cold dead. Moshe drew Liam's attention to the fact that he had also managed to bring his arms in front of himself, steadily moving up behind Lao. His diminutive height should have been a factor but in one swift move he threw his hands over Lao's head, using the bonds as a vice, trapping the arms of the terrorist. The remaining two others were now perplexed as whether to protect their leader or defend against the next attack. Momentarily lost in confusion, they let their guard slip and both were hit in corresponding shoulders as they turned, knocking them to the ground. Liam ran over, picked up one of their guns, kicked the other away and then stood over them, glowering menacingly. The lights flickered back on as Moshe and Lao struggled against each other. Lao, superior in strength was beginning to win the battle. Jabir strode in accompanied by Pizarro.

"So we meet again and this time in entirely different circumstances. It has taken me years to finally catch up with you."

Jabir walked up to Lao and punched him in the stomach, so hard that he doubled up and wilted. Coughing, Lao sneered back.

"The last time I saw you, was when my brother prevented me from

224

neutralising your sorry life. You call this a worthwhile existence, protecting the people that made you?"

"It's certainly better than trying to create a master race. Without mankind we wouldn't exist."

Jabir looked across the body strewn floor then continued.

"It's wasted breath anyway. Even your girlfriend finally drummed some sense into herself."

"Suicide is senseless. You of all people should know that."

Pizarro cut Liam's bonds. Once free he rushed over to Ama, putting his arm around her while the hostile altercation brewed to a fever pitch.

"Give me one good reason as to why we should keep you alive? All of your flock is either dead or heading towards extinction, your brother is a captive and your plan is foiled."

"At least give me an honourable death. You owe me that much."

Jabir without hesitation whipped out a knife and sliced across his counterpart's neck. Lao's face was one of release and faint relief, Jabir's of sorrow for a former friend and great adversary.

Both Liam and Ama looked at each other in shrugged acceptance as if they had been subconsciously aware of Jabir's nature all along. Moshe no longer had to restrain a lifeless body so he let Lao slip though his arms.

Liam immediately set about applying the explosives to the portal, linking them to a microscopic transmitter which he placed on the underside of his left wrist. The two remaining terrorists lay writhing in agony on the floor. Without a modicum of remorse Moshe finished them off with one of their handguns. Stepping over the bodies, they turned their backs on the portal and made their way for the exit, for what they hoped would be the last time.

Once they were out in the corridor, Tega felt like a different place. The dark, dank passageway was now alive with colour. The sea of misery existed no more. They hurried on until they felt that they were far enough away to breathe again. Ama clung onto Liam, almost catatonic in disbelief.

As they made their way through the labyrinth of passageways, Boy bounded towards them. Rejuvenated and as if nothing had happened, he jumped up at Ama first, licking her face, almost knocking her over whilst pushing Liam sideways. Once he'd established his mistress's welfare he sat in front of Liam with his tongue out as if to wait for his next command. With a couple of clicks of the fingers, directions were given and they filtered out into the atrium, exhausted but positive; vindicated and most of all alive.

Liam proffered his left wrist, baring it unblemished, for all to see. He then pressed the underside of his left wrist. He pressed again and then held. There was an almighty rumbling from within the bowels of the base and then silence.

All the specialists stood still, marking this moment. Only five were aware of what had taken place, the rest were oblivious to its significance. Yet everybody stopped what they were doing and waited for further explosions; none came. Knowing that they had been successful, the five cheerfully looked at each other with collective relief as a warm breeze rolled out of the corridor from whence they came. When the right time presented itself, Jabir spoke.

"Well that was interesting. If it hadn't been for Pizarro, we'd have completely forgotten about the small factor of the cell still being on board. I was so wrapped up in dealing with Voegel it had passed me by."

"Well I guess we owe our thanks to you." Liam cut in, looking at Pizarro and shaking his hand. "Jabir, we owe you a debt of gratitude - everyone aboard. If only they knew. How strange that it took one of their own to finally bring them down. I for one didn't see that coming. How long have you been on their trail?"

"I was developed with the sole purpose of being my father's bodyguard. I acted on his behalf for many years. I am nothing but loyal to my family and his friends. Laozi Veda was one of those friends and I was placed on the Repertega as a safeguard against anything such as this happening. That was a very wise move on your former benefactor's part."

"It was indeed. At least I can mourn his passing properly, now that his dark side has been retired. What is to become of Zi and the other two?"

"Up to you Liam; you are our leader when out there. I can take care of the ship and all its contents but what happens on Kepler stays on Kepler as they say."

"The way I see it, the duplicates have a choice; either form a prison state on New Zealand or face certain death at the hands of the World Council. Either way, their options are severely limited. As far as Voegel and Peel are concerned they have been blinded by their own stupidity and so therefore must remain incarcerated aboard the ship until it returns to Earth."

"So be it. What of Tega and the specialists, what are we to do now?"

"I have my meeting with the council representative tomorrow and I think it is as good a time as any to come clean; to explain the entire situation to them, therefore regaining their trust with honesty."

"What? Expose yourself as a fraud and risk everyone's lives with it?" Moshe chipped in uncharacteristically.

"Not at all, they won't care whether my name is one thing or another, that's not important, they will want the originals to stay but be accounted for, as part of those who are destined to remain and set up the village of Tega. They'll understand the situation with the duplicates as this is not the first time that anything like this has happened and it won't be the last. That is why the prison states are as they are, for times like these. The Great Book carries a lot more information. It's all about interpretation.

"As for me, I have to stay to protect Prithvian interests and set up Tega. The only thing left to organise with them is the timing of your departure as it is clear that they will not want the Repertega to stay much longer, risking another clandestine assault on their planet; leaving one final question mark hanging over the entire reason for this trip; the cure to our mark."

Liam removed the micro transmitter and bared his naked wrist once more as he continued,

"Earth's human population has been rapidly decreasing for many years, through faction friction and an exponential growth in suicide amongst teenagers. Duplicate development has stemmed the tide. With the extinction of the duplicate race, numbers are again on the wane and we need to arrest this problem. There is a cure; in many ways think of it as a portal, like the one we have just destroyed but this time keep it in your mind's eye."

Ama turned to stroke Liam's face, gently caressing his cheek with her fingertips as she looked longingly into his eyes. Deep in the blue caverns of his irises, she found what she was looking for and whispered.

"You can't go back, I can't stay with you."

Liam nodded slowly, knowing this to be true. Ama picked up the reins, laying his thoughts out for everyone to hear.

"This portal that he speaks of is the cure. It transmits a human to a place of peace, serenity and understanding. We need to unlock this portal in our brains, to generate acceptance through education and faith. In time and with belief we will evolve to lose our mark yet everyone must buy into the process. The war with the duplicates, the decimation of our cities and the preceding years of chaos amongst all our cultures, leaves our people waiting on the return of the Repertega and our well documented mission. The time is perfect for us to restore order to our shores.

"I have to spread the word and I need your help; everyone's aboard. We are the chosen ones who can make that difference. We have been lucky enough to be given the opportunity to explore our minds physically, we have stepped through the portal and been saved. Let's go back and tell everyone how they can too. Let's show them how. Let it take root. When mankind truly accepts its place in the universe and gives in to nature, once and for all, the succeeding spring will bear new fruit, unblemished, succulent and ripe for the future."

Liam had to cut in, only to add weight to her words.

"Spoken like a true Keplerian."

Jabir knew that he would have to return to Earth, loyally protecting human interests for as long as he was useful. As he processed his thoughts and their ideas, he finally responded before either Moshe or Pizarro could offer any protestations.

"Ama you have me as your protector. Liam, I will ensure her safety as she conveys the message for the salvation of the Prithvian people."

"Thank you Jabir, the irony is not lost on me but we will be eternally in your debt. It will be through her music that she will connect with all of our people, through the stories that will unfold; those that will unite everyone together. Ama is the key."

The group huddled close defining the moment seeing it as the birth of a path to all their futures. No one spoke as they listened to the many sounds of the atrium. Shattered and fatigued, they nodded in each other's direction and then departed towards their respective quarters.

Liam and Ama walked in silence. When they reached her rooms they went inside without a word, undressed slowly, carefully, contemplatively and lay down beside each other, holding, staring at each other, until their eyelids sagged and they simultaneously succumbed to a deep but dreamless sleep.

The next morning they got up habitually and as if nothing had happened. They made breakfast in communicative silence, acknowledging Liam's meeting with the representative from the Kepler Council later that morning. It was one final hurdle that needed to be overcome and one that needed to be handled carefully. When the time came for him to leave, he patted Boy briefly and kissed Ama goodbye before heading out into uncharted territory.

The hours passed by slowly. Ama looked out of the window as she had done when the ship first arrived, wondering whether Liam would be successful. A part of her hoped that their plan would be undone where they would be allowed to stay on the continent and everyone else deported. She knew that this was impossible. She couldn't help feeling scared and extremely alone with the task that she herself had set.

Liam did not return at midday as he usually did after these meetings nor did he return mid afternoon. Ama's mood turned from personal fear, to extreme worry on his behalf. Boy sensed her trepidation as she paced up and down the living room. Her thoughts compounded into exasperation until finally the front door opened and he strode in with a gleaming smile.

"They've accepted the truth and agreed to terms."

Not knowing whether to laugh, or cry, Ama leapt up from the chair and into his arms producing tears of both fear and joy. He held her lovingly; gently explaining the ordeal of the negotiations and the subsequent terms of the truce. There had been initial resistance to who he was and how he had come to be there. However the representative had already been instructed by the elders to treat him as one of them regardless of whatever it was that he would reveal. They were glad that the duplicate uprising had been brought under control. They were upset that the portal had been built in the first place, let alone brought to Kepler and in such a clandestine manner. They were concerned with there being similar devices hidden away unbeknownst to him. He had assured them that this was not the case.

The bottom line was that the Repertega would leave in two week's time and 84 specialists would remain behind. The remaining originals would stay where they were and the nine who had gone in search of them would be given first right of refusal to remain, likewise the rescue team including Liam. These Prithvians had all seen enough of Kepler to understand life as it was yet were in the unfortunate position to use that information against the

Keplerians if they were put in a compromising position back on Earth. It had already been decreed that they should be persuaded by Liam to stay.

Jabir as a duplicate, loyal to human race would return to Earth and no doubt his human counterpart, Pizarro would follow him. They agreed that Zi, Iso and Kal would be sent to Karkara for all eternity without being included in the final 84. They could fight it out with those there as to whether they were worthy of making up the numbers.

Liam let them know that Ama was the vessel. That much was agreed. This left 60 places available, via ballot, for those specialists who wished to stay.

When the parameters had finally been set and after much deliberation over timing, the representative had left the yard to make a call to the council in order to get their agreement sanctioned. He later returned with a piece of paper outlining the terms to their mutual benefit; laid out as nine bullet points. Once both parties had looked over the document and accepted the terms, they signed the paper, gestured the Keplerian farewell and had headed back into their respective territories. Liam had gone to the Department for Security, made copies of the agreement and returned to their quarters.

Now sitting on the long chair, waiting for Ama to ask him about the terms, he casually took out the piece of paper, briefly allowing access to her prying eyes. When she asked to see it properly, he playfully kept it from her until after a brief tussle she finally managed to wrestle it away from him.

He moved away to let her have the time and space to take it all in. It was best to leave her with them. He got up, walked over to the window and looked outside, without uttering another word. The points were more than pertinent; they were guidelines for their survival.

o   Universe - is in and around one and all, ever evolving and deeply diverse.
o   Nature - do not create beings unnaturally or put mankind before nature.
o   Individual – has freedom of expression, celebration and belief.
o   Vision – ultimate reality is achieved through perception, emotion and understanding.
o   Energy – is a continual ebb and flow, throughout eternity.
o   Remembrance – of family, past, present and future.
o   Shrines – create places of community, in reverence of nature and the cosmos.
o   Acceptance – life is infinitely finite, death is energy and matter redefined.
o   Love – we are one family, never steal from, cheat, nor harm your family.

Chapter 26

He packed his backpack, pulled on his threads and laced up his Chameau's for what felt would be the final time. He crouched down on the floor, cupped Boy's muzzle in his right hand whilst clicking his left index finger against the thumb, commanding his charge to lie down next to him. He whispered a few words into Boy's ear, patted him on the underside of the belly before running his hands up to the scruff of the neck and playfully rubbing his head, brushing the soft fur forward into a Mohican. He looked at Ama with a furrowed brow,

"Losing you again was never part of the plan."

Ama glanced at the clock on the wall in her quarters without responding. The last few weeks had been those of change, organisation and much deliberation where they'd agreed to spend their final hours out on the plains of Adhara. The idea was to while away the time, soaking up the morning rays with a walk to a copse not far from the ship. He gazed around the room as if taking a photo for his memory bank and paused to look at Boy before picking up his pack and slinging it over his left shoulder.

They ventured out through the maze of corridors into the atrium. They were confronted by a crowd. He looked upwards, still marvelling at the sheer brilliance and magnificence of the structure. There was an excited buzz as all the specialists, ship's crew and personnel had gathered in the centre to see off those who had chosen to remain. They pushed through the well wishers; he smiled at a few familiar faces and pressed on heading for the Department for Security.

There was only one way in and one way out since an accord had been reached. Jabir was the gatekeeper. He stood at the entrance as if he had been waiting there for quite some time. Walking towards them with his arms outstretched, grinning. He and Jabir bear hugged each other before he spoke without a hint of irony.

"You take care of her, you hear? I don't want to spend the rest of my days worrying that you've reverted to that abominable lust coursing through your veins. You guys have a purpose and one that needs to be addressed immediately. I'm counting on you Jabir."

"I guess I deserve that. Not a problem, I'm here to serve."

"Thank you. You're a shining example to your kind. You made a choice that none of us could ever have made back there. I guess it is in your nature not to question the morals of your actions. We owe you. Anyway, I don't want to make a song and dance of my departure so let's get on with it."

They proceeded through the double doors, passing the well trodden stairs to the briefing room into a makeshift departure lounge. Part of the Kepler Concord, as it was now known, was that all personal transmitters and electronic devices were to be handed in, preventing any further distress signals being sent out into space, encouraging passing traffic to make an unscheduled visit, no matter how unsuccessful it may be. His pack was removed by a security specialist and was thoroughly searched, scanned and placed on a conveyor belt, taking it to the gates of the compound on the perimeter. They walked on towards the exit as Jabir stopped and turned to him.

"This is where I must leave you. Fare well my friend."

"Stay true brother."

They hugged once again but this time with a lot less bravado, parting with a firm handshake. Jabir sauntered back to his department as Ama took Liam's hand in hers and gently pulled him in the opposite direction. She led him through a full body scanning device. He turned and gazed upon the inside of the ship for the last time. With security cleared and no one left in their way, they crossed over the threshold and down the gangway into the compound.

It was early morning and the chill breeze had already taken on a hue of Indian summer. Perhaps it was the occasion but autumn seemed to have been kept at bay in honour of the departing Prithvians where the fields were still lush and alive, with green and flower. Birds, bees and an assortment of lowland creatures had also assembled in the area as if to wish the Repertega and all her passengers, a fond farewell.

They hurried through baggage collection and out into Adhara for real, heading north with the intention of leaving them all behind. Even if it was to be for only a fleeting moment it was a chance for them to be truly alone, at peace and one with each other.

They took a wagon for a short distance and jumped out beside a hedge that bordered a large corn field. They found the gap that they'd made only a few days before and fed through onto a pathway leading to the banks of a hill, overlooking the plains of the lowlands. Without a word, they progressed over the ruts in the sun scorched ground, over a stile and into the next piece of patchwork that Adhara was famous for.

Holding hands they pressed on until they reached the intended copse at the crest of the hill which featured a myriad of roots and branches. He lay a rug down and beckoned for Ama to join him. With sorrow and fear in her heart she sat down whilst fighting back the tears.

"Being separated just fills me with an emptiness, one of which I don't think I'll ever be able to control."

"We've been through our plans, nothing has been left to chance, we are prepared and in our mind's eye we know that this is the only way. This is it. Remember what I have always said to you of love, family and compassion. It is the memory of us that keeps us alive forever; we live on physically through our progeny not our own reinvention."

"I know but it doesn't make our parting any sweeter."

"I will always be here. You will forever know where I am."

They sat listening to the sound of the local livestock as the wind rustled gently through the trees. The lulling lilt of chirping birds was accompanied by the mewing protestations of Keplerian cows and sheep. It was a countryside paradise. One that Ama had no desire to leave.

After a short while he leant over and took her in his arms, holding her tight as her father had done not too long ago. Her fears subsided and she basked in the net of his eternal love whilst reminding herself of the good fortune that they had at least been afforded the chance to reignite their flame. They lay back on the rug with her head on his chest. Ama spoke softly,

"Do you think he's really dead?"

"Who? Laozi?"

"Yes. I know I shouldn't, yet I can't help but feel a tad sceptical of his original intentions; but then again we'll never know."

"He was immense; a man of absolute character, undone by his blind conviction."

"All I do know and can agree with is that he led me to you and for that I am grateful."

The balmy air toyed with them, letting her words ring out, lulling them into an energetic daydream, fuelled by hope and their vivid imaginings. As their minds wandered the sun left the east, rising up above them.

Falling asleep, he pictured a thousand suns being fertilised by a million planets, exploding into new life within the Omniverse. The constant ebb and flow of energy was infinitely finite in its entirety. He knew that he was at peace; he knew that he had found his home.

Ama lay silently, willing the Repertega to leave without her, willing it to leave her with him forever. She sighed as she soaked up these final moments, knowing that no matter the interpretation, the reality of staying was impossible. She pictured a utopian life on Earth; a family of her own. Although she had found peace, she knew that she had to go home.

A klaxon sounded, reverberating through the trees, whisked along by the breeze. Neither moved as the resonance rolled across the plains in every direction. There was complete silence. The wind ceased and the air went strangely chill. The hairs on their arms pricked up, neither noticed. Both shivered silently as he awoke.

"You're leaving soon." He said languorously, having a momentary lapse of reason. Ama lay still. He snapped to attention. "Ama, wake up. It's time to go." She didn't move. "Ama, seriously, you cannot stay."

He sat upright, pushing her upwards, forcing her awake. She looked at him in half recognition as her mind adjusted to the situation. The reality dawned on her like a wave of pure emotion.

"I can't do this. I can't take on such a responsibility. To be entrusted with the cure is something for someone far more qualified than me. I am not worthy."

"Ama, listen to me. You are that person. You should have fear. Fear is good. It makes you stronger. Once you set the ball rolling, it will gather pace without too much trouble. No matter what the mark has done to us all, everybody is still looking for an explanation, for a reason. No one has ever really listened to a preacher or a politician, at least not for hundreds of years. It's the musicians, the songwriters who are the storytellers of our past, our present and our future. It is your turn to fill that void, to give the people reason, to give them a chance to believe, to give them hope, to restore their faith."

"So long as you are there to guide me - but you must understand that I am more than a little daunted by the task."

"Of course I do - I felt exactly the same when Laozi asked a similar thing of me but I see it now as being part of his grand design. He was far better informed than we ever gave him credit for. His deep and rich sensibilities were akin to the Keplerians. I have absolute faith in you Ama, as he had in me."

"How will I know that I am doing the right thing?"

"I'll always be there with you. Hold me here, keep me in your heart and I'll live on. We are one Ama. We will always be."

Wasting no more time, they rolled up the rug and stepped carefully over the cracks in the ground, where the roots of the trees were bursting through.

"It was easier leaving you the last time."

"This is farewell but not goodbye my love. In any case you'll have Boy to keep you company for many years to come."

"Yet he'll always be a reminder of what I've left behind."

"I will always be here, with no limits, no mark determining my existence. You know that I am here. You've got so many years ahead of you; years that will bear fruit like your rivers of Amalaka. Remember that my soul is there continuing on with our journey."

"Do you think that your lifetime has changed?"

"Yes but to what I do not know. The not knowing is liberating. I'm free of our curse and I'm here for the duration, whatever that may be. I must live in the present, the here and now; there is little point dwelling on the past or trying to shape my future. It is what it is."

"In many ways I am glad that this is so, as I'll know that you are always here, waiting for me, for whenever I am invited to return."

"I'm willing it so. But for now, you are the key to human survival. I must build on our legacy here. Besides I have Ban and Yakov to keep me company and even my good friend Moshe has opted to stay."

"That doesn't make it any easier."

"You are the perfect messenger, the perfect vessel to bring word back to our people. They'll believe you as they do in your music. Ours is not a religion but a system of beliefs, of codes of conduct, of morals, ethics and principles; those that we should all adhere to. This code guides us through the quagmire of science and reason, giving balance to our understanding of nature and the cosmos. Through education comes this understanding, through understanding comes peace. Our churches, our mosques, in fact all of our temples for the gods of the ancient world should be converted into shrines to the Universe. Isn't it time that we put our abundant technology to good use, rather than using it against ourselves?"

"Yes but how can I possibly do all that in my lifetime?"

"It's not a small task but as with any fruit, all it takes is just one seed, carefully positioned in the right place, at the right time. The rest you just leave, as they say, to nature."

"If only my father were alive to hear us now."

"He's very much alive in your thoughts and through you his genes live strong."

Once they reached their destination, they stepped through the gap and arrived at the familiar wagon stop. He knew that each moment was vital, that whatever he said now would be forever held in her heart.

"We've agreed that this is where our journey must come to an end. I will be here waiting. I'll return to the copse and watch the Repertega leave. I'll head for my cottage in Samanya and take up my position on the Council for Utsima as before. Once all of us who've remained finally find peace we will return here to Adhara and start building the Prithvian monument to mankind. I will mark this day and your departure, it will never leave me. You will never be far from me nor I from you."

The sound of hooves resonated from behind the brow of the undulation in the road. The springy tarmac vibrated beneath their feet. Like in a proverbial hourglass, the last grain of sand hit the bottom and they knew that their time was up. Ama spoke almost in desperation, her husky tones adding to the poignancy of her words.

"I will find your mother, I'll find your brother; I will tell them where you are and what has become of you. I will let them know of us and that you have set us all on the path to salvation."

The same wagon that delivered them pulled to a halt. The asvahs reared and bucked as if in disagreement with this enforced separation. Neither looked up nor cared at this juncture, knowing that if their eyes parted for a split second they would miss out on that final moment.

Ama's hair waved in the breeze as if it too were saying goodbye. Her unblemished, caramel skin shone with light perspiration. She grabbed him, throwing her arms around his neck, looking into his blue eyes one last time. All the fear of the future welled up from deep inside as she gushed her last words to him.

"I love you Hansel Laurence."

"And I love you Ama Pepper Clark."

They stood locked for a few moments more before she mustered every shred of will and determination to turn and climb up the side of the wagon into a seat out of view. As quickly as it had arrived the wagon moved away down the undulation. He gazed upon the rear of the carriage, hoping to catch a final glimpse of her. It was a hope in vain but it was just as well as it would only make their parting harder. He did not linger further nor did he want to look forlorn in the circumstances so he disappeared back through the hedgerow and headed for the copse. He would get a ringside seat for the Repertega's departure.

The atrium loomed magnificently in the distance like a gargantuan glass bullet reaching high into the sky. It was a monument to mankind's existence and one that he knew he'd use for inspiration. Rather than link up with the others who were staying behind, he'd already made arrangements for his journey to Utsima, alone. He had agreed with Moshe, Yakov and a whole host of others that they would meet at the landing site, the next year at the same time, regardless of whether they had been in communication or not.

The Prithvians had been persuaded to leave far sooner than all preceding visitors before them. He knew that Prithvian society had a long way to go before they would grasp the message. But he had faith in Ama, faith in the philosophy and most of all, faith in his people.

There would be no further contact between the two planets, until Earth had resolved its problems and this could take many millennia. He knew that the Prithvians would forget this visit; that it would be written down, consigned to the annals of history as a dead planet with a hostile atmosphere, nothing more. Yet it was the seeds planted in the minds of the specialists, which would be handed down through generations that would rid them of their mark.

He felt elated that the cure was now in the hands of a woman, built with unwavering devotion and constitution; a woman driven by affection and compassion, who'd reach every corner of the globe through her words and music.

Ama was pure love and that was what the world needed.

Perhaps it was as Laozi had intended; to drive a wedge between the two of them only to reconnect them at the most pertinent time, giving them the impetus to drive each other, to ensure the success of his mission. Perhaps Laozi had unwittingly created the cure, but whatever the truth was he thought upon fondly of his former mentor, knowing deep down that it had to have been entirely of his own conception. He was glad to have been of use and now had uncharted territory to explore, a life of acceptance and understanding; a life without boundary.

He climbed the hill once again, taking his seat under the trees, facing the Repertega. He waited till noon, never taking his eyes off the horizon. He thought long and hard about everything that they had said and done. The sun lay directly overhead and burned down on the tops of his shoulders. At first there was a crack, akin to an oversize twig snapping under Goliath's foot and then there was a gargantuan boom which was shortly followed by a tidal wave of air, cast out in every direction. All creatures in the vicinity, great and small, stopped to look at the enormous ship gleaming in the midday sun. The Repertega levitated gradually, briefly hovering above the ground, before tipping a wink in his direction.

He knew that Ama and Boy would be looking out from their viewing deck, so waved, before adding the Keplerian gesture of farewell. The undisturbed pale azure sky was momentarily obscured by the behemoth of Prithvian technology before it glided past, rising higher, heading north. He turned, following its line until faced by the stern. Its broad beams gave way to the atrium which protruded like a tiller less rudder, guiding it home.

He thought of its precious cargo and the secrets that they now held. He thought of their individual journeys and what they might have all made of their experiences. He doffed an imaginary cap at the crew, believing that whatever the consensus and the stories that would unfold, they had been successful. The ship increased in speed, pulling away from Adhara, rapidly shooting up into the sky before finally disappearing out of sight and into Kepler's atmosphere.

As soon as the vessel vanished, he collapsed onto a bed of exposed roots and shook violently. He lay on his back as the energy passed through his veins to the tips of his toes and back again. It was a convulsion like he had never experienced before. Yet the moment passed not soon after and he was finally able to regain his composure. Giant beads of perspiration ran down the sides of his temple as he took out a flagon of water and sipped it gently. It was as if half of him had left with her.

After a while he picked up his pack, slung it over his shoulder and proceeded through the copse to the other side of the hill, heading west. The sun beat down on his back, changing the remnants of the cold sweat to a more comfortable warmth. Fighting back the nausea he strode on; never looking back, never looking south.

As planned he headed for one of the great lakes of the region, Astikya, six hours walk from Tega. He knew he'd be able to get a boat across the huge expanse of fresh water before continuing with his intended journey.

He looked into the distance. The lake shimmered, beckoning him on. He was not alone, there were many others faced with a similar voyage. His role was clearly defined, it kept him focussed. This new world welcomed him, as he did them. He had never let his guard slip but still they had welcomed him in. His job was done; he had guided her as Laozi had guided him.

With each step the strength returned as he thought of his father, his mother and his twin brothers. He hoped for the futures of all of them as in Prithvian terms he wanted their memories to live on. For everything that he had been taught, for everything he had learnt, this was the true awakening. He hoped that one day they would all be able to join him.

He reached the river station in good time, to find it empty. It was as if it had been expecting him. He found the white wooden rowing boat that he'd been allotted and clambered in. He pulled the oars towards him, allowing them to run free through the rowlocks. The boat slipped into the stream, carrying him with its current towards the considerable body of water that laid in wait. The banks were steeped in reeds and bulrush, vibrant and alive. The smell of the hot autumnal day fused with the crisp clean air of the lake as he was spat out, through the funnel of an imaginary estuary into a glorious sea.

Facing west, he was privy to a majestic view of the setting sun, half sunk beneath the water. It glowed red whilst resting on the curvature of the horizon. He stopped and stared for as long as he could until dusk threatened to steal the limelight. There wasn't a cloud in sight. He knew that he would be able to navigate by moonlight. He turned the boat round, using both oars in forward and reverse and started to row. He felt fresh, awake and elated; the voyage had only just begun.

Epilogue

A year to the day, as we had intended
I reach the box, that's casually suspended
Upon the site, where the ship had landed
This glorious monument to our visit
Is gleaming back at me, so monolithic
In hope, I place both my hands upon it
Unlike for those who went before me
My palms won't allow my mind to see
My fists rain down upon its sides, tellingly
In frustration I exhale upon its surface
And it bursts alive with hope and promise
For this, as projected, is a spiritual device
It sucks me in and transports my mind
To home, to her, to life of another kind
I see my child through her eyes, unsigned
A daughter, unblemished by the mark
Untainted, unscarred, free from the dark

The End

Timeline

2014 Discovery of air as fuel

2014 The Mark first appears

2024 Discovery of Kepler System and Kepler 3

2091 Oil Wars end

2092 Duplicate development begins

2093 World Economy rebases to World Credits

2099 Vedas Corporation acquire the moon

2099 Mass production of duplicates

2101 Moon Resort – Phase 1 begins construction

2119 Termination of duplicate development

2122 Air fuel development begins

2133 All transport powered by air fuel cells

2136 First 'light travel' vessel developed

2141 Etihad and Vedas Corp merge

2141 Rover to Kepler

2142 Nephthys sets off

2144 Jupiter Mission successful

Map of Kepler

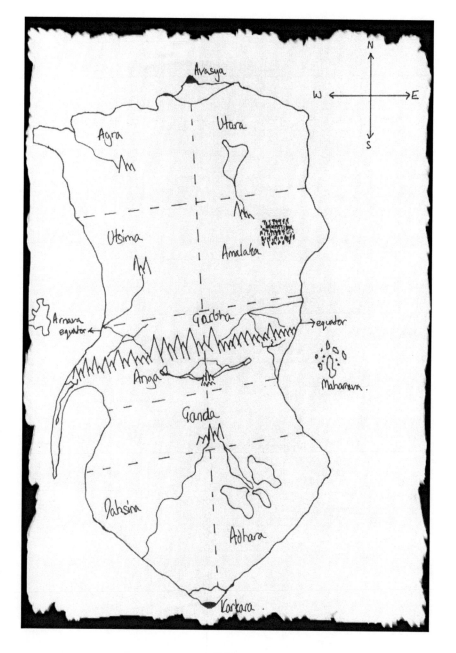

The Repertega

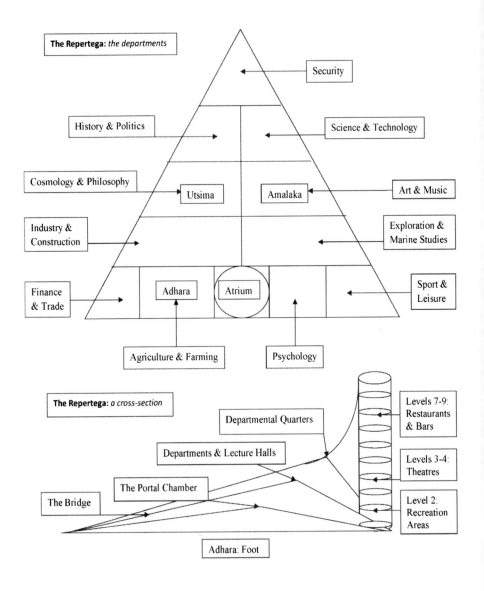

The Repertega: *the departments*

Security

History & Politics

Science & Technology

Cosmology & Philosophy

Utsima

Amalaka

Art & Music

Industry & Construction

Exploration & Marine Studies

Finance & Trade

Adhara

Atrium

Sport & Leisure

Agriculture & Farming

Psychology

The Repertega: *a cross-section*

Departmental Quarters

Levels 7-9: Restaurants & Bars

Departments & Lecture Halls

Levels 3-4: Theatres

The Portal Chamber

The Bridge

Level 2: Recreation Areas

Adhara: Foot

Keplerian Metropolises 2

Village/ Town/ City
layout:

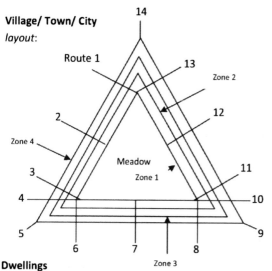

Kingdom
numbers:

Villages	126
Towns	42
Cities	1
Units	5,342,148

Dwellings
total:

Village	20,468
Town	61,404
City	184,212

Village
numbers:

Zone 1	84
Zone 2	3,528
Zone 3	5,880
Zone 4	10,976
Dwellings	20,468

Kepler
Population:

Estimated	48,079,332